ASSASSIN'S BREACH

A NOVEL BY O. NICHOLAS CICERO

A Third Street Creations, LLC Production

ASSASSIN'S BREACH

By O. Nicholas Cicero

ISBN-13: 978-0-9912534-1-8

Copyright 2013 Third Street Creations, LLC

For questions and comments about the quality of this book, please contact us at AuthorONC@gmail.com

Dedicated to my grandfather Liborio, who held me in his arms when I was a young boy and told me – "Never let anyone choose your path to success"

To my parents, thank you for your hard love and requiring that I develop into, and pursue the life of, an educated man...

To my sister Leenie, thank you for your countless hours of reading. My manuscript came to life due to your dedicated and merciless eyes...

To my son Alexander, I love you. Thank you for coming into my life and for providing me with the motivation to be greater than what I could have ever imagined...

To all of the aforementioned and beyond…Let's do this –

~ O. Nicholas Cicero

PROLOGUE

Prior to becoming a political appointee, Augustus Peña was an assassin for National Intelligence Covert Operations [NICO]. He believed his past was behind him. Yet, when he starts to write fiction that bears a resemblance to his experiences, his former director, Milken, elects to silence him.

The decision to eliminate the Peña threat stems from Milken's paranoid perception that recent military intelligence tell-all books and video games have permanently damaged the clandestine community.

Targeted for assassination, Augustus must kill in the name of family, as opposed to country, to fend off the assailants…in this Series opener.

ONE

Augustus Peña scurried, preparing for the inevitable. Blood rushed through his arteries, causing pain in his neck. *This cannot be healthy,* he thought, gathering equipment for his journey. He was flustered, unable to recall when he had packed his satchel so full for an operation. However, he could take no chances. He might be gone for days or even weeks. This was by far his most demanding mobilization. After stuffing it to capacity, he made a haphazard sign of the cross, cheaply offered for any extra power he might need. In the hours ahead, he would face challenges for which he was not, by his own admission, properly trained. Nothing in his background with National Intelligence Covert Operations sufficiently prepared him for the emotional rollercoaster he was experiencing.

"GO-TIME!" he shouted, as the moment requiring his immediate and decisive action arrived. Within a few hours, he would experience the most exhilarating and dramatic moment of his life.

"Mr. Peña, it is a boy. Your wife is doing great. She is going to make it," said the doctor emerging from the operating room. Augustus' wife, Jennifer Parsons, had just undergone emergency surgery to save her and her child's life.

Augustus reacted as any man would with his skill set in this situation – he bawled. Looking into his newborn son's eyes, he saw life's purity. He reflected deeply on how such innocence could ever grow to commit the horrific acts he witnessed firsthand. *Every piece of shit that I killed was once a beautiful baby too. Yet, their loss of virtue was not my doing. I am not a murderous bastard.* While not prone to softness, Augustus' heart melted with every tender breath his son puffed onto him. It was then, during the boy's first hour of life that Augustus pledged – "I will defend you beyond my last breath. No harm will ever come to you." Unbeknownst to Augustus, it was a pledge he would soon honor.

⌘⌘⌘

TWO

"To a reasonable creature, that alone is insupportable which is unreasonable; but everything reasonable may be supported." –
Epictetus – Discourses, Chap. ii

Old, tiled flooring combined with vaulted ceilings accentuated each echoing step. The three high-powered, regimented men taking this stroll did not speak. All eyes were ahead as they approached their destination. The men stopped in unison when a figure stepped towards them. They raised their right hands as if preparing to swear in. Instantly, their palms and fingers were subject to an intense infrared scan. They observed the glowing, yellow light that covered their hand. However, they were unable to see the single red light fixated onto the middle of their foreheads.

Although unable to see the beam, each of them was acutely aware of its presence. This was standard security protocol for entrance into The Chamber. Those seeking entry unequivocally understood one thing. If the scans failed to vet their clearance, the sniper guard would end their life with one shot. This procedure required a blind faith in the technology's accuracy. Yet, the men fanatically believed it to be necessary and patriotic.

Maxwell Prater stood still as the scan meticulously probed the contours of his hand. It took only forty seconds but felt like an eternity. Maxwell was the son of a Navy Rear Admiral and the grandson of a Naval Fleet Commander. His pedigree made him a perfect choice as NICO's Chief of Asset Control. As chief, he directed NICO's global corps of assassins. Unquestionably committed to his country, Maxwell did all he could to preserve its security.

On occasion, NICO voted on whether any of those assets required termination. Throughout his career, Maxwell voted affirmatively several times. He never thought twice about it nor did he ever question NICO's motivation. Maxwell strongly believed that blatant contempt for matters of national security must always result in termination. However, today was different. He was entering The Chamber to vote on a matter he strongly disagreed with.

The termination vote did not involve an active operative, but a former one. This fact alone did not trouble Maxwell. Assets knew they were required to honor their NICO commitment forever. Failure to do so meant slaughter. What troubled him was the logic behind the decision. His understanding was that the man received authorization to pursue a professional opportunity, but that NICO went back on its word. Maxwell was a sharp and critical thinker. He inherited his capacity for complex factual analysis from his family. He perceived the desire to terminate as ill conceived. He deemed it to be in NICO's best interest to move past this potential misadventure.

Maxwell met the subject only a handful of times. Still, he recalled sensing the power that the operative exuded. Even then, Maxwell knew that if ever warranted, it would take a colossal effort to dispose of him. Augustus Peña was not a creature you dragged into the shadows…those were his domain. Maxwell feared going into Peña's realm to commit a wrong against him. He knew that it was not only a suicide mission for NICO, but for those sent to carry it out.

The clearance for entry became evident when the laser's color changed from yellow to green. Irrespective, the men awaited verbal clearance. They did not want to cast doubt on their intentions with any sudden movement. A miscommunication, however slight, could have lethal consequences.

"All clear gentlemen," said the ominous figure. "Please proceed." Stepping in front of Maxwell as the others moved forward he asked – "Is…everything okay, Mr. Prater?"

This unprecedented occurrence rattled Maxwell. His voice crackled slightly – "Yes. Everything is ok...is…is there a problem?"

"Your heart rate recorded a higher level than usual. Moreover, thermal readings indicate perspiration developing above your temples. These are indicators of one's attempt at deception and its associated fear. So, I will ask you one more time, Mr. Prater, is everything okay?"

He answered nervously – "Thank you for noticing. Yes, I am doing well. Everything is okay. I was focusing heavily on the discussion I am about to have inside. I have no agenda of deception nor do I have any fear."

"Very well, please proceed. You should be aware that, as a precautionary matter, we will monitor your vitals for any signs of aggression."

Maxwell nodded and quickly entered The Chamber.

తతత

Sam Hepner sat in his oversized leather chair enjoying the view of Boston's skyline. It was close to midnight. Beads of rain slid down his high-rise office window. Sam looked at the cognac he just poured and toasted to his reflection in the window. He then chugged the liquor from his glass, "Ah – perfection." Sam Hepner was Vice President of Acquisitions for prominent Boston publisher Wickles & Nordquist. He was privately celebrating his success at gaining exclusive rights to publishing a specific series of novels. The stories loosely pertained to the experiences of one of the nation's most fruitful covert operatives. Several years ago, a Pentagon official introduced this man to Sam during a DC fundraiser. Sam observed him to be noncommittal about his experiences. The senior publishing executive knew there was a story to tell, so he befriended the man.

Over time, they developed a trusting relationship. Eventually, Sam engaged him in conversations about stories he might be able to write. Convincing the former operative to write informed stories was no easy task. He was extremely reluctant. Sam's pursuit consumed countless hours from his personal and professional life. Finally, his big break arrived. The man received approval from his former unnamed government agency to write stories. However, the stories needed to be laden with fiction. Wickles & Nordquist prided themselves on publishing only non-fiction works. However, after nearly three years, Sam was not walking away from this deal. Consequently, he signed a covenant with the former operative to publish a series of four novels. Writing was set to begin in the coming weeks.

Sam handled a picture on his desk of his wife and eight-year-old daughter saying – "This is going to be an amazing journey." He then called his wife to tell her he loved her and that he was heading home. Sam grabbed his briefcase, umbrella and turned off the lights. The towering office building was sturdy. However, a howling sound reverberated within it during windy rainstorms. Throughout the day, when it bustled with employees, the eerie sounds were non-existent. Yet, during the evening when it was empty, the sounds were remarkable.

Sam entered the elevator and listened to the ghostly echoes. *Wow…that is freaking creepy,* he thought. *I'm glad I don't work here overnight. I would go bonkers.*

He exited on the first floor. Normally, he parked in a reserved space underground. However, today he did not, due to a power outage that disabled the garage. Sam was on his way to the office when his secretary called, alerting him of the issue. By the time he arrived, power had resumed. Nevertheless, he did not want to risk being stuck in another glitch. Consequently, he parked in the firm's outdoor lot one block away, adjacent to a U.S. Coast Guard station.

Sam loved walking through Boston's cobblestone streets on cold, rainy nights. Times like these produced a Jack the Ripper-esque feeling. He arrived at his car and placed his items in the back seat. He opened the driver's door and turned to wave at the guard posted across the street. Sam customarily did this whenever he parked here. It did not matter who was on duty. He always waved…a show of support for their service. The guard shack was empty.

"Huh," he said. "That's a first." He could not remember a time when no lookout occupied it. Sam shrugged it off and entered his car. His cell phone rang. "This is Sam."

The caller's voice was unfamiliar, but pleasant – "Samuel, I am with Iowa's Safety and Intelligence Bureau. I apologize for the late call but my boss, Augustus Peña, asked me to contact you. He figured you would be working late. He wants to confirm the details for his meeting."

Sam was confused – "I'm sorry…what meeting?"

"He mentioned a meeting with your firm's team who will be working on his books."

Sam replied – "Uh…we WILL have a team. Right now, I am the only one with knowledge of this project. Can I get back to you tomorrow, after I approach my publishing board?"

"No, that will not be necessary."

Instantly, Sam's car exploded. It created a fireball seen throughout the adjoining neighborhoods. The blast rocked nearby buildings, producing a deafening rumble that bounced around the narrow Boston streets.

ॐॐॐ

Maxwell fidgeted in his chair as the other NICO bosses entered. There was no fanfare or small talk. The meeting started as soon as everyone sat down.

"This meeting is now in session," said Saxby Coles, NICO's Ambassador of External Affairs. As ambassador, he maintained the necessary outside relationships that ensured NICO's concealment. "On the floor for discussion and final vote is the termination of Augustus Peña." Saxby slowly scanned the rectangular-shaped table. He looked at all those present in their eyes, then said – "I motion to discuss."

"Aye, on the motion to discuss," said an older sounding voice. The voice belonged to C. Virgil Milken, NICO's director.

Maxwell, not wanting to appear disengaged, said – "I second the motion."

Saxby smiled and said – "Wonderful. Let us have a productive discussion then, shall we?"

At seventy years of age, C. Virgil Milken was a formidable individual. He stood almost six and a half feet tall and was as lean as he was mean. Age, however, had nothing to do with his coarseness. An executioner during Vietnam's Phoenix Program, he was revered for being a no-nonsense director. "You cannot be a leader if you are unable or unwilling to perform the very tasks you direct men to accomplish," he often preached. "Ask your men to fight…then prepare to fight for them, if they are weak. Ask your men to kill…then prepare to kill for them, if they fail." This mindset served him well in his rise to the top. Milken led NICO for thirty years and was as lethal now as when he started.

Milken spoke confidently, justifying his position. "Over the course of my service I have witnessed many things. I am proud of our existence and feel immense honor in all that we do. Nothing has caused me to stay awake. I am not cold or heartless, as some might whisper. Any action I have taken was the product of thorough and sincere analysis." Milken paused to sigh. "I analyzed this situation and visualized every scenario. Ultimately, only one conclusion captures the essence of who we are and what we do. Former NICO operative Augustus Peña is now a domesticated man. He has earned a great public reputation in the wholesome Midwestern State of Iowa. You might ask – is that a problem? My answer to you is – well, no."

Milken inched around the table. "Augustus served with the utmost distinction. No one respects him more than I do. He is a child of the Order. I recruited him myself when he was a teenager in New York City…the son I never had. It is, then, with a heavy heart that I dare utter these words. Augustus has become a massive security threat to this institution. ALL we have accomplished is on the cusp of ruins. Our concealment is at risk of exposure due to his reckless decision to exist outside of NICO's structure."

Maxwell, incredulous, could not refrain from interrupting – "Wait, the guy is retired and has a family. He is a public servant in…Iowa…and based on THIS he is a colossal threat to NICO's existence? Is that what I am hearing? Because, if that's what you're saying, I'm telling you, it sounds nuts."

Milken closed the distance between them in an instant. Pointing at Maxwell he yelled – "SILENCE, you behemoth of a fool. A book publisher has approached Augustus several times. Someone at the Pentagon with a hard-on for him apparently introduced them. Now, they want him to write novels based on his life's work. He came to me for authorization. I gave it to him, unwittingly and with conditions. However, I contemplated it further. I am perturbed he even thought this to be a possibility. He is directionless, and that makes him a threat. I have, as of this moment, neutralized the publisher."

Milken addressed the others – "What if his books spellbind the masses? Need I articulate the ruinous consequences of a public probe into our efforts? Borders will fall overnight. Our military and the militaries of our allies would come under a level of attack seen only in outright war."

Maxwell's face was red with anger. He resented Milken calling him a fool in front of the others. He continued to press –

"At what point did you decide that a well-disciplined operative, who decided to pursue a family, had it in his mind to expose us? I have met Augustus. The man radiated the kind of commitment to NICO you cannot genetically duplicate in a lab. Retired or not, he is an avowed officer. I intend on maintaining my faith in the inherent discipline that comes with such a commission."

"Are you willing to risk our entire existence upon inherent discipline?"

Maxwell replied – "Yes, absolutely."

Milken bellowed – "Where the hell was this inherent discipline when former special warfare officers published their stories? They wrote, of all things, about covertly assassinating the world's most wanted terrorist. Moreover, where in God's name did this inherent discipline go when active-duty operators provided classified, tactical information to a computer game maker?" Milken's voice thunderously roared throughout The Chamber.

Maxwell sensed defeat. He looked down, attempting to deflect further harshness from Milken, but to no avail.

"Young man," said Milken. "You sit in that chair and hold that position due to your pedigree. Do not ever forget that. If you are unable to uphold the leadership qualities of prior Praters, then I implore you to serve your country elsewhere. Do I make myself clear?"

An eerie stillness filled the room, making it seem colder than what it was. Finally, the awkwardness gave way to a gentle, Southern voice – "Gentlemen, I believe we heard a very powerful sermon from Virgil, don't you?" Prentiss Gates was NICO's assistant director.

Simultaneously, the NICO leaders agreed with him. One by one, each member of management articulated – "I approve the decision to terminate former operative Augustus Peña." Maxwell was the last to offer an affirmation.

Prentiss delicately clasped his hands in front of his chest. He let out a soft sigh of exuberance saying – "Well, isn't that just wonderful? Great job everyone, great job indeed."

Milken turned and walked away from the table as Saxby Coles shouted – "This meeting is now adjourned."

෧෧෧

This was the quickest voting Maxwell had experienced. There was no discussion or debate. He felt his participation was merely ceremonial. Incredibly, he was responsible for assigning the assets to accomplish this mission.

Maxwell considered which assets to appoint. He started experiencing the same anxiety that stirred curiosity at the checkpoint. He looked up to the monitoring station and said – "I know...I'm okay." He then looked across the table at his peers and said – "It's a long story."

Maxwell created the order and sealed it. He then brought it to the agency courier awaiting dispatch. Looking at the document he whispered – "I'm sorry, Godspeed."

⌘⌘⌘

THREE

NICO couriers made deliveries under cover of darkness to minimize exposure. They received no briefings or mission details and possessed zero intelligence. A captor seeking to learn the particulars of a dispatch would discover nothing. Only intended recipients knew how to decrypt these messages. The communications consisted of letters, numbers and symbols with different daily values…a perverse variation of the Julian date calendar. Assets typically consumed a day deciphering their mission.

Zachary 'Coop' Cooper was the courier chosen for this dispatch. He was especially adept in counter surveillance tactics. After graduating near the top of his class at Annapolis, he became an officer in the U.S. Marine Corps. There, he excelled in evasive strategies while serving on an expeditionary team. DEA officials recruited Coop at the end of his military obligation to hunt cartel members in South America. These experiences turned him into a master tracker in various environments. His proficiency caught NICO's attention when several of their missions crossed paths. Coop's service with NICO began almost two years to the day.

Maxwell exited The Chamber, handed Coop the sealed order and said – "I expect you to be as expedient and efficient as possible. You must double-up on your precautionary measures. I will be available on Sat-Comm-5. Contact me when delivery is made." Sat-Comm-5 referred to a satellite communication network. It only activated during heightened states of alert. NICO personnel accessed the network via proprietary Sat-Link devices, which they always carried.

Coop had only operated the gadget during training. He freaked for a moment, pondering the possibility of this delivery getting him killed. Coop returned from his momentary lapse into weakness. Upset at himself he thought – *What a pussy I am.* He then departed.

It would be an arduous journey. His destination was to location Alpha/X-ray. The recipient of the dispatch was the NICO assassin known as Ajax.

ॐॐॐ

It was an invigorating December morning in the Colorado resort town of Crested Butte. The ski season was in full swing and it buzzed with life. Typically, wintertime here was cold with heavy snowfall. However, this year was warmer than most with minimal precipitation. Manmade snow pumped out by blowers covered the slopes. Downtown, families filled the shops that lined the street while pub patio parties celebrated the warmer climate.

This was Ajax's third year living in Crested Butte. He became acquainted with it while working a job in a neighboring upscale town. He loved his experience in The Butte so much he made it his home.

Ajax had been a NICO assassin for five years. His father, a former KGB captain, trained him in the brutal Russian arts of interrogation. By eighteen, Ajax had earned a great reputation for inhumaneness. Proud of his son's achievements, the father positioned Ajax with foreign allies to enhance his aptitudes. By twenty-three, the Kremlin regarded Ajax as its most valued intelligence gatherer. Unlike his father, though, he never joined any of Russia's intelligence agencies. Independent by nature, he despised political idealism. Much to his father's chagrin, Ajax opted to freelance, concerned only with who bid the highest.

Ajax's clients were initially Russian bourgeoisie. Over time, he accepted assignments from western nations, including the American government. After working interrogation jobs for some time, Ajax pondered about his choice of profession. He was young and wealthy but did not have time to enjoy his spoils. He needed a change. Ajax thoroughly assessed his professional duties. He measured the length of time it typically took to yield profitable interrogations. By comparison, he evaluated how long it would take just to kill his targets. *I would still need to stalk my prey, so that would not change. Spend days interrogating or much less time to kill and dispose of them. These are my choices.*

The decision was a no-brainer. He notified his clientele immediately and was thrilled to bits that he would now have time to enjoy his wealth. It did not take long before NICO recognized his excellent work, discipline and efficiency. As a result, NICO placed him at the top of their preferred asset list for high priority kills.

Ajax's home was nestled high into a mountain, overlooking the town. He chose this location because of its view. Additionally, he enjoyed the seclusion. It was well off the beaten path. His property was at least five rugged kilometers to the nearest hiking trail. A person finding his home would have done so purposefully unless they were unbelievably lost. Part of Ajax's daily routine was a morning run. He did so to exercise and to survey the land for evidence of an incursion. His run on this winter morning was refreshing. He stopped along a tree line and inhaled deeply. *Ahh, very good*, he thought, enjoying the cool air in his lungs.

Like usual, he scanned the land for evidence of disruption. Ordinarily there would be nothing. Today, though, he saw something alarming. To the right of where he stood was a downed tree. It had been there for some time so this did not disturb him. What troubled him were the set of footprints on the ground in front of it. Someone sat on the log. Ajax had relaxed on it many times before. He knew sitting there provided a direct view of his home in the valley below. Ajax jumped into combat mode. He swirled, looking for the intruder. Like a primitive version of man, he went down on all fours. He tilted his head, listening intently to the sounds of the woods. All was silent. Nothing indicated to Ajax that the intruder remained in the area. Still on all fours, he quickly scampered to the footprints and assessed their freshness.

They are from last night, he thought. He discerned that the person did not attempt to wipe them away. It was the behavior of a brazen individual. Ajax looked around for other footprints. He could not find any. The soil was moist from slight rainfall in recent days. Any tracks getting to and from the log should be easily visible.

Ajax was confused. This tiny area of exposed soil was a natural dead end. Beyond this point was nothing but hazardous mountain terrain, under dense tree cover, for miles. The route

Ajax took was the only soft-soil trek up to that location. That route had no tracks on it. Any other course necessarily required hiking through the woods. Doing so is not only an arduous task during the day, but practically impossible for most recreational hikers at night.

This was no recreational hiker, thought Ajax. *No, this person had a purpose for being here.* He quickly returned home and armed himself for what he believed was an impending battle. Many thoughts raced through his mind as he barricaded himself inside. *The footprints belong to a scout. It will be an assault. They are going to attack at night like cowards.* He organized his weapons and ammunition saying – "I am fortunate that I am so good at counter-surveillance. If I did not survey my land daily then they would have succeeded in killing me. No, not this time…not ever. They cannot kill the Great Ajax!" He then jumped into his battle gear. Armed to the teeth, he sat silently…waiting for the approaching onslaught.

ॐॐॐ

Coop had always been fascinated with the historical struggles of people from around the world. Of particular interest to him were the exertions of the American Frontiersmen. Coop marveled what it must have been like for settlers who traversed the same lands he navigated.

Man, he thought, making his way through the Crested Butte mountain range – *How in the hell did settlers do this without technology and without knowing what waited for them up ahead? Shit, toss in a few hostile Indians and it is a freaking miracle anyone survived their journeys west.* He often conversed with himself to pass time while navigating to his destinations. However, getting to Alpha/X-ray was no simple task. His inward conversations on this journey were few.

He did not need a briefing to appreciate the inherent dangers of this mission. Ajax was a quick slayer, known to kill first and ask questions later. The man was so dangerous that NICO normally initiated contact with him via old-school espionage techniques. Those methods entailed marking mailboxes with distinctive lines. Over a period of three to four days, the lines became unique shapes. The markings served as an alert to Ajax that NICO would attempt communication with him in the coming weeks. This allowed him to anticipate the contact.

Coop thought of this as he stepped out of the dense woods and into a small clearing. It was eleven o'clock in the evening local time. He sat on a downed tree. According to his calculations, it overlooked Ajax's home. *Here I am…approaching a man so dangerous, that no one ever directly contacts him.*

Coop sat silently, staring into the dark valley below. The clear night sky danced with stars. They provided illumination to the cold world around him. "This is nothing like in there," said Coop, referencing his daylong journey. He entered the woods from Aspen, a town that was many miles away, and avoided all trails. "Well, we don't have a few weeks buddy," he whispered, regarding Ajax's normal timeframe for receiving notice of a NICO contact. "But I am not going right up to you either, man – no freaking way."

Coop studied the area, making sure he was not about to be pounced upon by Ajax. Intel showed that he monitored this part of his land for intrusion. Coop leaned forward, making deep footprints into the soil. He then positioned some shrubbery into a deliberate shape. "Let's hope you're as intelligent as everyone thinks you are," said Coop. He pondered the possibility that Ajax would not understand their significance. He then whispered, "Only a madman would be here right now if they didn't need to contact you."

Coop stood up, turned and jumped back into the woods for his return trek to Aspen.

ࣾࣾࣾ

Ajax remained hunkered-down in his fortress. The mere thought of someone watching his every move shook him to his core.

This is a peculiar feeling, he thought, warily scanning the windows for any signs of movement outside. *The awareness of someone stalking me for the sole purpose of wanting to kill me is debilitating.*

He noticed that his breathing, normally slow and controlled, was now erratic. "This must be how my prey feels when I hunt them down. This is beneficial for me. Now I know exactly how they feel when they sense I am coming for them. YES! YES! YES! This is going to make me even greater!"

Ajax was beside himself. He laughed loudly, running through his cabin checking every window and door. He had been so preoccupied with his feelings that he lost total track of time, and did not realize he had been holed-up in his cabin for three days.

❧❧❧

Coop went to downtown Crested Butte, hoping to make contact with Ajax. Intel showed he only appeared in public during the morning. He did so primarily to eat breakfast while drinking gallons of coffee. Although an abuser of the nightlife, Ajax only did so away from where he lived.

Coop strolled down the main avenue, sipping a coffee. He wondered where Ajax could possibly be. He never met Ajax, but had an idea of what he looked like from obscure photos. Coop's footprints by the log were markings designed to alert Ajax of a NICO communication. The footprints themselves signified contact by courier, as opposed to electronic or other means. The alignment of the prints was also significant. He placed the top of his right foot midway of his left one. This informed Ajax that contact was in one full day, left foot, and a half, right foot. Coop also created a message alongside of the footprints. He placed a large stone in the middle of some shrubs. This represented a town center. Coop's coded message informed Ajax of contact via courier, in a day and a half, in the town center.

This should have been simple enough given his upbringing, thought Coop. It was a logical opinion. However, he was unaware of Ajax's frantic reactions to seeing his footprints. Nor did he know that in the ensuing melee, Ajax's wild spinning destroyed his other efforts. *Hanging around these storefronts, sipping coffee day after day, is not wise. It is going to cause unnecessary exposure.* Coop contemplated going up to Ajax's home and knocking on the front door. He walked back to his car scowling – "Crazy bastard or not, this shit has got to get moving. If that prick fails to appear tomorrow, then I'm going up there and kicking in his fucking door."

ৡৡৡ

Ajax gained control over his anxiety. He emerged from his cabin prepared for war. It was mid-afternoon. He rolled forward out the front door with a camouflaged, pistol-grip shotgun in hand. He wore a modified utility belt that held a serrated knife and a 9mm handgun with extra ammunition. After completing a full roll he remained eerily still in a kneeled firing position. "Hmmmmm…nothing," he whispered, surveying the area. He stood and bolted up the mountain, hollering a war cry at the top of his lungs.

He dove several times, avoiding the almost certain barrage of gunfire being leveled at him from his envisaged executioners. Arriving at the tree line, where he noticed signs of the intruder, he stood silently. "I have a reprieve," he said softly. He then reflected – *Nobody shot at me. There is no one here to fight…oh no.* He then shouted – "This can only mean one thing. They have gone to get reinforcements because they know how difficult it will be to kill the Great Ajax!"

This troubled him. "I am great, that is true. However, even I cannot fight an army alone; and an army is what is coming for me. I must leave at once." Ajax's eyes were as wide as silver dollars. He convinced himself that his stalker left to get a militia. He turned abruptly and almost fell, slipping on loose rock. He then ran down the mountain, faster than when he ran up.

Ajax hurriedly packed for his evacuation. Clothing was not a necessity, but his tools of the trade were. Although no longer an interrogator, he became fond of several items he acquired along the way. No matter how rapidly he needed to flee, he would never leave them behind.

Satisfied he had what he needed, he looked around the cabin and sighed woefully. He placed his hand against a wall saying – "I really loved this place. I thought that I would live here for many more years to come." Ajax took a final look at the home he would never see again. He then armed the automatic defense system he personally wired and exited via the back door.

It was early evening. Ajax drove towards downtown, en route to the interstate system that would lead him out of this area. In all the years he lived here, he had not visited Crested Butte during the evening. He was more than just a little curious about what, if anything, he had been missing in the way of nightlife. He decided to drop in for a brief visit.

ॐॐॐ

It was late afternoon. Coop's patience had worn thin. Accordingly, he decided to contact Ajax directly. He packed his belongings and headed for Crested Butte.

As he got closer, he saw that darkness was quickly approaching. He reconsidered his plan as reality set in. He overestimated his desire to contact Ajax at all costs.

Going up to that psychopath's home at night is not a good move, he thought. Instead, he opted to stay in town overnight and head up first thing in the morning.

ॐॐॐ

Ajax walked along the town's main street, taking in the evening sights. He observed that the quaint looking pubs were full-blown parties at night. Ajax giggled as he saw drunk bar patrons stumbling outside to light up their cigarettes.

Live music emanated from many of the establishments. Ajax found it pleasant to listen to, especially when the various musical tones intermingled in the evening breeze. He went to a café patio, planning to enjoy some steaming mocha lattes while listening to these blended sounds.

ॐॐॐ

Coop pulled into a parking spot across from a bed-and-breakfast. He had eyed this establishment during his morning trips here and thought it would be a nice place to stay. He went inside to inquire about room availability.

An elderly couple that owned the place told him to check again in an hour. They informed him that they held reservations until eight o'clock in the evening and that they anticipated an opening. Coop really wanted to stay there so he agreed to return.

Feeling a bit sluggish, he decided to get a coffee from one of the shops down the street. He arrived at a café and stopped to read the food menu posted on a sidewalk placard.

 ૐ૱ૐ૱ૐ૱

Inside, a female server chuckled when she saw Coop reading the menu. Her roommate, who also worked at the café, was chatting with some friends on the patio. The server went to her saying – "Hey, that creepy guy is back. He's reading the menu by the door."

Her roommate glanced towards the door and said – "What the crap? This guy is bad enough during the day, but now he's showing up at night?"

The girls laughed loudly, disturbing Ajax. The raucousness caused him to look at them. As he did, the roommate pointed past him shouting – "No, I'm serious. This dude has been walking up and down the street for the past few days. He hangs out with no one and is always looking over his shoulder. I think he is up to something, but what the hell do I know, right?"

The girl's words resonated with Ajax. He stared blindly past her, making a mental checklist of his weaponry. He was certain this was no coincidence. She described the predatory movements of a stalking assassin. *My distance from the menu might be too far for a knife,* he thought. *I will resort to my trusty handgun. YES, I will shoot my way out of here.* Ajax slowly turned his head to look towards the sidewalk placard. He cautiously reached for his gun with his right hand. The movement of his hand and the turning of his head coincided in tempo. This coordination was extremely effective at not attracting attention from those around him. Just as Ajax was able to put eyes on the killer…he entered the café.

 ૐ૱ૐ૱ૐ૱

Coop went to the counter and placed his order. He observed a café worker making mocking hand gestures towards the patio. A roar of laughter ensued. Coop sensed the hilarity was at his expense. He felt angered, but was not about to engage in any immature arguments.

"Fuck them, I'm exhausted," he said, under his breath. He stepped aside, waiting for his ham and cheese croissant to be prepared. He wanted to see the faces of the people poking fun of him.

Coop turned, leaned on the counter and looked outside. "A bunch of young chicks, figures. Grow the hell up." He then gave thought to how sitting on the patio while waiting to return to the inn would be perfect. *Yeah…it would have been perfect if not for those assholes.*

ॐॐॐ

Ajax watched the man enter the café. *He does not seem threatening. Maybe he really is just some pervert.* As he was about to dismiss the man's threat, he noticed his footwear.

"Those boots," said Ajax loudly. He composed himself and thought - *Those boots…the grooves on the bottom, and the size of his feet. They are practically identical to the footprints created by the assassin looking down at my home.*

Ajax moved quickly from one window to the next, trying to view the man's boots from every possible angle. He whispered – "I believe those are them…but, I cannot be absolutely–"

The man turned around, leaned on the counter and crossed his feet, causing his right boot to face the patio. Ajax shouted – "He has red soil on the bottom of his boot, just like where I found those tracks, it is him!"

Ajax was wild with energy. He wanted to crash through the café window and confront the assassin who dared hunt him. However, he knew this would be problematic in such a public place.

He ducked, looked over at the girls and said to them – "Hey, listen, that creepy guy in there has been following me all week. Can you believe it? Anyways, look, I am getting the hell out of here. I really cannot have him know which way I went. Can you please do me a favor? No matter how much money he offers, can you please not tell him which way I went? Huh? Please?"

The girls reacted with laughter and a couple of "awes." Nevertheless, they emphatically agreed on not telling the "creepy guy" which way he went. Ajax thanked them and slipped away into the dark, music-filled town.

~~~

Coop studied the large patio for a spot where he could sit, away from the group. Suddenly, he noticed a large, dark-haired man peering at him from under a window sign.

"Oh, what now?" he said. "That better not be some queer wanting to put moves on me." Suddenly, it became clearer to him, as the man moved from one spot to the next. "HOLY SHIT," he shouted.

At the same time the barista yelled, "Mister, your order is ready!"

Alarmed, Coop jumped and turned. "Yes, okay, thank you, okay." He turned back towards the patio, but Ajax was gone. "Shit!" yelled Coop, darting out the café.

He looked towards the patio, verifying that Ajax was not hiding in there somewhere. He was definitely gone but the annoying girls were still there. Instinctively, Coop asked them – "Did any of you see where the guy that was sitting here went to?"

The girls responded with laughter.

Coop was absorbed with figuring out what happened. He had no time to be upset at the girls' cackling and rude commentary. He was no longer tired. Adrenalin soared through his veins. *Why would he run from me?* Coop could not come up with a reason for Ajax's behavior. It was a little past eight o'clock. He needed to check on room availability at the inn.

He sensed a presence across the street. He quickly glanced, but saw nothing. Coop walked past the inn and continued for one and a half blocks. The avenue became less commercial and more residential by the step. He chose this path because it drew his pursuer away from the crowded business district. Coop wanted to avoid collateral damage if they clashed.

He stopped and turned, half expecting to see the pursuer – no one. He still felt eyes on him. Coop crossed the street, maintaining a clear line of sight from where he had just come. He stopped by a parked European vehicle after noticing damage to it. It had a mangled passenger-side mirror, facing upwards, as if pulled towards one's face.

No owner would damage his or her vehicle like this, he thought. Coop looked around and surmised that his pursuer was at this very location, observing his movements. He then whispered, "Hmm, so he pulls the mirror up at an angle to make it look like he has a purpose for being here, like grooming himself. That is clever. Yeah, it's Ajax."

Coop saw a small alleyway about ten feet behind the vehicle. There was some debris on the sidewalk leading to it. It consisted of white pieces of plastic, the same color as the vehicle. Coop figured the fragments clung onto Ajax's clothing, after he broke the mirror, and fell off as he fled into the alleyway. *So that is where he ran off into, huh? No way am I going in after him...no way.* Coop tapped his finger on the damaged car mirror, pondering his next move. He then looked at his watch and kept walking.

He decided it best to go to his car before entering the bed-and-breakfast. He retrieved all of his items. He needed to avoid making multiple trips between his car and the inn. Coop knew that Ajax was somewhere in this town, watching him at this very moment. Leaving was not an option. He needed to deliver NICO's message. *There is no way in hell I am getting back into this car now that this psychopath knows it is mine.* Coop feared that Ajax would rig his car with explosives. He closed the door and went to the bed-and-breakfast.

Coop was determined to stay, even if there was no opening. As he arrived he said, "I will beg them to let me sleep in their basement. I need to stay out of sight the rest of this evening and keep my perimeter tight." He entered the inn, put down his belongings and went to speak with the owners. There was no one around. Coop called out – "Hello. I was told to come back after eight o'clock to find out if you have a vacancy."

A television was on in an adjoining room. An elderly voice replied – "Oh, yeah, come on back…just watching the game."

Coop was unaware of any games currently on. However, he was not alarmed because he did not follow sports closely. He had no reason to be suspicious. This was his first time here since attracting Ajax's attention. Consequently, this place was not on Ajax's radar and was clean. "Clean for now, at least," he muttered.

He walked around the desk and into the room. As he entered he asked – "What game you talking about?"

Coop felt a cold, pinching sensation in his neck as Ajax stepped out of the shadows saying – "The game of cat and mouse…I win."

ॐॐॐ

Coop awoke from the shock of iced water slamming onto his face.

"Wake up you pathetic, little man," growled Ajax. "How dare you come to my humble sanctuary to kill me? You were going to kill me, were you not? Or, were you going to take pleasure in torturing me first?" He did not allow Coop to respond and yelled – "SPEAK TO ME!" Ajax punched Coop along the left side of his skull, knocking him onto the floor.

All tied up, Coop tried to speak. However, something in his mouth muffled his voice. It felt like a rag and tasted like it was soaked in kerosene. Coop gagged as the fumes of the rag overpowered him.

"Ah…looks like you're ready to speak to me now, aren't ya…hmm?" He sat Coop back up onto the chair and pulled the rag out of his mouth.

Coop exhaled harshly and coughed violently, almost to the point of vomiting. Finally, he was able to put together a couple of words – "NICO…contact…asshole!"

Ajax jumped backwards, as if struck by a jolt of electricity. He had a crazed look on his face. "What do you know about NICO? Why do you dare speak of this to me out loud?"

He kicked Coop, sending him backwards. He then leapt on him like a lion on an elk. He tore open Coop's shirt, looking for a listening device. He found nothing. Next, he flipped Coop over, ripping his pants apart with a hunting knife to see if there was a device on him below.

Coop screamed – "I'm with NICO. I have a transmission for you!"

Ajax stopped instantaneously and said, "Uh, you…you're with NICO then, huh?"

"Yes, you deranged fuck! Now, pick me up and untie my ass." Coop took a moment to calm down. He then explained to Ajax why he approached him the way he did. Coop looked in his satchel for the sealed document.

"What are you looking for?"

"Your orders," replied Coop. He fumbled around some more, then said – "Ah, here we go. I was hoping you didn't lose this while dragging my ass here. Hey, where are we anyway?"

Ajax, still a bit leery, replied – "Don't worry about that. We are safe. Now, let me have what you refer to as my orders." Unbeknownst to Coop, Ajax had rapidly made his way through the inn killing all of the occupants while he was at his car.

Coop handed him the document. "Here you go. You know the drill, crypto and all."

Ajax grabbed the document, raised his right eyebrow and said – "Yes, yes, of course – encrypted like always…ha ha…hmmm."

"You know how to decode the message…do you not?"

Offended, Ajax roared back – "Why, hell yes I do. I just, you know, do not have the proper equipment right here with me. But, I will get it done soon."

Coop replied angrily – "No, not soon you buffoon, now. You have already wasted enough time with the bizarre notion I was here to assassinate you. What was it that you said to me? Oh, yeah, that's right – with my army of assassins."

Ajax glanced at Coop sideways and said – "Well…it is possible, you know."

Coop pulled out the Sat-Comm-5 device and held it up saying – "We are a couple days off schedule. I know you still need to decode that document. However, I need to report that I made contact with you. If I don't, they are going to get their panties all bunched up."

Ajax, recognizing the device, replied – "Yes, okay, I suppose you are correct."

Coop entered the coordinates for NICO's satellite into the device. He then typed his personal code. He waited close to two minutes for a secured connection to be established. Finally, a dampened ring, as the call went through.

"Personnel, how can I direct your call?"

Coop replied – "I have some new-hire paperwork to process. Can I get an overnight address for where to send it? I was delayed in getting the necessary documents together."

"Hold on, please."

Another minute passed, then – "Prater."

Coop spoke quickly – "Sir, there has been a delay. However, the ball is now in play."

Maxwell frowned deeply and asked harshly – "Why the hell is it taking so long?" Coop began to speak but Maxwell cut him off – "Put him on."

Coop raised the device to Ajax saying – "He wants to speak with you."

Ajax snatched it and said – "Talk to me." He listened intently. The proverbial wheels inside of his head were spinning as he made sense of it all.

Maxwell impressed upon him the sensitivity of the mission and the necessity for timeliness. Next, Maxwell broke NICO's standard operating procedure. He revealed the mission as opposed to letting Ajax decipher it. "All collateral tactics shall be your decision to make. Your performance and awareness must be at its highest level. This is a zero sum engagement on Augustus Peña. You know these details ONLY because of your delay." The line fell silent.

Ajax kept the device to his ear after the conversation ended, meditating on what he just learned. *Augustus…I cannot believe my ears. The last I heard he was retired, married and working for a small state government in the middle of the country. Idaho, I think it was.* Ajax paced slowly while scratching at a scab on the top of his head.

Coop retrieved the Sat-Comm-5 device from him and repacked it. "All squared away?"

"Yes, everything is very clear to me now."

Coop replied – "Good. Make sure there is nothing here that can identify us so we can get the hell out. I'm going to sweep from the back of this room forward to clear it."

"Yes. Do that."

Coop went to the rear of the room. "Hey," he said to Ajax, stepping backwards. "You didn't happen to wire my car with explosives did you? I mean, before you knew who I was you thought I was here to kill you. So, I'm just asking…did you?"

"No, but, that would have been good too, I suppose."

Coop froze – "Too? What the hell does that mean?" He spun around and saw Ajax screwing a silencer onto his weapon. He said – "Oh, fuck," and leapt towards him.

Calmly, Ajax dropped the hand he used to fasten the silencer. Without shifting his stance, he shot Coop several times, striking his chest and neck. Coop plummeted onto the floor. He was still alive, but barely.

Ajax walked over nonchalantly saying – "You see, little fellow, you were always going to die. NICO wants me to kill the great Augustus Peña. He is a family man. A man that no longer poses a threat to those targeted for assassination; or, to anyone at all for that matter. Yet, they urgently want him dead. They are even open to collateral damage."

He stood directly over Coop – "What we have here is an eradication campaign. A zero sum event, that means his family, too." Ajax chuckled slightly and said, "NICO is going to kill everyone associated with this job that was not on the planning committee…including me. Well, they only think they can kill me." He then bent over slightly, put the nozzle of the silencer two inches from Coop's forehead and said – "Well, there you have it. Goodbye." Ajax pulled the trigger and watched as Coop's body jerked violently in reaction to the fatal shot.

Ajax grabbed Coop's satchel and put his orders in it for safekeeping. Next, he used the canister of kerosene he soaked the rag with earlier to splash the room. "Who knew how handy this would turn out to be?"

With the remaining kerosene, he splashed the inn's main area. He then went to the kitchen and pulled out a live gas hose from the wall. Finally, he lit all of the flares from Coop's satchel and tossed them around so that they landed on the kerosene.

Walking upright and confidently, Ajax exited the premises through the front door. He disappeared into the Crested Butte night as the bed-and-breakfast exploded into a ball of fire behind him. As he walked away, he whispered – "Do skoroy vstrechi, Augustus. See you soon."

⌘⌘⌘

FOUR

"Anyone can get angry - that is easy; but to do this to the right person, to the right extent, at the right time, with the right motive, and in the right way, that is not for everyone, nor is it easy." –
Aristotle, Book II, 1109.a27

Jennifer Parsons rushed to get her son ready for his visit with grandma. "Nathaniel," she called out. "Come on buddy, let's get your shoes and jacket on to go visit Nana."

She could hardly believe how fast time had flown by since her traumatic birthing of him. Nathaniel was two weeks away from his second birthday. Like many children his age, Nathaniel liked to shout the names of things that interested him. Most recently, he developed a keen interest in cartoon characters that appeared to be wearing eyeglasses. He would point to them and shout – "Glasses on." Of course, in response to such great observation, both Jennifer and Augustus would congratulate him and say – "Yes, Nathaniel, great job. You are correct, that character has glasses on."

The boy squealed with delight upon hearing Jennifer say he was going to grandma's house. He ran the length of the long hallway between the kitchen and living room yelling – "NANA, NANA, NANA."

"Ugh…" Jennifer exclaimed as they were about to leave – "I forgot to pack extra apple snacks."

As Jennifer returned to the kitchen she heard Nathaniel in the front of the house yelling – "Glasses on…glasses on."

Jennifer chuckled affectionately. The television was still on. She knew that Nathaniel was watching a television show with animal characters who often times wore people clothing. She picked up the package of apple snacks and cheerfully declared – "Yes, my love, the animals have glasses on." She then took ahold of Nathaniel's little hand and exited their home for the ten-mile drive to Nana's house.

❧❧❧

Ajax peered at Augustus' home through a pair of binoculars, observing the movements of mother and child. He was inside of an electrical utility truck parked across the street. Suddenly, their child appeared at the front window, pointing directly at him while saying something. Ajax knew the boy was barely two years old. It startled him to no end to think that the youngster observed and called him out. Ajax immediately put down his binoculars and started up the truck.

"How the hell did that kid see me?" Ajax wondered aloud as he watched the two of them get into the mother's SUV. "I have to be more careful. There is no room for error. I am taking nothing else for granted. I will do this job quickly and make my escape from NICO forever."

Ajax salivated at the thought of completing this job. He was positive that NICO intended to kill him afterwards. However, the reputation-building benefits of eliminating Augustus and his family were enormous. They outweighed the efforts and risks associated with countering and surviving NICO's intentions. Ajax grunted as he watched the SUV cautiously back onto the roadway.

෴෴෴

The Peñas did not approve of having a television in the back seat to entertain Nathaniel. Instead, they used the time on their drives to talk and sing to him. Nathaniel loved these moments with his parents. He would start to hum song notes once the vehicle went into motion. Being that it was only ten miles to Nana's house, Jennifer chose to sing a short song.

She picked one about numbers that Augustus made up. It blended English and Spanish in a counting sequence. Jennifer started by singing – "One, two, three, four, fiiiiive, six…seven, eight, nine, ten." She then followed that up with – "Uno, dos, tres, cuatro, cinco, seis…siete, ocho, nueve, diez." Jennifer then said – "Okay, Nathaniel, now your turn." Nathaniel enthusiastically complied and began to repeat the song.

It was a quarter to ten in the morning. Jennifer turned onto the main avenue on her way to the interstate. She drove along the city's scenic country club when suddenly her windshield exploded. The world outside appeared to circle her at breakneck speed. She was extremely dizzy and felt as if she were about to pass out. However, she held on to consciousness in order to check on Nathaniel.

She looked to where the rearview mirror should have been. It was gone from the implosion. She painfully turned around and observed Nathaniel. Naturally, he was screaming. He appeared to be doing so from fright and not from injury. Jennifer touched her abdomen and felt a sharp pain. A rush of panic rushed through her. She glanced down to where she just touched and observed that there was no blood. However, her pain was severe. Although not medically trained, she knew she had sustained a massive internal injury. Jennifer looked back at Nathaniel and gently said – "I love you, sweetie, everything is going to be alright. I'll come get you very soon, sugar pie, I promise."

Jennifer slowly turned to look out the front of her vehicle, to see if help was on its way. Instead, she saw a man…a very large man, approaching her side of the vehicle with a gun in his left hand. Jennifer Parsons almost vomited with fear. She knew exactly what this meant, although she had no idea why it was happening.

Helplessly, Jennifer watched as the man pointed the weapon at her. She then heard the muffled shots pop out. Simultaneously, she felt the bullets tear into her chest, as she screamed – "NO…"

🙠🙠🙠

Ajax anticipated the duo would travel this route to access the highway. He had surveyed the area for several days. This stretch was the least populated portion of their route during this time of the morning. Accordingly, he decided to do the killings here.

Ajax drove an official electrical utility vehicle that he acquired. He knew its weight was more than sufficient to spin the SUV if he employed a tactical crash. He had to work quickly. An accident of this magnitude would unquestionably draw emergency personnel to the scene within minutes.

He watched from his vantage point as the SUV approached his predetermined kill-box. When it came time to attack, he careened into the unsuspecting SUV. At a speed of over eighty miles per hour, it caused the SUV to spin wildly out of control. The impact caused the SUV's windshield to implode. This served Ajax well. It cleared away any obstruction, providing him with unhampered shots at the woman.

Ajax jumped out of his truck with amazing speed. He could hear the woman scream as he approached. She understood what he was about to do. Her cries instantly stopped as he pumped three rounds into her defenseless body.

He quickly went to the driver's side, where the window blew out as well. He peered in over the woman's lifeless body and looked at the now hysterical baby boy. *Cute kid,* he thought. Without hesitation, he lifted his weapon and shot at the child. Concurrently, as if somehow reacting to a pang of guilt, Ajax felt a slight wave of nervousness come over him. This caused the shot to go high. Ajax looked into the back seat again and saw that he missed the boy. The child was in such a state of hysteria that he was no longer making noise. His face was as red as could be. Tears and snot covered it; and his mouth, was wide open with streams of saliva leaking out.

"There's no way I am not going to do this," exclaimed Ajax. He checked his weapon to make certain he had another round chambered. Ajax had experience executing family members of all ages. This was not a moral dilemma for him. He heard sirens in the distance. He had just seconds to complete this kill and move on to Augustus. Ajax returned to the blown-out driver's window. He leaned in, confirmed he had the proper angle for a kill shot, and said –"Goodbye, kid."

The child started screaming again, until the gunshots rang out. Nothing but silence filled the cabin. Ajax stood up and looked towards the distant sirens. He had to get out of there quickly. He took off towards a getaway car he stashed close by. Suddenly, his vision became blurred. Everything around him appeared cloudy and white. The sounds of sirens quickly disappeared and Ajax could feel himself falling over.

What just happened to me? He tried to crawl away from the scene but could not move. He felt no pain but knew he was losing blood very quickly. Ajax looked down at his hands. Dark blood covered them. He looked further down and saw his abdomen torn open…a portion of his intestines protruding. "Jesus Christ...how could this…"

Ajax saw the source of his condition. Although the loss of blood distorted his vision, he was able to make out the boy's mother. She crawled over his blood-soaked body, like a zombie emerging from its grave. She said something to him as she spat out blood and had a terrifying look in her eyes.

ॐॐॐ

Jennifer did not know the barbarian who committed this savage act. It did not matter. She was determined to end the life of the demon that dared such an atrocity. She had no experience with combat, or with any form of violence. However, she perceived that her time was quickly nearing the end. She was cold, and getting colder. She was weak, and getting weaker. She knew that she was about to die…but not before she ended this outrage.

She slithered painfully towards him, agonizing over every move. A current of exhilarating energy overcame her, providing the necessary might to continue forward. She climbed onto this large man, now reduced to a severely injured sack of meat.

Jennifer spit up blood as she snarled at him in a deep, guttural voice – "You may have killed me, you mother fucker, but you will not kill my baby!"

ॐॐॐ

Ajax felt hatred in the woman's grip as she grabbed ahold of his hair and harshly pulled his head towards her. He then saw the ominous hunk of metal distinctive of a .357 magnum that she had in her right hand.

Helplessly, Ajax watched in terror as she rammed the barrel into his mouth, breaking several of his teeth…

ॐॐॐ

Jennifer heard the muffled sounds of sirens. She used her left hand to wrap the man's long, matted hair tightly around her palm.

She squeezed as hard as she possibly could and forcefully pulled his head towards her.

Jennifer took one final, deep breath. She then lifted her .357 magnum and crashed it down into the bastard's mouth. The man shrieked in agony as the gun's barrel smashed through his teeth, ripping his gums. She did not waver, and pulled the trigger.

An intense calmness came over her. She felt inexplicably joyous upon seeing the top of his head blowout onto the roadway. Happiness turned into sorrow. Her eyes welled up with tears.

She attempted to call out to her son – "Naaaathaaaa…"
Before she could finish his name, everything went silent.

෫෫෫෫

Augustus Peña was the director of Iowa's Safety and Intelligence Bureau. The state's governor had appointed him to the position three years prior. His colleagues were aware that he came to this office having earned high honors and distinction in service of his country. However, none of them knew exactly what those duties entailed, nor did anyone ask. It was enough, for all those concerned, that a powerful figure in Washington recommended him. The scuttlebutt in the state capitol building was that Augustus previously served as a high-level spy for the CIA. They further surmised that the agency relocated him to Iowa to quietly end out his public service career. Augustus was aware of this speculation. However, he had neither the time nor the inclination to discuss his past.

It was slightly past ten o'clock in the morning. Augustus was in a regularly scheduled meeting at the Bureau's headquarters. His deputy director, Chad Molander, entered and sat next to him. Augustus greeted him with a smile.

Chad whispered, "Sir, we have news breaking out of our westernmost suburb. It appears to be a random carjacking, not far from your home. Local PD and State Patrol are on the scene."

Augustus personally selected Chad for this position. When identifying candidates, he made it clear to his peers what he was looking for. He was determined to find a solid, honest and hard-working individual to be his right hand assistant. Someone not corrupted by political ideology. Nor was he interested in some gung-ho, military type fueled with ego and testosterone. Most of all, Augustus was not interested in legacy applicants. He had no time for cronies whose sole achievement, often, was that they were born into an influential family. After months of scouring resumes and profiles, Augustus found what he was looking for.

Chad Molander was a native Iowan, the son of third generation farmers. He received his baccalaureate degree in French from a small local college. He went on to receive his Juris Doctorate degree from the state's nationally ranked law school. Upon graduation, Chad sat for, and passed, the Iowa bar examination on his first attempt. Augustus was impressed when the young man's application came across his desk. He was even more fascinated after they met in person. Chad was young, intelligent and untouched. Augustus could trust him…and groom him.

Augustus put aside his briefing notes. "Here you go," he said, handing Chad the television's remote control.

"Thanks boss."

Augustus scrutinized the broadcast, immediately struck by what he saw. "Turn the volume up," he demanded. Chad immediately complied and began to share Augustus' intense interest. They then listened to the report's frightening details.

"This just in to the KDSM newsroom…an apparent carjacking in the metro west area has left several people dead. Details of the incident are hard to come by. There is no word on the victims or their identities. Officials have stated that information will be available to the public as soon as possible. Both local police and the sheriff's department are currently on the scene. It appears from where we stand that the State Patrol has just arrived as well. Our news crew will remain here and share any information as soon as it becomes available. Stay with KDSM so that we can keep you posted, up to the minute, as this drama unfolds."

Augustus shot an incredulous look to Chad as the news clip ended. He pointed to the television and was about to say something. Suddenly, the Bureau's phone lines lit up. A cacophony of telephone rings ensued, causing Augustus to swirl around in his chair. The newscast left him numb, accompanied by a bad sensation in the pit of his stomach. He did not know why.

He possessed the ability to handle horrific situations with calmness and professionalism. These were traits absent in most people during these types of situations. Accordingly, news about several murders, irrespective of brutality, should not have affected him. He became concerned. He felt his mouth get dryer by the second.

The office staff scrambled to pick up the ringing phones. Chad ran to answer the one closest to them. As he addressed the caller, Augustus' cell phone buzzed. He looked at the caller ID. It was from the State Patrol.

ॐॐॐ

Iowa State Patrol Trooper Paul Hoffmeyer was the region's most senior officer. He had almost twenty-seven years on the job. Although mostly an administrator at this point in his career, he still had occasion to get out on the road. The State of Iowa's budget woes saw to it that he had his fair share of field time. He did not mind it one bit. Sitting behind a desk and dealing with politicians was an affront on his straightforward, sensible nature.

I love this shit, thought Hoffmeyer as he navigated the Des Moines morning traffic. Hoffmeyer was working the beat on Interstate 80. He was about to run the license plate of a slightly swerving semi-truck when the call came through –

"All units in the vicinity of the metro-west country club…local PD have been advised of a 10-31 and possible 10-32. This is a 10-39. Please advise your availability, over."

"Okay," said Hoffmeyer to the semi in front of him – "Looks like you get a pass today. I have a crime in progress involving a man with a gun and they want me to get there with my lights flashing. You are one lucky bastard." Trooper Hoffmeyer confirmed his availability with dispatch. He then took off like a bat out of hell with his lights flashing and his sirens blaring.

Hoffmeyer arrived on scene less than five minutes later. He instantly disliked what he saw. People had congregated along the roadway where the alleged incident occurred. The local police department was on scene as well as the sheriff's department. Medical personnel were just arriving. Additionally, it appeared that some media outlets were milling about the haphazardly cordoned-off area. Hoffmeyer observed two bodies on the pavement and went towards them.

As he walked, he grabbed his radio and said – "Control….this is 2-5. I am on scene and am about to engage and assist local PD….over."

The radio crackled – "Roger, 2-5. Please be advised that units 3-1 and 3-6 are en route to your location. Notify us of situational status upon inspection, over."

"10-4, Control." He walked to the two bodies and addressed the sheriff's deputy – "What do we have here?"

"Well," said the deputy – "It seems like this guy here got his brains blown out by that woman over there after he tried to rob her or something. It looks like they got into an accident before all of this happened. Maybe a road-rage incident…I don't know."

"Who was driving what?"

The deputy replied – "We believe she was driving the SUV, based on the blood trail. It looks like he crashed into her with the electrical utility truck that is on the mound across the street. We haven't had time to inspect the vehicles yet."

Hoffmeyer asked – "Witnesses?"

The deputy replied – "Yeah. There are a few. They were the first ones to arrive. However, they say that when they got here the woman was about ready to kill the man. They just assume the SUV was hers since there aren't any other vehicles out here other than the truck."

Hoffmeyer replied – "Wow…how wise of them." He looked over at the truck. He agreed it appeared to have hit the SUV before winding up in its current location. "So, an electrical utility worker gets into an accident and gets his brains blown out as a result." Hoffmeyer then said, "Get those witness statements in writing. With all of these people out here, I'm certain somebody can clarify how this went down."

Suddenly, a medic shouted – "SHE'S ALIVE!" Out of thin air, medical personnel swarmed over her to perform triage and take her vitals. The woman tried to speak, but was unable to get out any sound.

Hoffmeyer grabbed his radio and took a few steps back to report the situation. He felt the woman's eyes upon him. Hoffmeyer tilted his head, looked down and made eye contact with her. He had a very strong intuition that she was trying to communicate something to him. Then, he noticed her eyes look towards the SUV.

ﾐﾐﾐ

Trooper Hoffmeyer felt a chill come over his body. He instinctively bolted to the vehicle. He stopped short of it and realized they were mistaken. Something occurred here that was much worse than what any of them had initially thought. Hoffmeyer un-holstered his weapon and slowly inspected the vehicle as he approached. Nothing moved inside of the large SUV and the air within it was dead still.

Upon observing this, the sheriff's deputy and a local police officer hustled to the SUV. They approached Hoffmeyer from behind and asked him if the vehicle was clear. He did not reply. Instead, he dropped his weapon onto the pavement and lunged into the SUV without explanation. The men were stunned. They went to the vehicle to assist.

The deputy got there first. He could not believe his eyes as he observed Hoffmeyer unstrapping a toddler from a car seat. "Jesus Christ, what the blazes went on here?"

Hoffmeyer shouted – "I don't goddamn know. This was not an ordinary carjacking or road-rage incident. There are bullet holes all around this kid. He has no visible wounds. He is not moving and his eyes are closed. However, his breathing is low and fast and his eyelids are moving rapidly. This child is in shock and needs medical attention, NOW."

The deputy sprung from the SUV and shouted towards the medics working on Jennifer – "There is a male toddler in the vehicle that needs medical attention ASAP. He is in shock. There are multiple gunshot holes around him but we believe he has not been hit…move it."

The medics froze for a moment before scrambling to the SUV. Two of them remained with Jennifer while three others responded. Hoffmeyer met the medics with the boy in his arms. Tears streamed down his face as he gently handed him to them.

The deputy placed his hand on Hoffmeyer's shoulder after observing his reaction. "We need to move quickly to find out what happened here. Jurisdiction has to be decided so that there are no hiccups along the way. I am going to call the sheriff at home, right now. Are you okay, trooper?"

Hoffmeyer took a deep breath and replied – "Yeah...yeah, I'm okay." He then grabbed his radio to provide a status update to headquarters.

⋙⋙⋙

Police Officer Ryan Hobbs was a rookie with the local police department. It was his first month on the job. His duty was to identify the affected parties in this disaster. It was a tedious process. In a case like this, it began with checking ownership of the vehicles involved.

"Ryan," his fellow officer called out. "Where are we on the SUV?"

Officer Hobbs replied – "I'm striking out. The state's vehicle database does not recognize these plates. All I keep getting is some error-code." Hobbs wrote the license plate number and error-code down on his notepad. He tore the sheet off, and gave it to the other officer – "Can you do me a favor and check with either the sheriff's deputy or one of the troopers to see if they have better luck? I think I am screwing something up. I'm going over to run the truck."

"Sure rookie, no problem."

Hobbs walked to the truck and gave the exterior a once over to assess the damage. It was a commercial utility vehicle. The company logo along the outside and the lifts on top confirmed it. Identification of ownership was not an issue. However, he needed to identify the dead driver on the pavement. Hobbs knew that utility services tended to have a fleet of vehicles. He needed to locate a specific identifier for this truck to determine that man's identity.

Hobbs went to the back of the truck to obtain license plate information, but it was missing. He then glanced around the immediate area to see if it had fallen off, but he saw nothing. He went to the front. Hobbs was unable to determine from the severe damage if the impact embedded the plate. Frustrated, he decided to go inside to look for some other form of identifying information.

He turned to inform his fellow officer about his plan to enter the truck. When he did, he saw a trooper exit the SUV with a young child in his arms. "Holy –," said Hobbs. "What the heck is going on over there? I better get this information quick and go help them out. This whole thing is getting crazier by the minute."

The truck had sliding doors. They were made of heavy, thick metal. Hobbs pulled hard to get the passenger-side door to open. It appeared that the crash's impact knocked the sliding mechanism off a bit. He opened it as far as it would go. He used his flashlight to look for a spot to get his footing. Because the collision tossed everything around, it was potentially hazardous to walk freely. Once inside, he went to the cockpit area. Hobbs understood that fleet vehicles often had paperwork identifying the driver. However, in this instance, there was none.

Hobbs decided to search the main cabin. He thought, *maybe the driver carried a set of tools with his name on it to mark ownership.* He slowly stepped towards the rear, moving debris along the way. Hobbs stopped dead in his tracks. He drew his weapon and focused his flashlight onto a shadowy figure several feet in front of him. It appeared to be a man.

"Police….don't move!" yelled Hobbs. It seemed as if the man was just sitting there, lying in wait, as if to ambush him. The shock from the encounter wore off. Hobbs was able to refocus his eyes. He observed that the man was in a chair in the rear, and tied with rope. Moreover, his mouth had a rag stuffed in it. Finally, Hobbs was able to see clearly that the man was as dead as a doornail.

ॐॐॐ

Hobbs' fellow officer approached two troopers who just arrived on scene. He sought their assistance on running the SUV's plate information, saying – "Our rookie working the ID process screwed something up. He cannot get a read on this plate number. He keeps getting this error code. I would go check but...I have to maintain the perimeter. Can one of you guys help us out?"

One of the troopers agreed to assist after checking in with Hoffmeyer, and took the piece of paper. Suddenly, Hobbs spilled out of the utility truck, screaming wildly about someone dead inside of it.

"Awe, shit," said the officer, "looks like the rookie just found a dead passenger in the vehicle…probably not wearing a seatbelt. What do you guys think?" The officer signaled Hobbs to come his way. Instead, Hobbs made a beeline to Hoffmeyer and the deputy. The officer said – "What the hell has gotten into him? I mean, yeah, this is definitely a wild scene, but he needs to get a grip."

෨෨෨

Hoffmeyer was providing a status update when he saw Hobbs run frantically towards him. He shot a glance at the deputy standing alongside him. The deputy understood the look to mean he was to take care of this. He stretched his arm out towards the approaching Hobbs and said, "Whoa…slow down son, you're liable to hurt yourself. What's going on?"

Hobbs was short of breath, both from an adrenaline rush and from running too fast. He could not articulate his words.

The deputy, a little concerned, looked at his nametag and said – "Take a deep breath and try to calm down, officer…Hobbs, is it?"

Hobbs used his hands to gesture what he saw in the truck. "Yes, yes, it's Hobbs…that's right. Look, there is a dead guy in the truck. He's…he's in a chair in the back, and tied up with something in his mouth."

The deputy's eyes grew wide with disbelief. He looked at Hoffmeyer, and said – "This is getting worse every damn second. First, we have a woman who is almost dead and a man whose brains she apparently blew out onto the pavement. Next, we find a baby boy shot at from close-range. And, now, there is a dead guy in the back of the utility truck who has been…what did he say…tied up?"

Hoffmeyer informed headquarters that new information surfaced suggesting another fatality. He then signed-off, clipped the radio to his hip and addressed Hobbs. "Officer Hobbs, you're working on identifying these vehicles and their occupants, is that correct?"

"Yes sir. That is correct. I'm a rookie, you see, so...the department has me gathering data for notification purposes."

Hoffmeyer said – "Outstanding. Look, I need what you have gathered so far. Our first order of business is to notify the family of the SUV's occupants. We also need to speak with company representatives from that utility vehicle. We must determine what connection, if any, existed between the occupants of these two vehicles...to figure out why the hell so much violence occurred as a result of their encounter here today."

Hobbs replied – "Yes, of course. However, I don't have that information yet." Hoffmeyer looked at him incredulously. Hobbs quickly jumped to his own defense – "No, you see, I tried several times to run the SUV's license plate. However, the system would not provide ownership information. Instead, I kept receiving an error-code message. I must have messed something up, so I gave the plate number and error-code to my colleague. He is going to see if one of the other agencies can run it through their system. That is why I went to the utility truck. I figured I could at least get license plate data from it. However, the truck had no plates visible. That is when I went inside to look for driver identification and, instead, found the deceased."

Hoffmeyer's posture stiffened straighter than normal. He carefully looked at the crime scene around him. A picture emerged in his head. It was one that he did not like, not one bit. "Where is your colleague now?"

"He is over with the two troopers that just arrived."

Hoffmeyer marched towards them and shouted – "Have either of you run the license plate on that SUV yet?"

"No, sir, we were waiting to check in with you first," responded one of the troopers.

Hoffmeyer said – "Let me get that info from you – I'll run it."

The trooper handed him the piece of paper and said – "Sure, have at it pops, no problem here."

While returning to his car, Hoffmeyer read it. The plate number was nothing special. He did not recognize it from his many vehicle encounters – 401636Z, Dallas County. Hoffmeyer then looked at the error code... EP4CRO and he immediately found the source of his concern. This was not an error code. It was a security protocol set in place to shield the identity of certain high-level officials and their families. If a system hacker with bad intentions ever ran a protected license plate, they would only receive an error message. No amount of effort would yield the type of personal information they may have been seeking.

The codes varied greatly, and were uncommon. This one, however, he knew very well from his protective detail duties at the state capitol complex. It represented Executive Privilege for Cleared Reviewers Only. This was a license plate assigned to a member of the state's executive branch. Only individuals with a particular level of security clearance could inquire into this plate owner's identity. Hoffmeyer's pace picked up. He began trotting to his vehicle. Then, the trot became a quick jog and, finally, an all-out sprint.

Hoffmeyer dove into his squad car's cabin, through its already open door. Miraculously, he avoided colliding with a laptop propped-up on a stand by his steering wheel. "Come on, come on," he growled, fumbling with the laptop's keyboard. "This is not the time for fat fingers." Hoffmeyer entered the plate's number. When the fictitious error-code appeared, he pressed the F7 and F11 keys simultaneously. This activated a search of the license plate in the database's back systems. Next, he called Control to obtain an extra code. When entered, the extra code would release the identifying information to him. Hoffmeyer waited impatiently. Finally, Control responded and the trooper's heart jumped into his throat.

"Sir, the code for the next forty-five seconds will be XT687NMH3, do you copy?"

Hoffmeyer offered a quick affirmation and hurriedly entered the nine-digit code. Then, his eyes bulged. The identifying information appeared on the screen…Augustus Peña.

દ્ય દ્ય દ્ય

Hoffmeyer bolted from his squad car. He touched his chest. His heart raced uncontrollably. He completed a three hundred and sixty degree scan of the area. He did so in such a hasty manner, it made him woozy. He had a strange taste in his mouth. Hoffmeyer was uncertain of what he was looking for. Finally, clarity of both vision and thought came to him. He realized what he needed to do.

He put both hands up by the sides of his mouth and hollered –
"SECURE THE AREA NOW. THIS WAS A TERRORIST
ATTACK!"

A trooper ran to him and asked – "Sir?"

Hoffmeyer explained – "This is not a typical crime scene.
This was not a carjacking gone wrong. This was an assassination
attempt!" The young trooper seemed stunned as he listened to
Hoffmeyer explain – "That woman is the wife of Augustus Peña,
the director of our Safety and Intelligence Bureau; and that child,
presumably, is his son. By the looks of it all, that man with his
head blown off is the one who tried to kill them. We need to lock
this area down right now and get into contact with Safety and
Intelligence. I will handle making contact with them – you get this
area secured. Move the perimeter back and get those fucking
reporters behind the line! I do not want them repeating anything
we say. Get them back far enough so they can't hear a goddamn
thing, do you read me, trooper?"

The young trooper returned a crisp and loud "yes, sir!"

Hoffmeyer grabbed his radio to issue an emergency alert to
headquarters. Gasping for air, he said – "Control, this is 2-5,
over."

The radio crackled – "2-5, this is Control, go ahead."

"Control, the status of this situation is grave. Our initial
assessments were incorrect. This was not a carjacking. It was an
assassination attempt. We are now on high alert. Do you copy
Control? Over."

A slight pause, then – "2-5, we copy. 2-5, what is your
verification for high alert status? Over."

Hoffmeyer responded – "Control, the victims are immediate
family members of Director Augustus Peña. Evidence suggests a
high probability of deliberate targeting. Indirect confirmation of
who the intended victims are came from the vehicle's license plate
registration. It carried a security protocol code. Registration data
was verified as belonging to Director Peña."

"2-5, are there any signs of the director?"

"No, no sign of the director at all. However, there is a corpse
inside of the utility vehicle…it has not been identified."

"2-5, we are placing calls into both the director's office and his mobile phone. Please maintain communication to provide live situational data."

Hoffmeyer replied – "Roger that."

Shortly thereafter, Control said – "2-5, we have made contact with the director's office. He is there. His assistant is getting him now. Please phone in so that we can conference everyone, over."

Hoffmeyer got into his squad car to call. As he dialed, he observed his troopers in an all-out effort to secure the area. *God help us all,* he thought.

࿇࿇࿇

The caller ID on Augustus' cell phone showed it was from the State Patrol. At the same time, Chad handed him the landline receiver he was just talking into, and said – "Sir, State Patrol headquarters needs to speak with you immediately."

Augustus frowned and replied – "It is obvious that they do. They just called my cell." He took the receiver – "Augustus Peña, how can I help you?"

The communication was blunt – "Sir, there appears to have been a violent attack on your wife and child this morning, not far from your home. We have troopers and local law enforcement on scene right now. The situation is fluid. I have Trooper Paul Hoffmeyer on the line. He is one of our most senior administrators who happened to be on patrol this morning. Trooper Hoffmeyer, go ahead please."

Hoffmeyer provided Augustus with a gut-wrenching account of what appeared to have transpired. The horrific details caused Augustus to stand abruptly. He lost his balance, stumbled backwards and almost dropped the phone. Augustus then asked, "My baby…my wife…where…?"

"Emergency personnel transported them to City Hospital just minutes ago."

Augustus steadied his composure and said – "I will be at the hospital shortly. Please…call me directly on my mobile phone with every update."

After Augustus provided his mobile number, Hoffmeyer replied – "Yes, of course, sir." Hoffmeyer then queried – "Sir, although it has not been officially discussed, I'm guessing that State Police will assume jurisdiction over this matter…in conjunction with your office? Is that correct, director?"

Augustus placed his right hand to his forehead to wipe away droplets of sweat. He looked over at Chad, then replied – "You are correct, Trooper. State Police will have concurrent jurisdiction with Safety and Intelligence. It would be best, as I see it, if you personally took charge of the scene and remain our point of contact there. However, you need to check with your commanding officer on exactly how to handle that detail. My office will officially make that request in the coming minutes."

"Yes, sir – understood."

Augustus then said – "As far as my agency's role is concerned, I'm afraid that I have been compromised due to the attack on my family. Consequently, all orders from our office will come through my deputy director, Chad Molander. He will be this agency's point-of-contact going forth. Is that clear, trooper?"

Hoffmeyer replied, "Absolutely, sir."

Augustus hung up the phone. He looked at Molander and softly said – "Someone just tried to kill my baby…and my wife. I need to get to City Hospital as soon as humanly possible. You are officially the acting director of this agency until further notice."

Chad's voice quivered with emotion and asked – "Who would do such a thing director?"

Augustus opened his drawer and retrieved his service-weapon. He holstered it along with a few extra clips of ammunition. He then looked at Chad with a chilling, enraged expression and replied – "I don't know…yet."

❧❧❧

Hoffmeyer's men were moving people up and away from the area. Media personnel did not approve of the tactic. "Under whose orders are we being moved?" asked one reporter. A separate news team was recording their broadcast. Suddenly, they needed to dismantle their setup and get behind the newly created perimeter. "Why are you doing this? Who is in charge of this scene?" asked an angry reporter.

"I am," said Hoffmeyer, suddenly appearing in front of the protesting reporter. "My name is Trooper Paul Hoffmeyer, and this crime scene is now under the direct jurisdiction of the Iowa State Police." The reporters all scrambled to write this down. "Now, get moving past the line so that we can continue processing the area." Hoffmeyer turned and motioned to Hobbs and the deputy to come to him. "Okay, this is the situation," he said. "The circumstances surrounding this ordeal are worse than what we initially thought." Hoffmeyer addressed Hobbs – "Junior, you didn't screw anything up. In fact, you did one hell of an excellent job by reporting what you perceived to be an error." He then explained all that he knew, including State Police's jurisdiction.

"Holy shit!" exclaimed the sheriff, who arrived as Hoffmeyer started his briefing. "Yes, yes, of course this is state's jurisdiction, no doubt about it. Do the Feds need to be notified?"

Hoffmeyer replied – "If or when the Feds get involved is beyond my role and, quite frankly, not my concern. They will let us know if they are taking this over, you can count on that." Hoffmeyer looked around and continued – "As a matter of precaution, we are getting extra personnel to process this scene. We are also going to search the surrounding area for potential evidence. Sheriff, make certain that onlookers and the media remain far enough back to prevent them from peppering us with questions. If you leave it up to those assholes, they'll have this case solved by the evening news."

Hoffmeyer paused with a pensive look on his face and said – "These acts were extremely wanton and brazen. They exhibit the perpetrator's total disregard for the sanctity of human life. It is possible there are bodies we have yet to find. We need to perform a complete sweep of the vehicles involved and work our way out to the existing perimeter, and then beyond. Again, until otherwise advised, I am in charge of this scene and all orders come through me. Are there any questions?"

The officers replied in unison – "No, no sir…not at all," as they fanned out.

Hoffmeyer looked at the road beyond his squad car. He saw a parade of flashing law enforcement lights off into the distance. "Here come the cavalry," he said.

❧ ❧ ❧

Augustus and Chad sprinted as fast as they could through headquarters. When they arrived at the black, oversized SUV, Chad said – "Sir, please, let me drive." Augustus nodded in agreement. Chad floored the pedal and the large engine roared to life as he sped to City Hospital in record pace. Augustus jumped out of the SUV before it came to a complete stop. He then ran like the wind towards the emergency room entrance. Augustus held his shield high in the air, yelling – "I am Augustus Peña, director of Iowa's Safety and Intelligence Bureau. Where are my wife and son? They are victims of a violent attack and are now here. WHERE ARE THEY?"

Chad ran directly behind Augustus, panting, and operating on pure adrenaline. He noticed a doctor off to the left signaling them – "Sir, that doctor over there…to the left…he's motioning towards us. Let's go to him." Augustus tore off towards the doctor without saying a word and Chad flew right behind him.

"Mr. Peña, I am Doctor Mark Broderson and am the physician on duty. Come, I'll take you to your family." Surmising that Augustus was in no frame of mind to walk, the doctor ran. Augustus followed suit…and so did Chad. Doctor Broderson stopped and pointed to a room on the right, saying – "Your wife is in there. She is in critical condition. You need to be extremely cautious about how much you interact with her. Stress would not be good for her. I sedated her heavily to get her vitals stabilized. Mr. Peña, your wife suffered internal trauma due to the collision. She also sustained multiple gunshot wounds to her upper torso. Luckily, the bullet wounds, while traumatic, did not cause massive internal damage. Nevertheless, the blood loss alone from these events has devastated her body, and can be fatal. I'm sorry, Mr. Peña."

Augustus stepped to the room and peeked in to see Jennifer. From where he stood, he could see her legs and the lower portion of her left arm. Most of what he could see was machinery and all of the wiring and tubing associated with it. Augustus retreated. He put his back against the hallway wall and knocked his head against it. Then, slowly, he asked – "My son?"

"Come with me, Mr. Peña." Augustus hesitated. Doctor Broderson whispered – "He is alive and is doing fairly well. I wanted to step away from the room before talking about your son in the unlikely event your wife wakes up. If she is going to survive, she absolutely cannot be preoccupied with the details of her child's recovery."

Augustus nodded, and asked – "What has he sustained?"

Broderson replied – "No physical injuries. This is fantastic news, and quite a miracle I might add, given the circumstances. However, he has sustained quite a bit of shock. Your son is, what, about two years old, is that correct?"

"That is correct, why?"

Broderson said – "Even as young as he is, he was very much able to appreciate most of what happened. The severity of what he saw is traumatic enough for someone our age. For a little guy like that, though, it is extremely serious. He is at Children's Hospital next door, which is the north wing on this floor. I sedated him as well. He will remain that way for the next ten hours or so. I had to do that to settle down his little nervous system, to avoid the possibility of seizures resulting from his shock."

Augustus replied – "I fully understand, doctor. But, I still need to go see him."

Broderson replied – "Oh, yes, of course – let's go."

They walked quickly to Children's Hospital. Augustus' cell phone buzzed. He looked, expecting it to be an incoming call or text. Instead, it was a calendar reminder, set to go off two hours before he was to pick Nathaniel up from his Nana's house. The cruel irony of the moment was too much for Augustus to take. He let out a loud, emotional wail – "WHY?" His voice echoed down the hallway. It caught Doctor Broderson and everyone else around them entirely off guard. Broderson put his hand on Augustus' shoulder. Augustus cupped his face in his hands and they both continued the rest of the way, silently.

When they arrived, Augustus made a beeline to the bed and knelt by his son. He reached up, held the boy's chubby, little hand, and said a silent prayer. Augustus stood up, kissed Nathaniel's hand and stood over him while parting the boy's hair to the right. He always did this whenever Nathaniel's hair got a little messy. Augustus bent over, gently wrapped his son in his arms and placed his cheek alongside of his baby's face. He remained motionless and listened to every deep, innocent breath his boy took.

Augustus whispered – "No hay nada en este mundo que es más importante en mi vida, Nataniel, que tú. Mi hijo, yo te amo." A surge of tears and raw emotion rushed over him. However, he could not give in. He could not afford to risk his family's safety by falling into an emotional breakdown. Augustus did not know why this happened to them or who was behind it…or if the danger was over. No matter how tempting it was to curl into a fetal position and cry, he needed to be strong. Augustus kissed Nathaniel on his cheek and forehead and gently removed his arms from around him.

He looked up at the doctor and said – "I need to have State Police agents stationed around-the-clock by my family. If this presents a challenge to the care of other patients, then I suggest you make the necessary arrangements to have them moved."

Broderson was a bit startled by Augustus' sudden change in demeanor and replied – "Yes, yes, of course…right away."

Augustus glanced at Nathaniel once more and then exited the room.

 తతత

Chad was outside communicating with various law enforcement agencies. As the newly designated point-of-contact, he was the busiest he had ever been. Chad's heart almost stopped when he saw Augustus emerge from the hospital. He feared what he might learn about the family's condition. Chad was on a call with the State Medical Examiner's Office. He cut the call short and asked Augustus – "How are they, sir? Are you okay? Is there anything that I can do in there?"

Augustus gave him a look of sincere gratitude and said – "No, Chad, Gracias. The doc has got them squared away. I need you to continue doing a great job out here. But thank you, I really do appreciate it."

Chad nodded in affirmation, and said – "Okay, here is the status so far. The scene's perimeter is under control. It sounds like Trooper Hoffmeyer is kicking some serious buttocks keeping everyone in line and on task. Extra personnel are on hand to conduct a wider search of the area. The State Medical Examiner's Office, as opposed to the county coroner, is going to have jurisdiction over the two deceased. They're taking over based on the intended victims…ugh…sorry."

Augustus replied – "No, that's alright. You are doing a great job. Go on."

Chad continued – "Okay, that's pretty much it. Except, the State Medical Examiner's office cannot collect the bodies for at least another two hours. They have a staff shortage due to the recent budget cuts. So, identification of the deceased assailant and the other person won't be for some time yet."

Augustus scrunched his lips in frustration and said – "Just because the deceased are not officially identified doesn't mean that I can't see who they are. Dial up Trooper Hoffmeyer. Tell him to email you a photo of, at the very least, the son-of-a-bitch that my wife killed."

Chad found some humor in the matter-of-fact way Augustus described his wife's action and smiled as he made the call.

അ‌ അ‌ അ‌

True to Chad's assessment, Hoffmeyer was indeed kicking ass and taking names amid the hectic scene. "Is there a particular reason why that reporter is setup below the line? Move your ass and get her back over it!" he yelled to a trooper. He then said to Hobbs – "Son, you found the dead body in that truck. I believe that it is your honor to perform preliminary identification. It is okay if you are unable to ID the stiff. The State Medical Examiner's Office will do it once they get their sorry asses down here. Do you need gloves?"

Hobbs felt slightly disgusted at the prospect of working on a recently deceased body. It was unheard of for a rookie to be doing this type of investigative work. Yet, he recognized the fact that Hoffmeyer's suggestion was well intended. It was a professional gesture for having done great work. *Heck,* thought Hobbs. *Who knows what I can find next? I can move up the local ranks in no time if I keep uncovering stuff. First, it was the license plate code followed by the dead body in the truck. Man, this could be great for me.* Hobbs accepted the duty and said, "Thank you, Trooper Hoffmeyer."

Hoffmeyer pulled out a pair of latex gloves from his utility pouch and handed them to Hobbs. He nodded his head and tipped the rim of his hat saying – "Let me know what you find in there, son." Hobbs waved the gloves in the air confidently. He then ran to the truck and went inside. Hoffmeyer's mobile phone rang.

"Trooper Hoffmeyer, this is Deputy Director…uh…Acting Director Chad Molander."

"Ah, yes, sir. What can I do for you?"

Chad said – "Sir, I was just explaining to Director Peña the delay we are experiencing with the SME's response time. If possible, can you get us some digital pictures of the deceased assailant? Director Peña wants a visual of who did this to his family."

Hoffmeyer replied – "Absolutely, sir. However, you need to know, it is a mess. Facial recognition is going to be a bit of a challenge. The fatal shot took off part of the forehead as well as the top of the skull."

"I understand."

Hoffmeyer said – "I will get some photos sent to you in the next ten to fifteen minutes." The men terminated their call. Hoffmeyer shouted to a trooper who was already taking pictures of the scene – "Take half a dozen shots of the alleged assailant's face and bring the camera to me immediately afterwards."

The trooper complied and took six photographs from several different angles. "Here you go, sir," said the trooper handing the camera to Hoffmeyer.

Hoffmeyer hurried to his squad car and connected the camera to his laptop. He uploaded the pictures and sent them to Chad's smartphone.

࿇࿇࿇

As Augustus spoke with a team of doctors about his family's recovery, Chad informed him that the pictures were coming through. Augustus excused himself and went to him.

"We've got four of what appears to be six images coming through."

Augustus replied – "Okay. I'm going to wrap-up with the doctors then come back to check them out." He returned to the awaiting physicians and completed his conversation. Afterwards, he took a deep breath. *Time to see who the animal is that did this to my innocent, beautiful family.* Augustus inadvertently snatched the phone. Chad understood Augustus' anger. He was not offended.

Augustus stared at the first couple of photos. He felt deep wretchedness that this figure tried to murder his family. However, this feeling morphed into immense pride for Jennifer. As injured as she was, she succeeded in inflicting the lethal damage contained in these photos. *She really fucked him up good,* thought Augustus. *I cannot figure out what he looks like.* Augustus moved onto the next few photos. These showed the lower portion of the deceased man's face…and he dropped the phone.

Augustus instantly retrieved it and looked at the photographs again. Although the upper-half of the man's face was un-discernible, his jaw was still intact. It was a unique jaw. Augustus had seen it twice before, but on two different people. The first person was a highly ranked KGB officer named Afon. Augustus met him decades ago while doing wet-work in the Middle East. The other person was Afon's son, named Ajax. Augustus knew Ajax to be a NICO asset. The jaw in the photo belonged to a man much younger than Afon. Consequently, that would mean that the man Jennifer killed earlier today…was Ajax!

"WHAT THE FUCK?" Augustus exclaimed. "This can't be. Why would he do this? Why would they?" He weighed the possibility of this being someone else having nothing to do with Ajax, Afon or NICO. "I cannot jump to conclusions," he said.

Chad overheard everything Augustus said and stated – "I'm sorry sir, but I don't quite understand what it is that you're saying."

Although clearly somewhere else in thought, Augustus asked – "The other deceased man was tied up in the truck, correct?"

"Yes, he was. His mouth was gagged as well."

Augustus moved closer to believing that this was in fact Ajax. The man perversely enjoyed tying up and torturing people he intended on killing anyway. He considered this his calling card. A flash of recollection entered Augustus' mind. He opened his eyes wide and said to Chad, "Get me Hoffmeyer on the phone, fast."

ॐॐॐ

Hoffmeyer was walking the perimeter when his phone rang. He answered and asked – "Acting Director Molander, did the pictures go through okay?"

"Trooper Hoffmeyer," said Chad. "They did. Director Peña needs to speak with you urgently…hold on, please."

Augustus grabbed the phone and started talking – "Trooper Hoffmeyer, some of the photos lead me to believe that the deceased is a professional killer. I can brief you later on the details. However, of great importance now is that you and your men traverse the area with extreme caution. If I am correct, he would have left something on the scene to create a diversion as part of his getaway plan."

"What are you thinking he might have left?"

Augustus replied – "I'm not sure, but I am having Molander call in the bomb squad just in case. In the interim, keep your units in the open until they arrive."

Hoffmeyer said loudly, "Absolutely." He then unlatched his radio and addressed all personnel on the scene. "This is scene command. All units…stop what you are doing right now, and report to me immediately. We suspect that an incendiary device might be within the perimeter. We are to stand down until the bomb squad arrives. I repeat, stop what you are doing and come to my location immediately. I will be at my vehicle…scene command, out."

ॐॐॐ

Officer Hobbs moved about confidently within the utility truck. He felt convinced that he would not flinch if he came across another body. After determining there were no more, he proceeded to the deceased male in the back. Hobbs placed the end of the flashlight into his mouth while he put on the latex gloves. "Okay buddy," he said to the corpse. "Let's find out who you are." Hobbs worked through the pockets plainly visible on the deceased man's clothing, but came up empty.

He jumped slightly when his radio crackled. He heard Hoffmeyer's loud voice issuing a directive to meet at his vehicle. The remainder of the message was static-filled and garbled. All that Hobbs was able to discern was that Hoffmeyer wanted to meet at his squad car. "Ah crap, just when I was really starting to have fun. Alright, see you in a few," he said to the corpse.

Hobbs was about to remove his gloves when he saw a rectangular leather wallet on the floor. "Well lookie here," he said, reaching for it. He pulled up on the wallet. It did not move. Hobbs observed that the wallet had a chain across it. Believing it to be a traditional motorcycle wallet, he thought nothing of it. He assumed the chain was stuck on something. Hobbs gave it a hard yank…and pulled up towards him. The wallet released and a loud, metallic CLANK reverberated throughout the truck's cab.

෨෨෨

The explosion rocked the entire crime scene. Debris from the truck flew in every direction. A ball of fire accompanied the debris. It set Jennifer's SUV ablaze, in addition to two law enforcement vehicles. The blast's force sent Hoffmeyer airborne across his squad car and onto the pavement beyond. Fortunately, the other officers were already by Hoffmeyer's vehicle. Most of the shrapnel did not reach their location. Nevertheless, the blast was powerful enough to disperse them throughout the air as well.

Hoffmeyer laid flat on his back. He had the presence of mind to understand what just happened, but did not know what blew up. He felt a deep soreness around his temples and had the sensation his brain was spinning inside his skull. He took several breaths. Then, he rolled over to his stomach and slowly pushed himself up to stand.

Once upright, he became acutely aware of the explosion's source. Flames engulfed the now gutted utility truck. He observed that the SUV and two squad vehicles were also on fire. He became alarmed that the smoldering autos would explode. With no fire crews on scene, Hoffmeyer knew he had to move the personnel to a safer distance. He quickly made his way, albeit wobbly, to the sprawled out officers.

"Get up, get moving, those cars are going to explode," he yelled. Hoffmeyer looked up to where they recently moved the media and other onlookers. He was incredibly thankful for their distance. It appeared that none of them sustained injuries. Looking at the fiery scene, Hoffmeyer observed that the deceased perpetrator's body had caught on fire as well. "Ain't that the damnedest thing?" Hoffmeyer shook his head as he watched Ajax's body burn to a crisp.

It was at this point that he realized the sad reality of Hobbs' demise. He knew the young rookie was dead because they were all waiting for him to come out in order to start the briefing.

Hoffmeyer felt lightheaded and sat down on the curb as he grabbed his radio.

⌘⌘⌘

FIVE
"No evil can happen to a good man, either in life or after death" – Socrates

An echoing rumble filled the air. To the untrained ear, it sounded like a passing storm in the distance. However, Augustus was well versed in the sounds of detonations. He was certain of what he just heard. "God-damn-it," he shouted running to Chad. "Call Hoffmeyer and find out if something went off there." Chad did not need to. The call came into him. He received confirmation of the destructive blast. Augustus had not been entirely sure that the jaw he saw in the photo belonged to Ajax. Now, there was no doubt in his mind. The diversionary explosion was a hallmark NICO exit strategy that Augustus himself had employed in the past.

Sweat poured down Augustus' face. The realization of NICO sending an assassin to kill his family sank in. *Presumably, I was the main target,* thought Augustus. Then he said aloud, "and I still am." The wheels churned rapidly in his head as he tried to figure out exactly what was going on. *Was it because of the books? Milken cleared me for fictional stories. That cannot be why.* He did not care why NICO was trying to kill them, only that they were. He needed to determine their next move.

Augustus was convinced NICO's plan did not contemplate Jennifer thwarting Ajax's aggression by blowing his head off. He paced about frenziedly and thought – *They send a top operative to kill us all. This is something they will make sure does not remain in the minds of anyone outside their management structure.* He dug deeper into his analysis – *This operation would be a clean sweep. Kill the marks...then, kill the assassin. My God, NO.*

He sprinted into the hospital and went straight to Jennifer's recovery room. "There is a second assassin here," Augustus whispered. "Their job was to kill Ajax after he took care of us. Ajax is dead without having completed the job. Consequently, the secondary will finish what he failed to accomplish. I have no time to spare. They are already here." Augustus had to think and act decisively to protect his family from what he knew was an imminent attack. He had no idea who the next assassin would be. He could not even surmise whether it would be a man or a woman. Irrespective, he knew they were coming…and soon.

NICO is very thorough and efficient. They will waste no time in attacking again. He called Chad and ordered him to bring his vehicle to the ambulance docking area by the emergency room. "I can't explain. There is no time, but get it done – now." Augustus issued more orders. "If there is an ambulance there, have it moved under my direct authority for public safety. I need you to back my vehicle right up to the doors…and leave the engine running."

Chad responded – "Yes, absolutely, on my way to get it now." He whizzed across the parking lot thinking – *What in the world is going on now?*

Augustus left Jennifer's room and ran at lightning speed to Nathaniel. When he got there, two doctors were leaving his son's recovery room. Augustus yelled out to them at the top of his lungs – "FREEZE. Show me your identification."

The doctors froze and one of them asked – "Mr. Peña, are you okay?"

Augustus pulled out his weapon and growled – "SHOW ME NOW." Both doctors trembled as they reached for their identification badges. Anyone could easily forge a hospital ID. However, their frightened reactions convinced Augustus they were not assassins. The fear they exhibited was not an emotion NICO operatives were capable of experiencing. Augustus waved them off and ran inside to retrieve Nathaniel.

He wrapped Nathaniel in the blankets from his bed. He then gave his son three rapid kisses on the forehead. "I am very sorry for disturbing your sleep, Papito, but we must go now," said Augustus. He then bolted out the room and down the hallway, past the still frightened doctors.

సా సా సా

Chad backed the large SUV into the empty ambulance docking area. He was explaining to the EMT officer in charge of the dock his orders. Suddenly, Augustus barreled out of the gangway yelling – "The Station, Chad…take my son there. I will join you shortly!"

Chad gave a bewildered look and asked – "The Station, sir?"

Augustus replied – "Yes Chad, the Station! There is another assassin on the way, if not already here, to kill my family and me. I am going to get my wife now. However, I need you to take my son away from here right now." Augustus laid his deeply sedated toddler along the wide floor of the rear passenger area. They had no car seat and no time to locate and install one.

Augustus reached into a compartment along the rear floorboard. He pulled out a 9mm handgun kept in the vehicle for emergencies. He confirmed the ammunition clip was full. He then chambered a round and handed the weapon to Chad. "Safety is off," he said calmly. He then said – "I know you have not qualified with weapons for this position. However, you come from a rural family. I have to believe that you've at least shot at something while you were growing up." Chad gulped hard and Augustus said – "Chad, understand this. If you choose to not fire this gun for the sake of wanting to reason with whoever is threatening you, then you will die…and so will my son." Chad nodded quickly and Augustus said – "Now…get the fuck out of here – GO!"

෨෨෨

Chad sped off at an alarmingly high rate of speed. Then, he remembered that Nathaniel was on board, so he slowed down. Upon exiting the hospital's parking lot, Chad engaged the vehicle's emergency flashing lights. This allowed him to navigate through traffic without having to constantly stop-and-go. Chad kept looking back at Nathaniel to make sure he was okay. *He actually seems snug in that spot,* he thought. *Now, all I have to do is remember how to access the Station.*

The Station was a subterranean medical facility built underneath the Iowa State Capitol Complex shortly after the September-eleventh attacks. It was part of a Continuation-of-Government plan. The Station could provide all necessary medical care to injured heads-of-state in the event of a catastrophic attack that rendered all other medical facilities useless. The public, and most government officials, were unaware of its existence. It was still in its infancy stage of development. Military medical personnel, holding top-secret security clearances, routinely inspected and maintained the equipment and medicines.

Ironically, Chad became aware of this facility only three weeks ago. Due to the secretive nature of its existence, Augustus had to be certain that Chad was trustworthy enough to possess this knowledge. Thankfully, he was, especially given the situation they currently found themselves in.

Chad arrived at the state capitol parking structure. He drove down to the lowest level. Here, he would gain access to a tunneled roadway that led to the Station. Chad pressed his index finger onto a camouflaged pad, located inside a heavily pockmarked cement wall. Next, he entered an alphanumeric code. Chad successfully gained access and the wall in front of him opened sideways, revealing a dimly lit road. Remembering that the walls remained open for only thirty seconds, he hurriedly re-entered the vehicle and drove through.

Chad looked back to check on Nathaniel and then out the rear window. He was comforted to see that the opening behind them began to close.

ॐॐॐ

Augustus was in full operational mode. After seeing Chad off, he grabbed the EMT officer on duty and verified his identification. He then informed him of the imperativeness of having an ambulance at-the-ready for immediate evacuation. He also impressed upon him the absolute need for secrecy.

The EMT officer acquiesced, but informed Augustus that he had no medical personnel available to go along.

"I'll take care of that," said Augustus, as he jetted to Jennifer's recovery room. Suddenly, it occurred to him that NICO most certainly compromised his cell phone. To overcome this handicap, he snatched as many mobile phones as he could find. *You can always depend on people leaving their shit unattended,* thought Augustus, as he pocketed devices. He ran so fast that he slid into Jennifer's room, even as he tried to stop his momentum.

He gently, but quickly, touched her all over to make sure she was still alive. "Oh, thank God," said Augustus, grateful he arrived before anything happened. He kissed her on the nose. He then whispered into her ear – "Baby, we have to get out of here. I am taking care of it. Nathaniel is safe. I love you so much."

Augustus assessed the room to determine if there was another way out. He wanted to avoid going past the staff posted just outside of it. It was a large suite. It looked like it could house multiple patients, but she was the only one.

Jennifer had a lot of machinery hooked up to her. Multiple tubes ran to and from her body. *Getting her out of here is not going to be as simple as it was with Nathaniel,* he thought. *Her transport must be cautious and professionally done. If not, this can end tragically for us all.*

He stepped out of the room, and called for Doctor Broderson. The doctor responded from down the hall. Broderson trotted over and asked how he could help. "Doctor, can you please come in with me?" They both entered Jennifer's room.

Augustus said – "I understand the hospital has protocols that it must follow. I greatly respect that. However, this is a unique and dangerous situation. I need your help. I must have my wife moved out of this hospital as soon as possible. There is an imminent threat to her life…again."

Broderson replied – "I…I don't know what I can do. What do you want me to do?"

"I need to transport my wife to a location outside of this hospital. However, I need to do it in a way that does not draw attention."

Broderson replied – "That is impossible! I can't do that."

Augustus yelled – "STOP." They both looked at Jennifer. Augustus put his index finger to his lips while motioning his eyes towards her. The doctor nodded in agreement. Augustus whispered, "Doctor, at the very minimum, can you help me move her into the area back there?" He pointed to a space on the opposite side of the room. The lights were off and it appeared to be next to a stairway door.

Broderson replied – "That area is not suitable for care. We use that to store equipment –"

Augustus interrupted – "Not for care, doctor, for hiding." The doctor gave him an inquisitive look. Augustus then said – "Doc, there is another killer coming for her. I already evacuated my son.

But, her condition is such that I cannot simply whisk her away on my own without revealing her evacuation to the killer."

Doctor Broderson exclaimed – "My God. Who is it? We need to notify the police."

Augustus shot back – "We have no time Doctor Broderson. The killer is coming." Augustus was confident that his family's condition did not impede his judgment. He sensed a predator and knew that time had run out for an evacuation from the hospital. The NICO assassin was close…and coming for them.

დდდ

Kjas Brüder walked coolly across the hospital's parking lot. He wore formal attire and donned an official physician's jacket. On his left breast was displayed an identification badge that read FEMA – Visiting Surgeon. Above it, a nametag bore the fictitious name Dr. Kurtis Swaim. Kjas Brüder was NICO's Field Asset Control Manager. An eighteen-year NICO veteran, Kjas monitored the organization's assets. He never developed any personal relationships nor did he have a place he called home. Accordingly, Kjas had a sociopathic-like contempt for those who did. His tolerance was even lower for those in his trade that even dared toy with the concept. Thus, when the Augustus project materialized, he was extremely eager to participate. Initially, Kjas was unaware of the plan to kill the family too. However, when he figured out what Ajax was up to, his bloodlust for the project grew. He fully supported it.

Kjas experienced guilty pleasure watching Ajax fall at the hands of the woman. He monitored the events from a getaway car Ajax thought he had securely stashed. With Ajax dead, the duty to complete the mission was now his. It felt like a dream come true. Besides, Kjas had taken a liking to Ajax. The "mad Russian" made Kjas laugh when discussing his victorious adventures with women from around the globe. He would have pitied killing Ajax. He was thankful to the woman for her ferocious attempt at saving her and her child's life.

Kjas stopped to address a doctor and a police officer who were talking by the hospital's entrance. In his best backwoods Kentucky drawl, he said – "That explosion just now makes me think we've got more business coming this way. I'm gonna get on inside and scrub-up." The doctor and police officer agreed with his assessment. They departed to prepare for any potential incoming patients. Kjas thought – *Good God...no challenges from the doctor or the officer. They took my word as authority. Things are going very well.* Kjas then slickly made his way into the emergency room area to locate the Peña family.

෯෯෯

Augustus and the doctor quickly cleared a path to get Jennifer into the back area. The space was extremely dark. Broderson reached to flip on the light switch but Augustus stopped him. "No, leave it dark. We will move slowly. Besides, the light emanating from the stairwell is sufficient for me to guide her bed. I just need you to make certain the equipment is properly moved and that everything is still attached when we're done."

Broderson reluctantly agreed. They moved Jennifer as far back into the space as possible. The doctor checked Jennifer to make certain she was not medically at risk. He then checked the machinery to see if it was still functioning properly. "Can I get a little light to make sure?" he asked.

Augustus reached into his pocket. He pulled out a phone he had just thieved. He then randomly pressed a button on it so that it would illuminate. Augustus faced the phone towards Broderson and said – "Here you go."

The doctor made his final checks and said – "We're all good."

Augustus assisted him up from the floor and said – "Thank you very much, doctor. There is something else I need your help with, though."

"I kind of expected you to say that. What do you need?"

Augustus said – "I need you to make certain that there is an ambulance at-the-ready in the docking area. I do not intend on waiting around to see if a killer is coming tonight. She is safe here with me, in the dark, in the event someone does appear with mal intentions. However, if no one does and the ambulance preparations are complete, then we must move fast. This ward will need to be locked down while we discreetly remove her to the ambulance."

Broderson replied – "My God, man, you are being impractical. I cannot shut down an entire ward. Nor can it be done in the expedient timeframe I assume you need it in."

Augustus stepped towards him and said – "Doctor, please, go check on an ambulance, now. Precious time is slipping by. If you have any misgivings about my actions and plan on reporting this to the proper authorities, do not waste your time. I am that proper authority. I am the director of Iowa's Safety and Intelligence Bureau. An assassin, Doctor Broderson, attempted to murder my wife and baby today. They came to this hospital to recuperate only to be targeted by a second assassin who, I assume, is also coming after me."

Doctor Broderson appeared sheepish and fully understood the gravity of the situation. He nodded his head, and offered a heartfelt apology.

"Doc," said Augustus. "No one else needs to know about this right now. It would cause panic and that works to the killer's advantage. Also, even if you secure the ambulance in the coming minutes, please wait for me to call you to let you know we are ready. I need to make the necessary security arrangements before having her transported. In the interim, you should try to stay away from here."

Broderson replied – "I agree. I will alert the staff here that you need absolute privacy." He then left the room to see about the ambulance.

৵৵৵

Augustus bounced into action as soon as the doctor left. He successfully convinced him that an escape was still possible. However, Augustus knew this was not true. Broderson had served his purpose, for now. Augustus needed to get rid of him in order to continue his preparations. He grabbed a gurney stored in the back area, as well as a pillow and sheets. He carelessly tossed them onto the stretcher and positioned it where Jennifer's bed had been. Augustus inspected his handy work. *This appears naturally situated for anyone coming into the room.* He then said – "I need bait." Augustus stepped into the hallway. He waved at a young, blonde nurse who had administered medicine to Jennifer earlier.

The nurse came over, smiled at Augustus and said – "Yes, Mr. Peña…is everything okay?"

"I'm not sure yet. Come, look at what I mean." He led the nurse into the room and silently locked the door behind them. Augustus positioned himself by her side. The nurse turned and said – "I don't understand, where –"

As she spoke, Augustus struck her on the side of her neck with the bladed edge of his open hand. She instantly dropped to the floor. Augustus hoped that he did not kill her. However, he needed to strike hard enough for her to pass out silently…and for a long time. He picked her up over his shoulder and carried her to the gurney. He covered her with the sheets and propped her head up on the pillow. Augustus then ran to check on Jennifer. She was doing well.

Augustus opened the stairwell door next to Jennifer's bed. He loosened the light bulb above the doorway until it blinked. He reentered the room and wedged open the door by placing a small container on the floor, where the door met its frame. Augustus then exited the room through the main entrance, which he locked from the inside.

"Excuse me," Augustus said to a woman in the nurse's pod as he pointed back to the room. "She's knocked out cold. I am going to visit with my son for a little bit. Can you see to it that she is not disturbed? If you must go in, I really need to be here. Please, phone me before you do. Here's my cell number." Augustus handed the nurse his business card, certain she did not know he had already evacuated Nathaniel. He relied heavily on his perception of a severe lack of communication within the medical community. He moved swiftly down the hall towards the Children's Hospital wing.

Augustus looked back to see if anyone watched him. Nobody did. He then darted to the stairway entrance on his right. Augustus bolted to the level below and emerged breathless. He took a brief moment to determine his surroundings. He needed to locate the stairway leading up to Jennifer's room. This floor's plan was set up a bit differently, so it was not readily apparent to him where that staircase would be.

He chose this strategy so that the staff believed Jennifer was alone in the room. Augustus knew, unfortunately, that if the killer appeared seeking entry that the nurse would fail to call him. That is why he locked the door from the inside. However, it was not foolproof. It would only cause delay until the nurse obtained a key. His heart raced with fear at the thought of Jennifer being up there, alone, and vulnerable. He figured out the floor plan and darted to where he believed the staircase to be.

The room contained two patients and several visitors. Augustus entered it, pointed to the staircase door and said – "Coming through…sorry folks. I just need to make sure that these doors are all unlocked. Safety codes, you know?" He did not wait for a reaction and walked through the stairway door. He looked up to the floor above and saw the reflection of a blinking light. "Perfect," he said. Augustus ran up the two flights of stairs several steps at a time.

ॐॐॐ

Kjas sought someone unlikely to challenge his credentials when inquiring about the family. He singled out an overworked yet eager intern running from room to room. *Ah,* he thought. *She would know.* The intern came out of a room and Kjas said – "Excuse me, ma'am, can you please point me to where the female victim with multiple gunshot wounds is at? She was recently brought in with her child." She eyed Kjas' nametag and smiled at him. Kjas thought, *Bingo.* He seized the moment to continue his story. "I was sent clear over to the other side of this here wing, but that was incorrect. I need to report back to my superiors about her condition…their conditions, to be exact."

The intern moved closer to him and said – "I always wanted to work disaster areas for the federal government. You do such great work. I didn't realize this was the type of event your agency responded to. That is really exciting."

Kjas nodded, and added baritone to his voice to play into her affinity for his FEMA credentials – "It's getting bigger and more dangerous by the minute, sugar. Maybe, we can use your assistance if it gets rough. What do you think?"

The intern practically jumped to the ceiling and said – "Oh, yes, absolutely. Wow…disaster work!"

Kjas raised his right eyebrow and queried – "Um…the victims?"

The intern replied – "Oh yeah – follow me." Moments later, she stopped just shy of Jennifer's room. Her beeper went off. She looked down at it and said – "Oh shoot, I'm sorry mister, but I have to go. The mother is in this room. The baby is in the children's hospital wing, which is through that long hallway and to the right."

"Thank you kindly, ma'am. I will be sure to look you up before I leave. What is your name?"

The intern, thrilled that he wanted her contact information answered – "Oh, wow! Um, my name is Ashley…Ashley Duggleby."

"Much obliged, Ms. Duggleby," replied Kjas. "Uh, one more question, please. The husband…is he here too, do you know?"

The intern twisted her lips and looked up as she thought about it. "Oh, no…he left not long ago to visit his son. I saw him about fifteen minutes before you arrived, going down the hall saying he was going to be with his son for a while."

Kjas replied – "Much obliged young lady…much obliged," and the intern boogied to her next assignment. Kjas turned towards Jennifer's room. He reached inside of his right pants pocket and clicked off the safety to the .22 caliber pistol he brought to accomplish the job.

☙ ☙ ☙

Augustus arrived at the stairwell door to Jennifer's room. He disabled the blinking light to eliminate any illumination into her area. He quietly entered the room and listened closely. "We are still alone," he whispered. He then checked on Jennifer. Her condition had not changed. Augustus hopped over to the nurse and checked her pulse. "She's alive, good," he said. Next, he drew the room's curtain halfway to separate Jennifer from the nurse. Finally, he unlocked the room's door.

He took position midway between Jennifer and the half-drawn curtain. He tried capturing every spoken word in the hallway. Everything seemed normal. Augustus continually looked back to Jennifer for any signs of distress. The hospital hummed. He felt it to be rather peaceful, given the circumstances. Most of the conversations he heard were somewhat distant from the room. It provided him with a sense of comfort that they were located away from a heavily trafficked spot. Suddenly, the peace Augustus felt dissipated into the darkness of the space around him.

He heard a man with a fake southern drawl ask about his wife. The voice was far off, but he knew this was it. An expert linguist, Augustus fluently spoke more than a half-dozen languages. More importantly, he was an expert at distinguishing native from non-native speakers of most dialects. This expertise enabled Augustus to identify fraudulent attempts of one's linguistic origin. It did not matter if he was able to speak the particular language. The inflections and vocal pitches informed him whether the sounds were natural or forced manipulations. Augustus was not only alarmed that someone asked about his family, but that the person faked an accent.

He heard the echoing of a beeper, followed by the stranger's – "Much obliged young lady…much obliged." Augustus reflected on what just occurred – *Thank goodness, whoever that was did not come in with him. God was with her today.*

The room door opened halfway, then, shut slowly. The nurse remained unconscious in the dimly lit corner. Her condition would not seem out of the ordinary for a recovering patient. Augustus heard one slight step as the figure moved quietly across the room. *He is good,* thought Augustus as he tried figuring out who it could be. Then, he heard the distinctive sounds of a silencer being screwed onto a gun…followed by the cocking of its hammer.

❧❧❧

Kjas Brüder entered the room and quickly shut the door. The intern assured him the patient was alone. Nevertheless, he needed to get this done swiftly. Father and child were next. Kjas took two long strides and stopped at the bed. He screwed on the custom silencer for his .22 caliber pistol. Kjas raised the weapon to the recovering woman's head and pulled back on the firing pin until it clicked.

THWACK-THWACK-THWACK. The startling pain caused Kjas to squeeze the gun's trigger as he fell onto his knees. The single shot went high into the wall, safely above the unconscious nurse. Kjas touched his ribcage area and felt metal objects sticking out. "What is this?"

Augustus stepped out of the darkness and said – "Surgical knives…the throwing kind." He moved cautiously to Kjas' rear. It was possible the would-be assassin might continue attacking. Although the lighting was dim, Augustus quickly recognized Kjas. "So, NICO wants me dead I see. I don't suppose you are going to tell me why, are you?" Augustus shuffled his footing and got closer. His voice quivered with rage. "In what alternate universe does NICO reside where the taking of my wife and child are justified?" Kjas did not answer. Instead, he tried to turn around. Augustus stabbed him in the back with another surgical knife. Kjas shrieked in pain. "Who else is coming?" Augustus demanded. Kjas offered nothing. Augustus stabbed him again.

Kjas did not engage Augustus in conversation. Nor would he, regardless of how much pain he suffered. He knew his time had come, regardless of whether he talked. Augustus tapped the knives sticking out of Kjas' ribcage and said – "These are surgical knives." He then reached into his boot and said – "But this, this is a hunting knife." Augustus placed his left forearm across Kjas' forehead and pulled it back to brace against his thigh. He then made a deep, slow slice across Kjas' neck. He let go, and Kjas' lifeless body dropped onto a pool of blood now formed beneath them.

Augustus looked at the large knife in his hand and at the blood dripping off it onto the floor. Tears welled up in his eyes. These were tears of profound sadness. Augustus had truly come to believe that he would never take the life of another person. That belief was obviously wrong. He now had a clear and absolute understanding of what occurred. The most proficient society of assassins in modern history decided that he and his family must die. Kjas was just the first of many more he would have to kill. He knew this. It was his only choice if he and his family were to survive.

"Es una pena, por cierto," he whispered regarding the shamefulness of this situation. Augustus learned to kill for a cause, and at all costs. For many years, he did so proficiently and without hesitation. It was purported to be for the greater good of humanity…and he bought into that. Staring at the dead assassin sent to execute him and his family, Augustus acquired a distinctly different motive to kill. It was more beneficial than what any particular form of world order could provide. It led to an end transcendent of the greater good at all levels of cognition…mi familia…his family.

Augustus glanced at the nurse to confirm the bullet missed her. He then dropped the knife besides Kjas. Augustus knew he crossed the line of no return. There will be questions regarding the attacks on his family, and about this kill. There will be repercussions. He was not concerned. Focusing on securing his family, while simultaneously formulating a counteroffensive plan, was the only thing that concerned him now. Augustus sat on a stool by Jennifer. He then placed the final call he would ever make from his personal phone.

"Trooper Hoffmeyer, this is Director Peña. There has been another attack. I need your assistance immediately. Please, come to the hospital." Augustus leaned back and took in the relative tranquility around him. He concentrated on the rhythm of his wife's breathing. *It will be some time before I can enjoy peace like this again*, thought Augustus as he closed his eyes…

꙰꙰꙰

Within minutes, City Hospital swarmed with law enforcement personnel. Doctor Broderson was at the docking area, preparing for Jennifer's transport, when they arrived. At first, he thought it had to do with the explosion that recently rocked the crime scene. "Here come more casualties," he said to the EMT officer. However, that thought changed when he saw a tall, mature state trooper jump out of his vehicle. The trooper ordered the other officers to secure the area around Augustus Peña and his family. Doctor Broderson yelled –"Oh my God the other killer has struck!" He ran wildly towards Hoffmeyer yelling – "I can show you exactly where he is…where Augustus Peña is. I was with him less than thirty minutes ago."

Hoffmeyer immediately acknowledged Broderson and instructed his tactical units to follow the sprinting doctor. Broderson led them to Jennifer's room. He backed off as the men got into formation to breach and clear it. An agent forcefully kicked the door open. He entered the dark room, using the light on top of his assault weapon as illumination. Immediately, the agent yelled – "We've got a body." That was promptly followed by, "FREEZE, STATE POLICE." The remaining agents stormed the room. After Augustus' identity was established, and a determination made that no threat remained, they announced an "all clear."

Hoffmeyer was in the hallway speaking with Broderson – "Doctor, you say that the boy has been evacuated from this hospital?"

"That is correct."

Hoffmeyer asked – "By whom…How?"

Broderson answered – "I am unaware of how it all transpired. Mr. Peña briefly mentioned it to me. I haven't been able to check with the Children's Hospital staff…given the urgency to evacuate his wife."

"Huh, okay, that's interesting. I'll check with Director Peña to make sure everything is okay with his son."

Hoffmeyer entered the room and saw the body. It was in a pool of blood and there was a knife alongside of it. He stepped past the tactical agents and towards Augustus. He observed that Augustus had a distant stare in his eyes. Hoffmeyer stopped and took a knee alongside of him. "Sir, you okay?" Augustus did not look at him but nodded affirmatively. Hoffmeyer stood up and leaned on a gurney. He attempted to bring some levity to the moment by pointing at Jennifer and asking – "Did she do that to him?"

The question successfully drew Augustus from a deep meditation. The thought of Jennifer taking out two highly trained assassins in one day amused him. Augustus replied, "No…it was me."

Hoffmeyer looked at Augustus, placed a hand on his shoulder, and asked – "Director Peña, please, tell me. What exactly is going on here? How did you know that there would be a bomb at the crime scene? Who is the deceased on the floor? Why did you have to kill him? Obviously, there will be an official inquiry into today's events. However, I need you to provide me with some insight into why this extreme violence occurred. There are security measures that must be employed to protect not only you and your family, but the personnel under my command as well."

Augustus took a deep breath and replied – "Trooper Hoffmeyer, today's actions have rattled me to my core. I could never have expected them to occur. I, too, am quite perplexed at the dedicated level of violence directed against us. With that said, a picture is emerging in my head that will eventually explain today's events. It is not something that can be covered over a brief conversation, nor is this the appropriate time or place to discuss it. However, I am comfortable with speculating that these attacks directly relate to my prior service to this country. I apologize. I simply cannot furnish any more details right now."

Broderson entered the room. He gasped when he saw the bloodied corpse. However, that reaction paled in comparison to the reaction he had upon seeing the nurse on the gurney. He practically leapt over the corpse to get to her yelling – "What happened here? Why is this nurse in this gurney?" He felt her head and touched the soft part of her wrist to get a pulse. She was alive, but breathing erratically. Doctor Broderson went straight to Augustus and shouted – "I demand an explanation. What happened? Why is that nurse unconscious on a gurney situated where your wife was lying previously?"

Augustus stood up slowly to address both Hoffmeyer and Broderson. "That man on the floor came here to kill me and my family. He was here to finish the job that the first assassin failed to accomplish earlier today." He then looked at the nurse – "He was going to kill anyone and anything in the immediate vicinity of his intended victims. That nurse was simply in a really bad place at a very wrong time." Augustus then looked at Hoffmeyer, "I intend on giving an official statement of all that transpired here. However, I cannot do so until my family is in a secure location."

Hoffmeyer nodded and asked – "Your son, sir?"

"I had him evacuated by my deputy director. He is safe…for now. I need to get my wife evacuated too, as soon as possible. Once they are reunited, I can safely plan on getting them to a secure location elsewhere."

Hoffmeyer asked – "Where did you have him evacuated to?"

"I will show you, but there are parameters requiring unconditional secrecy. Can you do that?"

Hoffmeyer said – "I am too intrigued to say no. Yes, I can."

"Great. Now, can we get my wife out of here?"

Broderson scratched his head in a hectic manner and said – "I need to go too."

Augustus replied – "I assumed you would accompany us during her evacuation."

The doctor stepped closer and said – "No…I mean, beyond. You said that after your wife and son are reunited, you are taking them to a secure location. That is where I need to go." He continued – "Mr. Peña, I understand your obvious concerns about my going with you. However, your wife and child are in grave need of continuous medical care. Only a physician with full knowledge of their unique conditions can be of use to them." He looked at Hoffmeyer, and back at Augustus, and said – "Unfortunately, for me, I am that physician."

"Doctor," said Augustus, somberly. "I cannot guarantee your safety."

Broderson replied – "Mr. Peña, I cannot guarantee that your wife will live." The two men locked eyes, acknowledging the dangers. Broderson then said – "I need at least thirty minutes to gather enough supplies to get us through week's end."

Hoffmeyer said – "Heck, doctor, take the time you need. This hospital has tactical units up the wazoo right now and is as safe as Fort Knox."

Augustus cringed at Hoffmeyer's intimation that Fort Knox was a solid reference for impenetrable security. It brought back memories of an operation where he breached Fort Knox to reach a target under guard inside. Augustus knew the NICO playbook well, and was certain that Kjas was the last operative in the area. Nevertheless, he was in unchartered territory, and so were they. Undoubtedly, NICO did not anticipate losing two of their best operatives in a single day whilst all of the intended targets survived.

Although Augustus could not determine their next move, he knew one thing. This level of failure will send a shockwave of fear throughout NICO's management structure. That fear would result in more unprecedented measures put into play. Surviving these attacks meant that his family was now in even greater danger. If few people could be trusted before, even fewer were trustworthy now. It was time to rely on old, faithful friends who would lay down their lives so that you may live another day. However, he first needed to get his family to the Station.

"Doctor," said Augustus. "Please, proceed quickly. Do not fret if there is something you cannot find. We are going to a location that is a full service medical facility. All that you would need is already there. In addition, you can pack at a much more leisurely pace there for the next leg of our journey."

Augustus looked at Hoffmeyer and said – "No offense to the tactical squads here and their impermeable lockdown. However, the place where we are going is more secure. You see, by analogy, Fort Knox is a known location…as is this hospital. The facility we are going to is known to only a select few."

Hoffmeyer looked at Augustus, then over at the corpse, then back at Augustus and said – "Let's get the hell out of here."

ॐॐॐ

Doctor Broderson quickly grabbed some medical supplies. He also packed some surgical smocks, due to their lightweight and disposability. He had no idea how long they would be gone and had no time to obtain other types of clothing. Broderson announced his readiness for departure.

Twelve tactical officers lined the halls waiting to escort them to the ambulance. They surrounded the evacuees and slowly shepherded them down the corridor. Augustus pushed Jennifer's bed while Broderson managed the accompanying machinery. They completed the lock-stepped, chaperoned march without incident. Broderson securely fastened Jennifer's bed into the ambulance and they were ready to depart.

Augustus went to the driver's door as Broderson closed the rear doors of the ambulance from inside. He then said to Hoffmeyer – "Visual escort only. It is crucial that we maintain radio silence. Are these men capable of following that directive?"

Hoffmeyer's expression was one of nervousness as he said – "I will inform them that their very lives depend on whether they can stay off the wire."

"Very good," said Augustus, climbing into the ambulance's cab. "I'll wait for your signal to move."

Hoffmeyer yelled out for the men to gather around him. They promptly complied. He issued a directive for radio silence and confirmed that each of them understood. He then turned and waved Augustus on.

Augustus saw Hoffmeyer's signal. He placed the ambulance's gear into the drive position and slowly exited the hospital dock. He looked into the rearview mirror and said – "Here we go, doc. Are you ready?"

Broderson replied – "Hell no," and offered a fragile smile.

⌘⌘⌘

SIX

"The light shines in the darkness, and the darkness has not overcome it." – John 1:5

Maxwell Prater wandered edgily about his large plantation-styled home. It had been two weeks since he signed the fateful order to assassinate Augustus. He anxiously awaited news from the field. As was typical with all orders, the exact time, manner and location of execution was unknown. Not knowing these details was a necessary component to these missions. It allowed operators the freedom to determine their own tactics. Maxwell understood and appreciated the inherent necessity for this lack of information. However, not knowing them in this particular case was eating him alive. He was a nervous wreck.

"I better get a grip of myself or I'm the one who's going to wind up on a stretcher," he said aloud.

He chose to relax with his favorite morning beverage, a mint julep. He gulped his drink, prepared another and sat down in his recliner. He then turned on the television. There was nothing worth watching on the local channels. Consequently, Maxwell scrolled through cable stations to find something that interested him.

He flipped past a national news channel that he often watched. They were not reporting news. Instead, they were doing a feel good piece on service dogs for the blind and the joy they brought to those whose lives they touched. *This works for me,* he thought. He kicked back the recliner to rest his legs as he sipped his drink. The story had a soothing effect on him. Suddenly, an Emergent News Alert interrupted the program.

"Good morning, I'm George Peters with the American News Bureau in for Scott Wells, who is out on assignment. We apologize for interrupting the current programming but we want to share with our viewers an emerging tragedy out of the Midwestern State of Iowa. The American News Bureau, through its local Iowa affiliate, has just received word of an apparent series of shootings and explosions just outside of that state's capital. Details are sketchy, and it appears that some of the initial reports have already changed. However, ANB can confirm that a mother and her young child were the apparent victims of a brazen and violent attack that resulted in the death of the alleged assailant. The identity of that assailant has yet to be determined. Moreover, officials are not releasing the identities of the intended victims. However, we have received unconfirmed reports that the victims are close relatives of a high-ranking State of Iowa official. Stay with the American News Bureau, as we will keep updating you on the harrowing details of this horrific story as they continue to emerge. Now back to the scheduled program."

Maxwell reacted to the news alert with such shock that he thrust his legs into the air. The momentum caused him to flip backwards over the recliner. He crashed onto a glass table and landed on the floor. Stumbling to his feet, Maxwell reached for the remote control. He checked other news channels to find more coverage on the story. He was unsuccessful, so he went back to ANB and left it there for their promised upcoming reports.

Maxwell dashed into his den and grabbed his cell phone. "Damn it," he shouted, looking at the call history. "No freaking calls." Next, he checked the Sat-Comm-5 device. "Jesus Christ…nothing here either." Maxwell was convinced that the news story out of Iowa directly related to the Augustus project.

He ruminated over what he just learned. *Why the family, my order did not mention killing them?* He recalled his conversation with Ajax. "I specifically authorized collateral damage and told him it was a zero sum event. Oh, dear God," he said. "The Russian ape interpreted that to mean the family was also an intended target." Maxwell's uneasiness increased. He paced and talked to himself at full volume. "I screwed up. I should not have mentioned this to be a zero sum. He most certainly knew what that meant. Why did I do that? I have not heard from the courier. Ajax must have killed him. This is devastating. Oh, my God, Milken is going to have my balls."

Maxwell's head spun as he continued to consider the situation. "But, if Ajax knew that we intended on killing him, why would he do the job anyway? He could have just gone off the grid." Maxwell was perplexed. However, he settled on the one obvious answer to this question – "Invincibility…the man believed he was invincible. So, he chose to complete the operation and then thumb his nose at NICO by disappearing forever."

Maxwell returned to the toppled recliner and picked it up. He glanced at the television hoping to see an update on the story, nothing. Staring off he reflected – *The news report said the alleged assailant was dead. Does that mean Ajax is dead? Does that mean the family is still alive, including Augustus?* Maxwell considered the possibilities. "The secondary," he whispered, referring to Kjas Brüder's role in the operation. "He will certainly step in and complete the objective, but I have yet to hear from him too. What does this mean?"

He sat down and massaged his forehead…thinking. *Was this lack of communication symbolic of the secretive nature of field tactics or was it indicative of something much worse? Kjas is a NICO manager. If Ajax died, he would have certainly notified me of weakened operational integrity.*

Maxwell feared what would happen if he sat idly, waiting for a communication. There was no room for error. He had to operate under the assumption that at least one of his assets was dead.

He returned to his den and picked up the Sat-Comm-5 device. As he held it, he said – "I need people on the ground in Iowa, to poke around and report back. Kjas is extremely effective, so I do not need more assassins. I'll send an Intel team." Maxwell contacted NICO's Intel unit and had a two-man team dispatched to Iowa. Afterwards, he sat in the now upright recliner, stared at the television and waited on another news update.

ॐॐॐ

Prior to Jennifer's evacuation, Trooper Hoffmeyer addressed the medical staff at length. The substance of his speech related to the imposition of a temporary media blackout. "The lives of the director and of his family are in grave danger. Whoever sent that dead son-of-a-bitch to kill them will undoubtedly monitor the airwaves for news of the outcome. Now, we understand full well, that it is simply a matter of time before this all gets out. Nevertheless, we need your absolute commitment to silence until it is no longer feasible. Every minute gives us more time to get them to a secure location. Do I...do we...have your assurances that you will comply?"

Augustus gave thought to Hoffmeyer's emphatic declarations. Those words yielded an overwhelmingly positive response from the staff. Augustus was thankful to have such a highly competent law enforcement official assist him. He arrived at the capitol complex parking structure and stopped the ambulance. He got out and walked to Hoffmeyer's vehicle. "Sir," said Augustus. "I would appreciate it if you were to accompany me. However, the rest of the team would be best utilized elsewhere."

Hoffmeyer understood what Augustus was trying to convey – "Proper clearance needed for this point forward, huh?" Augustus affirmed. "I'll take care of it," said Hoffmeyer.

"Good," replied Augustus. "I'll meet you at the lowest level." He drove down and stopped in front of the pockmarked wall. Hoffmeyer arrived shortly thereafter. He met Hoffmeyer by his squad car and explained the entry process. Augustus alerted him of the thirty-second window of time for getting both vehicles through. Hoffmeyer nodded his head in a manner suggesting disbelief as he listened to Augustus describe it. "The wall is going to open sideways and reveal a road. We will drive on that road for about a mile, at ten miles per hour. Remember, the wall will automatically close after the thirty seconds has expired. You got it?"

Hoffmeyer raised his eyebrows and replied – "Uh huh."

Augustus turned and ran to the wall's hidden security pad. He tapped the ambulance as he went by and asked the doctor – "Everything okay in there?" Broderson replied in the affirmative. Augustus entered the sequence of code required to activate the entryway. The walls began to part and Augustus dashed back into the ambulance to take the wheel. He gave Hoffmeyer the thumbs up and drove forward.

Hoffmeyer watched in amazement as the ambulance drove through the opening. "Well I'll be a monkey's ass," he said, following the ambulance. Hoffmeyer looked back after entering the tunnel and observed the walls beginning to close. "Isn't that something?" he whispered, shaking his head and chuckling.

⋙⋙⋙

Chad's heart almost flew out of his mouth when he heard the vehicles approach. He had not been in contact with Augustus and did not know when he would arrive. Chad felt an overwhelming sense of elation when he saw Augustus step out of the ambulance. He ran out to greet him. "Director Peña! Oh, thank goodness. I had no idea if it was you or…or –"

Augustus placed his hand on Chad's shoulder and said – "You are a great man, Chad. Thank you for all that you have done for my family today. How is my son?"

"Your son is doing very well, sir. Uh, from what I can tell anyway," replied Chad. "He's still sleeping peacefully, the way he was when we came here."

"That is great news," said Augustus as he walked to the rear of the ambulance. "Chad, Trooper Hoffmeyer is here. He is in the second vehicle gathering his things. My wife is in the ambulance. Also, we have a doctor with us to help keep her and my son medically safe."

Chad exclaimed – "Sir that is wonderful news. I mean, that you were able to get her evacuated before anyone else could try to harm her."

Augustus gave him a somber look. He was about to reply when Hoffmeyer shouted – "Holy shit, Director Peña. I have watched some wild movie scenes in my time. I always wondered how in the world the producers could come up with that kind of stuff. But, I'll tell you, nothing in those movies ever prepared me for what we just went through, wow."

"Trooper Hoffmeyer?" queried Augustus.

"The sliding walls and the underground roadway that brought us here," exclaimed Hoffmeyer. "I've been a trooper for damn near thirty years. There is not much that I can honestly say either shocks me or otherwise throws me for a loop. However, the short trip into this place might have done just that."

From inside of the ambulance Broderson said – "I'm sorry, did I miss something?"

"Only the best Hollywood spy-movie entrance into this place," shouted Hoffmeyer.

Augustus turned to Chad and said – "Can you please take Trooper Hoffmeyer inside so that he can get acclimated? The doctor and I will be in with Jennifer soon. I need to talk to you once everyone is settled. The situation has actually gotten worse."

"Of course," he replied. Hoffmeyer followed Chad into the facility as Augustus and the doctor prepared to move Jennifer.

"Should I leave some of these items here?" asked Broderson regarding the supplies he brought. Augustus gave the doctor an inquisitive look. "To avoid having to carry them back out when we depart," he explained.

"No, take everything. We won't be leaving in this ambulance."

"Oh," said Broderson. He then rapidly gathered the supplies.

They speedily got Jennifer inside the Station and hooked her up to the facilities' equipment. Broderson then made several trips to the ambulance to retrieve his supplies while Augustus waited by the entrance.

"All done," said Broderson.

"Excellent," responded Augustus. "I'll be inside shortly. Can you please check on my son? It's been some time since a doctor has taken a look at him."

"Absolutely, Mr. Peña, on my way," said Broderson and he went inside.

Augustus reached into his pocket and pulled out one of the phones he snatched from the hospital. "The time has come to rely on old friends," he said. Augustus proceeded to dial the number of a true friend…a man willing to die for him. "I don't need your life," whispered Augustus as he put the phone to his ear and listened to the phone ring. "I just need your loyalty and willingness to kill."

❧❧❧

Cal Baker was at home on his ranch in Richfield, Kansas. He was watching the early evening news as he sipped on a cold beer. "What is wrong with people?" asked Cal aloud as he listened to the newscast. The developing story was about a violent carjacking attempt on a mother and child in the State of Iowa. The report was weak on details and intimated it might have been gang related.

The story infuriated Cal to no end. "These punks today," he growled. "They don't have the balls to serve in the military, where they can not only kill...but be killed. Instead, they earn their bravery from a goddamned video game and go shoot mothers and their babies."

Cal walked away from the television in disgust. He grabbed the remote and changed the channel to a different station. A hunting program was on, which was fine with him. However, there was a crawler at the bottom of the screen describing the same details he just heard on the newscast. "Goddammit," he yelled, shutting off the television.

"Caleb, what the hell is going on in there?" grumbled Pappy, Cal's father, from the adjoining room.

"Nothing pop...sorry," replied Cal. "Sorry to stir you up."

Pappy leisurely strolled into the room and said – "Sure as hell didn't sound like nothing, son. What's up?" Cal explained to his father the reason for his outburst. "Son," said Pappy. "Life already don't make sense most of the times. But, when you try to square away in your mind how people behave, through the disciplined eyes of a military man then, son, you are in for a world of troubling pain." Pappy sat on the sofa and rested his right hand on his knee. "Caleb, what those news folk are talking about, that's happening there in Iowa, that is something awful to be sure. Nevertheless, it ain't your fight and ain't for you to get all worked up over. Now, just go and relax the old fashioned way...by reading!"

Pappy chuckled as he got up from the sofa, patting Cal on the shoulder. "I'm going to the kitchen to check on the concoction your brother Bo is putting together for supper. It scares the stuffing's out of me when he says he's got a new meal put together that he is dying for me to try." Cal laughed inwardly as Pappy left the room.

Cal Baker was a retired U.S. Army Major. He served a majority of his twenty-year military career as a member of the elite and secretive Delta Force. Upon retirement, Cal entered service into what folks around these parts referred to as the Baker family business. Since before the days of Wyatt Earp, every generation of Baker saw a majority of its men serve in the U.S. Marshal Service. Pappy loved telling the boys about his early days on horseback, hunting down fugitives through rugged terrain. Even to date, the boys sat wide-eyed with childlike anticipation as they listened to Pappy tell of his days as a fugitive tracker.

The methodologies used to track absconders changed dramatically with the advent of new technologies. Nevertheless, the thrill of chasing fugitives was highly addictive to Cal, the leader of a fugitive removal team. He was currently on leave after having been on assignment for three straight months. He was trying to wind down and relax when he came across the news coverage that upset him so much.

Pappy's right, thought Cal. *This is not my fight. I cannot be fired up each time something tragic happens.* Cal looked at the blank television screen and said – "And that was, by all means, tragic." He walked over to the family library and pulled a book off the shelf. "Let's see what we have here," he said, looking at the title. "Moby Dick." He then sat down and began to read.

☙☙☙

It was about an hour later when Cal's service-issued mobile phone rang. "Awe, crap," he said. "I'm actually enjoying this book." He quickly answered it – "Marshal Baker."

"Amigo," said the voice on the other side of the line. "Soy yo, Augustus…"

"Augustus?" replied Cal, somewhat thrown.

"Yes," he replied. "My family is in grave danger, compadre. I most desperately need your help. Someone tried to kill them today."

Cal looked at his television. He immediately recalled that his greatest savior was currently a state official in Iowa. "Hermano," said Cal. "Do you mean the mother and child from the news reports?"

"Yes," he replied. "I see it has made it to your ears."

Cal froze. He dared not ask about their status. He did not have to.

"Jennifer and Nathaniel are alive. They are safe for the moment. I need a place where no one can get to them," said Augustus.

"Say no more," shouted Cal. "Let's get them to the ranch. They will be safe, I promise you."

Augustus knew he called Cal's service phone and was uncertain of his exact location. He needed Cal but could not impose upon an active operation. "I crave your help, amigo. However, I cannot have you pull away from your duties. Are you in the field?"

"No, hell no," exclaimed Cal. "I recently got back to the ranch after being gone for about three months. I am on leave for a few weeks to rest up. Shit, I thought you were my division commander calling to take me off leave for another assignment."

"Okay," replied Augustus. "I don't want more people pissed at me. I already have enough of those."

"Hermano," said Cal. "I know we will talk about this at a later time, but, who did this?"

"You would not want to believe me if I told you," replied Augustus. "I will tell you my suspicions when we meet in person. It is better that way." After a brief pause, Augustus shared the details of his family's medical condition. He also informed Cal that a doctor was coming along to care for them. Afterwards, they discussed the logistics of the transport.

"We need a rendezvous point," said Cal. "Although tempted, I will not ask your whereabouts."

"Thank you," replied Augustus. "I am fairly confident my location is unknown. To avoid leaving an electronic trail, I am not using personal devices. Instead, I acquired several phones throughout the day. I will use each of them only once and then destroy them."

"So, you'll contact me and not the other way around is what I'm hearing."

"Exactamente," replied Augustus. "On a different note, I'm the only gun coming on this transport. I would feel safer if we met halfway."

"To hell with halfway," said Cal. "I'll meet you along the Iowa/Missouri border. It's about ten hours from here, depending where we meet."

"That's a long haul for you," said Augustus. "I don't think —"

"Stop right there," interrupted Cal. "I owe you my life. Even if I didn't, I am now consumed with wanting to come to you and your family's aid…ASAP."

"Caleb," Augustus said, in a failed attempt at cutting him off.

"No, Caleb, nothing," replied Cal loudly. "It's a done deal. By the way, this is easy, hermano. The tough part comes after I tell Pappy what happened to you and your family. You know how it is. Once you get that bronco all riled up, there ain't no corralling him. I'll be lucky if that tough, old son-of-a-bitch doesn't take off to the Iowa border on horseback."

"Thank you, Cal."

"I love you, brother."

"I love you too, man." The two old souls settled on a time to meet in the border town of Hatfield, Missouri.

Cal shut his phone. He looked up and saw Pappy in the doorway with a plate of food in his hands. He had a troubled look on his face.

"What's going to rile me up so badly Caleb that I'm liable to ride on horseback to the border?"

"Pa," said Cal. "That news story we talked about."

"Yeeaahhhh?" asked Pappy slowly.

"That was Auggie's family and they need our help real bad." Pappy dropped the plate of food on the floor. The look of concern on his face gave way to an ice-cold grimace of pain and disgust. "I told him we would get them and keep them safe," said Cal.

"You're damn straight we are," replied Pappy. "I'll go let Bo know and have him load up the truck. Where we headed?"

"Hatfield, Missouri. We leave tonight." Cal leaned on his desk and let out a huge sigh as Pappy left. He could not imagine how horrific this must have been for Augustus and his family. He reached into a drawer and pulled out a glass and a bottle of whiskey. He poured himself a stiff drink, and sat down. His thoughts quickly went back twenty years, to the day he first met Augustus. Auggie, as Pappy liked to call him.

It was an unplanned encounter, but one written in fate. To this day, Augustus has not spoken of why he was in that rebel camp, deep in the Columbian jungles…and Cal never asked. Augustus' sudden arrival that day sparked an eruption of violence, resulting in the swift deaths of Cal's captors. Cal would have certainly perished from the torture his imprisoners prepared to inflict upon him. "That was a November of fury and Auggie was a true angel of death," whispered Cal. He slugged half his drink. "Now, it's my turn to save you, hermano," and he emptied his glass.

෬෬෬

After completing the call, Augustus opened the phone's rear panel. He removed the battery, as well as the SIM card, and crushed the telephone by stomping on it several times. He twisted apart the tiny SIM card. After gathering the broken pieces, he placed them into a makeshift burn bag. He then went inside.

Hoffmeyer and Chad were in a hallway between Jennifer and Nathaniel's recovery rooms. Both rooms had clear plexiglass windows surrounding them. From here, the men were able to keep watch as the patients slept.

"Gentlemen," said Augustus as he approached. "How are they doing?"

"They are sleeping peacefully," replied Hoffmeyer.

"They seem to be doing well," offered Chad.

"That, plus their safety, is all I can ask for right now," said Augustus. He then took a seat on one of the cushioned chairs in the waiting area. "Trooper Hoffmeyer," he said, clasping his fingers. "I need your help with some operational details."

"You got it, director, how can I help?"

"Here's my problem. I asked you to come here in anticipation we would be leaving fairly soon. However, it appears my family and I will need to spend the night."

"That's not a problem, sir. I am fully prepared to stay with you if that's a concern."

"No," said Augustus. "That's not my concern. What concerns me is the fact that your superiors will be looking for you, if they are not already. This is a secret location, so they do not know you are here. There are people looking to kill my family and me. Allowing you to call your superiors, to inform them of your safety, is not an option. That has the potential of revealing our position and is a risk I cannot take."

"What do you suggest, sir?"

Augustus answered – "As much as I value your assistance and, quite frankly, that weapon on your hip, I think you must leave for the safety of my family."

"Director," responded Hoffmeyer. "I feel I should be a part of this. At the very least, I would like to see you and your family through the night."

Augustus replied – "If a manhunt for you ensues, the last officers to see you were the tactical units outside of the parking complex. That fact alone might be enough to prompt one of the few people who know about this location to step forward."

Hoffmeyer said – "I see your point, director, but –"

Augustus interjected – "The people who attacked my family are highly organized and very much dialed into things. You can bet your ass that, at this very moment, they are monitoring all communications…and not just electronic."

"What exactly are you saying?"

"Several hours have gone by since I killed the second assassin. Whoever sent the duo will get restless when they do not hear back from them. Restlessness leads to curiosity. Curiosity, leads to people looking around on the ground."

"So, you're thinking that there are folks poking around amongst our people to find out where you are?"

"Yes," replied Augustus.

"Pardon my saying so, sir," said Hoffmeyer. "But, for someone who is not certain of who THEY are, you sure do seem to know a lot about what THEY are going to do."

Augustus smirked and said – "Now is not the time, Trooper Hoffmeyer. I need to get my family to safety first. Then, I will be able to provide what little information I have."

Hoffmeyer nodded and said – "I understand. I may not agree with you not sharing whatever information you have but, I do understand." He followed that up by saying – "I have an idea. I think it might just work."

Augustus responded – "Oh…do tell."

Hoffmeyer shared his idea with Augustus and Chad. He came up with a ruse. Augustus deemed it to possess great potential for success. It could buy much needed time by throwing off any NICO operatives monitoring the flow of information.

"Okay," said Augustus. "Let's do it. However, you'll need to use one of these phones instead of yours."

Hoffmeyer appeared appalled when Augustus opened up his satchel. It contained numerous mobile phones of varying types and models. "Where the hell did you get all of these?"

"People leave shit around unattended, what?" Augustus coyly replied.

"I can't use a hot phone," scowled Hoffmeyer.

"They're not hot, trooper. I just borrowed these for an indefinite period of time...for security purposes." Hoffmeyer did not appear amused. "Besides," continued Augustus. "Everyone working this case knows that the last person you were seen with was me. We are both now missing. It seems obvious that anyone looking for us will have put a trace on our phones to locate us the moment we use them."

Hoffmeyer looked at his phone as he pulled it out of his pocket. "Shit," he said. "I had no freaking idea. That possibility just did not occur to me. I'm sorry."

Augustus laughed loudly and said – "No need to apologize. I'm just glad you didn't use it since getting here."

"Actually," said Hoffmeyer. "I used it once, to call my wife."

The partially jovial expression Augustus had from laughing disappeared. A look of concern replaced it. "What's done is done. We cannot change the past," he said. "Let's get your plan into motion and hope that it will be enough to get us through the night."

ೊೊೊ

Hoffmeyer took a phone from Augustus' satchel and turned it on. Next, he dialed the home phone number for his commanding officer, Dan Teale. As expected, Commander Teale's wife answered.

"Sherri," he said. "This is Paul Hoffmeyer."

"Oh, yes Paul, how are you? Um...Dan is not home now, you know?"

"Yes, yes, I know that, Sherri," said Hoffmeyer. "Listen, I need for you to get a message to Dan for me. It's an emergency. I am calling you from some fellow's cell phone. I lost my phone and radio in a scuffle and I cannot remember Dan's new number. Besides, I need to get moving fast."

"Oh, my," said Sherri. "Are you alright, Paul?"

"I'll live, thanks for asking," replied Hoffmeyer. "Say, can you please call Dan and inform him that I am executing an emergency transport of endangered victims in an unmarked vehicle? Dan knows this means I will be out of contact for several hours or longer, for security purposes. Can you do that for me, Sherri?"

"Why yes, I most certainly will, Paul. Oh, hey…will he know where you are? Do you want me to tell him where you are going?"

"Tell him I am going to where we both wished we had transported to the last time we did this."

"Oh…okay…I'll do that, Paul. I'll do that right now, right after I hang up with you."

"That's great, Sherri," said Hoffmeyer. "Thanks a bunch."

"Uh…okay…be careful, Paul."

Hoffmeyer shut the phone. Augustus reached his hand out motioning towards it saying – "Can I get that from you, please?" He handed the phone to Augustus, who then promptly destroyed it. "Just one use," he said, in response to Hoffmeyer's confused look.

"I can see why you needed to lift so many phones," said Hoffmeyer, sarcastically.

Augustus stuffed the broken pieces into his makeshift burn bag and asked – "So, where is this place you told her you were headed?"

"Orange City," replied Hoffmeyer. "It's over four hours from here, in the northwestern portion of the state. Not far from the South Dakota border."

"I've been there," replied Augustus. "It's very beautiful."

"The locals refer to the area as God's country," said Hoffmeyer.

"That's good," replied Augustus, "because we're going to need a fucking miracle to get past the fact that you used your phone. Can I have it?"

"Have what?"

"Your phone, I need to destroy it. Otherwise, it can be remotely turned on via satellite to determine your exact location."

Hoffmeyer reluctantly complied. "Shit, I loved that phone."

૰૰૰

The Intel team's chartered aircraft arrived in Des Moines at seven thirty in the evening. The two men exited the plane and settled into a government vehicle waiting for them on the tarmac. They then sped out of the airport and headed straight to the initial attack scene. Their orders were straightforward. Confirm Ajax's demise and pick up Kjas' trail. The men intended to work the locals for as much information as possible about all that occurred.

Peter Dunn and Kurt Spindle were two well-seasoned intelligence agents. They officially worked for the National Security Agency. However, NICO often borrowed agents from that agency for domestic intelligence-gathering operations. The two institutions had an interdependent relationship and served as annexes for one another. NSA field agents held identifications for various federal agencies and retained full authority to use them as necessary. For this operation, the two agents were using credentials from the U.S. Department of Homeland Security. Ajax was a foreign national and Augustus an appointed official. These facts provided the perfect cover for their inquest…assuming Ajax was the assailant killed.

Typical to NICO Intel investigations, the agents' arrival on scene would be unexpected. Consequently, establishing a rapport with local law enforcement was crucial for success. Their role was to snoop around without hampering ongoing local efforts. The agents were not assassins. Nevertheless, they had the authority to use lethal force as they saw fit. It was a sanction that agents Spindle and Dunn had a penchant for exercising.

The pair arrived at what they dubbed the 'kill zone'. The cordoned-off area appeared to be about the length of a football field. The heavily guarded stretch consisted of tactical units positioned at every possible angle.

"Look at this big city shit," mused Peter Dunn.

"Somebody needs to tell these hayseeds the attack has ended and send their asses back to the farm," said Kurt Spindle.

The agents surveyed the charred remnants of the vehicles with wild bewilderment.

"Woo-hoo," said Dunn loudly. "Somebody had themselves a cookout."

"That's some heavy shit," said Spindle. "How many vehicles total?"

Dunn replied – "That looks like it used to be a truck…that's part of an SUV. One, two, three cop cars…at least five vehicles knocked out of commission from what I can gather."

As the two agents spoke, a tactical officer approached them with two others in tow.

"Oh, now, look at this," said Dunn, gesturing towards the oncoming units.

"Gentlemen," said the lead officer. "This is a secured crime scene. Is there something I can help you with?"

"Agents Spindle and Dunn, U.S. Department of Homeland Security," said Spindle as they presented their badged credentials.

The lead officer motioned with his head to the officer on his right, who then stepped forward towards them. "Can I get those, please?"

"Our badges?" asked Dunn in a mocking manner. "You want us, to give you, our badges?"

"Fuck this," said Spindle to the officer. "I'm not going to be treated like some goddamn boy scout and I am definitely not handing you my fucking badge." Spindle looked at Dunn and said – "Let's go."

The lead officer raised his submachine gun and pointed it at the two agents saying – "Hold it right there, gentlemen, and not another step forward. Turn around with your arms in the air and your palms facing skyward and face me…slowly."

They turned to face the officer and Spindle said – "You have got to be fucking kidding me, right? What is this all about?"

The lead officer replied – "Gentlemen, you presented us with badged credentials for the purpose of gaining access to this highly sensitive area. Given the level of violence that occurred here today, we are under strict orders to vet anyone attempting to enter the perimeter. Simply turning away and leaving will not cut it. You flashed it, now we've got to check it out." The officer then made a sterner facial expression, and said – "Your badges, please."

Dunn, with a slight smirk on his face, said to the officer – "You do realize that your weapon's safety is still on, don't you?"

Instantaneously, a metallic CLANK-CHUNK echoed throughout the cold Iowa night air. "Weapons hot," exclaimed the three tactical officers, as they released their safety switches and pointed their weapons at the agents.

"Nice job, asshole," Spindle said to Dunn as he slowly handed his credentials to the officer closest to him. Dunn followed suit without saying another word.

Close to ten minutes later, the officer who took their credentials returned. "Sir," he said to the lead officer. "These guys check out with Homeland." The officer returned their identifications saying – "See how easy that was?"

"Don't be a smart-ass," said Spindle.

"More like an asshole," muttered Dunn.

"Look," said Spindle. "We just need to pass through the kill zone to see if we can find some clues regarding who else may be involved, besides the dead assailant."

The lead officer replied – "Have at it. However, just so you know. We don't tend to glorify, with bravado-like zeal, the description of a scene like this."

"What are you trying to say?" asked Spindle.

"I'm not TRYING to say anything. What I AM saying is that you two bozos need to show some respect for what happened here today. This is not a kill-zone, as you so eloquently put it. This is a crime scene where people died. You got that?"

"I got it, I got it," replied Spindle, walking past the officers towards the heart of the scene.

"Holy shit," said Dunn. "What the hell is up their asses?"

"I don't know," replied Spindle. "I don't want to be out here any longer than necessary, though. Ten minutes, tops, and we are gone."

The agents walked the scene, using their flashlights to illuminate the darkness around them. They found nothing that helped them with their search, so they headed back to their vehicle.

"Thank you, gentlemen, you've been most helpful," said Spindle. He directed the comment towards the lead officer, who smirked without saying a word.

"The female victim," said Dunn. "Has anyone had a chance to debrief her yet?"

The lead officer replied – "You have to check with the units stationed at the hospital where they were both taken. Of course, her husband should be there by now as well."

"You mean Augustus Peña?" confirmed Spindle.

"That's Director Peña to you," replied the lead officer.

"Right…right…that whole respect thing, right," replied Spindle.

"Which hospital was that again?" asked Dunn.

"City Hospital, in downtown Des Moines," replied the officer.

"Thank you," said Spindle. He then motioned to Dunn to depart the area. Before leaving, Spindle asked – "Say…down at the hospital. I'm not going to run into more trouble with badge checkers, am I?"

The lead officer replied – "With your guys' attitudes, they're more likely to pump a few rounds into your asses BEFORE going on to check your credentials."

"Where ARE we?" asked Dunn, incredulously.

One of the officers overheard him and said loudly – "Welcome to Iowa, gentlemen."

ॐॐॐ

The agents walked back to their vehicle, muttering obscenities under their breaths. Spindle started the engine, looked at Dunn, and said – "I'm thinking that maybe we should approach the folks guarding the hospital a little different."

"Yeah, right…I'm with you there, man," replied Dunn as he looked back towards the tactical officers. "That is not a bad idea. Not at all…"

Spindle put the vehicle into gear and drove away. "I don't want these assholes to drop lead on us for speeding away from their perimeter," he said, justifying his slow exit. He then drove down the street and turned onto the interstate.

The highway leading into downtown Des Moines was desolate, with only sporadic traffic. "Two more exits," said Dunn as he read the GPS unit's directions. He then checked his weapon to make certain it had a round chambered.

"We're just here to check things out," said Spindle as he eyed Dunn working his piece. "There's no need to be gearing up for a fight."

"What's the matter? Those dudes back there scare the shit out of you, Spinds?" mocked Dunn. "Since when have you been opposed to brining a gun to a pillow fight?"

"Don't be a prick with me," growled Spindle. "You just got to use your head a bit here. That is what I meant by needing to approach the next group differently. That scene was some heavy shit, and I don't mean the fucking farmers with their guns, either." Spindle slowed down in response to some traffic building up ahead of them. He continued speaking – "Those were heavy explosives used back there. The locals know it and this town is at a paranoid level of alert. The news is lit up about the targeting of the Peña family. The last thing the Agency needs is for us to agitate the shit out of the locals and get into a goddamned shootout. Can you imagine what would happen to us if that occurred? The press would have a field day. I can see it now. NSA agents shoot it out with local cops, while attempting to gain access to the Peña family."

"But we're carrying credentials from Homeland Security, man," replied Dunn, nonchalantly. "There's no NSA connection, bro. You just need to chill out. Look, it's just a few more cops with attitudes guarding the hospital. I agree with you, that we should approach them a little differently than we did back there. However, I am not going to be a bitch and take it up the ass from them. If they want to play big city cop and point guns, that's cool. But, you know, I'm going to let them know that I've got one too, you feel me?"

Spindle shook his head in disbelief. He navigated the car around a bend. Suddenly, he slammed on the brakes. Spindle looked at Dunn the way a father would at an errant son and said – "What was that crap you were talking about just now regarding only a few cops with attitudes guarding a hospital?"

"What the hell is going on?" Dunn asked, staring out the window.

At least three helicopters hovered closely overhead, lighting up the Iowa evening sky. Directly ahead of them were several modified SUV's, flashing their bright law enforcement emergency lights. Alongside the exit were scores of heavily armed police, moving about in a hurried fashion. Beyond the modified SUV's was a command post, comprised of blue field tents and mobile floodlights that illuminated the entire perimeter.

"Awe, fuck…here we go again," said Dunn as several of the units jogged towards them.

"I hate being right all the time," said Spindle, putting both hands up so the approaching units could see he posed no threat. "I suggest you do the same, junior." Dunn promptly complied without uttering a sound.

An officer tapped on the driver's side window. Spindle lowered it. "Your destination, gentlemen?" asked the officer. Spindle and Dunn identified themselves and the officer had them pull to the shoulder. The officer followed them and opened the driver's door when they stopped. He asked Spindle to exit the vehicle. Another officer did the same at Dunn's door. An officer asked for their credentials. They were in no way prepared to resist this time around. The officer who took their credentials held them up and said – "I'll be right back with these. I just need to run a check on them."

Spindle and Dunn nodded simultaneously, saying – "We know the drill. Have at it."

འའའ

There were occasions when NSA field agents had their credentials challenged by local authorities. Protocol required agents to turn over their identifications without protest. NSA had a support system in place to verify an agent's identity and their professed affiliation with the respective agency involved.

The process, code named Boricua Posse, entailed a complex sequence of computerized events that diverted the inquirer to NSA's Personnel Status Center. Located underneath the Arecibo Observatory on the Caribbean island of Puerto Rico, the center operated round-the-clock. Its sole purpose was to provide real-time support to the hundreds of NSA field agents conducting operations across the globe.

Sergeant Keith Hanson of the Iowa State Patrol trotted to the command post with Spindle and Dunn's ID's. He laid them down on a table, picked up the command post phone, and called Homeland Security's LEO support line. Each set of official government agency credentials had a serial number associated with an agent's identity. The DHS verification specialist who answered asked Sergeant Hanson to provide those numbers to her. She entered the serial numbers into her database and a profile for both agents displayed on her computer screen. The summary authenticated Spindle and Dunn as being DHS agents. This procedure represented the first layer of NSA's field support system.

Located prominently in each agent's profile was a standing order. It mandated immediate contact with their unit's commander to inform him of the inquiry. The directive provided two sets of telephone numbers to call. Unbeknownst to the verification specialist, those numbers dialed into the PSC. Moreover, she had no idea that the database inquiry she just entered generated a secret electronic message. Even before she called, a communiqué automatically transmitted to the PSC alerting them of the probe.

U.S. Army Colonel Hank Boultry was the Commanding Officer-on-Duty at Arecibo. Staffing regulations at the center dictated a five-day rotation. As a result, all personnel were required to reside at the center for one hundred twenty hours and be available for all of them. This was Colonel Boultry's third evening within the rotation. He sat in a small, metallic chair reading his favorite book – The Holy Bible, King James Version.

"Oh…oh boy…" he chuckled, reading aloud. "That Korah, man, he should have known not to cross Moses like that. Whew, getting swallowed up by the earth is exactly what he deserved." Col. Boultry had a reputation for getting excited while reading his Bible verses. The other personnel found his overtly zealous readings entertaining. It was often mused that he read Bible verses the way an adrenaline junkie watched high-octane sports.

Boultry completed his reading for the evening. He marked the page where he stopped, and closed his Bible. "I am whooped," he said while yawning and rubbing his eyes. "Lieutenant," said Boultry to the young naval officer managing the phones. "She is all yours. I am jumping into the rack for a few."

"Aye, aye, sir," replied the lieutenant.

❦❦❦

Boultry awoke from his nap to a rapid succession of knocks on his door. It was the lieutenant. "Sir," he said. "I just received a ping from the DHS database. A second inquiry is commencing on agents Spindle and Dunn."

"Really?" replied Boultry. "Wasn't the first one just a little while ago?"

"It was, sir," replied the lieutenant. "It was fifty-two minutes ago."

"Is it possible this is the same inquiry being run through again?" Boultry asked.

"Negative, sir. The system requires a unique string of code before categorizing inquiries on an agent as being new. The network automatically generates the sequence whenever the respective agency initiates a new search. Consequently, we are not talking about human error…if there is any error at all. Moreover, the ping is on both agents. An error causing two inquiries on both of them would be highly coincidental. The improbable alternative is a massive system failure causing repeat pings."

"How long do we have before the call comes through?"

"Any second," replied the lieutenant.

"Let's get up to the pit," said Boultry, referring to where the phones and network connections were located.

When they arrived, a petty officer had just received the call. He raised his hand upon seeing them and said to Boultry – "Homeland Security on the Alpha, sir."

"I'll take it from here," said the lieutenant.

"Aye, sir," replied the petty officer.

Boultry frowned, walked to his desk and said – "Switch them over to high-comms, lieutenant." High-comms was internal jargon for patching a call into super-strength speakers located high above the pit. Boultry normally did not use high-comms. However, given the circumstances, he felt it important for the staff to understand exactly what was going on. His experience told him something unusual was unfolding in the field tonight. Boultry sat down and grabbed the microphone on his desk. He then looked at the lieutenant and waited for the okay.

"She's up, sir," said the lieutenant, giving the thumbs up.

Boultry squeezed the microphone's activation lever, which resembled a large trigger, and spoke into the oval tip – "Homeland Security, this is Section Chief Boultry. To whom am I speaking with?"

"This is Sergeant Keith Hanson with the Iowa State Patrol, sir. I apologize for disturbing you at this hour, but –"

Boultry cut him off saying – "Let me guess, sergeant. You need to check on the credentials of my two agents on the ground there...Spindle and Dunn...is that correct?"

"That's affirmative, sir."

"How did I know that, sergeant?" yelled Boultry – "I know because less than one hour ago, I received a similar call from some other Iowa cop looking to verify the same freaking thing."

"Uh, sir," Hanson tried to speak –

"Who is the scene commander there? A sergeant cannot possibly have command of a crime scene large enough to require multiple verification checks of the same federal agents. Am I correct, sergeant?" yelled Boultry.

"Sir...there are two separate crime scenes and –"

"And that proves my point even further!" bellowed Boultry. "Put the highest ranking officer at your location on the phone, right now. My agents need to do their job and I need to get some sleep."

"Copy that, sir," replied Hanson.

Boultry looked at the lieutenant and winked an eye while displaying a large shit-eating grin. "Jumping Jehoshaphat," he said after clicking off the microphone. "What in the world have those two gotten themselves into?" Boultry shook his head in a disapproving manner and said – "I cannot judge...that is the Lord's work. Instead, I shall do all I can to preserve their hides lest they wind up taking their trip to blazes a tad bit earlier than when they ultimately will anyway."

The personnel in the pit all laughed at Boultry's short sermon.

"Sir, they're back on," said the lieutenant.

"This is Commanding Officer Dan Teale of the Iowa State Patrol," said the voice on the other end of the line.

Colonel Boultry quickly got back on the microphone and replied – "Commander Teale, this is Section Chief Boultry with the U.S. Department of Homeland Security. Thank you for taking the call. I seriously hope that you can provide some sort of order to the fiasco involving my agents on the ground there."

"Now hold on just a moment chief," growled Commander Teale. "That is an unfair assessment of this situation. You need to understand the circumstances surrounding this matter."

"Who in God's name do you think you are talking to?" erupted Boultry. "My division has two special agents there who can't get crap done because everywhere they go they get sidetracked with this credential verification bull. I am a firm and obsessive disciple in the practices of security and diligence. I understand the need for tight controls. However, once a cleared and verified presence is established, I expect that to suffice. It does not matter how many active scenes you have. You don't ask every uniformed officer for their identification and run them through the wringer every time they move from one scene to the other, do you?"

Commander Teale felt angered by Boultry's intimation that the crime scenes under his command were not properly controlled. However, he also understood where Boultry's anger and frustration came from. "Chief," said Teale. "Look, I apologize for all the confusion and for the obvious impediments that have been placed upon your men. This has been one hell of a cluster-fuck and it just keeps getting worse. Besides, it's not like we were notified that your guys were coming…so, my men are all on edge."

"Okay," said Boultry.

"Chief Boultry, I promise this will not happen again," said Teale. "I will provide them with official State Police ID's. I will also inform my units that your guys will be moving about the scenes and are to be left alone."

"Well, I appreciate that commander."

Commander Teale said – "I'll bring your men to scene command and provide them with a full briefing. As I understand it, your agency is not seeking to take over this investigation, is that correct chief?"

"Thank you for getting them up to speed, commander," responded Boultry. "As far as taking over is concerned, we are not yet ready to do that. It all depends on what my men find out." Boultry shrugged his shoulders and looked at the lieutenant in a manner suggesting he had no idea what else to say. The lieutenant placed a hand over his mouth to cover a smile and shrugged back at him.

"Roger that," replied Commander Teale.

"Well," said Boultry. "I'm delighted we were able to get that squared away. I'll contact my men later to follow-up on your briefing."

"I will let them know."

The conversation ended and the center fell silent. Colonel Boultry twisted his mouth, expressing deep contemplation. "You know what?" Boultry asked aloud to nobody in particular. "I am just a little wound up after that whole exchange. I think I will kick back and read some more. Yeah, I'm in the mood for some good ole' Solomon…that's what I'll do." Boultry retrieved his Bible, opened it and located the stories he wanted to read. "Ahh," he said, kicking his legs up on the desk. "Lieutenant, she's still yours…I am going back to biblical times."

The pit echoed with "Aye, colonel," as the lieutenant acknowledged the directive.

༄༄༄

Commander Dan Teale went to agents Spindle and Dunn and personally returned their credentials. "You're all clear," he said. "Can you please come with me? I need to get you some official ID's so that you're not constantly being stopped in your tracks."

"Much obliged," said Spindle.

"Yeah…thanks," said Dunn.

Commander Teale escorted the two agents to the command tent, set up at the end of the highway's exit. "You gentlemen take a seat. I will be right back to provide you with a full briefing. I'm going to get someone working on your ID's."

When he left, Dunn leaned into Spindle and jokingly whispered – "Score."

"Quit fucking around," said Spindle. "This could be incredibly good for us or it can be incredibly bad, so cut the shit and focus."

"Damn, dude," replied Dunn. "Chill out."

Commander Teale returned not long after. A couple of officers came in with him and sat down towards the front of the tent. The commander looked at Spindle and Dunn and said – "I've got headquarters working on your guys' temporary ID's. Word is going out over the wire that you two will be conducting your own investigation at each scene, as they continue to arise. Like I assured your chief, you will have unfettered access."

"That's great news, commander, thank you very much," said Spindle.

"Yeah, that is great," said Dunn, followed by – "Um, you said each scene as they continue to arise. Can you explain?"

Commander Teale ignored Dunn's question and began his briefing – "As of right now, this is all we know. At approximately zero nine fifty this morning, a woman and her two-year-old son suffered a violent attack on a major roadway in our westernmost suburb. We believe the assailant acted alone. That assailant is now deceased and was apparently gunned-down by the woman in self-defense. Unfortunately, the assailant was able to inflict serious, life-threatening injuries upon her. The child was in severe shock but otherwise uninjured. Although, evidence at the scene does suggest the assailant took several close-range shots at the boy without hitting him."

"What the –" whispered Dunn, stunned at the assassin's inability to hit his target from close range.

Teale disregarded the interruption and continued – "Local PD and the sheriff's department arrived on scene first. State Patrol responded shortly thereafter. While processing it, we learned that the intended victims were the wife and child of Augustus Peña. He is the director of Iowa's Safety and Intelligence Bureau. Emergency medical personnel transported the family to City Hospital under heavy escort. The hospital is just down the street from here. As a matter of housekeeping, State Police has full jurisdiction. As the highest-ranking officer in our organization, I am in charge of this operation until otherwise notified by the proper authorities." He took a deep breath and said – "Now, this is where things start to go downhill."

"More?" asked Spindle, genuinely intrigued.

"Oh, yeah," replied Teale. "A delay within the State Medical Examiner's Office caused the assailant's body to go untouched for several hours. We needed to keep the investigation moving forward. Consequently, in addition to the victims, vehicle identification was necessary too. While obtaining this information, another deceased body was located inside of the truck the assailant used to attack the Peña family. That body bore signs of torture and its identification depended on the SME's arrival as well. It is unknown why at this point, but a local PD officer returned to the truck, triggering a high-explosive device. The blast not only killed the officer but also decimated the entire crime scene. We believe the assailant planted the device to assist in his escape, which, of course, his demise prevented. That scene remains fortified, as you already know. We are waiting for a residue expert to arrive from Maryland to help us trace the origin of this explosive."

"Sounds like there's a part three to this saga," said Spindle.

"There is," replied Commander Teale. "And it doesn't stop there."

Spindle and Dunn leaned forward to listen intently. They believed that whatever Teale was about to say could help shed light on Kjas Brüder's whereabouts.

"The hospital," said Teale in a tired voice. "The mother and child were taken to City Hospital and placed in separate wards. According to our information, after the explosion occurred, Director Peña evacuated his family to an undisclosed location. However, prior to doing so, he apparently accessed and rendered useless the city's entire video surveillance network. With this action, he effectively eviscerated our ability to track his movements after he left the hospital. We are literally in the dark when it comes to knowing his progress from that point forward. The evacuation itself is quite interesting. They were removed separately…the son went first. We do not know for sure who evacuated him. However, we believe it was Deputy Director Chad Molander. Mrs. Peña's condition caused a delay in her evacuation. While preparing for her removal, there was yet another attack by a different assailant. As we understand it, Director Peña killed the assailant just inches away from her recovery bed. Hell, he damn near decapitated that son-of-a-bitch."

"Holy shit," exclaimed Dunn.

"Yep…" said Commander Teale. "Interestingly enough, it is rumored that Director Peña rendered unconscious a nurse who resembled his wife and used her as bait for that assailant. This action, if true, suggests to us that he knew who his attackers were.

Furthermore, his going into hiding implies his anticipation of more attacks."

"Do you know who evacuated the wife?" asked Spindle.

"Yes," responded Teale. "That's where these two gentlemen come in." He pointed to the two tactical officers who entered with him. "These men were at the hospital when the director evacuated his wife. They were under direct orders from the scene commander, Trooper Paul Hoffmeyer, to seal the hospital. They also had to keep silent the fact that another attack occurred. Presumably, this allowed the director to get his family to safety without alerting other would-be assailants of yet another failed attempt. Where he intends that safety to be is anyone's guess…we simply do not know."

"So, who was with him when he evacuated his wife?" asked Dunn, rather impatiently.

"Oh, right, sorry," replied Commander Teale. "Director Peña and his wife were escorted out of the hospital by the tactical unit these men belong to. In addition, a doctor accompanied them. His last name is Broderson, I believe. Trooper Hoffmeyer went with them as well."

"Has anyone heard from the doctor or Hoffmeyer?" asked Spindle.

"Negative," replied Commander Teale. "It's as if they've all disappeared into thin air." He then said – "Regardless, we cannot take anything for granted and must assume these attacks will continue. We may not know the whereabouts of Director Peña and his family, but that does not diminish our duty to their security. Of course, it would make it much easier to protect them if we knew where they were."

Commander Teale walked towards the back of the tent and said – "Well, that's all I have gentlemen. I will make sure to get those ID's to you as soon as they arrive. In the interim, you can interview these two officers if you think it would help."

"Yes, thank you commander, we will do that. I believe it would be very helpful," said Spindle, followed by – "Oh, one more thing, commander, before I forget."

"What's that?"

"Have you identified the hospital assailant?"

"Nope," replied Teale. "Forensics is working on that as we speak."

"Do you have a description of what he looked like?" asked Dunn.

Teale replied – "Male, late forties or early fifties…hard telling, really. He had blonde hair, groomed mustache and a goatee. I say he stood about six-foot one to six-foot two, would be my guess. Why, remind you of anyone?"

"Nope," replied Spindle. "We are just curious and eager to get this investigation moving forward is all."

"Yeah," said Teale. "I understand. Oh, wait," he blurted. "How the hell could this slip my mind? The hospital assailant had a phone on him. Naturally, our officers went through the contact list and called the few numbers saved there to identify the body that way. No one picked up these calls, with the exception of one. On that call, the SME picked up."

"Come again?" asked Dunn.

"Don't you see?" said Commander Teale. "The State Medical Examiner's Office was answering the phone that was on the first assailant. They both knew each other."

Immediately, Spindle and Dunn stood up. Spindle said – "Sir, we'll be back. We need to provide the information from this briefing to our command."

"No problem," said Commander Teale. "Heck, perfect timing. Here come your ID's."

ॐॐॐ

Agents Spindle and Dunn thanked Commander Teale for his briefing and for the ID's. They then hurriedly returned to their vehicle to inform Maxwell of Kjas Brüder's fate.

"That kid has got some scary, bad-assed parents," said Dunn as they walked. "Mom and dad both take out A-1 assassins in one fucking day."

This is not going to be received well, thought Spindle, reflecting on the call he was about to make to Maxwell.

Dunn persisted with his immature observations of the events that unfolded – "That dude, Augustus, that's one cold mother fucker Spinds…ice cold! Did you hear what the commander said?

He knocked some bitch out simply because she resembled his wife. THEN, he used her ass as bait to lure in Kjas and then…WHAT? He almost decapitated the man! Come on, man…that is some of the coldest shit I've heard…damn."

"Is there something about the attempted murder of a two-year-old that doesn't strike you as cold, agent Dunn?" asked Spindle.

"Shut up," replied Dunn, effectively ending the conversation.

The two agents got into their vehicle and drove to an area away from the noisy command post. Spindle dialed Maxwell and waited for him to pick up. "This is going to suck," he said as he listened to the phone ring.

ల్ల్ల్

"**M**other of Christ!" yelled Maxwell, after hearing Spindle's report. He had just showered and dressed prior to receiving the call. The rawness of the account was too much for him to handle. Maxwell's body unleashed an unforgiving barrage of liquefied emissions that he was powerless to control. Too frightened to be angry or embarrassed, he tore open his dress shirt while fumbling to remove his tie.

He hyperventilated and believed he was having a stroke. He managed his way into the master bathroom and lunged into the bathtub, still partially dressed. He turned it on and stood under the steaming shower. Suddenly, he coughed violently, as condensation from the hot water infiltrated his lungs.

Get a hold of yourself, thought Maxwell. He wept hard, almost to the point of hysteria. He knew this was the end for him. He slammed his fists into the wall, suffering from pangs of guilt for allowing this matter to be set into motion. Maxwell understood there was nothing he could have done to prevent it, given Milken's steadfastness. Irrespective, he felt accountable and at fault.

Maxwell removed his clothes and cleaned up from his multiple accidents. He remained motionless under the running water, staring off into an unidentified distance. Maxwell pondered what new horrors lurked in the darkness ahead, and then vomited.

ల్ల్ల్

Spindle briefed Maxwell. On the other end, he heard what
sounded like muffled growls, followed by crashing and things
breaking in the distance. Spindle decided that Maxwell needed
some time to digest what he just learned. He pulled the phone
away from his ear, gave it a bewildered look, and hung up.

"What's up?" asked Dunn.

Spindle slowly lowered the phone to his knee, looked at Dunn,
and said – "I think he just shit himself."

"You know," said Dunn. "I normally would laugh my ass off
over some shit like that, but, I kind of feel for the dude, given
everything we learned." Spindle glanced at Dunn and nodded.
"So, do we bother going to the hospital?"

"Well, I suppose Peña's whereabouts are still an issue,"
replied Spindle.

"That wasn't our mission. Besides, I ain't into doing bad shit
to the family, Spinds," said Dunn.

"Who the hell said we need to do anything to anyone?"

"I'm just saying this shit is all jacked up. Those are some sick
pups, tormenting the family like that by continually going after
them," replied Dunn.

"Ah…I see that special agent Peter Dunn, the brave and
unmoving NSA field operative, has had a change of heart,"
mocked Spindle.

"Nah…nah," responded Dunn. "You see, you've got me read
all wrong, partner. The concept of what they initially tried to do is
not that troubling to me. It is the fact that they screwed it up and
now the family is on the run. Look, they tried and failed. Done
deal, leave them alone. The family won. Don't torture them with
that shit anymore."

"Okay, Mr. do-good. So, we just what, go home?" asked
Spindle.

"No, dude, fuck that!" replied Dunn. "We most definitely go
after Augustus Peña. He got that shit coming to him, absolutely.
We don't, however, need to be feeding leads on the family is what
I'm saying."

"He's with his family, dumb-ass."

Dunn replied – "True, as far as we know anyway."

"Look," said Spindle. "I admire where your head is at, I really do. However, we cannot drop the ball on providing his whereabouts just because he is with his family. That's not what we do…you know that." Dunn looked at Spindle without saying a word. "I'm hungry," said Spindle. "Let's go grab something to eat before going to the hospital."

"What the hell is open around here at this time?" asked Dunn.

"I saw a twenty-four hour convenience store on the way here. Let's go check that out," replied Spindle.

"Ooh…yum," said Dunn, sarcastically.

≈≈≈

They arrived at the local chain, known for its above average offerings of grab-and-eat items. Dunn had never been in Iowa and was not familiar with the store's brand name or reputation. "Fast Travel?" asked Dunn, reading aloud the name of the convenience store while they pulled up. "Why do I have the strangest feeling that the name of this joint relates to how fast the food from here makes it to your ass after you eat it?"

"You're a piece of work," said Spindle, exiting the vehicle.

They entered the store. Dunn walked around the brightly lit mart, skeptically checking out the food. When he arrived towards the front again, he faced a small rotisserie-type cooker. He looked at Spindle, who was preparing fixings atop a hamburger, and asked – "Oh, man…what the hell is this?"

Spindle looked up from his hamburger and laughed. He sucked some ketchup off his fingers and replied – "Why don't you ask the nice young lady at the counter?" The woman heard Spindle and looked over towards Dunn. Spindle said to the woman – "My buddy is from the East Coast and has never been in Iowa before. What is even more remarkable is the fact that he doesn't recognize the food he's looking at right now."

"Oh…is that so?" she replied. "Well, that is a corn dog, and it is the exact kind that they sell at the State Fair," she said proudly.

Dunn, perplexed, had the woman describe the way a corn dog was prepared. "Well, shit, Spindle," said Dunn, after receiving the explanation. "I'm going to eat a whole bunch of these. I love corn bread and I love hot dogs." Dunn grabbed the remaining half-dozen corn dogs from the cooker and walked over to the counter to pay for them. As he laid the items down for the woman to ring up, he glanced at a digital lottery display above the register. The board informed customers of current jackpot totals for the three lotteries sold in Iowa. "No sir!" Dunn shouted gleefully. "Spinds…they play Hot Ticket in Iowa too. I always buy me a ticket back in DC."

"It's up to $16.5 million dollars as of this afternoon," the woman said to Dunn.

"Well, it's a done deal," exclaimed Dunn. "I'll take the corn with dogs, or whatever you call them, three Hot Tickets and this bottle of water too." The woman rang up the purchases. Dunn paid for them in cash and went to the car to eat.

Spindle returned to the car shortly thereafter. "Lottery, seriously?" asked Spindle as he got into the vehicle. "And what do you plan to do if you win a large prize?"

"I plan on cashing the mother fucker in, why?"

Spindle shook his head as he ate his food, then asked – "How the fuck did you get this job anyway?"

"Affirmative Action, bitch!" replied Dunn as he roared with laughter. He then opened the glove box and placed the three lottery tickets inside. After closing the compartment, he looked at Spindle and said – "For safekeeping. Don't let me forget to check them."

"Go screw," said Spindle.

੭੭੭੭

Spindle and Dunn returned to the command post and gained entry with no hassle. They waited a few minutes to see if Commander Teale would appear with any new information. He did not show so they decided to enter the hospital. It was extremely hectic. Spindle turned to Dunn and said – "I'm on point. Follow me and do not mouth-off to anyone. We are supposed to be keeping a low profile and have failed miserably up to this juncture."

Dunn nodded his head and replied – "10-4, Cochise."

Although the attack inside of the hospital occurred several hours prior, the stress remained intense. Some staff members were crying, ostensibly from pure nerves, and law enforcement personnel were present at every turn.

"They must believe he is still in the hospital somewhere," whispered Spindle, trying to make sense out of the heavy armed police presence.

"Do you think he's still here?" asked Dunn.

"I don't know," replied Spindle. "I mean, it makes sense that he…they…would be here, given the medical condition of his wife. Plus, the child is going to need some sort of medical care."

"Is there another hospital nearby?"

"I'm pretty certain there is," replied Spindle. "This is a fairly large metro-area. They can't have just one."

The duo contemplated poking around other local hospitals when they heard their names called out. They looked towards the voice and saw Commander Teale walking quickly towards them.

"I was told you two just came up this way. I forgot to provide you a radio for communicating with scene command. I'm glad you are still here."

"What's going on?" asked Spindle.

"Follow me." They went into a nearby room. Teale gave a nod to the officer who came with him. The officer proceeded to check the room for any other occupants.

"She's empty, sir," said the officer to Teale.

Commander Teale directed the officer to close the room door, and said – "I've received word from Trooper Hoffmeyer. He was the original attack scene's commander, if you recall."

Dunn sprung from a cot he was leaning against and exclaimed – "Hallelujah! Where is he?"

"I don't really know for sure."

"What did he tell you?" asked Spindle.

"He didn't tell me anything," replied Teale. "He left a rather cryptic message with my wife almost an hour ago."

"Uh, come again?" asked Dunn. "I'm confused…your wife?"

"Trooper Hoffmeyer and I go way back. Our families know each other very well. It is not out of the ordinary for him to pass a message through my wife if he is unable to reach me."

"Commander," said Spindle. "What was the message?"

"My wife tells me that Hoffmeyer called her from someone else's phone. He apparently lost his communication equipment in some sort of scuffle. He didn't say with who, though," replied Teale.

"Hmmm...very interesting," said Spindle.

"Yeah, it is," replied Teale. "But, what is even more interesting is his claim to have forgotten my new telephone number."

"Shit, that's no big thing," said Dunn. "Forgetting new phone numbers is common, isn't it?"

"Maybe, but I've had the same phone number for five years."

"Okay, that is interesting," replied Dunn.

"Commander," said Spindle. "Maybe he did get into a scuffle and is injured or otherwise disjointed. This could cause him to not remember your number or the fact that it has not changed."

"I suppose that is always a possibility," replied Teale. "However, he also provided my wife with some specific information as to where he was going. It was in a somewhat coded fashion, which would require a decent amount of clear thought."

"Where is he headed?" asked Dunn, looking at Spindle with an exaggerated look in his eyes.

Commander Teale shared the details of Hoffmeyer's message, to include the exact location of the safe house in Orange City.

"How far away did you say that was?" asked Spindle.

"It's a good four hours if you're going non-stop. But, with folks requiring medical attention and monitoring, I'd imagine it would take them longer," replied Teale.

"So, you're saying he is already on the road?" asked Dunn.

"It would appear so, especially since he called a little over an hour ago. It sounded as if he was in a big hurry, according to my wife."

Spindle looked at his watch and walked over to the window to look outside. He bit his lip as he thought, then said – "Commander...the roads up to, where was that, Orange City?"

"Yes."

"Is it interstate all the way?"

"Nah," replied Teale. "There really is no quick way to get there from Des Moines, mostly county roads. Most of it is paved and limited to fifty-five miles per hour."

"And they are in an unmarked vehicle, from what your wife tells you, is that correct?" confirmed Spindle.

"That is correct," replied Teale. "What are you thinking?"

"Nothing specific," replied Spindle. "I'm just thinking aloud, trying to make sense out of all the details."

"Yeah, me too," said Dunn. "I'm totally lost."

Spindle shot Dunn a glance that conveyed, in the strongest possible terms, that he wanted him to shut his mouth. Dunn noticed Spindle's glare, made his way to a corner of the room, and sat down on a visitor's couch.

"Commander," said Spindle. "Can I get a pair of those radios so that we can be in constant contact?"

"Yes absolutely. I'll get those to you immediately." He then said – "Although Hoffmeyer is on the move, I am keeping this command post operational. Having those radios will be a very good thing."

"I couldn't agree with you more," replied Spindle, followed by – "Commander, what is your plan going forward, since Hoffmeyer is moving to a safe-house?"

Teale looked at both agents, and said – "I'm not sure yet. I have no choice but to assume that he is moving the director and his family. This is an extremely sensitive situation. The media is starting to fill the airwaves with absurd speculations. We have to be extremely cautious. Any misstep, however slight, could cost folks their lives." The commander placed his hands on his hips, and said – "I…we…have to operate under the premise that whoever attacked the Peñas are looking for another opportunity to strike. I really would like to avoid being the dumb-shit who gives away their location to sadistic killers hell-bent on murdering that family."

"It's a good thing you have this place locked-down tight," blurted Dunn, unable to resist the urge to speak.

"We'll take those radios," said Spindle, while staring blankly at Dunn.

"Will do," replied Teale, followed by – "Say, are you guys hungry? It's going to be a long one."

"No, thank you," replied Spindle. "We grabbed something quick to eat at the Fast Travel down the road."

Dunn chimed in – "Yeah and I bought some Hot Tickets!"

Teale bellowed in response to Dunn's remark. "I'll be back in a few with those radios." He then exited the room with the officer that accompanied him in.

తతత

Immediately after Teale left, Spindle unleashed a flurry of expletives upon Dunn in an angry, whispered voice – "What the fuck is wrong with you? Are you trying to cause them to question our presence here and suspect our motives? Huh? Speak to me you reckless fucking moron!"

"Dude," said Dunn, calmly. "I ain't gonna whisper-fight with you. That's just strange."

Spindle threw his hands up in the air in total frustration and turned around.

"Look, man," said Dunn. "Just cool out, I'll quit dicking around. But, you've got to admit Spinds...some of that shit I said was funny, right?" A moment of silence passed between the two agents and Dunn finally said – "Alright, I'm sorry. Can we both just agree that I am an idiot and move on?"

"It's about time we both agreed on something."

Dunn moved past Spindle's anger with him and focused on their conversation with Teale. "Spinds, why'd you look at your watch, and then look out the window, when you asked the commander about the roads leading up to that place?"

Spindle turned and wagged his long, skinny index finger at Dunn. He spoke quickly, and in an agitated tone – "You see...this is the very thing that disturbs me the most about you, special agent Dunn. You are incredibly intelligent and remarkably astute. Yet, you fail to use that intellect on a consistent basis. It is frustrating...and it is dangerous. I implore you to keep your head out of your ass or you are not going to find humor in how your career ends up."

Dunn was visibly confused about Spindle's response, and said – "Alright man, alright."

Spindle returned to the window and said – "We don't have much time. The commander will return with those radios soon. You are wise with your observation. At that moment, I pondered the possibility of Augustus being on the move to Orange City, and determined he has not yet left. I came to that conclusion based on several factors. The first factor being that it is now late into the evening. The roads leading to Orange City, per the commander, are county roads. I surmise, given the infrastructure of this state, that those roads offer little to no roadway lighting. Add to that an abundance of deer that populate this state, and you have a situation that makes night travel extremely treacherous. Throw in a critically injured wife, and a child, and you have a man who is going to evacuate his family at dawn."

"That makes a world of sense," commented Dunn. "No, I'm serious. I'm not trying to shine you on," he said in earnest.

"Thank you," replied Spindle, followed by – "But the question is…from where does he leave?"

"Maybe the tactical dudes Hoffmeyer talked to can provide us with a clue as to what part of the city they could be laying low in right now," said Dunn. He then said – "Nah, forget it. They are just as much in the dark as we are. Shit, if they knew where to look, do you think they would be in such a frantic mess?"

"Let me think about that some more," replied Spindle. "They're not looking at this situation the same way we are. Consequently, they might be able to provide us with a tidbit of information that places us near Augustus and his family. Yeah, it might not be a bad thing for you to talk with them. If we can identify their whereabouts, we can tail them from afar for NICO to intercept."

Dunn, uncomfortable with the idea of providing the family's location to NICO, nodded his head and said – "Yeah, I suppose that's what needs to be done."

Spindle looked at him, scratched his chin and walked back to the window to think.

ॐॐॐ

Commander Teale returned to the room. "Gentlemen, here are your radios. They are preset for the channels and frequencies our units are on, both here and at the original attack scene."

"Anything special we need to do to use these?" asked Spindle.

"No," replied Teale. "You just click and talk. Now, what you do need to know is that these puppies are always on. They will go for days without needing a charge. Since they are always on, there is no power button. If you want the damn things to shut up, you'll need to lower the volume on the side here." Teale demonstrated where the volume button was on the radio.

"I don't suppose there is a mute button?" asked Dunn, jokingly.

"Nope," replied Teale. "These radios are comms-hot. They also have GPS tracking technology, so we'll know where these suckers are at all times if we need to look."

Spindle raised his eyebrows and opened his mouth to say something when the commander cut him off –

"Forget it, I already covered it," said Teale. "At the present time, only dedicated-channel scene command radios, like these, are enabled with GPS. The type of communication device that Trooper Hoffmeyer had was a field model, so there's no way of pinpointing his exact location that way."

Spindle gave Teale a look of approval. He was surprised by the commander's ability to figure out what he was about to say.

"Agent Spindle," said Teale, in response to Spindle's expression – "This isn't my first trip through the cornfield."

"No, I suppose not," said Spindle. *Shit, he is sharper than what I gave him credit for,* thought Spindle. *I had better watch my ass. I am glad he showed his cards before I said something stupid to raise his suspicion.*

"Agent Spindle," said Teale. "Are you alright? Looks like you might have drifted off there for a quick moment!" Teale laughed as he made the statement.

"Welcome to my world," joked Dunn, prompting Teale to laugh louder.

Spindle feigned offense, and said – "Sorry, commander. Yeah, I did kind of drift off. I have to believe there is some sort of technology on Hoffmeyer's equipment that allows us to triangulate his general location. It would be great to know where they are on their trip to Orange City, to provide them safe passage."

Commander Teale replied – "Ah, agent Spindle, now you have done the mind reading. We tried locating Hoffmeyer, Director Peña and Deputy Director Molander via their cell phone registrations."

"The SIM cards?" asked Dunn.

"That's correct," replied Teale.

"And?" asked Spindle.

"They were all off-the-grid, so to speak," replied Teale. "My people tell me the SIM cards must have been destroyed. Our techies sent ping signals to communicate with those cards. They were unsuccessful. Not even a tiny hiccup, as they put it."

"Would Hoffmeyer know to do that?" asked Spindle.

"Heck, I'd be shocked if he knew the darn things even existed," exclaimed Teale.

Spindle let out a sigh of frustration. He realized that Augustus undoubtedly was the one who destroyed those SIM cards in his effort to go black.

"No worries," said Teale. "I decided to put some birds in the air to cover the typical routes to Orange City."

"And the atypical routes?" asked Spindle.

Teale replied – "I'm leaving one of my senior troopers in charge of this command post and breaking off several squads to cover those routes ASAP. I am going on the ground too. Do you wish to accompany me? We will maintain constant contact with our air units. One of us will locate them, I'm certain of it."

"Commander," said Spindle. "We must politely decline your offer. We continually need to brief our command and could very well be required to pursue other leads on a moment's notice. That, I am afraid, would be disruptive to the process you have put into motion. I hope you understand."

Teale nodded in agreement and said – "I most certainly understand, special agent Spindle. I realize that my jurisdiction ends at the Iowa border and that yours extends way beyond that. Anything you gentlemen need within my dominion is at your disposal."

"Thank you," replied Spindle.

"It was great to meet both of you. I am leaving in about fifteen minutes. Here's my cell phone number, in case you need to call me," said Teale.

"Safe travels," said Dunn.

"And you as well," replied Teale. "Oh, and be sure to try one of our pork fritters before you leave Iowa. If you love corn dogs, you will go crazy over our homegrown pork sandwiches. Suckers are about this big around," said Teale, laughing, as he estimated the size with his hands.

"That's freaking crazy," exclaimed Dunn.

Commander Teale howled with laughter as he exited the room, saying – "Take care, gentlemen," and he walked away.

ॐॐॐ

Maxwell thanked God he did not throw away the remaining valium prescribed to him several months prior. He kept them just in case he had an unmanageable emotional crisis. The current events fit that bill. Stricken with the mother-of-all-panic-attacks, Maxwell decided self-medication was the only logical solution. "Come on, come on, come on," he said frantically, while mishandling the pill container. "Oh, dammit," he growled, as the drugs flew across his bathroom the second he opened the bottle. Maxwell dropped to the floor, and seized upon two tablets that landed by his feet. He picked them up with his trembling hands and shoved them into his mouth. Maxwell swallowed hard and felt the pills slide down his gullet.

Acutely aware the valium required time before having any impact, Maxwell laid on the floor, in anticipation of the drug's calming effects. Several minutes passed and his vision became blurred. Maxwell did not recall this experience the previous times he took the medicine. *I will close my eyes and wait for everything to settle down.* He turned his head, placed his left cheek on the cold tile, and shut his eyes…

ॐॐॐ

"**S**on-of-a bitch, pick up!" screamed Spindle, as he placed his third call to Maxwell.

"What's up?" asked Dunn, observing Spindle's agitation and aggressiveness.

"This shithead is not picking up his phone and it's pissing me off," replied Spindle.

Dunn mused, "You did say that he took a shit on himself. So, you know, maybe he's just taking a really long bath."

Spindle replied – "I don't know. Look, I need you to go talk with those two tactical officers that were in our briefing earlier. Like you suggested, they can at least point us in a general direction."

"I was just talking shit, Spinds. I don't really think they can do that. How do you figure that they can?"

Spindle replied – "For one thing, they broke contact with the trooper at some point. I want to know the exact details of that moment. I also want an exact make on their evacuation vehicle. We know it was an ambulance, but I need more specifics. Augustus appears to be skilled in the art of deception. I want to figure out what a modified version of the ambulance might look like. However, in order for me to speculate on a modification, I need to know original specifications. Got it?"

"Got it…I'm on it," said Dunn as he exited the room.

"Dunn," shouted Spindle.

"Yeah?" replied Dunn, reemerging into the room.

"Try not to be a complete asshole out there, okay?"

"You're a dick, Spindle."

Spindle walked back to the window. He leaned forward and placed his palms down on the sill. Looking towards the sky, he said – "I know you're out there, Augustus, and that you are not far. I do not know what you have done to cause this reaction from NICO, but it must be something terrible. I will find you for them. However, one awkward move, and I will kill you without qualm." Spindle then reached for his phone and placed another call to Maxwell.

ॐ ॐ ॐ

Armed to the teeth and fully supplied, the Baker men tore off from their ranch under the midnight moon. Their quest to save the Peña family had officially begun. Bo drove while Cal rode shotgun. Pappy, always on the ready, sat sideways across the last row of their oversized suburban, keeping watch.

Tapping the assault rifle that lay across his lap, Pappy said – "Boys, this here is something real serious and is gonna require our hides to be extremely vigilant."

"What you thinking, Pa?" asked Cal.

"Caleb," replied Pappy. "Whoever went after Auggie and his family is not your average, everyday hooligan. No sir, this smacks of something more organized than that."

"We already figured it was an organized attempt," replied Cal.

"Okay," continued Pappy. "But, did you figure out what type of organization?"

"A gang, Pa," offered Bo.

"Beauregard, keep your eyes on the road…and, no, it weren't any gang," shouted Pappy.

"I think he meant a drug gang, Pa," offered Cal.

"Nah, it ain't no gang, drug or otherwise," replied Pappy. "This seems to be much more professional than that. I saw on the television, right before we left, that there was another attack on Auggie's family…in the hospital where his wife and boy were taken."

"What?" Cal shouted.

"Yep, turns out it occurred hours before being reported to the media. I suspect that when Auggie called you, the hospital attack already happened. So, he should still be fine," opined Pappy.

"Those mother fuckers!" yelled Cal.

"Mind your tongue, Caleb," said Pappy. "Nah, that ain't no gang. That rings to me like some sort of government operation. Something that is clandestine, brutal and professional."

Cal said – "It could be a foreign intelligence agency going after Auggie, for work he may have done in the past."

"Why does it have to be a foreign intelligence agency, Caleb? We have those right here too you know," said Pappy.

Cal asked – "Pa, why in blazes would you even suggest that our own government is trying to kill Auggie and his family?"

"That would be wrong, Pa," said Bo.

"Beauregard, don't make me tell you again," shouted Pappy. "Stick to driving and keep your eyes peeled on the road. There will be critters running all around these back roads for several hours yet. Auggie needs us to get there in one piece."

"Sorry Pa. I won't do it no more," replied Bo, sheepishly.

"Well, think about it son," Pappy said to Cal. "When you were in the Army, you were part of a unit that the U.S. Military, to this day, has not officially acknowledged the existence of. It was on one of their secret missions that you met Auggie. Rather, he met you. As I recall from your side of it, you and your Delta command had no idea how he got there. Nobody knew what organization he belonged to or his purpose for being there. Your secret unit, with the resources and aspiration to know all global matters, was ineffective at detecting the activities of whatever organization Auggie belonged to. Moreover, they continued to fail in their attempts at identifying them afterwards. This even after Auggie presented himself and exposed their existence."

"Yeah, but I don't see –" Cal started to say.

Pappy continued – "Let me finish, son. That level of secrecy comes with an enormous amount of bureaucratic roadblocks that need navigating. That means political connections. In turn, that means politicians. Only one form of organization contains politicians, and that is government. If history has taught us anything, boys, it is this. Governments will employ all measures in order to maintain their secrets, up to and including murdering their own citizens. Oh, they call it assassination so as to make it sound more important, but it is murder nonetheless."

"We're not the only government with politicians, Pa."

"That is true," replied Pappy. "But, the amount of hostilities that have occurred in this calamity would be considered an act of war if it came at the direction of a foreign entity. I don't see how anyone would want to go there with us."

Cal frowned after listening to Pappy's analysis. He then recalled his conversation with Augustus. "You would not want to believe me if I told you," were Augustus' exact words. Those words, coupled with Pappy's analysis, convinced Cal his father was on to something. "Okay," said Cal. "I buy into it being a government attack. The question is, why?"

"Beats the heck out of me," replied Pappy. "I suppose that is something only Auggie can answer. I just don't know, Caleb."

"I sure hope it's not our government," said Cal, staring out the passenger window.

"This much is going to be true regardless of who it is, so hear me out," said Pappy. "Any government planning these attacks would have done their homework. Not only on Auggie, but all of his associates too. You two may not be golf partners, but you are extremely close. You have an official history with him, Caleb."

"What are you suggesting, Pa?"

"That you…we…became involved way before Auggie called. The second their attacks failed, Auggie became a ghost for them to find. Naturally, they would have thought to check us out, to see if he has contacted us. Either that, or round us up for something much worse," said Pappy.

"Worse?" asked Cal.

"Yes," replied Pappy. "Kill us. That would serve their purposes twofold. It would eliminate the need to keep constant watch over us. Moreover, it would send a crippling message to Auggie, that they know his every move and that he has nowhere to hide." Pappy grabbed a better hold of his weapon and said, "It's a damn good thing Auggie called us, lest we'd have been taken by surprise…it was a damn good thing. They are out there, boys. It's just a matter of time before they present themselves to us." Pappy shifted his sitting position and leaned back further into the vehicle's dark cabin. He stared wide-eyed out the rear window, looking for any signs of a pursuing enemy. "And I'll be waiting…" he whispered.

෴෴෴

Spindle gave up on calling Maxwell. He decided to take ownership of the mission. *If that son-of-a-bitch doesn't find it important to pick up my call, then I'll make the tactical decisions.* He checked his watch and said – "Where the hell is Dunn? Did he disappear too?" Spindle picked up the scene command radio to get a status from Dunn. He saw the other radio on a chair across the room. "You know…" Spindle said loudly, in disgust. "I am sick and tired of being partnered up with this piece of shit."

"What piece of shit?" Dunn asked, as he entered the room.

"Ah, you know, some loser, wannabe federal agent, who forgot his radio in a potentially hostile environment. That piece of shit," replied Spindle, stunned by the timing of Dunn's arrival.

Dunn ignored Spindle's hostility towards him. He recognized that he screwed up again by forgetting his radio. Dunn offered no explanation. Instead, he briefed Spindle on what he learned. "Spinds," he said. "Those tactical dudes hooked us up, man. They knew a lot more than what I thought they would. As it turns out, things didn't work out the way we thought."

"What's different?" asked Spindle, concerned.

"For one thing, they left in multiple vehicles, not just by ambulance. Here are the exact details of their makes and models." Dunn handed a sheet of paper to Spindle with the information. "Augustus, his wife and a doctor were in the ambulance. The trooper, Hoffmelter, or some shit like that, followed them in an unmarked vehicle. The deputy director took the boy earlier in the day in Augustus' official state vehicle…an SUV. That info is on the sheet of paper too."

"That's what the commander speculated happened…about the boy, that is."

"That's right," said Dunn. "So that checks out. However, the rest of the story is interesting. Those two officers from our briefing had me speak with another officer who escorted them from the hospital."

"What?" Spindle replied, incredulous.

"Yeah, and it was one hell of a lucky-assed break for us too, let me tell you. It apparently was a sizeable convoy. The officers who took part in the escort have all taken off to the Orange City area, except for this dude. He was the only one here that could speak to me about what happened. Crazy, right?" said Dunn, excitedly.

"Sure…sure…crazy Dunn. Where the hell did they go?" asked Spindle, impatiently.

"The officer says he doesn't know for sure because that trooper, Hoffmuncher –"

"Hoffmeyer, you dumb fuck," interrupted Spindle, angrily.

"That trooper…Hoff…mey…er…" mocked Dunn, "broke contact after directing the escorting officers to disengage and disperse."

"So they went off the grid mid-escort," said Spindle, almost more to himself than to Dunn.

"Correct."

"Did he tell you where they broke off?"

"Yeah, inside of a parking structure, next to the state capitol building."

"Huh, so they went inside a parking garage and broke contact with their escort?" confirmed Spindle.

"That's what the guy says, Spinds. You know, now that I think about it, it makes total sense."

"Please tell me how that makes any sense, Special Agent Dunn," asked Spindle, in a somewhat fatigued voice.

"From what little I know of this Augustus dude, he's one cold and calculated mother. A guy like that obviously knew NICO would continue to hunt him down. So, he has the trooper call his men off and Augustus goes into hiding somewhere nearby that only he knows about."

"A location where he evidently felt safe enough to be alone," pondered Spindle aloud. "You know, that actually does make sense. I mean, we already surmised that Augustus was aware NICO would continue to hunt him down, so that's not an epiphany."

"Damn...thanks, man," said Dunn, sheepishly.

"No, wait, I'm not done," replied Spindle. "I'm being serious here. That much we knew. However, multiple vehicles breaking contact, at a location away from the hospital, is new. And, so, by your analysis – which I agree with, by the way..."

"Thank you," interrupted Dunn.

Spindle continued – "Which I agree with...Augustus would necessarily have to be somewhere close to that structure. Close enough to where he did not need the escort anymore. Yeah, good job agent Dunn, good job."

"Go on, Spinds, cut that out. You going to make me blush you keep that up."

"Alright," said Spindle. "Grab your shit and let's go."

"Where to?" asked Dunn.

"To the parking garage."

"Why the hell are we going there? There ain't nowhere for them to hide, unless they remained in their vehicles all this time."

"Maybe not," replied Spindle. "But, that is the location where Augustus felt safe enough to be without an armed escort before disappearing. I still believe that he is waiting for dawn to boogie out of Des Moines. If he felt safe there before, then he might once again, prior to his final departure."

"Maybe he will use it like a staging area for their getaway," suggested Dunn.

"Could be," said Spindle. "But, we won't know for sure until we get there to see for ourselves."

"Are you going to check with Prater first?"

"Fuck that guy," said Spindle. "By the time he gets back to me, Augustus will be old and retired. No, I'm making the operational calls out here until he decides to contact us."

Dunn nodded his head in agreement and the two agents exited the room. They then left the hospital and departed for the Iowa state capitol parking structure.

అఅఅ

Augustus was by Jennifer's side when she showed signs of waking. She moaned slightly. The moans became more frequent and a little louder. Augustus ran to get Doctor Broderson, who was getting some much-needed sleep. "Doctor…my wife is waking up…she is sounding a bit distressed."

Broderson woke up immediately and rose to his feet as Augustus described Jennifer's condition. "I must sedate her again. She might go into shock if she comes right out of her induced state," he said, quickly grabbing his supplies.

Augustus returned to Jennifer's side and held her hands. Her eyes began to open, but it was apparent she was unable to focus on her surroundings. "Todo está bien, mi amor," said Augustus, calmly assuring her that all was well. Augustus did not truly believe that Jennifer could hear him. However, he felt that a calm and soothing voice of assurance could not hurt.

"Nathaniel…" Jennifer said in a low, weak voice. "My ba…by…"

Augustus' eyes welled up with tears as he listened to her call for their son. "Nataniel está aquí, mi amor…él está bien…él está vivo, mi cariña," he said, telling her that their son was alive and well.

The doctor arrived. "This dosage is not quite as strong as the first," he explained. "But, it will still last for many hours. The idea is to bring her out gradually, with shorter intervals between awakenings, as opposed to suddenly. I am doing it this way so that her nervous system can adapt to the reality of the situation…to avoid shock." Broderson administered the next dosage. Within seconds, Jennifer fell back into a peaceful, deep sleep.

Augustus looked up at the doctor and asked – "My son?"

"Same concept," replied Broderson. "I will prepare a smaller dosage for him. He might only need one more, given his age, but we will see about that."

"Do we wait for him to wake up?" Augustus asked, uncomfortably.

"No," replied the doctor. "I will prepare it now. Then, I will check his vitals to see where he is in his sleep-cycle. I can tell from that whether he is beginning to wake." He looked at Jennifer and said – "We were extremely fortunate to catch her before she awoke. It could have been damaging if I did not dose her in time." He then looked back at Augustus saying – "I must do this for your son immediately, excuse me." Broderson walked away without waiting for a reply.

Augustus went to Nathaniel and gently rubbed his head. "I love you immensely, hijo, but I cannot seem to describe how much." He clutched Nathaniel's tiny hands. He then raised them to his mouth and kissed them serenely. "I am so sorry for bringing you into this world, hijo. It was incredibly irresponsible of me, knowing the life I have lived. You and your mother lay in pain, while I remain standing. This is my fault. I do not deserve your love. I do not deserve it, but I accept it, with the greatest honor and privilege. I will protect the love you both have so graciously bestowed upon me with extreme prejudice. Te lo prometo…I promise."

He knelt down, still holding onto Nathaniel. He closed his eyes. Feeling the presence of Nathaniel's hands, Augustus prayed the Lord's Prayer in Latin – "Pater noster, qui es in caelis, sanctificetur nomen tuum…"

Broderson arrived at Nathaniel's room, but stopped when he realized Augustus was praying. Although not a man of faith, Broderson felt moved at what he witnessed. The visual of Augustus kneeling, while holding his baby's hands, seemed to have a powerful connection to the words he was saying. *Is that Latin?* Broderson thought. It was a surreal encounter for him that incorporated a deep and modern love with an ancient ritual of faith.

Broderson stood silent as Augustus' words echoed throughout the large recovery room.

"…Et ne nos inducas in tentationem, sed libera nos a malo. Amen." Augustus stood up and made the sign of the cross over his chest.

Broderson waited before approaching. "Mister Peña," he said quietly, "may I?"

"Of course," replied Augustus, stepping away from Nathaniel. He took a seat in a nearby chair and watched as the doctor checked Nathaniel's vitals. A thought occurred to Augustus, so he asked – "Doctor, should I change his diaper?"

Broderson looked at Augustus and explained the physical effects this type of sedation has on the human body. "Thus, the fluids and nutrients they received have been absorbed by their bodies, with little to no evacuation of waste. Consequently, they are both perfectly fine. However, since it is unknown when they will be at another stable location such as this one, a quick bath might be in order, as a matter of hygiene."

Augustus quickly stood up and said – "Yes, absolutely, I will get on it right away."

"I can handle your son, if that's acceptable to you?" offered the doctor.

"That would help tremendously," replied Augustus, and he made his way to Jennifer.

ରେ ରେ ରେ

Agents Spindle and Dunn arrived at the parking structure and slowly entered through the main entrance. "Which way?" asked Spindle.

"Hell if I know," replied Dunn.

"You mean to tell me, that with all the great information you received, you were not told which way they went after breaking contact? Or, for that matter, where exactly in this building contact was broken?" asked Spindle.

"Look, Spinds," replied Dunn. "All he said was that they turned into the structure and that Hoffmeyer walked up towards them, so they stopped."

Spindle assessed the ramp while tapping his fingers on the steering wheel. "Okay," he said. "That helps."

"How?" asked Dunn.

"If the trooper walked towards them from the right, he would be walking down. If he approached them from the left, he would be walking up. You said he walked up to the escort. So, I'd say that he came from the left," proffered Spindle.

Dunn replied – "Whatever."

Spindle steered left and slowly drove down the ramp. He stopped again, just beyond the first turn, and asked – "I don't suppose your source speculated on where they might have ended up after breaking contact?"

"Dude," replied Dunn, agitated. "Don't be a smartass, man. No, he did not. All he said was that he assumes they left through the rear exit. However, he didn't actually see them do that, so it was only a guess."

"Rear exit, huh?" said Spindle. "Okay, let's go find it then, shall we?" Spindle drove deeper into the structure, seeking the rear exit. He drove as far as he could go and came upon a wall. "I don't know about you, but I didn't see an exit on the way down here...rear or otherwise," said Spindle.

"Maybe we should have turned right," said Dunn.

"Yeah, maybe," replied Spindle, surveying the lowest level. He maneuvered a U-turn and drove up the way they had just come down. They drove past their initial point of entry, and continued another level, before arriving at the structure's north entrance/exit. Spindle placed the car into park and got out after determining this exit was at the rear of the garage.

"What you looking for Spinds?" asked Dunn, exiting the vehicle.

Spindle did not answer. He walked out the exit and crossed his arms. He observed the Des Moines neighborhood nestled just beyond the garage. Spindle pointed ahead as he spoke – "There's the highway we were on. It is not far from here at all. It allows for a quick escape, once they decide to head out...if they haven't already."

"What?" Dunn asked, stunned. "Now you think they have already left?"

Spindle lowered his head in contemplation and remained silent for almost one minute. He emerged from his deliberation saying – "No, I do not. I was simply articulating an obvious possibility. My intuition, Dunn, strongly suggests they have not yet left, but, that they will be Oscar-Mike in the coming hours."

"Do you want to wait out here?" asked Dunn. "It's early Saturday morning, so we shouldn't see many other cars driving around besides theirs, right?"

Spindle led Dunn back to their vehicle saying – "Not out here, get in." Spindle maneuvered another U-turn and drove down. He then said – "The likelihood is extremely high they are hiding within the surrounding neighborhood. The last thing we need is for them to spot us as we stand outside bullshitting."

"Okay, I can dig that. But, where are we going now?"

"Back to the bottom," replied Spindle. Dunn gave him a perplexed look, without saying a word. Spindle responded to his expression by saying – "From the information we have, Hoffmeyer broke contact with the escort inside of this structure. That trooper was with Augustus. Assuming all we were told is accurate, he walked up towards the escort, meaning, from the direction of the lowest level. The escort member you spoke to speculated they might have exited this structure via the rear exit, which is on a higher level. Both of those observations are contradictory. However, they still may independently hold true even though the rear exit is not where they traveled towards when they initially entered this structure."

"Bro, are you hypo-glycemic or something?" quipped Dunn. "You're not making any sense."

"What I am hypothesizing is that after breaking contact with the escort, they went to the lowest level to finalize their plan."

"So, why go there now?" pushed Dunn.

"Did you notice what was missing down there?" asked Spindle.

"No."

"Cars, you asshole, cars; this is a freaking parking lot and there aren't any goddamned cars parked down there. Even though it is an early weekend morning, this lot already has a shitload of vehicles parked in it…except for in that lowest level," said Spindle, excitedly.

"So, there are no cars parked. I don't get what you're trying to say, man. I mean, come on Spinds. Are they going to breakdance down there…what are you getting at?" Dunn asked, seeking clarification to his confusion.

Spindle replied – "For some reason, that area is cleared of vehicles. There must be a sign somewhere directing people to not park there, but that doesn't matter. What does matter, however, is that Augustus must be aware of this. If so, he knows this is always going to be an excellent place to gather. Especially, if they plan to do something like swap vehicles or meet with others who are assisting them. Daybreak is in another couple of hours. So, if my theory is correct, they will come here for a short respite before booking it for that highway and off to who knows where."

"And what if your theory is wrong?"

"Then, agent Dunn, we return to headquarters having done all the reconnoitering possible for NICO," replied Spindle.

"And if your theory is correct?"

"Then, we do what needs to be done."

"No family," said Dunn, sternly.

"No family," echoed Spindle.

Spindle drove to the lowest level. He parked parallel to the wall that covered the ramp leading down to it. He strategically parked the car so that an approaching vehicle would not immediately spot them. He turned off the car and its lights. "When the first vehicle turns onto this level, we won't know if it contains Augustus. However, we still have to engage. I will wait until they fully turn towards us and then slam on the high beams to stun them. As I do that, you jump out and engage the occupants to determine if Augustus is amongst them. If he is not, we will have to quickly detain whoever is in that vehicle and wait on Augustus to arrive. As you engage, I will drive up alongside of you. I will assist in engaging the vehicle's occupants once I drive right up on them. You got that?" asked Spindle.

"Got it," replied Dunn.

The two agents sat in the darkness, eagerly anticipating the events to come.

"I want a corn dog," whispered Dunn.

❧❧❧

Augustus finished folding the towels he just used to wash Jennifer. He stepped forward to kiss her. As he bent over, he glimpsed a rapid succession of yellow lights. Augustus stopped short of kissing Jennifer. He looked around to determine their source. The lights did not flash again. Unable to ascertain what they were, or where they came from, he continued and gave Jennifer a long, soft kiss on her lips.

"You look beautiful, mi cariña. I am taking you and Nathaniel to stay with my great friend Cal and his family in Kansas. You both will be very safe with them, I promise you. I will need to return to Des Moines –"

KNOCK…KNOCK…KNOCK… The noise cut Augustus off mid-sentence. He left Jennifer and opened the door.

"Sir," said Chad. "I wanted to make certain you were okay and to see if I could help you in any way. I went to the other room and the doctor had just finished cleaning up your son. So, I decided to get fresh clothing for him from the bag your wife packed to take…to take…to take this morning." Chad broke down into tears and voiced a flurry of words that Augustus was unable to comprehend.

"Chad," said Augustus, compassionately – "Aye, mira, venga aquí...come here." Augustus stretched open his arms and stepped towards him. He embraced his deputy director tightly, saying – "Never in a million years, Molander, could I have imagined you would be exposed to something as tragic, and emotionally compromising, as this. I have yet to sit down with you one on one, to discuss what I believe is happening. I am so very sorry, Deputy Molander…so sorry."

"Whoever these people are, sir…are they going to keep trying to kill your family? Are they going to kill you? Me?" Chad sobbed. "I'm sorry, Director Peña, I really am. It's just, it really hit me hard when I pulled out Nate's clothing from his bag. The tag inside his shirt showed the size of 2T and…and…his pants are so small. I couldn't imagine what kind of person would want to kill him…I'm sorry," he said as a new bout of crying ensued.

Augustus continued holding him. "Shhh, Shhh," he whispered. "There is absolutely nothing to be sorry about, Chad, nothing at all. I, on the other hand, must apologize for everything. The time has come for me to be as forthcoming with you as possible. Please, wait here while I finish tending to my wife. I am almost done."

Chad wiped away his tears and had a sheepish expression. "Okay."

Augustus returned to Jennifer. His stomach churned slightly due to Chad's emotional distress. "I must tell him the truth. It is the least I can do. I know I can trust him implicitly," he whispered. Augustus completed tending to Jennifer. He then left the room, to engage in one of the most honest conversations he ever had the courage to have. He emerged from Jennifer's room rolling down his sleeves. As he buttoned the cuffs, he said to Chad – "Vamos…let's go have a chat."

He motioned Chad towards a small conference room a few steps away. The two men entered and sat closely to one another. Augustus spoke fervently and concisely and laid it all out for him. Chad was like a young boy, digesting the frightening words of spooky tales, as told by a family elder. Augustus stopped talking and sat silent.

"Director Peña," said Chad, after mulling it over. "If it were not for today's events, I would have a very hard time believing this to be true. However, I have no basis to doubt any of what you just told me. I believe you, sir…and I trust you."

"Thank you, Chad. You do not know how important it is that you both believe and trust me. I am truly grateful."

"These are the things of conspiracy theorists," continued Chad.

"Sometimes, those theories bask in the truth." He motioned for Chad to stand. The yellow lights flashed again. This time, they flickered without abatement.

"What are those about?" asked Chad. "I saw them go off while walking to you from Nate's room."

"I don't know," replied Augustus. "How long did they last when you saw them?"

"I only saw a couple of flashes. Nothing like this, though."

"Yeah, me too," said Augustus, curious as to their meaning. He then said – "Let's go to Hoffmeyer, after checking on my son." Chad nodded and they hustled over.

"Do these lights have significance?" asked Broderson as they entered the room.

"I'm sure they do," replied Augustus. "But I don't know what it is." After checking on Nathaniel, they went to the main console area.

"What the –?" asked Hoffmeyer.

"Don't know yet," replied Augustus, sharply.

"You mean to tell me, you are one of just a handful of people who know about this place, but you have no idea why these lights are flashing? Is there a fire somewhere?" asked Hoffmeyer.

"No, no fire," replied Augustus, ignoring the remainder of Hoffmeyer's inquisition.

"How do you know that?"

"Because the fire warning system has not been triggered," replied Augustus, pointing to the red fire alarm button on the console.

"Oh," said Hoffmeyer.

Suddenly, the Station came to life. A soft, computer-generated female voice said – "Caution…weight differential of four thousand five hundred fifteen pounds detected on deck for ten minutes…caution." The voice repeated this warning twice, and then ceased. The lights continued to flash.

∝∝∝

The announcement jarred Augustus' memory. He recalled an impromptu meeting he took part in the year before. He had met with members of a DC funding committee, secretly empaneled to build and maintain this facility as a pilot project. The conversation focused on some contemplated technological upgrades. One of the enhancements considered was a surface detection system. In theory, the system would provide added protection by continually monitoring the surface weight of the garage's lowest level. This was important, they proposed, because that is where the secret entrance is located. Augustus was stunned. "I thought the funding for this enhancement was ultimately dropped and the project scrubbed," he said aloud.

"Sucks to be left in the dark, huh?" said Hoffmeyer, sarcastically.

"This is no time for sarcasm or attempted humor," growled Augustus, recognizing the likely meaning of the lights. "They know we are here…"

⌘⌘⌘

SEVEN

A warm, mighty breeze from deep within the Tyrrhenian Sea blew across the French island of Corsica. Typical to the island, the long stretches of beachfront were desolate. They lacked the grotesque masses of tourists that such tropical paradises attracted. The absence of beachfront tourism was not the result of a downtrodden or depressed economy. Rather, it was eerily desolate by design.

The political elite on this island were fanatical about maintaining their independence from France. However, they were even more obsessed with keeping Corsica from becoming the commercial circus that plagued their neighbors in Cote d'Azur. Preventing multi-billion dollar industries from developing Corsican beachfronts was no small task. It not only required a strong commitment to principle but, often times, an accompanying strong hand.

A powerful and generations-old criminal underworld thrived in Corsica. At times, it found itself at odds with the island's politicos, themselves a commanding force. Typically, these differences were resolved peacefully with concessions from the Corsican government. They varied greatly and ranged from a greater share of the island's profits to the highly prized privilege of prosecutorial immunity from French authorities.

The politicos preserved Corsican beachfront property with religious fervor and enforced it with merciless terror. In recent months, a three-mile stretch of explosions rocked this tiny island onto its side. The blasts were a response to a direct threat to that preservation, and represented the politicos' unwavering commitment of maintaining a developed-free Corsican beachfront.

In the months leading to the dreadful explosions, several prominent European resorts sought to develop Corsica. In their pursuit, resort executives communicated with a Corsican billionaire landowner...a criminal underworld boss. Soon afterwards, they signed a private land deal for development. The tycoon was convinced the politicos could not withstand the pressures that both he and this European conglomerate would bestow upon them. Shortly after closing the unprecedented covenant, the developers broke ground. They brought in excavation crews from elsewhere in the region, to avoid work stoppages. Concurrently, the conglomerate engaged the services of several marketing and public relations firms. In turn, those companies blanketed the region with advertisements of the impending enterprise.

Reaction from the politicos was decisive and swift. In addition to the swath of decimated land, the errant billionaire's one hundred sixty-four foot yacht inexplicably plunged into the Ionian Sea, engulfed in flames. All fifty guests on board died with him. A tense moment eventually resulted in peace, and the Corsican shoreline remained liberated from unwanted influences. The Tyrrhenian Sea's air once again blew across the shore, unobstructed, and free.

Mauricio di Pecha was a resident of Corsica and a longtime enforcer for the island's political elite. He picked up his glass of red Corsican wine and unceremoniously gulped a large quantity. He followed up this barbarous act by emitting a sound of pleasure. He then placed his glass down and returned to his favorite local dish of Tianu, a slow-cooked meal of game stew. Mauricio was privately celebrating his fruitful role in ensuring the island's conquest of the conglomerate's aggression. He enjoyed his dining and gulping of wine over several course servings. When finished eating, he would sit back and wait for the servant to replenish the bowl of Tianu.

"Bè, ví ringraziu," responded Mauricio, thanking the servant for the new helping. When it came to his consumption of wine, however, the process was not as relaxed.

Mauricio habitually cleared his glass after each gulp. Consequently, to his right, stood a different servant prepared to fill it. Mauricio was extremely particular about the exact amount of wine he wanted poured. The servant had to be exceptionally vigilant to avoid overfilling it. Failure to do so would hinder Mauricio's enjoyment of his meal…an act that had devastating consequences. "Un mì dirangeti micca," Mauricio would growl, directing the servant to not make him upset, if he gaffed monitoring the wine.

Mauricio was about to make such an utterance when his beeper chimed. "Merde," he said, cursing the bastard who dared interrupt his meal. Although passionate about enjoying his meals undisturbed, he exhibited great discipline. Mauricio understood that the beeper never went off for a trivial matter. He reached into his chino pants and retrieved it. He looked at the return number displayed on the thin, rectangular screen. This was not a job associated with the needs of the politicos. It was much more important. The numbers on the screen read 24.13 and were the corresponding numbers for the Roman alphabet letters X and M.

He returned the beeper to his pocket. At the same time, the servant closed in to refill his glass. Mauricio waved the servant off and said – "Ùn sò micca interessatu," declaring he was not interested. "Una buttiglia, per piacè," said Mauricio, requesting a bottle instead. Frustrated with having his meal interrupted, Mauricio smacked the Tianu off his table and snatched the bottle of wine from the approaching servant. He then left to contact the mercenary consortium that just reached out to him...XM Investments.

જ્ઞ જ્ઞ જ્ઞ

XM Investments was a multi-trillion dollar consortium that adopted the persona of an investment firm. However, nothing could be further from the truth. Functionally, the organization operated as a society of mercenaries. They were available on a global scale at a moment's notice. Based in the Central American country of Belize, XM Investments was a ghost. Known as "The Trust" by its clients, XM provided no public information regarding its company's leadership or personnel. XM maintained its anonymity by continually feeding millions of dollars into the openly corrupt Belize government. In turn, XM enjoyed exemption from Belize's corporate reporting laws while politicians, made wealthy from their inducements, ignored their existence. The result was a name-only firm, with no physical location, and no known employees. They were, in effect, a phantom enterprise.

Anonymity within Belize was crucial for XM's survival. However, what mattered most was remaining invisible to the outside world. The advent of modern day technologies made life off the grid virtually impossible. However, this presented no challenge to XM. The firm embraced those same technologies and reengineered them to their advantage with wild abandon. The result saw XM deploying countermeasures, at every turn of the hi-tech continuum, effectively extending their spectral existence from the physical into the technological.

The governments that contracted with XM did so without knowing the identities of the firm's leadership or personnel. However, those governments needed XM…to complete missions they themselves could not legally perform. This degree of anonymity caused concern amongst leaders worldwide. However, XM's silent yet powerful reputation for being able to monitor anyone and deploy anywhere, overrode such fretfulness. A statement, once made by an electronic voice to a high-ranking U.S. figure, quashed some trepidation – "Our anonymity ensures we cannot be implicated. Implication equals involvement. Who, then, can accuse you of illegality if it was accomplished by an entity that was not involved?"

అళ అళ అళ

Mauricio di Pecha led an action-filled life. The child of a Sardinian father and a Sicilian mother, he only knew Corsica as his home. Born and raised in Corsica, Mauricio was notorious for being a staunch proponent for the expulsion of influences corruptive to her culture.

Handsome and well built, a politico approached Mauricio when he was only seventeen, to exploit these traits. The politicos had business interests in Barcelona. However, an authoritative figure there was asserting his influence against them. "Questo può essere risolto solo in camera da letto," the politico said, explaining that the matter could only be resolved in the bedroom. With that blessing, Mauricio traveled to Barcelona where he effortlessly seduced the authoritarian's young bride. The man lost face within his influential circle. His colleagues incessantly mocked him about his wife's joyous fornication on the beach, before hundreds of beachgoers. As expected, the authoritarian ceased his attempts at sacking the politicos' business efforts.

Success for the politicos translated into success for Mauricio, and it came quickly. The politicos utilized him for their criminal underworld dealings. During a period that locals refer to as the "Corsican Wars," Mauricio's talents and violent tendencies blossomed. These displays eventually drew the attention and admiration of XM Investments.

Mauricio quickly advanced to his villa along the wave-crashing shoreline. He entered and walked through the parlor into the adjoining kitchen. He pulled aside a large, tri-colored piece of canvas that hung behind the stove, and walked into the dark room behind it. He knelt, feeling for an unseen handle, and pulled up hard. He then used the glow of his mobile phone to navigate a steep flight of slippery, metallic stairs. Mauricio felt grateful whenever he successfully navigated these steps. He earned respect for them after losing traction one day. The event caused him to be at the mercy of Newton's law of gravity and, as he believed, a merciful Devil.

Mauricio went to a small desk at the rear of this sub-basement, and sat down. There was a small, black phone on it…a replica of the type American telephone operators once used. He picked up the cylindrical earpiece, put it to his left ear and tapped the handle on the phone's base twice. He established a connection, evidenced by the sound of intermittent static and beeping. Mauricio said – "Chamada a cobrar por favor," stating in the Brazilian dialect of Portuguese that he wanted to make a collect call.

"O quê foi o futebol pontos?" replied the voice on the other end of the crackling line, asking Mauricio for the score of the soccer match.

"É vinte e quarto a treze," replied Mauricio, stating the score of the contest was twenty-four to thirteen. These were the corresponding numbers to the letters X and M.

"Isto é um perfeito pontos," replied the voice, exclaiming this was a perfect score. "Um momento por favor."

Suddenly, the desk broke into four distinct sections and separated to the sides. The floor made a swoosh sound. A tiny opening appeared, revealing a smaller stairway than what he just navigated. The compact room below brightened. Mauricio hurried down these stairs and sat in front of a digitized wall. Embedded in it, were multiple dials. Mauricio fixed each of them to a predetermined sequence.

Once the final sequence was fixated, the wall lit up to a radiant green color. Immediately, an electronic voice addressed him – "Our most lucrative client has requested our services. Location is within the client's home country. Coordinates to the territory are as follows – 41.5339 degrees north and 93.6331 degrees west. Additional assets are at your disposal and awaiting orders. Further instructions await you in craft. You have two hours before departure." The voice fell silent, and the radiant green illumination dimmed.

Mauricio needed to scramble to depart on time. However, he had to satisfy his curiosity as to the location. He spun his chair around and reached for the world atlas he kept for reference. "Induva và stu nùmeru?" murmured Mauricio, wondering where these numbers would take him. He did not need an atlas to know he was going to the United States. He already knew they were XM's largest and most lucrative client. The question was…where within the United States was his destination. Mauricio hoped it would be somewhere fun, with a crazy nightlife. "Oh…Miami…" whispered Mauricio, looking up the coordinates, longing for such a gift.

"Des Moines?" blurted Mauricio in French, curious as to why he was going to do work in a city of monks. A few extra moments of research and Mauricio realized his error. The location did not involve an enclave of monks, which is what Des Moines connoted in French. Rather, the words made up the name of a US city. Next, he focused on the larger territory that contained it. "I…O…WAH," mouthed Mauricio, trying to pronounce the name of the state. "Merde," he said, disappointed at not receiving work in a nightlife haven like Miami. Mauricio slammed the atlas shut, replaced it on the shelf and exited the room. "Fucking Iowa," he said, in broken English, as he turned off the lights and disappeared into the darkness of his villa.

ๆๆๆ

Augustus racked his brain, trying to recollect exactly how to work this system once an alert sounded.

"So, exactly what is it you thought was not funded, but that is apparently being deployed at this very moment?" asked Hoffmeyer.

Augustus took a seat at the console and replied – "Surface weight detection."

"What…the…hell…?" said Hoffmeyer, loudly.

"It's a security system that monitors the surface weight of the garage's lowest level…where we came in through. In theory, that level is a no-parking zone. Consequently, there should never be weight on it beyond the surface's baseline tonnage. If there is, the system kicks in and figures out the weight, like a scale. It then reports, at ten-minute intervals, whether the extra weight remains present," explained Augustus.

"I don't recognize this State anymore. It's like something out of a movie," replied Hoffmeyer, walking away in disbelief.

"That's it," shouted Augustus. "Movie cameras…how could I forget? I shut down the entire camera network prior to us leaving the hospital." Augustus, frustrated with his forgetfulness, ran to the opposite side of the console. He located the controls for monitoring the city's cameras during a catastrophic emergency. He prepared to access the video surveillance network when a thought occurred to him. He realized that this action was certain to give away his location. Augustus needed a plan before engaging it.

"Trooper Hoffmeyer," said Augustus. "Commander Teale is most likely in charge of state-level efforts in this matter, is that correct?"

"That is correct," replied Hoffmeyer. "Unless someone in your bureau's chain of command has taken over. Why do you ask?"

"I need to access a centralized video surveillance network, to determine what is on the lower level. This is the same network I disabled prior to us leaving the hospital. I can bring the system back to life. However, it would be unwise for me to access it with my credentials. Doing so will almost certainly trigger an electronic alert to headquarters. Accessing it under another identity is a risk, but it might delay the inevitable long enough for us to get out. I am trying not to compromise our safety."

"If it's not already," said Chad.

An alert sounded concurrently with Chad's statement. "Caution...weight differential of four thousand five hundred fifteen pounds detected on deck for twenty minutes...caution."

Augustus looked at Chad and said – "I agree."

"I don't get it," said Hoffmeyer. "What does Commander Teale have to do with any of this?"

"Only someone with commander level credentials can access the network through this portal. I need to act quickly and can only think of Teale at this point," explained Augustus.

"So...Teale knows about this location and hasn't said anything yet?" asked Hoffmeyer.

"No...no..." replied Augustus hastily. "It's his clearance level that determines his access to the network. Having knowledge about this facilities' existence has no bearing at all."

Hoffmeyer pushed – "So, then, you're just going to type his name into the system?"

"Something like that," replied Augustus. "I need to figure out his access-point ID. I'm sure I can do it." Augustus typed as he spoke – "Unlike passwords, which are often complex sequences of random data points, access to this system is based on a mathematical calculation of one's surname. Each letter in the alphabet has a number associated with it. The letter A equals one, B equals 2 and so forth. This part is simple. The larger task is determining the proper equation for deriving the access-point ID. It could be that each letter's corresponding number is multiplied by a certain sum or is divided into a particular integer, etc."

Hoffmeyer responded – "Sounds pretty basic to me. Why the hell wouldn't the folks who put this whole thing together require something more difficult to get into the network?"

"This method may seem out of place with the level of security and overall secrecy associated with this location. However, I can assure you, it only seems that way. This is the product of a well-reasoned and purposeful tactic," replied Augustus. "This facility is designed to be used during a catastrophic event that threatens the very existence of our government. Consequently, in real-time use, that means individuals accessing these systems are in the midst of a calamity. Maybe even under siege. A situation like that would be nerve-wracking. It is unfeasible to expect someone with zero combat experience to recall complex sequences of characters and symbols...the type that typically make up one's password. No. Instead, you have to assume they would recall their last name, no matter how frazzled they were. All they would be required to remember is the mathematical equation associated with it and they are off to the races."

Hoffmeyer chuckled and said – "Yeah, well, I think all of this money and secrecy is a waste. Especially since now I know that anyone armed with a last name can waltz right in here and access the controls you're on."

Augustus faced him and said – "Not just any last name will work. It must be one of a very few select individuals. More importantly, if someone just waltzes in here with the last name of one of those individuals, then we are all fucked anyway." Augustus returned to typing.

Hoffmeyer blinked several times while nibbling his lip and said – "Well put...I got it. Roger that Director Peña."

"Do you need some help, sir?" asked Chad.

"No, not yet," replied Augustus. "But I will."

Hoffmeyer looked up at the flashing lights and said – "I think this is as good a time as any for a weapons check." Augustus gave him a look of approval. Hoffmeyer then retreated.

Augustus paused to gather his thoughts. *What is the best way to go about this?* He then said aloud – "I don't have all day to figure out this guy's mathematical equation. Shit, not even he knows, since he is unaware of this facility. He obviously wouldn't be sitting here trying to access this network unless brought here by someone like Molander or I –" Augustus recognized something in what he just said and yelled – "Oh shit, right. Great, okay, now let's try..."

"What is it, sir?" asked Chad.

"Oh, Chad," exclaimed Augustus. "It was the break we needed. Mira, this Commander Teale, he technically possesses the proper level of clearance to access this network. However, he is currently not privy to the Station's existence. Consequently, he can only access it after receiving instruction. Because of this reality, which has not yet occurred, he does not know that his access-point ID exists. Therefore, it is set to a default mathematical calibration...one he would be required to change after initially activating it."

"That's great sir!" shouted Chad.

"Yes…yes it is," replied Augustus, rapidly entering the default mathematical equation for each letter of Teale. Next, Augustus input a remedial virus code, to reverse the effects of the malicious string he used to disable all of the city's cameras. Approximately three minutes elapsed. "BRAVO," yelled Augustus, as he brought the system back to life under the identity of Commander Dan Teale.

"Okay," he said in a serious tone. "It's time to find out who is hanging out on the lowest level of this garage…and why."

෨෨෨

Over the prior decade, the Des Moines area had been laden with thousands of surveillance cameras. The devices were equipped with panoramic video capabilities and ultramodern audio capturing technology. The residents of this emerging metropolis were largely unaware of their presence. Typically, the unassuming devices were no bigger than a library desk lamp. Usually installed atop streetlights, they were often mistaken for emergency traffic beacons.

Augustus possessed great competence working the video surveillance network. This proficiency allowed him to make the crucial split-second decision to disable it. If left operational, his whereabouts would have been instantly determined. The surveillance network was incredibly sophisticated and complex. Nevertheless, it posed no match for Augustus' level of skill.

"Let's see…city code, enter…east village neighborhood, enter…capitol vector, and enter. Boom…¡aqui estamos!" exclaimed Augustus at the end of his narration. A joystick-like throttle controlled each camera. He accessed one and maneuvered the throttle to get a panoramic view around it. "Okay…todo se ve bien," said Augustus, indicating that everything looked good.

"Do you have our location yet?" asked Chad.

"No, not yet," replied Augustus. "I am verifying the system's integrity."

"Sounds difficult," replied Chad.

"The difficult part was bringing it back to life and getting the cameras to sync-up and start working with each other again. This is more time consuming than anything else. I will have to teach you some day."

Chad stared away, pondering Augustus' words. He felt uneasy, wrestling his intuition that Augustus would never again have the chance to teach him anything.

"Okay, I am on Grand Avenue. I can see the parking complex. The historical building has a camera on its roof with an excellent vantage point," whispered Augustus. He accessed it. "Next are the garage's security cameras."

"Sir, are you able to directly access the garage's security cameras? To avoid navigating through the other ones?" asked Chad.

"Excellent question," replied Augustus. "You see, I WILL be able to teach you something after all." Augustus smiled and winked at him, suggesting he was cognizant of Chad's angst.

"But how did you –?" Chad started asking.

"Know?" Augustus said, completing his question.

"Yes."

"I guess torturing and killing people provided me with telepathic abilities," responded Augustus. Chad regarded him with horror and shock. "Relax, Molander," said Augustus. "I was just fucking with you. It was pretty obvious what was running through your head, given your sorrowful expression."

Chad let out a huge sigh of relief saying – "You got me good, Director Peña."

"You always gotta have time to fuck with someone, Chad, don't you forget that. Life is too short. Humor is a requirement, no matter how bad the situation may be," declared Augustus. Chad smiled. Augustus then said –"Now, regarding your question, the answer is yes. I do have direct access to the parking garage's cameras. However, I felt the need to reconnoiter the capitol complex first. I want to avoid any more surprises."

"So, where are you now?"

"I'm about to access a camera on the garage's next-to-lowest level," responded Augustus.

ߪߪߪ

It was four o'clock in the morning. Navigating the outside cameras was not visually challenging. The city's streetlights provided excellent illumination. In the parking structure, though, it was pitch-black. The state did not leave lights on in the garage overnight. Augustus could not see a thing. He gave up, returned to the control panel, and scrolled through its settings.

"What are you looking for?" asked Chad.

"I believe these cameras are equipped with night vision. However, I can't seem to locate the command to activate it."

Chad peeked at the screen and said – "Try that one," pointing to a command word.

"Fura...what the hell does that stand for?" asked Augustus, thinking it was an acronym.

"It's Furasshu," replied Chad. "It's Japanese for the English word flash. I took Japanese in college. More importantly, I use that command to access night vision when I am online gaming. It is called Emperor's Fu –"

"STOP!" yelled Augustus. "A gamer...you are an online gamer, Chad?"

"It might work, sir," continued Chad, exhibiting childlike humor.

Augustus clicked the hypertext link for the word Furasshu. The dark screen turned greenish, revealing the garage's details. "Son of a bitch," said Augustus, raising his eyebrows in astonishment.

"Looks like this high-tech system was programmed by an online gamer," said Chad.

"This country is screwed," retorted Augustus. He meticulously scanned every inch of the next-to-lowest level for evidence of an intruder. He saw no threats, and said – "Huh, I half expected a raiding party to be amassed on this ramp in support of whoever is down below."

Hoffmeyer reemerged with weapons in hand and asked – "Are you disappointed?"

"No," replied Augustus. "I'm just wondering what kind of plan would put all of its resources on the contact level, that's all." Augustus prepared to switch over to the camera on the lowest level when he caught a glimpse of something. Opposite the ramp's wall was a slight registration of heat. "Well…looksee here," said Augustus. "We have a heat registration against the other side of the wall."

"These cameras can detect through walls too?" asked Chad, excitedly.

"No," replied Augustus, pointing to the screen. "The interior ramp walls have large spaces between them. You can more or less see it here. The heat signature is passing through that gap and registering on the night vision."

"Night vision…now we have night vision?" asked Hoffmeyer.

"Oh, you missed a lot," responded Chad.

Hoffmeyer looked at the shotgun in his left hand and the semi-automatic he just holstered and asked – "Are these going to be any good in this fight? I mean, what's next, laser beams?"

"You'll be just fine," said Augustus, shifting his focus to Chad – "How much weight did the system claim was on the lowest level?"

"One moment, sir," replied Chad as he reviewed his notes. "She said four thousand five hundred fifteen pounds. Why do you ask?"

"At first, I thought the weight represented an assembly of men on the lowest level, waiting for us to emerge. However, my suspicion now is that it is a vehicle," replied Augustus.

"Are you making something out that looks like a vehicle?" asked Hoffmeyer.

"No, but the heat registration is uniform and appears to be decreasing. This is not consistent with the type of heat a group of people would emit. There would naturally be fluctuations, due to each person's unique level of perspiration," explained Augustus.

"Is there a camera on the lowest level?" asked Chad.

"Yes, there is. However, it is located along the other side of that wall," replied Augustus. "I need to know the potential threat before accessing it." Chad seemed confused. Augustus clarified his actions – "In the world of espionage and counter-intelligence there exist devices that can detect ocular surveillance, you know, camera and video detection scanners."

"Woah," said Hoffmeyer.

"Yeah," responded Augustus. "I was not concerned about this when I thought it was a group of Neanderthals waiting for us to emerge. Now, though...this seems to be more covert."

"What's on your mind?" asked Hoffmeyer.

"The heat signature's dissipation suggests a vehicle that is cooling down. It normally takes a car engine twenty minutes to cool off entirely. This is consistent with the amount of time the alerts state the weight has been there," explained Augustus.

"I have a feeling that's not all you're thinking of," said Hoffmeyer.

"No, it's not," replied Augustus, who then looked at Chad and reaffirmed – "You say the weight reported is four thousand five hundred fifteen pounds, correct?"

"That's correct, sir," replied Chad.

"Okay," Augustus speculated – "The weight of a standard model Walrus sedan is right around four thousand fifteen pounds. Pack in two men at about 200 pounds each, with weapons and ammo, and we get to four thousand five hundred fifteen pounds."

"What in the world...a Walrus sedan? Why in God's name would you choose a particular vehicle?" asked Hoffmeyer, in an agitated tone. "And speculating about two men with weapons? Tell me, why not three smaller guys with weapons or...or...four guys with a baseball bat?"

With an exceptionally stern expression and matter-of-fact iciness in his voice, Augustus replied – "It was once in my purview to know such things for the purpose of assessing a detonation's effect." Augustus looked at all of them and said – "A Walrus sedan is the standard-issue vehicle for NSA agents. Moreover, they travel in pairs when hunting their prey."

"Jesus Christ director, have you lost your mind? Are you suggesting that the NSA is behind the attempts on your family? This is preposterous. I cannot go along with that line of reasoning. I think it is time we get out of here and address the situation in a normal fashion. No more hiding...no more conspiracies for Christ's sake!" hollered Hoffmeyer.

"Trooper Hoffmeyer cool your jets at once!" demanded Augustus. "Don't you dare forget your place here for one goddamned moment. These are affairs within my expertise, not yours. I implore you to defer to my proficiency, in matters of intelligence and espionage, when it comes to assessing the cluster fuck we currently find ourselves. Do I make myself clear?" The force of Augustus' roar shook a cup of water nearby. Augustus took a moment to let what he just said sink into Hoffmeyer's soul, and then continued – "Now, I won't know for certain what is on the other side of that wall until I access the camera on that level."

Hoffmeyer glanced at the heat registration as it glowed in the night vision and said – "My patience is wearing thin, Director Peña. Go ahead and check that level. If there is nothing there, then we all need to go back to headquarters and have them take the ball. Do you understand?"

"I understand," replied Augustus. "However, you also need to understand that in order for me to determine what is going on, I must dabble in the world of craziness. I mean, shit, one would have been deemed psychotic for remotely suggesting this would happen to us."

"Yeah, and I would have been the first one to call them that too," admitted Hoffmeyer.

"See? So, can you hang tight with me a little longer, until we know what is going on out there?" pleaded Augustus.

"Yes, sir," said Hoffmeyer, taking a seat next to Chad at a nearby table.

Augustus returned to the monitor. The heat registration had diminished. *They are totally cooled down and lying in wait.*

The overhead lights flashed again and the voice blared – "Caution…weight differential of four thousand five hundred fifteen pounds detected on deck for thirty minutes…caution…"

Augustus whispered – "We are running out of time." He felt the pressure mounting. It was coming from all angles…the presence in the garage, the cautionary alerts and Hoffmeyer's ever-increasing doubt and impatience. These issues created a dire need to formulate a plan for an earlier than expected departure. Additionally, it weighed heavily on Augustus' mind that returning the cameras online meant Operations Command would soon become aware of it. *They will trace the access back here,* he thought.

Augustus felt angered at the hastening of his departure from the Station. However, he could not dwell on it. "The time has come to advance. But first, I have to see what we are dealing with out there," he uttered, focusing the lens and night vision equipment.

෴෴෴

The surveillance camera was located along the inside wall of the down-ramp. Augustus focused the night vision and began scanning. He turned the joystick left, to where he suspected the weight presence to be…and saw a car. His heart skipped a beat. His suspicion of a vehicle was correct. Before focusing on it closer, he moved the joystick to the right, to ensure no other threats existed.

The rest of the level was empty. The vehicle represented the sole source of weight reported by the alert system. Augustus refocused onto the car and cursed as he confirmed the make and model, a Walrus sedan. He turned to the console's keyboard and entered a command.

"Is it not working?" asked Chad.

"It's working great," replied Augustus. "I'm turning up the sensor to pick up on body heat. I want to know how many occupants are in the car."

Chad stiffened as he realized that his boss' theory was at least partially correct. "So, there really is a car up there," whispered Chad, as if speaking louder would alert the vehicle's occupants of their location.

"Dare I ask what model?" asked Hoffmeyer, reluctantly.

"Walrus sedan," replied Augustus, forcefully. Hoffmeyer sighed. Augustus increased the heat sensory module's precision and zoomed in on the cabin of the car. He then studied the thermal images and said – "Two occupants."

"What are they doing?" asked Chad.

"Sitting and waiting," replied Augustus. "It's interesting, though. The car is facing away from the entrance wall. It's as if they expect something to come towards them."

"Is it possible they are an escort, waiting for us to emerge, while simultaneously keeping watch?" asked Hoffmeyer.

"Yes," replied Augustus. "It is perfectly possible for that to be the case."

"How do we find out for sure?" asked Chad.

"I suppose we can drive out of here and see if they shoot at us," replied Augustus.

"I don't like that idea," said Chad.

"That makes two of us," agreed Augustus. "But, we might not have much of a choice...wait...let me try one more thing." Augustus returned to the control panel and looked for the audio command. He found it and said – "Oh, look, a straightforward command for audio. How wonderful, no gamer jargon." Chad looked sheepish. Augustus chuckled, pleased at himself for giving Chad more shit about online gaming.

"I doubt these folks are going to be saying much. However, if they do utter something, it might be useful," said Augustus. He engaged the camera's audio surveillance package, zeroed it in to the vehicle's cabin and said – "Unfortunately, the audio surveillance cannot pickup conversations within confined spaces. In order for this to be useful, the occupants need to be outside of the car, which is highly unlikely."

Several minutes elapsed with no peep from the occupants. "I'm wasting time," said Augustus. Then, an incredible event occurred. The passenger opened his window. He held his arm out while apparently clutching on to something. A whispered conversation inside the car ensued and the audio surveillance picked it up:

Voice one – "What the fuck are you doing?"

Voice two – "I'm trying to get a phone signal, that's what."

Voice one – "Why the fuck would you do that?"

Voice two – "I have zero phone bars and I presume you do too. So, if Maxwell or anyone else from NICO is trying to reach us, we will never know."

Voice one – "Get your fucking arm back in the car and close that window you moron. The agency does not issue us standard civilian shit. Who gives a fuck about phone bars? NSA phones can be used in freaking tunnels and mines you shithead...now close that fucking window!"

Augustus' vision became blurred. He almost passed out. The color in his normally bronzed face gave way to a vivid paleness, noticeable to those around him. He bowed his head ever so slightly.

For the first time in his adult life, he experienced the sensation of defeat. He contemplated all of his options. *I can walk out and let them kill me, to spare my family any more bloodshed and pain. However, what guarantee do I have that their mission ends with the taking of my life? What depraved mind made my family open for assassination? Will the depravity cease to exist once I am dead?* These thoughts swarmed Augustus' mind, with the relentless and overwhelming force of a tsunami.

"Director Peña, are you alright?" asked Chad, greatly concerned upon witnessing the life disappear from Augustus' face.

Weakly, Augustus replied – "There are two men in that vehicle who are agents with the National Security Agency. They have been sent to kill me by the organization I briefed you on."

"And your family?" asked Chad quickly.

"I have to believe the answer to that question…is yes," replied Augustus.

Hoffmeyer stood up. He cautiously approached Augustus and placed a hand on his shoulder. "I don't know what organization you briefed Deputy Molander on. Regardless, whatever you need from me, director, I am in this fight too…you can count on me. For the record, any revelations you might suddenly want to share with me about your past are unwelcomed. I still believe you must brief the proper authorities about who is coming after you and why. However, it's above my pay-grade at this point and, quite frankly, I really don't want to know."

ॐॐॐ

Augustus acknowledged Hoffmeyer's sentiment and then said – "Start packing up, we are leaving immediately. I will finalize a plan of escape. We are Oscar-Mike…on the move…in thirty minutes. Chad, come with me. I need to let the doctor know we are evacuating."

They ran hurriedly down the long corridor to Doctor Broderson and informed him of the emergency evacuation.

"I half-expected this to be the case after seeing those lights and hearing the warnings. Consequently, I am ready to go and the patients are all set for transport," stated Broderson.

"Excellent work doctor," said Augustus. "As I mentioned to you earlier, we are not leaving via the ambulance we arrived in…come with me." Augustus led the doctor to a set of doors around the corner from the patient area. He opened them. The doorway led to a dock where a fleet of large vehicles stood parked at the ready.

"These look like tanks instead of medical vehicles," opined Broderson.

"They are mixtures of a combat medical Humvee, Bradley fighting vehicle and SUV. They are entirely bulletproof, including the tires and windows. They are also self-fueled, so no fill ups needed," said Augustus.

"Self-fueled?"

Augustus replied – "It is too complicated to explain in detail right now. Briefly, they are equipped with solar plates, which provide some of the energy. However, there are also state-of-the-art wind turbine propellers that generate electricity as the vehicle moves. The electricity synthesizes real-time and is available for immediate use. This obviates the need to refuel. It is an ergonomic breakthrough for travel and is top-secret. Our fighter pilots are already enjoying the extra distance they get from this technology."

"Huh," is all that Broderson was able to utter after hearing Augustus' explanation.

"Pick your vehicle and load up, we leave in thirty minutes," said Augustus.

"All of us in one?"

"That's correct," replied Augustus.

❧❧❧

He moved quickly, exhibiting the strength and vigor of the Augustus of old. He returned to Chad, who was keeping watch over Jennifer and Nathaniel. "Chad, I need you. Please come with me. They will be fine. The doctor is on his way to them." Chad quickly stood up and followed Augustus. They returned to the room they were in earlier.

"Chad," said Augustus. "I only have a few minutes to develop my plan of attack and I am relying on you to help me execute it flawlessly."

"Attack?" asked Chad, worriedly.

"Yes, attack," replied Augustus. "These men are here for one purpose only. It is to kill, and it is my intention to prevent them from doing so."

"How are you going to do that?"

"Let me worry about those details," replied Augustus. "What I need is for you to focus on, and fully comprehend, the following instructions."

"Okay, of course, go ahead," said Chad, nervously awaiting his directives.

Augustus did not lay out his entire plan. It had nothing to do with trust, as he absolutely confided in Chad. Rather, he did so because the situation was extremely fluid. A sudden deviation might fluster Chad...and he needed to execute his portion of the strategy without hindrance.

Augustus finished giving his instructions and said – "Okay...so, to make sure we are on the same page, let's go through all of this one more time. Number one...we will be in radio contact once I arrive at my point of attack, and not one second sooner. We have to assume they are monitoring the airwaves and we cannot lose the element of surprise. Number two...the second I engage you via radio, you will turn the key that is located on the console to open the entry wall. I will show you exactly where that key is located and how to access it. Number three...time is of the essence, Chad. It will make the difference of whether we all live or die. You cannot fail and must act swiftly. Number four...and this is for the best, my friend...you must stay behind..."

"Director Peña!" exclaimed Chad. "Is there any other way?"

"No Chad, there is not," replied Augustus. He then moved in, gave his deputy a great big hug, and patted him strongly on the back. "You are a great man, Chad Molander. I will never forget you." Augustus then broke off and said – "There is one more thing. Come, let's go see Doctor Broderson."

The doctor was preparing to move Nathaniel to the vehicle when they arrived at the room. "Ah, I was hoping that you'd come to help me," said Broderson.

"Chad will help you in a few," replied Augustus. "But first, I need you to put together a concoction for Chad that will guarantee he does not wake up for at least twenty four hours."

"I'm sorry…what?" asked Broderson.

"Director Peña?" asked Chad.

"I am leaving Chad behind as part of my plan," replied Augustus. He turned to Chad and said – "You are a remarkable young man, and I trust you not only with my life but with the life of my family. However, you will face insurmountable pressure from various government agencies to tell them all that you know. I hired you based on your extraordinarily honest nature, Chad. The thing is that honesty does not serve me well right now. Consequently, I need you to be inaccessible for questioning, for a significant amount of time, after we depart. The only way I can guarantee that you will not speak is to have you put out of commission."

Remarkably, Chad agreed with Augustus' logic for wanting him deeply sedated and said – "So it shall be, sir."

Broderson shook his head saying – "I suppose it wouldn't make much difference if I presented the numerous ethical and moral problems with this plan of yours, would it?"

Augustus turned to leave and said – "Let me know when it is prepared, doctor. Chad, please come with me." They arrived at the console area. Augustus showed Chad the location of the key that was to be used to open the wall, as well as the two-step process for accessing it.

"Hold the red button for five seconds. Then, while holding down on the red button, tap the yellow button three times. The key will appear from within the console," explained Augustus. Next, Augustus furnished Chad with the virus code for disabling the camera network and instructions on how to administer it. "Do this the moment our vehicle leaves the garage."

He retrieved two high-powered radios, designed post-9/11, for use in confined areas such as tunnels and other underground locations. "Remember," said Augustus. "Do not talk on this. I will turn it on before I leave and contact you on it when you need to access and turn the key. Do you understand?"

"Yes, sir...I do," replied Chad.

"Very well," said Augustus. "Please go help Broderson load the vehicle. I will go get Hoffmeyer and then prepare to execute my plan."

Augustus went to Hoffmeyer, who was making a final equipment-check and re-strapping his protective vest. Given Hoffmeyer's hesitancy, Augustus decided it best to offer a watered-down version of his plan. "A diversion," is what he would tell Hoffmeyer was the goal.

"I present myself...they give chase...and you get going. I will proceed to hustle my Puerto Rican ass over to the north exit and jump into the vehicle. As a precaution, I will have a riot-strength stun gun if they get too close. Once we are all in the vehicle, we will be safe, given its bulletproof nature."

"It is not a very good plan," responded Hoffmeyer.

"I agree," said Augustus. "But, it gets us out of here before anyone else arrives."

Hoffmeyer did not protest further, but remained unconvinced of the strategy's effectiveness.

෯෯෯

Augustus hustled to the console and searched the office directory for maintenance. "This is where blueprints of the surrounding tunnel system would be kept," he said. He located it and ran as hard as he could to the maintenance room.

He felt thankful beyond words that the door was unlocked. Augustus entered the small room and rummaged through every drawer and compartment like a mad man. He found nothing. "COME ON," he yelled in frustration. "There has to be a damn blueprint of this place." Augustus purposely fell backwards into a chair, so that he could think. The force of his descent caused his head to jerk upwards. He saw a small door in the ceiling. Augustus cursed as he sprung up and moved the chair directly beneath it. He climbed onto the chair and stretched his arms up to open the tiny door. He felt uplifted upon seeing the distinct paper of blueprints.

Augustus jumped and grabbed ahold of the opening's edges. He pulled himself up and maneuvered his body to dangle from it, using the sides of his elbows. It had been some time since he found himself in such a compromised position. However, his years of intense training and fieldwork ensured he would not fail. Hanging on by one elbow, Augustus used his other arm to reach into the area, to pull out the blueprints. One at a time, he dropped them onto the maintenance room floor. Augustus alternated elbow and arm in this fashion until he cleared all twenty of the rolled up blueprints from the crawl space.

He took a deep breath, and released it, as he let go. Augustus fell straight onto the floor. The breathing technique allowed him to absorb the impact from the nine-foot drop. It was a tactic he learned many years prior, studying ancient Japanese combat disciplines. Augustus landed with the swiftness of a cat and scampered straight to the blueprints.

He quickly dismissed several of the designs as irrelevant. Finally, he zeroed in on three of them. "Yes, this is exactly what I am looking for," whispered Augustus. He then studied the blueprints, which outlined a multilayered tunnel system underneath the capitol campus. "Got it," he said, "time to move." Augustus grabbed the architectural plans and went to the Station's weapon room.

When he arrived, he accepted the reality that he had to use his fingerprint to access it. *I have no choice,* he thought. *There is no time for an alternate plan.* Augustus placed his palm on the hand scanner, located outside the door. An orange light illumed as it scanned his digits. Several seconds later, the screen next to the scanner read – GREETINGS, DIRECTOR PEÑA. ACCESS TIME = 0510. Augustus read the message and said – "There's no turning back now." He then entered the room.

Augustus harnessed himself with a shoulder holster and placed a fully loaded 9mm handgun in it. He still had his service weapon on him, but he wanted extra hardware. He then filled his holster compartments with as many clips of ammunition as he could find. Augustus was abundantly equipped and ready to go. He ran out of the room, but then stopped, saying – "Ugh…Hoffmeyer."

He went back inside, to locate a stun gun. However, the Station did not stock those. Instead, he found a gun specifically designed to shoot rubber bullets. He grabbed the weapon, in addition to the clip of special ammo next to it, and took off.

ॐॐॐ

Augustus arrived at the console area and said to Hoffmeyer – "This is going to happen extremely fast. I need you to be at the entry wall, so that when it opens, you are gunning the engine and plowing right through with zero hesitation."

"Got it, sir," replied Hoffmeyer, followed by – "That's a lot of hardware you are carrying, for just going out to stun someone, don't you think?"

"My ass," replied Augustus. "If shit goes bad, I want to be prepared. In the interest of full-disclosure, I do not have a stun gun. This facility apparently does not stock them. However, these are rubber bullets, and this gun is specifically designed to shoot them," said Augustus, showing Hoffmeyer the gun and ammo.

"Very well," said Hoffmeyer. "These things work fine too. They'll knock the shit out of someone, and keep them from coming at you for some time."

"Well," Augustus said to Hoffmeyer and Broderson – "Load up."

"Mister Peña," said Broderson, handing Augustus the concoction he prepared for Chad, "the medicine."

"Thank you," replied Augustus, followed by – "Chad, let's get you set up by the console."

Hoffmeyer asked – "What medicine?"

Oye, pero que dolor en el culo es este tipo, thought Augustus, reflecting on how much of a pain in the ass Hoffmeyer had been throughout this ordeal. "Something for Chad's nerves," responded Augustus, as he shot a look at Broderson.

He sat Chad down and said – "If you have to go to the bathroom, the time would be now…well, after you and I are done here, anyway." Augustus smiled as he spoke.

"No, I'm good, thanks," replied Chad.

"This two-way radio is now on," said Augustus, as he brought the radio to life. "Do not move this radio, do not touch it, do you understand? Its only purpose is for me to convey to you when the time has come for you to open the wall."

"Yes, sir…yes, sir…I got it…okay," replied Chad.

"Now, you remember how to access the key, don't you?"

"Yes…yes…Director Peña. I hold the red button for five seconds…then….um…while holding it, I tap the yellow one three times…yeah…I've got it," replied Chad, who had begun to sweat profusely.

Augustus stared directly into Chad's eyes and said – "The camera on this screen is real-time. You may or may not catch a glimpse of what goes down. Either way, you must keep watch on this camera after we leave, to know when to administer the computer virus and take this medicine. Is that absolutely clear?"

"As clear as can be," replied Chad.

"You need to inject yourself in the thigh and take the whole dose. If you do not, then everything we are doing here is meaningless. Do I have your word, Chad, that you will do this? I want your word not as my subordinate, but as my friend."

"Yes, Director Peña, you most certainly have my word."

"Don't ever call me Director Peña again. Call me Augustus. I am your friend, call me that!" said Augustus, in a strong whisper, as he grabbed the back of Chad's neck and bid him farewell.

"Direct…uh…Augustus?" said Chad. "Will I ever see you again?"

"I don't know," replied Augustus. "I really don't know." He stood up and walked away.

"Augustus," shouted Chad, causing him to look back. "I forgot how many times to tap the yellow button…I'm so sorry." Augustus started to respond, but Chad cut him off – "I'm just fucking with you, sir," said Chad, followed by – "A very wise man once told me, that you always gotta have time to fuck with someone. He also said that life is too short, and that there is always room for a little humor, no matter how bad the situation is."

Augustus felt a surge of emotion, as he realized just how much he had come to respect and admire this young man. The sentiment gave way to a stomach full of hilarity. Augustus roared with laughter, as he ran down the hallway, towards the tunnel system beyond.

⌘⌘⌘

EIGHT

"Alea Iacta Est" – Julius Caesar, while crossing the river Rubicon…

Augustus entered the tunnel system that ran underneath the capitol campus with relative ease. The blueprint he used as a guide was flawless. Utilizing the underpass was imperative for success. It allowed him to reach his destination on the sly, and out of sight. The tunnel system's design dated to 1874. From that point forward, it had been a work in progress, until the entire complex underwent a massive renovation during the 1990's. Its intended purpose was for political appointees, and their designated staff, to navigate surreptitiously between buildings.

For reasons unknown, the parking structure did not access the tunnel system. Consequently, Augustus needed to locate an area from which to emerge, that offered minimal exposure. Surfacing into a state building would not work. Doing so would set off an alarm, causing state troopers to respond.

Augustus located the perfect spot on the blueprint, and hurried there with inconceivable speed. The egress he chose was located beneath a narrow alleyway, midpoint between the garage and the state's genealogical building. Upon arrival, he referenced the blueprint to locate the closest engineer ladder.

Engineer ladders peppered the tunnel system. They provided access to areas critical for maintaining the massive HVAC network of pipes. The ladders were short, narrow and led into voids of darkness. Luckily, Augustus brought a few glow sticks with him from the Station's supply room.

He found the nearest ladder on the blueprint. It was only a few feet away…conspicuously located behind a thick pipe that dripped with condensation. Augustus cautiously crawled under the pipe. He rose on the other side, making certain he lost no equipment. Everything remained properly secured. Augustus grabbed a glow stick out of the satchel he towed, and twisted it violently, to activate its radiant formulary. He then placed the stick in his mouth and climbed the ladder, to the crawlspace above.

Augustus clenched the glow stick with his teeth while scurrying along the tight space. He thought of himself as a tarantula, hurrying to attack its unsuspecting prey. Augustus knew, from his study of the blueprint, that he would come to an even narrower opening. The cavity would be on his right, approximately forty yards from the crawlspace's entryway. Augustus estimated each of his push-offs to be about one yard. He counted each of his scampering leaps until...*Forty!*

"There it is," he said, letting the glow stick drop from his mouth. The narrow opening led up to the manhole, in the alleyway, between the two buildings. Augustus surmised that once he got onto the alleyway it would be only a matter of seconds before he reached the vehicle. *I will call Chad on the radio the moment I get to the top,* he thought. He retrieved another glow stick from his bag, activated it, and slowly began his ascent.

After reaching the top rung of the ladder, he paused and took a breath. He then cautiously pulled out the radio. Augustus examined his bag to make certain there was nothing left in there that he needed. He then detached himself from the bag and let it drop to the crawlspace below.

He pushed open the manhole cover. "Ay, Díos mío...qué milagro," he said, hailing as a miracle that it opened problem free. Noiselessly, he moved the cover off to the left. He stopped once he had enough room to extricate himself. Effortlessly, he pulled himself out of the manhole.

He lay on the ground, on his belly, scanning the area around him. Guardedly, he moved his right arm to his hip holster. He retrieved his weapon and brought it up by his face. Augustus then switched off the gun's safety mechanism, giving life to its lethality.

☙☙☙

Throughout this crucible, Augustus managed to keep his cool. However, that coolness gave way to umbrage and hatred for the unavoidable actions he would take. Anger and hatred mutated into a raging fury. He thought not only of his family, and the agony inflicted upon them, but also of his own. Augustus grasped that there existed no scenario from this point forward where he could maintain a normal life. His great reputation and well-deserved directorate appointment would be lost eternally, regardless how this turned out. The establishment would regard him as tarnished goods for the remainder of his life.

His eyes grew wild with fury. The world around him went silent and saliva streamed from his mouth. The ferociousness overtook him, altering his persona into a wild jackal preparing to strike. Augustus bounded onto his feet. He no longer resembled the man who called himself husband, father, director and friend. Rather, he bore the appearance of a grotesque figure, released back into this realm, through the gates of hell.

He put the radio to his mouth and snarled – "DO IT CHAD...DO IT...DO IT." Augustus zoomed towards the garage and leaped over the three-foot wall in a single motion and screamed into the radio – "DO IT NOW, CHAD!" Augustus dropped the radio, and used all of his remaining discipline to return to silence.

It was extremely dark in the garage. However, daylight began to appear, casting an ethereal silhouette against the walls, as he charged towards the unsuspecting agents. In an instant, Augustus closed in on the vehicle and went airborne, to mercilessly attack his prey.

꒰꒱꒰꒱꒰꒱

Chad recoiled upon hearing the command come over the radio. The volume and texture of Augustus' voice scared the bejesus out of him. Ever the great assistant, Chad did not skip a beat. He held the red button for five seconds and then tapped the yellow button three times...the key appeared. Chad turned the key the moment it became accessible.

He was all alone now. The others were on the inside of the wall that was about to open. Chad wanted to see exactly what was going on. He slid his chair to the monitor and remained glued to the screen...watching...waiting...and wondering wildly about what could possibly transpire.

꒰꒱꒰꒱꒰꒱

"It's going to be light soon," said Spindle.

"Time to do some shit," replied Dunn, followed by – "Hey, how long we gonna wait if they don't show up here shortly after daybreak?"

"Why?" asked Spindle. "Do you have a date?"

"No, man," replied Dunn. "I just want to get out of here and check what Hot Ticket numbers came out, that's all."

"You dumbass," Spindle shot back. "You bought those tickets well after the drawing time, so it won't be until at least tonight. Lottery…wow…"

"Nah, nah, nah…I thought the drawing was –" said Dunn, leaning forward to reach for his lottery tickets, when he saw movement through his rearview mirror. "What the hell," he yelled.

"What…what?" Spindle asked nervously.

"Dude…no fucking way, no fucking way!" yelled Dunn. "Them mother fuckers is coming out of the wall behind us, Spinds! They not in a house somewhere…they were behind a trap-wall." Dunn acted like an uncontrollable child, laughing frantically and slapping his knees.

"Oh my fucking God," exclaimed Spindle. "It's them."

"Engage," yelled Dunn as he grabbed his gun and reached for the door handle.

Spindle yelled – "DON'T" as he glimpsed, through his peripheral vision, a shadow passing over the rear of their car. He then shouted – "Don't open the door!"

Dunn ignored Spindle's exhortation. He flung open his door and began exiting the car. As he did, dawn's emergence occupied the garage just enough to cast a chilling visual. Staring up at him from the ground were Augustus' devilish-red eyes.

Spindle screamed – "NOOOOO."

   ❧❧❧

The muzzle flashes from Augustus' weapon lit up the lowest level. He reloaded, forgetful about having another gun in his shoulder holster, and stood up. He went over to Dunn, who was quivering and shrieking in pain. Augustus knew that the driver was deceased. Half of his head was missing, and splattered throughout the car's interior. Without losing an ounce of fury, Augustus knelt down besides Dunn and said – "Call them, call them now."

"Who…who?" whispered Dunn, unable to put together a complete sentence.

Augustus pushed down hard on Dunn's most painful wound and yelled – "NICO."

"I…I," said Dunn, followed by a howling scream as Augustus pushed down again.

"Call now or you die an extremely painful death."

Dunn looked towards the car and said – "His pho…his pho…pho…"

"His phone?" asked Augustus. Dunn affirmed with a fast nod. Augustus stepped to the car and saw a phone by Spindle's lifeless body. He grabbed it and asked – "This it?"

"Yes."

Augustus looked through the phone's contact list. Unsurprisingly, he found nothing. "When was the last communication?"

"He kept…try…ing…couldn't…" Dunn tried to speak. He coughed up blood and choked.

Augustus checked the outgoing call logs. He saw the same number repeatedly. Knowing that the number represented their NICO contact, he hit the Send button. He then placed the phone to Dunn's ear saying – "Tell them you found me."

ॐॐॐ

Maxwell scampered along his bathroom floor upon hearing the phone ring. It was by his head. However, he was discombobulated, extremely disoriented and unsure of his whereabouts. The abrupt awakening caused his heart to race uncontrollably. He grabbed the phone and answered – "Prater," in a heavily drugged-up sounding voice.

Dunn yelled with all of his remaining strength – "AUGUSTUS PEÑA!"

Maxwell's disorientation and confusion disappeared. Dreadful fear replaced it as he listened to the name just screamed at him. The screeching ended, displaced by a loud boom. Everything fell silent…and the phone line went dead…

৵৵৵

Hoffmeyer raced to Augustus, screaming – "Don't do it Director Peña, don't you dare shoot!" The single shot reverberated throughout the garage. Hoffmeyer drew his sidearm. "Augustus Peña, I am placing you under arrest for committing murder. Lie flat on the ground. Get on your stomach and clasp your hands behind your head," bellowed Hoffmeyer.

"Don't be a fool Hoffmeyer," Augustus retorted. "I had no other choice but to defend my family."

"Shut it," shouted Hoffmeyer. "I'll have no more of it, do you understand me? No more! You have made a mockery of me and all that I stand for as well as tarnishing the reputation of this uniform I so proudly wear. You, Augustus Peña, gunned down these two men in cold blood. You ambushed them, with all the intent in the world of slaying them. To make matters worse, they were federal agents. That is a capital-level offense if I recall correctly…a capital-level offense mister Peña. Do you know what you just did…do you? You just bought yourself a ticket on Death Row and made me appear as an accessory to murder in the process. You manipulated me into believing that you were being attacked by multitudes of professional killers; where, all along, YOU, Augustus Peña, were the actual assassin."

Augustus's rage intensified. Explaining himself to Hoffmeyer was not an option. Moreover, there was no way in hell he would allow Hoffmeyer to arrest him. To do so would be suicide. Augustus was well beyond the point of being able to resolve this matter in conjunction with law enforcement. Time was running out and he needed to act fast.

"Get flat, mister Peña, or I will do it for you. On your belly and arms to the side," shouted Hoffmeyer, training his weapon on Augustus.

Augustus did not say a word and compliantly spread his arms out to the side. He then dropped forward, hitting his chin on the pavement as he landed. Once prone, Augustus placed his hands behind his head and clasped his fingers.

"Stay still, I really do not want to hurt you…but I will…you must understand that," said Hoffmeyer.

Augustus did not utter a sound.

Hoffmeyer grabbed a set of handcuffs from his belt with his left hand, while training his gun on Augustus with his right. He then reached forward to place the first bracelet on Augustus' left wrist.

Upon feeling the handcuff's cold metal on his skin, Augustus raised his chest off the ground with great power. This ability was the result of many years' worth of jungle missions that required Augustus to dangle lifelessly from triple-canopy treetops, waiting for his quarry, from whence he would spring to an upright position and make his kills.

The force with which Augustus lifted himself from the pavement stunned Hoffmeyer, throwing him off balance. In one swift, circular motion, Augustus rose onto his knees and held Hoffmeyer's head under his armpit.

Hoffmeyer felt dizzy and could not comprehend what just happened to him.

Augustus swatted away Hoffmeyer's gun. He knew that he could easily kill the trooper by snapping his neck…but there was no need for that. He was most certainly frustrated with Hoffmeyer's rigidity. However, he also recognized that the trooper had a duty to protect and serve the citizens of this great state by enforcing its laws.

He looked at Hoffmeyer and said – "You will not die here tonight." He dropped his center of gravity, what Asian martial artists refer to as Chi, onto Hoffmeyer's body. Simultaneously, he squeezed hard on the trooper's twisted neck, and held that position for ten seconds.

Hoffmeyer's body slumped inertly towards the pavement. An audible hissing sound emitted from Hoffmeyer's lungs, as air rushed out of his body.

Augustus gently laid him down onto the pavement and stood up. He then retrieved the trooper's gun and ran back to the idling vehicle that contained his family and the doctor.

"It's just us," said Augustus to Broderson, as he climbed into the vehicle.

Broderson was horrified…but he dared not say a word.

"He's not dead," Augustus said, referencing Hoffmeyer's sprawled out body. As he drove, he said – "But those two bastards are," pointing to the bodies of agents Spindle and Dunn.

☙☙☙

Chad watched the video monitor with bewilderment and disbelief. The rapidity with which everything occurred caused him to feel queasy. Chad looked away when Augustus leveled a barrage of bullets into the car. He waited a few seconds and looked again.

The video quality was grainy. However, Chad discerned a severely injured man lying against the passenger side of the car. Chad imagined that the man would receive medical aid once Augustus left the scene. However, his idea of a civilized ending to this encounter was shattered. He observed the man make a palpable plea for his life just as Augustus shot him in the forehead.

Chad leaned sideways in his chair and vomited onto the floor. When he sat up, he looked back at the monitor and saw a state trooper pointing his weapon at Augustus.

"My God…that's Hoffmeyer," Chad said aloud, wiping vomit off his face. He grew more nervous and confused and wondered how this would alter Augustus' plan. "What the –" Chad said, as he witnessed Augustus overcome Hoffmeyer. He could not determine whether Hoffmeyer was dead or merely injured.

Desperate, Chad jumped out of his chair and administered the malicious code, disabling the camera network. Next, he grabbed the syringe of sedative and chewed off the safety cap. Although he could not recall the last time he used foul language, Chad stuck himself in the thigh with the syringe saying – "Fuck this…"

☙☙☙

The eeriness of the phone's sudden silence had the unusual effect of clearing Maxwell's mind. Without hesitation, he went into his den to contact Milken, to inform him of what just occurred.

Milken listened intently as Maxwell spoke. He struggled to comprehend how Augustus was able to achieve such a feat. He pursed his lips, lowered his head, and reflected on the matter further. "So," began Milken, breaking the long silence. "Augustus Peña is now on the loose after somehow identifying our reconnaissance team and then…killing them."

"That is correct," replied Maxwell, somewhat disturbed by Milken's lack of emotion.

"Well, then, it's going to take a little longer and a few more resources than what I have set into motion," said Milken.

Confused, Maxwell asked – "What other resources?"

"I took immediate action, after not being able to reach you for several hours."

Embarrassed and ashamed of himself, Maxwell tried to explain his lack of communication – "Oh…I…uh…well, let me tell you what happened."

"There is no point explaining it to me now," said Milken. "Besides, this has truly worked out for the best. You see, not being able to reach you concerned me. I assumed that Augustus had found and killed you. Consequently, I thought of other options. Obviously, I was wrong to be concerned. You were apparently off doing God knows what, with God knows who, while NICO assets were being slaughtered. We will address that at a later point in time."

"But Virgil, I wasn't –" responded Maxwell.

"Quiet, you blunderer!" shouted Milken. "I am not interested in your pathetic excuses, nor am I your friend. Do not call me by my first name for the rest of your contemptible life. Now, as I was saying, your unavailability consumed me. I had no choice but to take immediate and decisive action. Consequently, I made the necessary arrangements to have our primary vendor reinforce our efforts in the field. Of course, I had no idea at the time how extensive the problem was, so I only made a request of minimal proportions. That now needs to be changed. Therefore, Prater, I must take leave from this insightful conversation with you and upgrade my request of the vendor."

"You've employed the services of XM Investments?" catechized Maxwell.

"Why…yes," replied Milken.

"They are barbarians, lacking of discipline, who are devoid of all respect for the sanctity of innocent human life, Milken. They will kill everyone and everything in their path," shouted Maxwell, unafraid to show his disgust at Milken's decision to employ their services.

Milken replied – "I am calling a Chamber meeting for this evening. We can discuss this further when you get here. I must go and ensure that we have enough assets on the ground."

For the second time in less than an hour, Maxwell's telephone line fell silent.

ॐ ॐ ॐ

Milken contacted XM management to expand their scope of operations. As he spoke, a phone in his office beeped. Milken did not answer. He needed to complete this communiqué. Besides, the caller had to retry, at every two-minute interval, until establishing contact.

Milken completed his conversation and took a seat by the Sat-Link phone. As expected, it sounded within two minutes of the prior attempt. "Please tell me something is actually going well for us," said Milken when he answered.

"I would much rather wait to see the outcome before professing any form of success," replied Saxby Coles. "The game pieces are now in play, and I eagerly await their results."

"Very well," said Milken. "See you at The Chamber tonight." Milken swiveled his office chair. He grabbed the remote for a large, flat-screen television across the room. He increased the volume and listened to a news report out of Boston.

"Authorities are still looking for leads on the massive car bomb explosion that rocked downtown Boston, killing prominent publishing executive Sam Hepner. Sources close to the investigation have suggested an organized crime connection gone sour. KBNB has learned that this theory stems from both the powerful nature of the bomb, and the mysterious circumstances surrounding the executive's need to park outside of the firm's indoor lot…"

"I can't say I saw that one coming," said Milken, regarding the organized crime hypothesis. "I'll have to save blaming the Chinese for a different time." Milken had wanted to put information into the stream of communication suggesting China's retaliation against Wickles for publishing memoirs of dissidents. Milken chuckled and turned off the television. He retreated to his quarters to get ready for his meeting.

⌘⌘⌘

NINE

Mauricio di Pecha arrived at the coastal airport in Calvi, Corsica with some time to spare. He sat by a terminal window to get a full view of the runway. Mauricio enjoyed watching planes take off and land. He often ruminated about how intelligent a person must be to fly an airplane. *I could not do such a thing,* he thought as the plane he observed touched down softly. *If I were a Pilote, it would certainly go straight into the ground.*

He continued looking at the plane as it taxied towards the terminal. When the small jet came to a halt, Mauricio stood up and grabbed his belongings. He went downstairs, to where the terminal led onto the tarmac. A French Passport Control Agent was on duty. Mauricio handed him $300 US dollars as he walked past. He did not need to pay the worker a dime. No one would dare stop him from going out onto the runway. Nevertheless, Mauricio made it his practice to engender favor amongst those who could turn against him if provided the opportunity.

Mauricio walked towards the aircraft as its fuselage door opened. A retractable stairway unfolded, extending to the ground below. Mauricio reached the bottom of the staircase. A woman wearing a short, red skirt appeared at the jet's doorway. She also sported stiletto heels, a satin tank top and, from what Mauricio could gather from his angle…no panties.

"A ringrazià ti," said Mauricio to the woman, thanking her for the gratuitous view of her privates as he walked past the staircase.

"Cacadori!" she shouted at Mauricio, expressing her anger at his obnoxiousness.

Mauricio chuckled and strode underneath the jet. On the other side, he swung his jacket over his right shoulder. A baggage cart pulled up in front of him.

"Je n'accepte que l'argent exacte," said the French driver, informing Mauricio that he only accepted exact money.

"Je n'ai pas d'argent exacte," replied Mauricio, notifying the man he did not have exact money. He then said – "Je suppose que je vais devoir vous payer un supplement," informing the driver it appears he will have to pay him extra.

The two men nodded and Mauricio boarded the cart. They remained silent for the seven-minute drive to the edge of a remote runway, where the tarmac met the Ligurian Sea. The chauffeur drove speedily down the middle, as if he intended on navigating into the sea. The cart slowed, and came to a complete stop inches from the runway's periphery. "Vos articles, monsieur. Dois-je vous aider?" said the driver, asking Mauricio if he wanted assistance with his items.

"Bien sûr que non," he replied, stating he did not. He then jumped off and grabbed his things. Mauricio went to the lip of the runway and turned back, facing the cart. He proceeded to squat very low and said to the driver – "Au revoir." He then grabbed ahold of the ladder embedded into the earth below him.

"Vais-je vous voir bientôt?" queried the driver asking if he would see Mauricio anytime soon.

"Seulement si le diable n'a pas d'autres plans pour moi!" roared Mauricio with laughter, replying it depended on whether the Devil had other plans for him.

"Eh bien, je vais attendre et voir! Au revoir!" responded the driver, stating he will wait and see and bid Mauricio farewell.

෴෴෴

Mauricio climbed down the two hundred-step ladder. It led to a three-foot ledge of earth below. He turned to face the water and raised his right arm. He held it across his chest as if looking at a watch. However, Mauricio wore a watch on his left wrist. This motion served to signal a speedboat that was circling about in the waters before him. The speedboat's engine rumbled as the navigator made a beeline to Mauricio's position. The craft closed its distance and maneuvered into a semicircle pattern. Parallel to the shelf Mauricio occupied, it stopped. An unseen person threw a large package out to him. The speedboat's engine thundered back to life, and took off down the channel.

Mauricio opened the package and retrieved a malleable-looking item. He unfolded it and opened a zipper that ran across its length. He then placed his belongings into the haversack-like container, and zipped closed its powerful interlocking fastener. Mauricio reached into the package again. He removed a specialized helmet and a miniature oxygen tank that went with it. He speedily connected the tank to the helmet and put on the headpiece. There was one last item in the package, a two-foot long pole. Mauricio grabbed it and clicked a button on its center. The length of the pole grew to four feet. A trident-spear emerged on either end. The spear was the most important tool in the package. It represented his sole defense against any sharks desirous of claiming him as a meal. Next, Mauricio threw the container with his belongings into the water, and watched as bubbles appeared around the sides as it sank to the depths below. He then looked at his trident spear, and plunged into the shark-infested Ligurian Sea.

Oxygen was available in the tank for a maximum of fifteen minutes. Upon expiration, the military grade epoxy contained within it would denature. Seconds later, the cylinder would self-destruct and dissipate into the vast ocean beyond. Luckily, for Mauricio, he did not need fifteen minutes to arrive at his destination. The dive to the cavern he sought would take him only five. However, delays could most certainly occur due to the schools of aggressive sharks that routinely lurked in these waters. On this day though, Mauricio would not need to resort to his trident savior. The sharks were most certainly around him, and unquestionably interested in his presence. However, the beasts showed no bloodthirstiness, and let him pass without menace.

Mauricio arrived at the cavernous opening with his items in tow. He swam to a small-scaled submarine, docked at the rear of this underwater cave. He pulled himself onto the vessel and entered a passcode to gain entry. After securing his items inside of the submarine, he returned to the top. Mauricio pulled the hatch shut and spun the iron wheel on its underside until airtight. He then hurried to the controls and activated the submarine's systems.

He turned on the sub's communication system to receive directives from XM. After bringing the sub to full power, Mauricio pushed full steam ahead for his deep-level trip through the Ligurian Sea. Exiting the cavern, he took notice of several large sharks feasting on a whale. Mauricio raised his eyebrows and thought about this great omen – *They do in the water what I do on land...and with the same amount of pity and remorse. Yet, they let me pass without incident. Truly, this is the work of both Demons and Devils. It is a sign from beyond that my objective is worthy. I have gained respect from the greatest eradicators on earth.*

ॐॐॐ

Mauricio monitored the sub's low frequency radar to locate his connection for the next leg of his journey. It showed no signs of vessel activity. He rechecked the navigation coordinates to confirm he was on course…Strait of Gibraltar. He was where he needed to be for the rendezvous. He then stared at the locator as if doing so would manifest the vessel he sought. Several hours elapsed, with no sign of the ship. Mauricio became increasingly agitated as each minute passed. *Something is wrong…something is terribly wrong,* he thought. *Contact should have been hours ago. I cannot linger in these waters…lest I draw attention of the Spanish Navy.*

Staring at the floor, he contemplated his options. He even considered the unthinkable…abortion of the mission and returning to Corsica. He immediately dismissed that as a choice. Mauricio looked at the radio, wondering if he should initiate contact with XM. That would not work either. Getting on the radio might alert authorities of his presence. He could not risk this. "Merde," he cursed, realizing he had no good options.

Many hours later…the radar flashed. He saw what he was looking for. The vessel appeared in the radar as a hexagonal-shaped figure. This was the result of ingenious XM engineering. It allowed identification of its vessels by radar, and boasted other functionality. The hexagonal-shaped vessel came to a floating halt. The vessel then emitted two deep, moan-like sounds, lasting less than two seconds each. Mauricio responded to this signal by pushing a blue button, located next to the radar screen. The submarine emitted sounds that resembled the language of dolphins. Shortly thereafter, the satellite radio beeped. Mauricio engaged the radio to receive the message.

"Rise," said the digitized voice on the other end of the radio.

Mauricio re-docked the radio and went to his craft's controls. He initiated the mechanisms necessary to ascend towards the awaiting vessel. Mauricio stopped the ascent when the surface measurement dial showed the top of his sub to be three meters from the vessel's hull. Next, the vessel lowered a half-dozen hooking devices. They automatically latched onto their respective clamps situated atop the sub. Once clamped, the vessel pulled the submarine until it locked perfectly into the ship's underbelly. The two vessels were now one, and the next leg of the journey was about to begin.

ॐॐॐ

Mauricio felt the sub lock into place. He checked the monitors, to confirm airtight connections, and then climbed up to the hatch. Mauricio spun the wheel furiously to get it open. He emerged into the belly of the vessel, screaming, seeking the whereabouts of the Greek crew's captain.

A crewmember replied that the captain was up on deck.

Mauricio raced topside, yelling for the captain. Eventually, a swarthy-looking man appeared, with a half-consumed bottle of Metaxa in his hand. The captain was drunk. This enraged Mauricio even further.

"You call yourself a captain, you piece of shit!" shouted Mauricio.

The captain smirked and responded sarcastically – "I got my ship here, in the dead of night, with no loss of crew. Yes, I shall say that I do call myself a captain." The captain raised the bottle of Metaxa and gestured it towards Mauricio for him to take a drink.

Mauricio slapped the bottle out of his hand while simultaneously punching him in his neck. The captain fell awkwardly to the deck. Mauricio then yelled out for the first mate.

A young man in his twenties appeared from the crowd of men gathered there. Mauricio looked curiously at the young man and said to him – "You cannot be the first mate…you are too young."

"But, I am…I promise you that I am."

"How many voyages have you embarked on?" asked Mauricio.

"Three," replied the first mate.

"Three?" repeated Mauricio, incredulous. He then asked – "How long have you been first mate?"

"Today is my first day," he answered proudly. Mauricio appeared very confused, prompting the young man to explain further – "I took over for the previous first mate because of his desire to quit. He had been doing this work, as I was told, for over 12 years and grew tired of being called out to sea at a moment's notice."

Mauricio could not believe his ears, and asked – "So, he simply turned over his duties to you and remained in Cyprus, to enjoy his peace and tranquility?"

"No," replied the first mate. "Actually, he is on this ship. He is below-deck, in the captain's suite. He quit being the first mate shortly after we left port. He has been celebrating his decision to resign with the captain…they are great friends."

Mauricio glanced at the captain, who was choking and holding his neck. He then said to the first mate – "Go get him."

"Sir?" asked the first mate.

"The former first mate, bring him to me."

The first mate whistled at two crewmembers and motioned them to follow him. The three men went to the bow of the ship and down some steps, disappearing into the deck below.

The captain, having caught his breath, attempted to stand.

Mauricio saw this and said – "Where the fuck are you going?" He kicked the captain square in the face, causing him to tumble backwards.

The three men reappeared from below deck, dragging a tall, lanky man.

"Sir," said the first mate. "He is so drunk that he cannot walk."

"Throw him down next to his friend," ordered Mauricio. They complied and the crowd gasped. Mauricio then addressed the crew – "For close to one day, I waited for this vessel to arrive. Do you know how dangerous that was for me and for this mission?" Mauricio scanned the deck and eyed each crewmember. He continued – "I did not come to this merciless sea for matters that are trivial. Nor did I travel here underwater for dramatic effect. We operate in this manner because the mission cannot succeed otherwise. Concealment and stealth…this is of the utmost importance to our employer, and is critical to our success."

Mauricio looked down at the captain and said – "You failed us all by choosing personal pleasure over your professional duty. That failure could have cost me my life and could have exposed this entire mission."

The captain looked up angrily at Mauricio and said – "How dare you disgrace me like this in front of my men? I am the captain of this vessel!" He sprung from his kneeling position and lunged at Mauricio with both hands stretched out in front of him.

Mauricio spun past him and picked up the bottle of Metaxa he had smacked out of his hand. He rose and swung the bottle at the captain's head. The bottle crashed loudly as it smacked his skull. Shards of glass covered the deck. Mauricio, from behind, reached over the captain's head. He stuck his fingers into the captain's nostrils and pulled back hard. Swiftly, Mauricio used the now jagged-edged bottle in his hand to slash the captain's throat from ear to ear.

"Feed him to the sharks," said Mauricio, as he dropped the captains' twitching body.

The young first mate looked horrified and asked – "Should I bring this man back down below?" referring to the former first mate.

"No," replied Mauricio. "Throw him in with his great friend. They can continue their celebration by taking part in a grand meal together."

The young first mate moved quickly, as did several of the men. They tossed the nearly deceased captain and his drunken friend into the water. The blood pumping from the captain's neck attracted schools of sharks to the ship's starboard side. Soon after, a cacophony of splashing sounds filled the air as the sharks feasted on the two men.

A truly remarkable prophecy, thought Mauricio, watching the sharks jump over each other to get a piece of the men into their jaws. *They did not attack me. In turn, I get to present them with a generous offering…I am truly blessed for success.*

ༀༀༀ

The first mate approached Mauricio and asked – "Will you be our captain now, sir?"

Mauricio placed his hand on the first mate's shoulder and said – "No, you are captain now." He then motioned his eyes to the sharks saying – "You have a great responsibility. Do not fail." The newly appointed captain gulped hard. Mauricio said – "I will go with you to the bridge, to set course. Come, we must move quickly…too much time has already been wasted."

They went to the ship's bridge to set sail. Luckily, for the newly appointed captain, he was well versed in nautical steering. Although he had never commanded a vessel, he grew up on the sea and possessed a masterful grasp of oceanic navigation. Mauricio pulled out the ship's atlas. He then pointed to their next destination.

"Yes, sir," responded the captain. He then set course for coordinates 18 degrees, 27 minutes north and 66 degrees, 4 minutes west – San Juan, Puerto Rico. Soon, the young captain appeared as comfortable and competent as any high sea commander, shouting orders to his eagerly awaiting crew.

"Very good," said Mauricio, as he observed the captain taking charge of the ship's crew.

"Sir," said the captain to Mauricio. "I believe this is meant for you." He motioned his head towards a leather box, bolted onto a table by the helm.

The box had a small, square light on it…and it was blinking. Mauricio opened the box. There was a telephone receiver inside. He picked up the receiver and put it to his ear.

"Our client has experienced significant loss since we last communicated," said the mechanized voice on the line. "Because of this, they have requested an expansion of our services. Fortunately, we have personnel in the client's home country, who have unexpectedly completed an assignment ahead of schedule. They will be re-routed to support your efforts. You are to remain on course. You will be contacted shortly before your vessel leaves international waters and into the client's shores."

The communication ended. Mauricio hung up the receiver and closed the leather box. "I am going to the captain's suite to rest for a while. Do not hesitate to come get me if something goes wrong." The captain and his bridge crew nodded and Mauricio disappeared into the hallway's darkness.

"Can he stay in the captain's suite?" asked a crewmember.

"That man can stay and do whatever the hell he wants," replied the captain. "Now, shut up, and stop asking stupid questions unless you want to be the sharks' next meal."

The bridge crew stared silently into the vast darkness of the Atlantic Ocean. The XM vessel hummed as it steamed through the harsh waters ahead of them.

⌘⌘⌘

TEN

"There is no hunting like the hunting of man, and those who have hunted armed men long enough and like it, never care for anything else thereafter." – Ernest Hemingway

A Purificação, translated – The Cleansing, was a clandestine unit of former military commandos. They worked for XM Investments, specializing in the art of chaos. The Cleansing achieved its objectives by creating subversions within targeted organizations. Soon after their engagement, rebellious bloodbaths would ensue, ensuring the target's destruction from within. Its latest venture brought it to the southwestern border of the United States. A powerful and brazen drug cartel had recently expanded its violent business model into the US. Unable to contain the cartel by legal means, American authorities contacted XM seeking an "unofficial, yet effective, resolution to the rising threat from the south."

Surprisingly, the cartel exhibited fortitude in withstanding any internal divisions. This resilience overrode The Cleansing's best efforts. Consequently, an operation designed to last five to six months, concluded in eight short weeks. The Cleansing's leader, C-One, decided to cut bait and perform a top-down eradication of the cartel. The wrap up campaign would be fast and simple.

At 2:30 pm local time, C-One drove an acquired Border Patrol jeep along a road that the cartel often utilized. C-One, and the rest of the team, posed as U.S. Border Patrol agents. They spotted and pulled over the cartel leader's eighteen-year-old niece, citing an alleged traffic violation. C-One arrested the girl and brought her to a recently abandoned Customs and Border Protection outpost.

He allowed the niece to contact her family. She informed them that she was under arrest and facing deportation. Like clockwork, the girl's mother arrived at the outpost to pick up her daughter. C-One demanded money from the mother. He threatened to send the girl to the most violent place in El Salvador if she failed to pay immediately. The mother called the cartel's leader, who was her brother. She relayed C-One's threats and demands.

C-One knew the cartel leader's machismo would get the best of him. He expected the leader to arrive at the outpost with reinforcements and, quite possibly, his capos. C-One also surmised they would not enter with guns blazing, since they would not want to shoot the women. The Cleansing understood this plan was brasher than what their client wanted. Nevertheless, XM always produced the desired results for its clients. In the case of this project, they were about to neutralize the rising threat from the south.

Approximately ninety minutes after his sister's frantic call, the cartel leader's caravan approached from the southeast. C-One positioned one of his men 100 yards west of the outpost, to provide sniper-support. The rest of the team remained inside. As per C-One's instructions, the vehicle with the $3 million cash payment he demanded backed into a vacant parking spot in front of the outpost. The driver, of his own volition, then placed the van's gear into drive. He kept his feet on both the brake and gas for a quick exit.

The doors of the two other vehicles in the caravan opened. Half a dozen heavily armed men spilled out from each of them. The cartel leader whistled loudly, directing some of the men to stand guard around the van with the cash. He then walked into the outpost with five of his comrades.

Inside, the leader demanded proof that the women were unharmed. C-One told him to check for himself. However, the leader insisted on having them inspected by a female family member, who was in the van. C-One did not protest and agreed to let the women leave. This lack of protest caused the leader to experience a bit of apprehension. "Are you not worried about the money?"

"I have no doubt you will do what I expect," replied C-One, smiling.

The women exited. Immediately after, a two-foot thick tarp dropped from the ceiling. It covered the entire length of the wall that faced the parking lot. Suddenly, a muffled BOOM rumbled from outside. The powerful blast shook the unsuspecting cartel members to their core. The parking spot that the van backed into unwittingly sat atop an intricate design of explosives, embedded into the pavement. The device activated when the van parked…and detonated when it attempted to drive away. The tarp that dropped inside the outpost was a shock-blast-refractor. It could withstand many more times the surge that just killed every living thing within 40 yards of the detonation. The cartel members suffered momentary shock and tried to comprehend what just happened. Without warning, C-One and the rest of The Cleansing tore into them with their semi-automatic rifles, until every sign of life vanished.

ॐॐॐ

The Cleansing prepared for departure to its base in Belize. The group did not address one another using personal names. Instead, they referred to each other according to their number in their chain-of-command. The capital "C" denoted the unit's name – Cleansing. Thus, C-One equated to the unit's first in command, and so on down the line.

C-One was packing his equipment when C-Three, the team's communications specialist, approached saying – "Sir, management wishes to speak with you."

"I thought my after-action synopsis was straightforward," replied C-One, somewhat annoyed. "What else do they need?"

"Dunno," said C-Three. "All I know is that I can't wait to get back home and have myself a shitload of mojitos!"

C-One smiled in response to the comment and went to speak with XM. C-One listened absorbedly. As always, he took no notes and committed everything to memory. Several minutes later, he said – "Copy that…I will look for further guidance in six hours…we are Furious George in fifteen…out." He turned off the communication device and locked it into place inside its specialized compartment. He then looked at C-Three and said – "You can forget about those mojitos, unless you know a place that makes them in Iowa."

"Come on, really?" replied C-Three. "Iowa?"

"That's right," answered C-One, followed by – "Alright everyone, let's bring it in." The group huddled around him like a sports team around their coach. He provided details of their new mission. They seemed genuinely stunned, and somewhat in awe, of both the situation itself and of the apparent abilities of the target in question. C-One concluded his briefing with – "Management realizes this operation is outside our primary area of specialty. However, they believe getting us into this op, while we are still in country, is advantageous over dispatching a wet-team from Belize. Like our original extraction, driving is the preferred mode of transportation. We have limited access to air support down here. Management thinks they might be able to have a flight team meet us, as we get closer. However, I will not know until our next communication. I will reopen comms in six hours for further guidance, as we will be closer to Iowa by then. Also, a word on command structure…the client has overall operational command."

"Spooks," said C-Three.

"No Such Agency as far as I know," said C-Two.

"Yep," confirmed C-One, followed by – "As an FYI, management has sent a lead hunter."

"Excuse me?" asked C-Two.

"Yeah…this thing went downhill so fast, it was determined more assets were needed. That is how we got involved. We are more of an afterthought, really. Our role is to provide heavy support to the hunter once he arrives. Unless, of course, the client wraps this up themselves by then," explained C-One.

"How far out is he?" asked C-Five.

"Somewhere in the Atlantic is all I know. Okay, time to go. Let's get moving, let's go…" ordered C-One as he hurried the team to their vehicles.

"Furious George, huh?" C-Five asked C-Three.

"Goddamned right, brotha," replied C-Three. "That means we are Fucking Gone and are hot on some poor bastard's ass!"

The team of five mercenaries loaded into their vehicles and sped northward to their Midwestern destination, which was over twenty hours away.

෩෩෩

Milken brainstormed every conceivable method for locating Augustus. The situation was unraveling quickly. After pinpointing Spindle and Dunn's whereabouts via GPS, he contacted the necessary players at Homeland Security on behalf of the NSA. During that exchange, Milken seized the opportunity to start the next phase of his quest to destroy Augustus. He engaged in character assassination.

Milken painted a false picture for DHS top brass. He depicted Augustus as a national security threat, based on information NSA obtained through various backchannels. Milken attested to reports of Augustus attempting to sell firsthand, compartmentalized intelligence to foreign spy agencies. The information involved US covert actions around the globe that spanned decades; to include the distasteful methodologies often employed in achieving those objectives.

"You know," Milken said during that conversation. "The rawness people romanticize about, when speaking of governments and spies, but that enrages them whenever that brutality becomes public."

"So...why the attack on his family?" asked one of the DHS officials.

"It appears," replied Milken, "that he solidified a deal with a block of smaller countries, but that he backed out when an offer from a larger and more lucrative nation was made. That, apparently, was not received very well by the original takers."

"That's truly remarkable," replied another of the DHS brass.

"Yes, it is," said Milken. "Not to mention...the quantum level of detail we are talking about could very well cause our allies to turn on us. Moreover, it could provide those who are already hostile towards us, a reason to attack this country on a massive scale."

"Holy shit," replied all of the DHS leaders on the call, with great concern in their voices.

Milken took advantage of this moment and "explained" NSA's need to use DHS credentials without their knowledge. "Indeed...which is why we needed to be as covert as possible, within the legal confines of our Constitution of course, to locate this son-of-a-bitch. We need to bring him in and determine what sort of damage he might have already caused our country."

Milken magnificently convinced the DHS leaders of Augustus' abhorrent nature. Moreover, he induced their belief of the extraordinary threat his continued freedom posed to the nation's safety. In essence, he created an all-out, top-secret manhunt for Augustus Peña. Milken felt pleased. DHS brass directed him to coordinate his efforts going forward with the regional special agent in charge. In addition, they guaranteed full cooperation in the hunt for Augustus, irrespective of NSA's lack of prior communication. After speaking with DHS brass, Milken chatted briefly with the regional special agent in charge.

"We want to keep this as airtight as you folks do," said the SAC to Milken. "We will release zero information to the public...meaning, a total media blackout."

"I couldn't be more content," responded Milken. "Please, keep me apprised of any emerging details."

"Absolutely," replied the SAC. "We have an investigator on the ground now. I will be on scene in under an hour."

❧❧❧

Milken boarded his private jet. He decided to check on the SAC. Nearly two hours had passed since they last spoke. He went to his office, towards the rear of the plane, and placed the call.

"SAC Eggert," answered Special Agent in Charge Monte Eggert.

"SAC, C. Virgil here...we spoke about the current situation earlier today. I was just checking in to see if you arrived on scene yet."

"Ha...yeah...I am on scene. We are going to be busy here for some time," replied SAC Eggert. "The dog team has swept the area for explosives. We are processing the scene as we speak for blood-spatter-patter analysis. We want to get an exact read on where the shooter was situated...or, at least, the trajectory of the bullets."

"Very interesting," said Milken, slowly, giving thought to the blood-spatter-patter analysis. He then asked – "Any thought, SAC, as to whether any of the agents' blood got on the killer?"

"My guess is that if the shooter was in close proximity, say three to four feet, then he definitely has blood on him somewhere. However, anything beyond that range is doubtful. Why do you ask?"

"Oh, just going back to Murder Investigation 101," replied Milken. "You know, evidentiary matter to be used at a later time to implicate the accused...just being hopeful, I guess."

"Well, that's the least of what you are going to be interested in," said SAC Eggert.

"Why is that?"

"For starters, alongside of the deceased agents' vehicle was a state trooper, laid out on the pavement. At first I thought 'oh my God...this is a massacre' but, it turns out the trooper was rendered unconscious. He suffered significant injuries to his clavicle area and has been transported under heavy security to City Hospital."

"Hmmm...interesting that he was not killed," Milken opined. "Is there anything else?"

"Oh, is there...directly behind the deceased agents' vehicle is what appears to be an opening to a tunnel or a cave. I am waiting for more agents to arrive before going in to check it out," responded SAC Eggert.

"I'm sorry...did you say...a cave?" asked Milken, in an incredulous tone of voice.

"That is affirmative. I think the suspect popped right out of that tunnel and ambushed your two agents."

"I do believe this explains a lot," replied Milken, followed by – "Thank you for your assistance, SAC Eggert. It has been most helpful."

"No problem, sir," replied SAC Eggert. "I will keep in touch."

"Oh, one more thing before I go," said Milken. "The media...have they caught wind of something being amiss?"

"Not a clue," replied SAC Eggert. "It looks like they are spending all of their time and resources focusing on other parts of the city."

"Yes...I suppose they would," said Milken. "Thank you again." Milken hung up the phone. He then picked it back up and made another call.

ॐॐॐ

"Gates," answered Prentiss.

Milken spoke the moment he heard his voice – "Hear me out as I speak, Prentiss. I recall discussions, several years ago, about creating a hemoglobin-tracking system via specialized spectrometer satellites. Do you know where that technology stands today?"

"Ah," replied Gates. "You're referring to our VGT satellite program, Virg. However, we have not tested field performance yet. Why do you ask?"

Milken cleared his throat and asked – "Can you run that acronym by me again, Prentiss?"

He smiled, realizing that Milken was clueless as to what VGT stood for and said – "I'm sorry, Virgil. The program has been around for only a few months at best. We have not received a full briefing on it yet. It's called V, G, T, - Voodoo, Gamma, Tango and the acronym stands for Virtual Genome Tracking."

"Virtual Genome Tracking," repeated Milken, letting the words absorb into his mind. "This sounds very promising, Prentiss. Can you explain it to me quickly?"

"I can provide you with a nutshell version of the program and what it does…uh…in theory, anyway."

"Go for it," said Milken. "I'm on the plane and have nothing but time until we land."

"Great," replied Gates, enthusiastically. He then launched into a descriptive narrative of the program. "Virtual Genome Tracking or VGT is our newest locator tool. It allows us to track targets globally, regardless of where they are physically located. Targets do not have to be outdoors for positive identification. As you are well aware, Virgil, traditional satellite technology requires a clear line-of-sight for positive ocular identification. Consequently, perceptive targets can avoid detection by knowing the time of day a satellite has line-of-sight on their positions. This creates a massive problem on our end. We can overcome this evasive tactic by re-tasking the satellites. However, doing so is a tall order. It negatively affects other operations relying on that same satellite at a different time of day. With VGT, Virgil, we have a specialized and dedicated satellite. It is, in essence, a space wandering spectrograph imager with transmission capabilities. The thing takes profound infrared images, seeking out the unique DNA sequences contained in a person's hemoglobin. It does this by separating single-stranded DNA fragments. The satellite then analyzes the infrared-like spectrograph images for a positive sequential match. Finally, it transmits the results back to earth, at the satellite's command headquarters. The Arecibo Space Station in Puerto Rico runs the entire project."

"I have never been more proud of my country," said Milken, with noticeable joy in his voice.

"Yeah, well, don't get too gushy, Virgil. A South African pharmaceutical company put this technology together. They wanted to market it to the insurance industry. Their pitch was going to be that monitoring an insured's DNA could determine if an illness was likely to manifest. In turn, the company could either increase their insured's premium rates or drop their coverage entirely before it happened," said Gates.

"Those rat-bastard insurance executives...they are the lowest form of bi-pedals around," said Milken, disgusted.

"You just can't trust them," agreed Gates.

"So...tell me more, Prentiss. How did we get it?"

Gates replied – "We accidentally identified their invention during one of our operations in the region. We then checked with our system developers to see if they could expand and reverse-engineer what the South Africans had put together thus far. After our engineers gave us the thumbs up, we proceeded to kill everyone associated with this project. We then stripped the company's facilities bare and deployed a barrage of high explosives and napalm, wiping the company's memory from modern day existence. We then blamed it all on –"

"Uh...I don't need to know that part," interrupted Milken.

"No...I suppose not," agreed Gates.

"Tell me," said Milken. "The DNA...what is the range of data that we have?"

"You mean, the population of blood samples we are able to genome track?" clarified Gates.

"Yes, precisely," replied Milken.

"Currently, we only have data for federal law enforcement and intelligence personnel that underwent a physical within the past two years to maintain their security clearance," replied Gates. "Look, Virgil, I appreciate where you are going with this. I really do. However, I have to tell you, this program started well after Augustus left NICO. Consequently, we do not have recent blood samples on file for him. We simply do not have in our possession what we need for this program to assist us."

"Does the blood need to be in the body for the tracking system to work?" asked Milken.

"I guess I don't know what you are asking," replied Gates, perplexed.

"Does the blood have to be naturally contained in its respective body for the tracking system to genome-type the DNA? Or can the blood, say, somehow evacuate its host, land on someone else's person, and still be traceable under this program?" clarified Milken.

"I do not know."

"Find out and get back to me pronto. If it is a possibility, then I will fill you in on what I am thinking. There's no need to waste time doing that now," ordered Milken.

"I do love a mystery every now and then," responded Gates. "I will contact Arecibo and get right back to you."

Milken walked to the minibar after speaking with Gates and poured himself a small amount of vodka. He then filled the remainder of the glass with bottled water. He reached into a compact refrigerator, extracted two perfectly shaped ice cubes, and dropped them into his drink. He raised his glass to about eye-level. He rotated the tumbler gently, scrutinizing the way the room's lighting interacted with its crystal-cut shapes. Finally, he put the glass to his mouth, tilted his head back, and cleared the contents in a single gulp. Milken looked at the now empty glass in his hand. He shrugged his shoulders and snickered while saying – "Fucking South Africans…that's another one I didn't see coming…whew."

ॐॐॐ

A world of exciting possibilities came to life in the tiny island of Puerto Rico. The Commander-on-Duty, Colonel Hank Boultry, listened to Gates' inquiry. He then asked an elderly man, recently brought out of retirement to oversee the VGT program, to join their conversation. The Arecibo crew had nicknamed the man Gums, due to his peculiar fondness of taking out his dentures when concentrating on a project.

"The possibilities are endless!" Gums erupted. "We can eventually monitor troop movements, heads-of-state. It could be the end of espionage, as we know it. The technology will literally eliminate a spy's ability to remain hidden, out of sight and undetectable!"

Gates already knew these concepts were on the table for potential uses, upon full implementation of the program. However, they all had one thing in common. They tracked blood contained within a live human body. Gates inquired into the potential of tracking blood physically located on someone else.

"Obviously, it would have to be the blood of someone in our records," said Gums, rapidly, with excitement. "Otherwise, it will not work. Moreover, there is a tiny issue. Okay a major issue, regarding how long after evacuation we can track the DNA. Do you know the subjects we are talking about?"

"I think it would be best if I get you conferenced in with Milken. He has all the details," replied Gates. He then asked Boultry to establish a cloistered and encrypted call between them.

Boultry responded quickly, and the three of them connected with Milken.

৵৵৵

The conversation lasted longer than any call that any of them could recall taking part in during their careers. It was lengthy due to the method of encryption utilized and because of the complex issues involved. Milken's airplane had already landed. However, he was not willing to break communication. Consequently, he had the plane taxi to its private docking area.

The conference call ended. Milken went to the pilot and said – "Have her fueled and ready to go in three hours. Well, give or take an hour. It all depends on how many matters I must tend to." Milken pat the shoulder of his beloved pilot as he spoke to him.

The pilot looked up at Milken, nodded his acknowledgement and smiled. He then glanced at Milken in an inquisitive manner.

"Puerto Rico, take us to Arecibo."

The pilot spun his chair. He started shutting down the plane to begin pre-flight preparation for their next voyage, and said – "I hear Rican women are freaking nuts!"

Milken's response was one that few people ever experienced. He roared with laughter and offered a follow-up joke to the pilot's humor. He then exited the aircraft.

ન્જન્જન્જ

Gates had some reservations about Milken's desire to use the VGT program in this effort. He felt it was not ready for implementation. Gates needed more information about the program's overall status.

Saxby Coles was already at The Chamber when Gates called. "You are kidding, right?" he asked, regarding Milken's intention.

"No, I am not," replied Gates. "Virg is hell bent on using the VGT. There is no talking him out of it, so I will not even try. Consequently, the satellite is going live and on the hunt. I thought it best to use this opportunity to check with you on the status of our external efforts. You know, with you being our ambassador of external affairs and all."

"Piss off, Gates," replied Saxby. "I have this thing handled. It's not my problem you cannot control the old man."

"Just give me a quick briefing on where we are, Saxby, that is all I ask," said Gates.

"Do you want it now or when you get here?"

"Now is fine. I have time before departing. I am not that far away."

"Alright, then, here you go. Just tell me when to stop talking. I can go on forever with this stuff. I'll start from the top, so bear with me."

"Time is ticking," said Gates, rolling his eyes as the long-winded Saxby spoke.

Saxby then began his briefing – "The VGT program has in its sights many scenarios for potential uses. However, we have many roadblocks to overcome. Of them all, developing an all-inclusive database is our greatest challenge. The program is only as good as the data we are able to analyze. Federal personnel samples work great for testing the system, but not for much else. It is too narrow in scope. We need to reach the general population. The greatest tool available for launching such a large-scale data-grab is our political process. Success, Gates, is contingent upon manipulating lawmakers into approving measures that would furtively feed us what we require. Both NICO and NSA have been deeply involved in America's lawmaking process without the public being the wiser. Our efforts on this measure will be no different."

"I am intrigued," said Gates.

Saxby continued – "Our solution is to reconstruct the American healthcare system. It will be a time-consuming process. However, it is necessary for this endeavor's survival. We will start the debate by claiming the need to streamline the healthcare system with electronic databases. The spin out of K-Street will be reduction of healthcare costs by minimizing medical errors. We will also add a green, paperless angle to it for the tree huggers. The use of electronic databases will become mandatory. Ultimately, Gates, what we seek is a national database of medical information that the VGT program can tap into at will."

Gates interrupted – "The satellite doesn't operate off of medical records, Saxby. It traces DNA. How in the world is that going to help the program?"

Saxby replied – "If you let me continue with my briefing, I will tell you."

"Go ahead," said Gates, looking at his watch.

Saxby continued – "As you quickly pointed out, Gates, the initial data grab would only contain raw patient data. Yes, this would be useless to the VGT program. However, as the required paperless network is implemented, new provisions of the legislation will emerge. Our friends on the Hill will extend the electronic medical records requirement to blood banks. Shortly after that is carried out, we will push for a national emergency order."

Gates asked – "What in the world?"

"Oh, this is the greatest part of the whole plan," said Saxby. "The President will announce that the nation is experiencing a blood shortage emergency. To remedy this crisis, he will sign off on legislation mandating individuals to make deposits of blood. Doing so will become a condition for maintaining their healthcare coverage. The legislation will require blood banks to clone and store the blood so that patients have enough of a supply should the need arise. Here is the back-story, Gates. Unbeknownst to the public, of course, is the proprietary software engineered by VGT program scientists. It will be installed at each of the blood banks and work round-the-clock stripping DNA from blood. Then, it will genome-type and individually categorize the results, followed by spectrographic transmission of the data to Arecibo for storage. Once at Arecibo, the spectrograph images will routinely upload to the VGT satellite for infrared searches on the earth below."

"That is the most ingenious method for gaining access to private data that I have ever heard, Saxby. I am ever so proud of you," complimented Gates. "It sounds as if this program is on sound footing and is going to be a major part of our arsenal someday. Luckily, our current needs are not for public data. We have what we need at our disposal. I just hope that Milken's plan does not destroy the great potential that your briefing has showed this program to possess."

"Me too," replied Saxby.

⌘⌘⌘

ELEVEN

Maxwell looked out the window of the small jet as it began its descent. The flight from his home to The Chamber was short. He reflected on his tenure at NICO and on the substance of his overall career. Maxwell wondered what his father would think of him if he knew the truth. *My dad is most definitely not a stupid man,* he reasoned. *Surely, he has at least tacit knowledge of what goes on at NICO; but does he really? Ugh, I don't know. I just think there would have been some indication from him about the rawness of it all if he did. Maybe I am being too much of a boy scout. I need to accept the fact my father is one of the many cogs constituting the whole of this violent struggle to maintain our nation's security.*

The plane was in its final approach. The pilot spoke over the intercom, asking Maxwell to prepare for landing. He fastened his seatbelt and looked back out the window. *What in the hell was Milken thinking? Is he out of his mind?* Maxwell felt troubled over Milken's decision to pull XM into the mission, given their unrelenting thirst for blood. He also felt unsettled that supplementation of NICO personnel, with these mercenaries, happened without a Chamber vote.

Maxwell recognized that his manic bout, and subsequent unconsciousness, contributed to Milken's decision. However, it happened so fast, that it appeared as if Milken had it in his mind all along to have XM involved with this mission. "And if Milken has it on his mind…it will happen," he whispered, as the jet's tires made solid contact with the awaiting runway.

Maxwell disembarked the aircraft. He got into the limousine that routinely provided transport between the airport and The Chamber. All was normal and nothing seemed out of the ordinary, with one exception. No other member of NICO management was in the limo with him. As a matter of routine, the transport carried several members to The Chamber at the same time. Doing so facilitated a smoother process for getting staff through The Chamber's security protocols. Maxwell figured the sudden demand for this meeting caught some of the others off guard, causing delays.

"Thankfully, I have a book to read while I wait for everyone else to get here," he said, after thinking the matter through.

The limo driver overheard him and said – "Actually, mister Milken already arrived. I had just gotten back from dropping him off when you landed."

"Oh, great," replied Maxwell. He then thought – *What, he couldn't wait the twenty minutes or so before I landed? What a prick.*

The limousine pulled up to an abandoned compound. In the middle of it, lay a large cathedral-styled structure. The driver got out to open Maxwell's door. However, Maxwell exited the limo first and stopped him by saying – "No need for you to get out, but thanks anyway." He then grabbed his belongings and shut the door. The limo driver tipped his hat at Maxwell, got back in, and drove off.

❧❧❧

Maxwell walked onto the compound. He admired the stonework all around him, the way he did whenever he came here. *Incredible how such beautiful vastness can emit a powerful aura of peace yet provide a gateway into such brutality,* he thought. At the end of the quad stood a stone pillar. Centered into it was a burgundy six-foot steel door.

He opened the door with a large, antique skeleton key. He entered the pillar. It was pitch-black inside. He knew where to locate the hand-scanner, due to the many times he had come here. He laid his palm flat inside of a non-assuming space of wall to the right. The darkness before him lit up. It revealed an oval enclosure with a chair. To the right of it was a mini elevator, designed for luggage. Maxwell placed his briefcase and jacket into it then took a seat inside the capsule. He buckled the seatbelt. This action activated the system. He placed both arms on their respective armrests. With both index fingers, he simultaneously pushed buttons adjacent to them. The capsule and elevator then lowered to a universe below.

The pod ride dropped Maxwell the equivalent of ten stories. It was slow and deliberate, and allowed for another probe of him and his items. *This is like TSA on steroids,* Maxwell jokingly thought. *I cannot see Milken sitting still long enough to make this ride. I bet he takes a regular elevator.* The capsule came to a smooth and quiet stop. "Ah…shit…here we go," whispered Maxwell, stepping out of it.

He felt awkward walking down the lengthy corridor alone. He could not recall a time when he did not have someone on either side of him, stepping stride for stride. Maxwell shifted his items to his left hand as he approached The Chamber doors. The corridor's energy seemed tranquil. It felt a little chillier too. He arrived at the endpoint of his march and stopped.

The guard that normally met him here did not appear. Before Maxwell could give it thought, a voice from the sentinel post above said – "Prepare for final clearance." He raised his right hand for scanning. It illuminated, the way it always did at this point of the entry process. Maxwell looked straight ahead. He felt a radiating discomfort from the scan. He could see the yellow color of the laser. Suddenly, the color changed from yellow to an intense red. Maxwell's fingers numbed. Then, his hand…finally, his entire right arm. His lifeless arm dropped like a boulder. The momentum from his plummeting limb caused him to drop onto one knee.

"Zero clearance? Oh no…" He looked in disbelief at his right arm. He saw a dime-sized red dot moving up from his hand to his head. Maxwell yelled – "Milken, you mother –"

The single shot reverberated down the corridor. A figure stepped forward, looked up at the sniper position and said – "Great shot Director Milken, you still got it."

Milken sat up, locked down the rifle he just used to kill Maxwell and replied – "I thought I was going to miss the squirrely bastard when he dropped to his knees." He then disappeared into the shadows behind him.

❧❧❧

Milken entered The Chamber and addressed Gates and Coles, who were sitting at the main table. "I never liked that twitchy little prick. I just could not respect him. I apologize, but legacy appointments just boil my craw. I have no time for them."

Gates replied – "That is all well and good, Virgil, but you know…that boy came from a highly respected pedigree."

"And what a pathetic representation he made of that family," Milken shot back.

"They will expect answers, you know?" offered Saxby.

"And they will get them," replied Milken. He then addressed Gates – "Take his body back to his home. Dump it there. It really does not matter where. Then, torch the place…and I mean scorch it. I want to make certain the only thing forensics can definitively determine is Maxwell's identity. Make sure the drop-team fully comprehends that nothing else can be detectable, such as the time of death. We will offer those looking into his death an explanation. Poor Maxwell's murder came at the hands of Augustus Peña."

"And how do we go about doing that?" asked Gates.

"I am glad you asked," replied Milken. He paced about slowly, using his hands for effect as he spoke. "Much to our astonishment and disappointment, it turns out that Prater was in cahoots with Augustus. He functioned as Peña's handler, for seeking foreign bids on our nation's compartmentalized intelligence. However, despite his momentary bout of insanity and treachery, Prater's sense of duty and familial pride eventually won the day…and he wanted out. Oh, wait, it gets even better in case you are wondering. You see, young Maxwell was an ardent idealist, and sought to expose us to the world as penance for his partaking in our actions. Unfortunately, he was not a field man, and no match for the brutal and morally bankrupt Augustus Peña."

Milken paused, looking at Gates and Coles with a hopeful look. He sought praise for his fantastic idea. However, there was none. Slightly offended he did not receive commendation, Milken lost his enthusiasm and said – "Right…so, well, the rest of it is pretty run-of-the-mill kind of stuff. You know, we say that they both met, Prater tried to convince Augustus to quit his pursuits and Augustus killed Prater with THIS gun…don't forget to take this by the way…and then torched the shit out of Prater's home…end of story."

Gates took a moment before saying – "Virgil, that plan is, well, rather sadistic is it not?"

"Our ranks teem with sadists and you are second in command of this organization, Prentiss. What does that say about you? Don't you fucking preach to me! Do you consider yourself to be an altar boy?" shouted Milken.

"No…I most certainly do not. Not by a longshot," replied Gates.

"Good," responded Milken. "Get this done ASAP. I am off to Puerto Rico. We are going to get this whole shit show wrapped up soon."

Gates and Coles looked at each other, raised their eyebrows, and did not say a word. They then left, to put Milken's plan into motion.

⌘⌘⌘

TWELVE

Milken arrived in Puerto Rico. Gums greeted him at the airport with a small security detail. He exhibited incalculable enthusiasm at the prospect of putting his greatest toy into action. "So, I have given a great deal of thought about how we should begin this process. I did not think you would object, given the time-sensitive nature, so I started the prep work."

"You are correct," responded Milken. "I do not object. Let us be clear, shall we? Any operational details related to this VGT program fall squarely into your lap, not mine. I am not looking to lay blame on you. This system, and everything it does, is beyond my knowledge base. I do, however, reserve full authority with what actions to take if and when the targets are acquired, is that clear?"

"Oh…yes…yes it is…very much so, Director Milken."

"Just Milken will do," he said. "So, what have you done thus far to start this process?"

"Uh, well…Milken…I had the vials that contained the blood of the two deceased agents brought to us from storage. We keep the samples here in Arecibo. Anyway, once we received the blood, we drew enough from each to obtain a good-sized specimen. We then placed the matter into our state-of-the-art genome sequencing device, to extract and identify each specimen's unique DNA sequence."

Milken asked – "How long is that going to take?"

"Oh, typical human genome sequencing takes from five to ten days, depending on the type of samples involved."

"WHAT?" Milken shouted. "We don't have that kind of time. It is ludicrous to even suggest that we could do this if it takes –"

"Um, if I may interrupt you, Milken?" said Gums. "Five to ten days is the typical timeframe, utilizing a traditional mainframe-sized machine. However, we at Arecibo utilize a much smaller, yet superior process that can yield the same results in a matter of hours." Gums smiled, reflecting his pride in being able to assuage Milken's fears and concerns.

"Oh," replied Milken. "Next time, just give me the actual status and not a historical narrative. I don't need a weather report…just the facts as they are."

"As you wish," replied Gums, showing no signs of fluster from Milken's rant.

"…About gave me a fucking heart attack," muttered Milken, looking out the car window as it whizzed towards the PSC.

☙☙☙

Milken sat at Colonel Boultry's desk as he spoke – "My position on the matter is absolute. However, it is ultimately up to you and your command structure as to how you will proceed."

Gums approached the two men saying – "Sorry for interrupting. Milken, I thought you should know. We estimate another ten minutes for completion of the sequencing."

"That is excellent news," said Milken. "I will go back with you in a moment. I was just telling the colonel, that I empathize with how rigorous these rotations can be on a man's soul. Nevertheless, I feel more comfortable with him retaining watch throughout this operation. He has exposure to critical matters that have already occurred during this ordeal. The alternative, bringing a fresh commander up to speed on the particulars of this mission, does not serve my nerves well."

Milken stood up and said to Boultry – "Please, let me know the moment you and your superiors come to a decision."

"Heck, sir, I'm staying," replied Boultry. "If I cannot remain for overall watch, then I will stay as special commander to this particular mission. Either way, I'm here for the long haul."

"I am very pleased with your decision, colonel," said Milken. He then said to Gums – "Alright, let's go see what your process has yielded."

☙☙☙

The pair arrived at the VGT unit's satellite command area. An officer assigned to the team said – "Sir, the sequencing is complete and ready for spectrograph imaging and upload."

"Wonderful!" responded Gums. "Bring her to life."

The team worked diligently to get the VGT satellite into position for image upload. Although line-of-sight was not required for the satellite to hunt, it was necessary for receiving spectrograph images. This ensured data integrity. The team navigated the satellite to a geostationary orbit above Arecibo. Once geostationary, it followed earth's rotation.

"Satellite locked into orbit," called out a team member.

"Spectrograph images ready for upload," shouted another.

"Okay everyone, let's get ourselves in order here," Gums said to his unit. "This is the moment we have all been hoping for; a mission-ready and live structure hunt." Gums sat slowly, reached into his mouth and removed his dentures. In a trancelike state, he stared at his team in the pit below, while simultaneously placing his dentures into a receptacle on his desk.

"What the –" said Milken aloud when he observed Gums do this.

"How do you think he got his nickname, sir?" asked an officer.

"Honestly, I thought the man must have chewed a shitload of gum," replied Milken, perplexed and stupefied. He then murmured – "In-fucking-credible…"

෨෨෨

The Bakers were within 100 miles of Hatfield when Cal's phone rang. "Baker," he answered.

"Caleb, this is Resident Agent in Charge, Lee Billings."

"Is that Auggie?" asked Pappy, loudly. Cal waved him off indicating it was not. "Sorry, thought he'd be contacting us right about now," said Pappy, as he sat back in place.

"RAC Billings, to what do I owe the pleasure?"

"I understand from your Duty Station Officer that you are on leave, Caleb. However, we have a critical situation developing in the Midwest. I need your squad," replied Billings.

Cal's instinct told him this had to do with Augustus. He knew RAC Billings well enough to regard the man as trustworthy. Nonetheless, he could not shake off all that Pappy brought up earlier about this being a government plot against Augustus. Cal's inclination was to ask Billings outright if this pertained to the Peña matter. He thought better of it and opted for nondisclosure. Cal would reveal nothing unless asked.

"Affirmative, RAC, I'm on leave. My squad returned from the field recently. I am off on a short field trip with my brother and dad to do some hunting. It will be a little bit before we can turn back. What's going on?" asked Cal.

"Shit, wouldn't you know it?" replied Billings. "One of the biggest manhunts in the nation's history is about to commence and this agency's top fugitive ops team is out of commission."

"Who's the culprit?"

RAC Billings dodged the question – "Word is the individual is wanted for questioning and, more importantly, his own protection." Billings cut the conversation short – "Hey, listen, I have to go. I'll get back to you if it becomes mandatory for your posse to report in."

Cal turned the phone off and said – "That was RAC Billings out of St. Louis, Pa."

"Yeah…what did he want?"

"Said he needed my squad to assist with what he called the largest manhunt in the nation's history," replied Cal.

"He has a penchant for being dramatic, doesn't he?" said Pappy, chuckling slightly. He then opined – "Didn't sound to me like you planned on turning back, Caleb."

"Nah…you're right, Pa. I told him we were all out enjoying a field trip together. Besides, it is not compulsory at this point. Billings said he would get back to me if it becomes mandatory for our team to report for duty."

"Auggie?" inquired Pappy.

"Must be, Pa…I can't imagine there'd be another major event in the Midwest," said Cal.

"Oh, he said Midwest then, huh?"

"Sorry, forgot to mention that…yeah, I'm certain this is about Auggie."

"Don't mind me asking, Caleb, but why didn't you ask him?" queried Bo.

"Cause Caleb knows as well as I do, Beauregard, that this here predicament is a government sponsored atrocity being propagated against Auggie. He ain't going to be a trusting any of them…that's why!" said Pappy.

"Pappy is right," said Cal. "I need to be cautious about who I share information with about any of this…regardless of whether they are in my agency."

Cal turned and addressed Pappy – "Although, you know, if the call comes for a mandatory report, I have to admit that I am picking up Auggie and his family. I will refuse to go in."

"It must be a hard decision to make, Caleb. Saving your job versus saving the lives of a man and his family…a man that not only saved your life, but also rescued you from certain torture," said Pappy.

"There's no choice about it Pa. I know what to do."

ৡৡৡ

Augustus careened south along Interstate 35 towards the Missouri border.

"Aren't you worried about the police stopping you for speeding?" asked Broderson.

"Absolutely not," replied Augustus. "All of the vehicles in the Station's fleet are equipped with police scanners. More importantly, they have special license plates on them. They have codes embedded into them. The codes indicate the vehicle belongs to a government agency conducting undercover or some other sensitive operation. Law enforcement cannot identify this vehicle or the agency to which it belongs. Consequently, they will not pull us over and let us go on our merry way."

"So, it's like we're invisible," opined Broderson.

"That's right," replied Augustus. "These are different from the ones assigned to my personal vehicles. Those have codes too. They identify the vehicle to law enforcement as belonging to a high-level State official. However, they do not identify the official or the agency. The license plate on this vehicle produces a message that says something like "sensitive, data not available." It provides no further information. Thus, law enforcement cannot tell whether the vehicle belongs to an official or not…just that they are not to pull it over. Basically, this vehicle does not exist."

"Does anyone have normal license plates anymore?" asked Broderson, sarcastically.

"Yeah…you," said Augustus, laughing and accelerating the vehicle's speed.

The painstaking process of uploading images to the satellite ate away at Milken's nerves. He paced uncontrollably and checked the countdown clock that estimated the time remaining. "Forty more minutes," he whispered. "Christ, you would think we were transmitting data from a whole army."

"Christ would not know how to regard our actions, Milken. Besides, an entire army would actually consume the better part of a week," Gums snickered. "I would very much prefer that you retreat to the cafeteria and allow my team to work unencumbered. Your presence here makes them a bit…anxious."

Milken turned, mumbling under his breath as he withdrew – "I would very much prefer that you put your goddamn teeth back in before speaking to me. Those gums make me anxious."

Augustus arrived at the state line without incident. *It is a good thing the Missouri border is not far from Des Moines,* he thought. *It will be just a matter of time before they discover the Station and locate these fleet vehicles.* Augustus was also thankful about timing. The other local individuals with knowledge of the Station's existence were in Beijing, on an agricultural trade mission. "I was not supportive of directly doing business with China. Now, I think it was the best idea this Governor has had in a long time," he said aloud. Augustus exited Interstate 35 and then drove west onto US-69 towards Hatfield, Missouri.

Cal's phone rang again. He thought for sure it was RAC Billings, calling to mandate his team's participation. "Crap...here it is," grumbled Cal as he picked up the call.

"Hermano," said Augustus. "Cómo estás? Is everything going well on your trip?"

Cal was elated to hear from him. "Oh shit man, it's really good to hear from you brother," he replied. Cal looked back at Pappy and said – "Sorry about the language, Pa."

"You go on, son," replied Pappy. "There ain't anything to apologize for. Be sure to give my best to Auggie and his family."

"I will, Pa," said Cal.

"I heard him...and thank you," said Augustus.

"Where are you?"

"I just crossed into Missouri. I am on US-69 west and about 15 miles from Hatfield. How about you?" he replied.

"We are slightly under 70 miles away...right around Clarksdale, Missouri. Bo has been blue-lighting it all the way at about 90mph, so we made great time," said Cal.

"Yeah...I have some advantages for speed too," chuckled Augustus. He then asked – "Have you heard anything over the air about this mess? I have not put the radio on."

"No, but I received a call from an agency higher-up requesting that my team join in the largest manhunt in the nation's history," replied Cal.

"Any mention about it being a manhunt for me?" asked Augustus.

"He provided no details...probably because I stopped him short. I told him I was on leave and busy with my family. Besides, it was more of a voluntary request. There is a high probability, though, that he will call back mandating my team to report for duty," said Cal.

"Man...I'm sorry hombre. I shouldn't have gotten you involved," said Augustus.

"Don't even think about apologizing," replied Cal. "I already made up my mind. It was not much of a decision, in case you are wondering. We are all in. Plus, if Pa is correct, which I suspect he is, we have been in this thing together since before shit hit the fan."

"Your dad is a wise man. It will do me well to see him again," said Augustus.

"Yes…yes he is," replied Cal. "Look, it's obvious that you will get to Hatfield before we do. Call me when you get there. We are going to punch it to 110mph to get to you!"

"Hermano, I do not feel comfortable with you keeping your phone on you anymore. It is time that you dispose of it. We should not speak anymore until we meet up, comprende?"

"I understand completely," replied Cal.

Augustus then said – "I want to push forth and meet you while we are both on the move. Are you taking US-169 north?"

"Affirmative, brother…I don't blame you one bit."

"Bueno…I will blow past Hatfield, continue on this road until I get to US-169, and then turn south. We will come up on each other in about another forty mikes," explained Augustus.

"Copy that, and this phone is now toast," said Cal, and he ditched it out the window after completing the call.

෯෯෯

Augustus pulled over to the side of the road. He destroyed the mobile phone he just used to speak with Cal. He then placed the pieces inside the burn bag. Looking into the rearview mirror at Broderson, he asked – "How are they doing?"

"They are doing very well, Director Peña."

"I am fairly certain I am no longer the director of anything. Let's just stick to Augustus from here on out."

He then shifted the vehicle into drive and tore down the desolate Missouri road before him. Soon, he would unite and join forces with the Bakers, against an unseen peril that was callously bearing down upon them….

෯෯෯

Gums practically tossed Milken from the operations area for causing anxiety with his franticness. However, he too experienced jitters. This was an incredible moment in human ingenuity. Not only was this a tool of espionage, but a weapon of war. It could deploy with wild abandonment anywhere that human blood existed. *We can track on earth, the moon, in space stations...everywhere,* Gums shouted in his head, pondering the potential applications. He gazed at each team member in the operations pit below and whispered – "This is amazing."

"Sir," shouted an officer. "She is all set and ready to hunt."

Gums snapped out of his dreamlike state, landing back into the moment with extreme clarity of thought. He put his dentures back into his mouth. He then shouted orders, reminiscent of a Marine gunnery sergeant addressing his platoon – "Unlock geostationary position. Resume manual navigation controls. There is a large area of land to cover. Precise coordinates are unknown at this time. Nevertheless, we do have a starting point. We will fan out from there. Lieutenant, coordinates will be on my mark in 5, 4, 3, 2, 1...United States...Midwest...41°35'27"N 93°37'15"W...Des Moines, Iowa."

Designed to capture high-resolution images of DNA particles, the VGT satellite needed to be as close to earth as possible. Consequently, once it was squarely positioned over Des Moines, Gums ordered – "Drop her to Low Earth Orbit." Gums told the guard standing behind him to get Milken. "Depending on what this puppy finds, and how fast she does it, we might need to turn this show over to him pronto."

"Yes, sir," said the guard, who promptly left to get Milken.

"On your order, sir," said an officer on the controls to Gums.

"Scanners hot," ordered Gums. The VGT spectrometer came alive, searching the world below for the agents' DNA.

Milken returned in a hurry. "Where is it now?"

"She is above Des Moines, Iowa, scanning from the city's center outward," replied Gums. He focused with great intensity on multiple computer screens. They displayed algorithmic data that would mathematically determine a match. Gums reached into his mouth. He stopped and looked up at Milken. He removed his hands saying – "I have impeccable hearing, Milken. I apologize for causing you anxiety."

Milken did not respond. Instead, he looked away, sheepishly.

"A MATCH," shouted Gums without warning, causing Milken to jump slightly.

"Christ, man, what the hell is wrong with you?" yelled Milken. "What are you yelling about?"

Gums pointed to a computer on his left and said – "There is a time delay from when data is captured mathematically on this interface from when it displays on the graphic platform above."

The team quickly closed-in on the graphics platform with expectancy. MATCH appeared on the screen in red capital letters.

"Son-of-a-bitch," said Milken, while the group congratulated each other. However, the celebratory mood in the VGT ops center was short-lived.

"Readings indicate a large quantity of the particular DNA sequences," said Gums. "This is more indicative of the body host as opposed to the narrow specimen we seek."

"Agents Spindle and Dunn," opined Milken.

"May their souls rest in peace," said Boultry, feigning belief the agents were in a better place. In truth, he believed that they were burning in hell and were exactly where they belonged.

"Okay," said Milken. "It is time to choose where to focus our efforts. Let's try north…to see if the bastard is headed up to Canada via Minnesota."

Gums ordered the re-tasking of the VGT satellite according to Milken's directive.

"I am stunned, to tell you the truth, that this worked. I mean, the damn thing really and truly did what we thought it would," said Milken, excitedly.

"It most certainly did!" shouted Gums right back. "The limitation, as I see it, is that we need to be in Low Earth Orbit in order to make the match. Conversely, a much higher satellite position is needed to efficiently scan a large region like the one we are attempting."

"Yeah, I agree," said Milken, as he walked away to call Gates.

ಎಎಎ

"Prentiss," said Milken. "We have positive DNA identification."

"That is incredible Virgil," exclaimed Gates.

"It most certainly is. The problem is the identification was of the two dead agents. It is still great news since that means this whole program is not a pile of bullshit. However, it does not serve our immediate need. We need to narrow the search, but who knows which way they took off. It is a total crapshoot right now. We don't have the time to dick around with this," said Milken, somewhat frustrated.

"What about known associations?"

"What about them?" Milken replied.

"Have we determined where he might go to receive help?" Gates asked. "I imagine that would have been the first thing we did."

Milken replied –"Yeah, we did, but that turned up nothing. Augustus kept few ties to anyone. Our agents were able to identify a couple of fellows he golfed and had drinks with on occasion. The thing is they are locals. They live something like two miles away from his home in Iowa. He is not going to hide out with them…no way. Besides, he met them after becoming a civilian. Consequently, not only are they unquestionably unaware of his previous life, they would not understand it. He is not going to ask them for help in keeping him and his family safe from people who want to kill them. Seriously, who has that happen to them, right? That kind of talk makes people think you are crazier than screwed sheep."

"And nobody from his past?" Gates asked.

"He's had minimal contact with a guy in Kansas, a Deputy U.S. Marshal. Our intelligence team reports that nobody was at home when they went to check if he had heard from Augustus. I suppose I should check back with Intel…to firmly rule out that possibility," Milken said.

"I will have Coles work the folks at Intel as well. Who knows, there could always be someone else that we've missed," said Gates.

"Sounds good…talk to you soon," said Milken, followed by – "Prentiss, wait…I forgot to ask, the Prater mater?"

"It has all been taken care of, Virgil," Gates replied. "The place is as lit up as a Christmas tree in Rockefeller Center."

"Bravo, Prentiss…bravo…"

☙☙☙

Milken contacted Intel services to get an official word on the Kansas acquaintance, and to inquire about any other leads.

"Sorry, sir, we have nothing new to go on," said the lead Intel officer to Milken.

"The acquaintance in Kansas turned out clean, correct?"

"That's affirmative," replied the Intel officer. "We had one of our sources, who works at that acquaintance's agency, reach out to him. The response we got back was that the acquaintance was away on a family trip."

"What time was this contact made?" Milken asked.

"Sometime around 0900," replied the Intel officer.

Milken pressed – "Did he say where he was?"

"Negative," replied the Intel officer.

"Have you tapped his phone line?"

"Negative, sir...we can't. He is the head of a US Marshal fugitive removal team. Placing a wiretap on his phone is impossible without a FISA court order...even for us."

"Alright...do me a favor and satisfy my curiosity. Can you at least run his cell phone number through GPS and get a fix on his location? There is no reason why we cannot do that from a managerial standpoint. I don't want to rain on his parade, so no physical surveillance," said Milken.

"Roger that," replied the Intel officer. "It shouldn't take that long."

"Talk to you soon." Milken hurried back to the satellite operations center to see if the new coordinates yielded any results.

"Nothing yet," said Gums, as he heard Milken approach.

"Time of death for agents Spindle and Dunn was approximately at sunrise. They would not have gotten much further than International Falls, Minnesota, by now, given their payload. Concentrate from that point southward," said Milken. His phone buzzed. It was the Intel officer.

"That was pretty darn quick...what's up?"

"I would love to take credit for speed, but it helps when we are tracing someone already in our database," replied the Intel officer.

"Do you have an exact location?"

"That will be up on my screen soon. We have the general vicinity. I wanted to call you while honing in on the exact location, so that I could give you a live status," the Intel officer replied.

"Excellent work," said Milken. "Where is the general vicinity?"

"He is pretty far from home. It looks like his family trip started early. He would have had to drive all night to be here at this time," said the Intel officer. He then said – "The general vicinity is…wait sir…we have the exact location. He is in the city limits of Clarksdale, Missouri."

"Where exactly is that?" Milken asked. "I am not very familiar with Missouri."

"It's approximately sixty five miles from the Iowa border," replied the Intel officer.

Milken felt a chill run down his spine. He then asked – "Which direction they headed?"

The Intel officer replied – "Um…looks like they were going north but the signal has stopped moving."

Milken erupted – "You imbecile, he is headed to meet Augustus. How dare you call yourself an intelligence officer? You pathetic, good for nothing waste of taxpayer dollars. I have half a mind to…" Milken stopped himself mid-thought and caught his breath. "Patch that GPS feed in to the PSC so that we can monitor it from here. Can you handle that?"

Milken ended the call without waiting for a response. He spun Gums around in his chair and said – "Re-task the satellite. We have about as good of a lead as we are going to get before those blood samples go bad and lose their traceability."

"Where to?" asked Gums.

"I have the name of a town, but no coordinates. Bring up a map of Missouri. Those dipshits at Intel are likely to give me coordinates for Alaska instead," Milken said angrily. The map of Missouri quickly appeared on the large overhead screen. "Clarksdale, where is Clarksdale?" Milken demanded. "I was told sixty five miles from Iowa."

"Right there, sir," said a team member, directing towards it with a laser pointer.

"US-169, huh?" said Milken, analyzing the situation aloud. "So, if he is headed to meet Augustus, and I believe he is, he can go straight north into Iowa. He can make his way to Des Moines on back roads. Except I cannot see Peña staying in Iowa, let alone in Des Moines. My guess is they will meet in Missouri. Augustus undoubtedly took the fastest route out, via the Interstate. Does he stay on the Interstate and circle back to meet up on these Missouri back roads? Alternatively, does he turn off and wait for his friend? I do not know…"

Milken addressed Gums – "I need the satellite to scan every inch from Clarksdale northward. That is the kill-box." Milken felt in his gut that Augustus had been on the move at top speed from when he killed Spindle and Dunn. "Drop her in on that position and start scanning now."

"Sir," said the lead officer. "The GPS from Intel is now up on the screen. It appears that the target is not moving."

"Intel informed me that the signal was moving north but then stopped," said Milken. He stared at the blinking cursor that represented Cal's GPS tracking signal, wondering what this could mean. "Could he have figured out that we are tracking his GPS signal?"

"It is possible, but highly improbable," answered Boultry, appearing at their location from the main center. "The technology used to sniff that out is complex and typically not issued to law enforcement personnel. It is more or less a counter-intelligence tool reserved for, well, intelligence folks. My suspicion is that their stopping is due to something entirely different."

߬߬߬

Augustus observed dirt swirling high into the air about a mile ahead of him. The roads in Missouri occasionally changed between paved asphalt and gravel. He surmised the road returned to gravel up ahead. Whoever was driving in that dust ball was approaching rapidly, with apparent purpose.

Augustus had no way of knowing if the disturbance represented friend or foe. Suddenly, out of the high-kicking cloud of dirt in front of his vehicle, emerged an extended cab truck.

߬߬߬

Bo maneuvered the truck so that it slowed to a stop while simultaneously sliding to the other side of the road, in front of the oncoming vehicle.

"That was perfect!" Cal shouted to Bo.

"Don't you ever do that shit again…you hear me!" yelled Pappy at both his sons, as they jumped out onto the road.

ﾑﾑﾑ

"**H**ammer that area," shouted Milken, convinced he pinpointed Augustus' location.

The VGT satellite went through all the paces on this mission. Multiple re-tasks with multiple re-deployments. Consequently, the VGT team was thrilled beyond comprehension at the satellite's mission-specific versatility.

"Sector targeting commencing, sir," shouted the lead officer.

"Follow that road north to the Iowa border," ordered Gums. "We are putting all our eggs into this basket and presuming our target is on it somewhere."

The officer maneuvered the VGT satellite according to Gums' orders. He then said – "Satellite on the hard-deck, sir."

"Wonderful!" replied Gums. "Let's take some pictures then, shall we?"

The satellite meticulously scoured the US-169 landscape in a northward trajectory. The PSC fell silent, and a mechanical churn became audible, representing the spectrometer's active hunt.

"Mother-of-God…there it is," said Gums, as the match appeared on the screen above.

"We have contact and are on-task," shouted Boultry, taking the comms.

"Your orders, sir?" asked Boultry of Milken.

"Follow them, well, Augustus, anyway," replied Milken. "I am stepping away for a little while so that I may deploy our solution to this debacle. Please, let me know if you somehow lose track of Augustus or if an urgent matter arises."

"The specimen must have been in large quantity on the target's clothing. Either that, or a sizeable amount must have gotten on his skin, coddled by body heat and sweat," said Gums.

"Huh?" queried Milken.

Gums replied – "The blood...it gave a strong reading on the spectrograph. It was nowhere near as weak as I anticipated it would be this many hours after...well, you know. I theorize this is either due to a large quantity of blood or that its properties somehow remained preserved."

"Oh, good," replied Milken. "That means you won't fuck it up and lose them...carry on." Milken then departed to put the next phase of the chase into motion.

ക്കക്ക

"**A**ffirmative...extraction point located on grid...we will be at the landing zone in two five mikes...out." C-One completed his conversation with XM command and then addressed his team.

"Ears up! Air support will extract us in about two-five mikes. Once airborne, we will engage our objective within the hour. We are no longer support on this mission...we are taking the lead and going in hot. So get your kill on...are we on it?"

"KILL IS ON," replied The Cleansing, in unison, securing their gear for extraction.

ക്കക്ക

"**M**onsieur," said the young captain to Mauricio, as he entered the suite. "An important message awaits your presence on the bridge."

"What do you mean waiting?" grumbled Mauricio. "Bring it to me...I am still resting!"

"I cannot, Monsieur," replied the captain. "It is on the big phone, in the box."

Mauricio arose, realizing there existed no physical message, but rather, an electronic one from XM. "Mère de Dieu," he said, brushing past the captain towards the bridge.

When he arrived, an officer said – "Monsieur –"

"Yes, I know...shut up!" snarled Mauricio, as he picked up the device.

The communication automatically began – "There will be an airlift extraction from your vessel's helipad. Due to significant changes in operational details, a shift in roles has occurred. Our client's time-sensitive needs caused us to designate the team currently inside their country as primary. They are currently en-route to commence contact. You are now secondary. Our next communication will be at the client's Caribbean base of operations."

Mauricio hung up the device. He glared at the young captain, and at the other officers in the bridge, and said – "Your former captain's inexcusable delay has caused me to lose primary status on this mission. You are all extremely fortunate I do not kill you just for being associated with that piece of shit!"

He slammed his fists hard on the table in front of him. He then tore off back to the captain's suite. He was furious for losing the lead in the hunt, and was convinced it had to do with the vessel's delay in getting to their rendezvous point.

અ અ અ

Cal ran to the vehicle. He hoped to God that it was Augustus. The driver's door opened and out stepped his emotional yet composed friend. Cal opened his arms as he closed in and gave Augustus a Baker-family-hug. According to local lore, that hug was strong enough to crush an adult male grizzly, but full of all the love in the world. Cal embraced Augustus and the two combat-hardened men cried like toddlers in a nursery.

"Mi familia, hermano…they are trying to kill my wife and baby boy," cried Augustus.

"I have seen many things, amigo, but this is beyond any description that I have," Cal cried, sharing in his grief.

Augustus' voice muffled underneath Cal's arms – "I am running, but I do not know where to go. I do not know what to do. I do not know how to keep them safe."

"We will figure this out together, brother. I am going to be by your side from this moment forward. I promise you," Cal declared.

Pappy, an unusually hardened and emotionless man, walked up to them with red, teary eyes and said – "Auggie…" Pappy joined in the emotional greeting. The men held close for what amounted to a minute. However, it possessed the energy of an experience lasting much longer.

Bo had met Augustus several times. He thought well of him, but never developed the kind of bond as had Pappy and Cal. Irrespective, Bo felt extremely saddened for him. He gently touched Augustus on the shoulder and said – "It bothers me something awful Auggie that this has happened to you. I am even more troubled about what happened to your boy and his mammy. I will protect them with my life Auggie…I will…Pa…I will."

Pappy counseled Bo – "I know son, I know. Calm down now, though. Auggie needs us to be boulders for him, you hear me?"

"I do Pa," replied Bo, "I do." Bo was a young boy when his mother passed away suddenly from an undiagnosed cancer. He was physically the largest member of the family and arguably the closest of all the Baker boys to his mom. Pappy often chided Bo during his early years for being what he called a "grand-ole momma's boy." Naturally, that chiding ended after her death.

Bo's mental and emotional health deteriorated significantly after her passing. It left him with a life full of loneliness and sorrow. Over Pappy's numerous objections, Bo undertook the role of caretaker for the family's ranch. He pursued no professional interests and saw his life as a continuation of his mother's. "This is what Ma did, and it was good enough for her, which means, it is good enough for me," Bo would say, in response to any suggestions that he do otherwise.

Pappy knew that Bo's emotional reaction to Augustus' plight came from deep within, stemming from the loss of his mother. Pappy also knew he needed to check that emotional tidal wave from developing. If not, Bo stood the chance of having a total meltdown, which was the saddest thing a father could observe his son experience.

Mrs. Baker provided the core strength of their family. As a tribute to that strength, Pappy buried her alongside of a centuries-old boulder that prominently overlooked their property. "Ma will continue to be our family's strength," Pappy would say to Bo after her burial. "She will always be our boulder."

Bo understood Pappy's reference about needing to be boulders for Augustus. They all needed to show the strength of his momma, to help Augustus and his family survive. Consequently, Bo found the requisite composure and contained his emotions.

Pappy grabbed Augustus by his shoulders, motioned his eyes towards Bo and said – "Auggie, there really ain't no one better than Bo to look after your wife and child, there really isn't."

Augustus nodded in agreement and said to Bo – "Thank you, Bo. I feel truly blessed to have you looking over my family. They are in the vehicle with a doctor if you want to see them."

Bo rushed to the vehicle and climbed in to meet the doctor and to see Jennifer and Nathaniel.

"We gotta get off this road," said Pappy.

"I agree completely," replied Augustus. He then grabbed Cal by the back of his head, looked straight into his eyes, and said – "You are truly my brother…thank you." He let go and retreated to his vehicle. Bo had already settled in besides the doctor. "You're staying with us I take it," observed Augustus.

"I am," replied Bo.

"That is good. I wouldn't have it any other way," said Augustus.

Cal leaned in through the window and whispered – "Don't wake them up Bo, and listen to everything the doctor tells you to do…you hear?"

"Yes, Caleb. Go on and tell Pappy that I understand," Bo responded. The two brothers smiled at each other and laughed silently.

"Amigo," Cal said to Augustus. "We have a safe house not far from here. We can stop there for the remainder of the day and head back to our ranch overnight. What do you think?"

"An agency safe house or a Baker one?" asked Augustus, jokingly.

"You know what…that just jarred my memory brother," Cal replied. "The place I just mentioned is one that our agency has used for witness protection. However, Pappy's youngest brother passed away last year. He had a farm about forty-five miles south of here. Nobody lives there. It is spacious and extremely isolated. Let's go there instead."

"That sounds perfect," said Augustus.

"Okay, follow me," said Cal, hopping back onto the pavement. The two vehicles resumed momentum, heading for their final destination of the day in Plattsburg, Missouri.

෯෯෯

They arrived at the 180-acre property. Bo immediately got out, surveying the conditions. Doctor Broderson exited the vehicle and took a long, well-deserved stretch.

Augustus popped his head into the back and peeked at Jennifer and Nathaniel. He then said to Broderson – "Man, you really knocked them out cold, Doc. How long do you anticipate before they wake up? I would like them to be aware of their surroundings before we take off again."

Broderson replied – "I administered a drug with high quality extended-release properties. Do not be concerned, they are both doing very well. These monitors indicate accurately any distress they might be experiencing. Previously, they both exhibited high levels of distress. They were most likely dreaming about their experience, which negatively affected their sleep patterns. However, they are both calm now. They are either not dreaming or whatever is going through their minds is no longer disturbing them. This is great news. I am amenable to drawing one or both of them into full consciousness, if you so wish."

Augustus looked at his family and said – "Let's revisit this in another hour or so. I don't know if I'm ready to disturb such peaceful sleep yet."

"Understood," replied Broderson.

"By the way," said Augustus. "How strong was the concoction you gave to Chad?"

"That medicine was a crude mixture and markedly different from what I used with these two. Not only will it knock him out for a minimum of twenty-four hours, it will also have a deleterious effect. When he wakes up, he will not remember his name…or anything else for that matter," explained Broderson, smiling.

"Poor Chad," said Augustus, with slight humor in his voice. "He didn't know what the hell he got himself into."

෯෯෯

"Target DNA is on the move, sir," said an officer.

"Alright…looks like they are going to a secure location. Let's keep on top of them," ordered Boultry. The Arecibo team monitored the DNA tracking signal intently.

Close to an hour later, the lead officer said – "They are stationary, sir."

Boultry replied – "Give it a couple more minutes. Once we are confident that this is their endpoint, I will pass the details and coordinates to Milken for action."

Time passed by, and the unsuspecting targets showed no signs of movement. Boultry presented the location data to Milken. In turn, Milken fed the coordinates to his assets in the field, who were awaiting final strike orders…

&&&

"Eight, five, two delta this is hop-trot Charlie. We have package in sight, over," said the extraction pilot, with a slightly exaggerated Texas drawl.

"Hop-trot Charlie, we are still a go," replied Arecibo command. "Be advised that upon extraction your call signature will be Whiskey November, copy."

"That is a big ten, four," replied the pilot. The charcoal-grey Seahawk-class chopper swooped upon the highway, approximately one hundred yards from the approaching vehicle.

The helicopter's blades generated heavy gusts of wind. It made visibility nearly impossible, forcing C-Four to stop driving well before he intended. "That's our ride…get your shit and let's go," shouted C-One.

The Cleansing ducked as low as possible and moved towards the chopper. Battering gusts of dusty wind hammered them as they clung onto their gear for dear life. Two at a time, the team jumped into the eagerly awaiting Seahawk.

"All clear," shouted C-One to the pilot. "We are mounted up."

The sound of the Seahawk's deep thumps reverberated along the cavernous, desolate highway as it ascended. The pilot welcomed The Cleansing onto his airship. He then called over the wire to Arecibo command – "Eight, five, two delta...package has been recovered. We are now call-sign Whiskey November, wahoo. ETA target forty-four mikes..."

ॐॐॐ

"Sir, the team has been extracted and is en-route to engage," said the lieutenant to Boultry.

"Get thermal imaging up on the screen for those coordinates, so that we can monitor it in real time," replied Boultry. He then left to inform Milken that the main pod area would monitor the assault on Augustus' position.

ॐॐॐ

A vast stretch of hayfields covered the property. It had not been cultivated for quite some time, and brush grew wildly throughout. The house was a large and beautiful Victorian style structure. It seemed out of place in this rugged terrain. However, the patterns and designs embedded into its woodwork suggested that dedicated agrarians once occupied it.

The men hustled between their vehicles and the house before settling in. Augustus knelt on the ground, re-staking a portion of fence that blew over. Suddenly, he stopped, stood up and paced erratically...like an animal sensing an approaching storm.

"¿Que pasa amigo?" asked Cal.

Augustus did not reply. He lowered his head, stepped a few paces north, then west, east and south. He raised his head and backed up slowly to Cal saying – "They're coming." Of the many competencies Augustus developed over the years, his most extraordinary was his awareness of the natural world around him. His NICO experiences converted him into a predator, making him cognizant of nature's elemental shifts during all types of occurrences. "It is like reading nature's energy-filled tea leaves," Augustus once said to a colleague. The unique stench of danger was not new to Augustus. It could only mean one thing.

"Get them inside now," Augustus shouted to Broderson, referencing his family.

"But...I don't know where to set them up," the doctor replied.

"Come with me," said Bo. "We'll take them to the storage area behind the kitchen." They proceeded to move Jennifer and Nathaniel inside.

"Law enforcement coming?" asked Cal.

"No...something much worse," Augustus whispered.

"It was that no good Lee Billings. I bet he got a trace put on your phone, Caleb," shouted Pappy. "Calling out of the blue and asking you to voluntarily come in for such an unprecedented manhunt...phooey. Caleb, I did not buy it for a minute. He is working with them and now they know where we are."

"I threw my phone out the window hours ago, Pa," replied Cal, worried and confused.

Augustus wondered if he led this approaching danger to them. *A trace on the Station's vehicle is not possible,* he thought. *The engineers specifically excluded that technological ability from the specs, prior to manufacturing the fleet.* Those in charge of the program foresaw scenarios where aggressors, to continue their attacks against heads of state, could use technology to their advantage. If the enemy hacked into the Station's systems and accessed tracking metadata, they could feasibly determine the whereabouts of each vehicle upon discovery. Knowing this, Augustus felt strongly that a trace did not come through him.

He then said – "I sense a colossal and determined foe approaching, hell bent on inflicting savagery. A person's energy affects the world around them. When Man is intent on exacting violence upon another, nature's scent becomes putrid to those who can smell it. We must prepare...right now."

Cal and Augustus moved the vehicles to the rear of the house.

Pappy leaned each weapon they had against the shed, with their corresponding ammunition placed carefully by them. "That's all we have, boys," said Pappy, looking down at the hardware. They had five M-4 carbine rifles, six 9-mm semi-automatic handguns, two .45 caliber pistols and one western Winchester rifle. "I don't know how many folks you expecting to hit us Auggie, but we'd better make all our shots count. These ain't gonna last very long."

"Unfortunately, I do not know. However, I have faith these will make do." Augustus then went inside to check on his family.

❧❧❧

Broderson asked – "What exactly is going on? Are we all in danger right now?"

"Take care of my family," Augustus growled, grabbing the doctor's shirt. "I don't know what exactly is going on but, yes, we are in real fucking danger." Augustus reached into his pants pocket. He pulled out a .22 caliber revolver and handed it to Broderson.

"I am a doctor, Mister Peña. I heal people, I do not kill them," protested Broderson.

"This is not for you to use on…them," said Augustus. "Doctor, you are a full-grown man, and have been with us since Des Moines. You potentially possess valuable information from your tenure with me. That means interrogation. Trust me, you will want this." Augustus looked at his family and said – "I don't know how much time we have. My family needs to be conscious. I believe they stand a better chance of survival if they are awake. Otherwise, the temptation of killing them as they slept might prove to be too great."

Broderson looked at Augustus with disbelief, saying nothing.

"If they make it into this room doctor, then the rest of us are already dead."

"Who in the world do you suspect is coming here?"

"Barbarians, Doctor Broderson, that's who," replied Augustus.

Bo appeared, and said – "Auggie, Pa' says people is coming here to hurt the boy and his momma…is this true?"

"I believe so," said Augustus. "I am really going to need your help on this one, Bo."

"There ain't no one gonna do that to them, Auggie…they is not!" Bo turned away and headed outside to gather his choice of weapons.

"Doc," said Augustus. "Wake them up."

❧❧❧

C-One shuffled up to the pilot and said – "Could you guys have picked a louder method of insertion? I think they can hear this fucking thing in Canada."

The pilot laughed and said – "Shoot, sir, what you worried about? These coordinates are for a property that is over one hundred fifty squared acres. That means no nosy neighbors. Besides, Command has this billed as being like shooting fish in a barrel. Just a couple of civilians with some handguns and maybe a shotgun or two…"

C-One smirked – "That's what they said, huh?"

"You got it, partner," responded the pilot.

"That's just fucking great," said C-One, making his way back to the team. Upon reaching his men he said – "Huddle up. We have a bit of an issue as it relates to tactics and security. Command has these pilots convinced this is going to be a walk in the park. I suspect that is why we are being transported in this groaning behemoth."

"What's your take?" asked C-Three.

"We enter in two squads," replied C-One. "Four through six, you will drop in the second we breach the property line. The pilot says it is over one hundred fifty acres, so you will need to boogie your asses to the LZ and meet up with us. By then, we will have already put down and engaged."

"Is it defended?" asked C-Two.

"I don't give a flying fuck whether it is or not," replied C-One. "What concerns me is that Command referred to this as shooting fish in a barrel. If that were truly the case then this would had been handled in Iowa. Someone down there has game. Consequently, I am not going in eating ice cream expecting nothing but clowns and drunken midgets."

C-One returned to the pilot and said – "It is imperative that you let me know when we are about to breach that property line. I am dropping in a team before our main entry. Slow down to about forty to fifty knots for the exit jump. Ten to twelve feet above ground will be just fine. There's no need to put down or to get lower than that…these Cinderella's can handle it."

"It's your ball, sir," replied the pilot. "Play it how you want…we are sixteen minutes out."

The chopper's humming seemed alive with knowledge of the impending mission, as its intensity increased with each passing second.

༺༺༺

"**W**here are we?" asked Milken.

"Chopper is less than twenty miles from the drop point," replied the lieutenant.

"The quality of the feed looks good," commended Milken, referencing the live overhead thermal imagery.

"She's a beauty alright," agreed Boultry.

"Is that them?" asked Milken, observing heat signatures moving around on the property.

"Affirmative, sir," replied the lieutenant. "Those are the targets."

"How long does this feed stay up?" Milken asked.

"She is good for twenty minutes, sir. She will then automatically go dark for a thirty-minute interval," described the lieutenant.

The thermal imagery satellite was separate from the VGT. Agencies typically deployed it to spy on suspected terrorist camps. However, many of those organizations had increased their counter surveillance capabilities. Consequently, the spy satellites automatically shut down their surveillance functions at pre-determined intervals. In theory, this decreased the likelihood of their detection.

"Okay," said Milken. "I want a fresh twenty, so cut her off. Bring her live right when we expect the team to arrive at the point of entry. I don't want to miss a thing."

"Copy that, sir," responded the lieutenant. He proceeded to shut off the thermal image feed from the satellite.

"Where is our cleanup man now?" asked Milken. "I don't want this to be lying around for weeks just for some hunter to find it."

"He has just been picked up at sea, sir," said the lieutenant, regarding Mauricio's status. "ETA, Arecibo, in one hour."

"Get his ass on a jet helo to Missouri the moment he lands. I don't want him to have time to contemplate taking a shit," ordered Milken.

ॐ ॐ ॐ

"My baby!" screamed Jennifer, as she awoke from her deeply sedated state. "Where…?"

"Shhh…sh…sh…sh…Mamita, he's doing great," said Augustus, holding her hands.

"Oh Augustus," cried Jennifer, throwing her arms around his head and shoulders. "It was so horrible. What is going on?" Jennifer reached for her stomach and cried out in pain.

"Here, Mrs. Peña, let me give you something for your pain," said Broderson. "You have some pretty serious injuries, but you are otherwise doing very well."

Jennifer stared at Broderson with astonishment. She looked back at Augustus and whispered – "Where are we? Where is Nathaniel?"

"We are in Missouri, baby. Nataniel está allá," said Augustus, motioning his head towards their sedated son. "You and Nataniel have been deeply sedated by this wonderful man, Doctor Mark Broderson. He was at the hospital when the both of you were brought in after…after…" Augustus looked away, subduing the rush of emotion and tears about to overcome him. "Mamita…there is so much for you and I to discuss; but we have no time to talk right now. I am at a loss for how to end this conversation with you."

Jennifer weakly raised her hand to Augustus' face. She grimaced slightly from her pain and said – "I know, my love. It is okay. I can tell from the look in your face that we are still in danger. I am just thankful that I have been provided another chance to see you…to tell you how much I love you…" Jennifer cried and said – "And our little, beautiful son…"

Broderson looked at Augustus and motioned his head towards the door, indicating he wanted him to leave.

Augustus took the hint and said – "Baby, the doctor is going to explain everything to you. I need to go and make sure we are as safe as can be. I love you, Jennifer…I love you so much." He leaned forward and gave Jennifer a deep, heartfelt kiss. He then looked at Broderson and said – "Tell her everything."

"Augustus," said Jennifer as he started to leave. "I need a gun."

Broderson was about to protest, but Augustus put his hand up to stop him from talking. He removed a .45-caliber semi-automatic weapon from his hip and laid it on her right side. "Full clip, one in the chamber, sweetie…make them count." He then left the room and returned to the men outside.

Broderson delivered a quick briefing to Jennifer on what had transpired and on what was possibly about to occur. He then proceeded to awaken little Nathaniel.

ฅ๖ฅ๖ฅ๖

Cal raised his hands into the air, with palms facing Augustus, when he heard him come out of the house. Augustus recognized the signal. He stopped dead in his tracks. Cal placed his left hand over his ear and twirled his right hand several times.

The clockwise motion alerted Augustus to a helicopter. He progressed slowly, making sure not to break Cal's concentration. Pappy and Bo stood silently. When he reached Cal, he signaled with his fingers to determine how many.

Cal whispered – "Sounds like one big fucker or multiple smaller ones in tight formation."

"Distance?" asked Augustus.

"A little beyond the length of this property, if I recall the layout of it…about five minutes away tops," replied Cal.

"Well, there it is," said Pappy. "Here comes the posse, boys. I don't think that they are coming to just round us up, either."

"Neither do I," said Augustus.

"Bo," said Pappy. "Get what you need and head inside with them right now!" Bo complied straightaway and hoofed it into the house with his weapons.

Cal looked at Pappy and Augustus and said – "Stop…shh…do you hear that?"

Augustus responded – "I do…that's a fucking Seahawk."

"Yeah," Cal said. "I agree, but it sounds like it stopped for a moment."

Augustus yelled – "Take positions. They put down a drop-team. If the helo lands here, that means there will be two waves of attacks. If it passes us by, then the drop team is it. Either way, we have no time. Get ready."

"I need your assault weapon Pappy…sorry…don't mean to take your best toy," said Augustus.

Pappy replied – "She's all yours, Auggie. I'm gonna stick to this here Winchester rifle and pick them bastards off one at a time. I'm a crack shot with this here thing, believe you me."

"Must be where your boy gets it," said Augustus, patting Pappy's shoulder. He then shouted – "CAL, SHOOT TO KILL."

Cal knew what Augustus meant and appreciated the last-second reality check. Cal was currently a Deputy U.S. Marshal, a federal law enforcement agent. His instinct was to avoid creating fatalities at all costs. However, this was something much different. Augustus' words amplified this reality into Cal's mind. An imminent conflict loomed, that could be brutal and carnage ridden. However, he had no other choice now, but to fight.

ৰৰৰ

"Satellite up," shouted the lieutenant. "She is on target and all thermals are clear."

Boultry sat at his desk, with the Bible open across his lap. He then started to read Psalm 23 aloud – "The Lord is my shepherd…"

ৰৰৰ

The chopper's mechanical screech preceded the wind gusts from its blades by a fraction of a second. The dark conveyor of death touched down forcefully onto the front lawn. C-One and his now divided team exited the craft and headed straight for the front door.

"Touchdown," said Milken, as he and all the others watched with anxious anticipation.

"How many members are on that team?" Boultry asked Milken.

"Six on this particular mission," replied Milken.

Per Milken's prior directive, the satellite feed started just as the chopper was about to touchdown in front of the house. Milken was clueless of C-One's decision to split up the team's insertion. As a result, it did not concern him when he observed six heat registrations on the chopper's landing zone.

"Well then, we have got company coming in from the rear," said Boultry.

Sweat formed above Milken's eyebrows as he observed three heat signatures approach the chopper by ground.

Milken shouted – "It's an ambush, patch in to that pilot now!"

કેન્કેન્કેન

"**C**ome again eight, five, two delta," said the pilot, when the alert from Arecibo came over the wire. "Eight, five, two delta, be advised, your recent communication was unclear, please revise…over…"

"Whiskey…CRACKLE…November…CRACKLE…amb…u …sh…"

The pilot made out the garbled word through the crackling static. He yelled to his copilot – "Fucking ambush!"

The copilot did not respond. Instead, his sunglasses flew off his face, accompanied by fragments of his flight helmet. The pilot did not understand what just occurred, and felt foggy. He looked down and saw a chunk of the copilot's jaw on his lap. The pilot jerked and swatted the jaw away. He yelled over the wire – "CONTACT," but, it was too late. The bullets that tore off his copilot's face made their way to him. He died instantly as the precision shots from Cal's M-4 carbine cut across his collarbone and neck.

કેન્કેન્કેન

The team approached the house. C-One raised his arms to direct C-Two and C-Three's entry pattern. C-Three acknowledged the order by raising his right hand, giving the thumbs-up. Suddenly, C-Three's thumb disappeared, along with most of his right hand, into a burst of blood and tendons. One second later, a portion of C-Three's right arm tore off at the elbow. The next impact was a fatal shot to his head.

The volleys were rapid and methodical. Pappy watched as his target fell dead to the ground, and said – "There ain't nothing like a Winchester."

C-One could not believe his eyes. He ducked and signaled to warn C-Two, who did not notice, and entered the house. C-One next saw the distinctive sparks of bullets striking metal. He noticed a man with an assault weapon, laying siege to the pilots. "Mother fuckers," he yelled, and charged towards him. Instantly, the ground around him spat up dirt and rock. He realized that an unseen defender was shooting at him. C-One changed direction and rushed towards the approaching drop-team.

ॐॐॐ

Augustus rummaged through C-Three's equipment, looking for useful items. He found two concussion grenades. He then signaled Cal to pursue the retreating intruder from a right flank position. He motioned his fingers, reminiscent of a crawling spider, to remind Cal that there might be others. Cal signaled his acknowledgment. The pursuit was on.

Augustus had seen one of the marauders enter the house at the beginning of the onslaught. However, he had to have full faith that Bo would address the threat. Augustus knew that if he were unable to have that faith, then the attackers would have the upper hand. Breaking away and abandoning his counter insurgence against their murderous plot would be a fatal mistake. Augustus needed to continue his charge to neutralize their capabilities permanently.

ॐॐॐ

During operations, The Cleansing maintained zero radio contact. Electronic footprints of their activities did not exist, thereby lessening the chance of exposure. They operated silently, using hand signals and knocking sounds, to communicate amongst their pack.

Unfortunately for C-Two, this lack of radio contact meant he had no idea what was going on outside. Instead, he progressed through the main level of the house, seeking his prey. He observed some movement by what appeared to be the kitchen area. C-Two cat walked a half step at a time while simultaneously raising his weapon. He saw a woman leaning against the far wall, with a small child in her arms.

"Fuck…this really is like shooting fish in a barrel," he said, as he prepared to rush in and make the kills. However, he suddenly stopped. C-Two's body tingled all over. He began trembling uncontrollably. He tried to look down, but his head could not move. Blood spewed through his mouth and nostrils. C-Two lowered his eyeballs and saw a large, bloody blade protruding from under his chin.

"You don't ever hurt a boy and his momma…not ever," said Bo. He then pulled out the knife as hard and fast as he could. C-Two fell dead to the floor. Bo repositioned himself…waiting…on any other attackers that might appear.

かかか

C-One put his hands up when he saw the approaching drop-team. He motioned his arms for them to spread out, which they quickly did. C-One took position next to C-Five, alongside a tall and wide pile of hay and said – "Goddamned ambush…Three is dead…pilots are dead."

"What the fuck?" said C-Five. "What about Two?"

"I saw him go into the house, but then all hell broke loose. I don't know."

かかか

Augustus saw the men spread out in front of him. He threw himself down and remained motionless. He counted their numbers. After a few moments, he realized this was all of them. He looked far to his right and saw Cal cautiously approach. He made a nondescript sound with his lips.

Cal immediately recognized it as coming from him, so he stopped.

Augustus gestured towards him. He held up two fingers on each hand, indicating there were binary groups of two. He then signaled an explosion by taking a closed fist and releasing all fingers upward. Finally, he thrust forward his fist and arm, directing Cal to charge straight to the two targets on the right.

Cal acknowledged and crouched into a position from which he could easily bolt.

Augustus did not hesitate. He activated one of the concussion grenades and tossed it between the two men to his right.

C-Four and C-Six saw something sail towards them. They had no time to react. The earsplitting explosion washed over them. They lay defenseless from the blast, unable to fight off the attacking, and now hollering, Cal Baker.

"They got fucking grenades too?" shouted C-Five.

"Double-back…we're getting the hell out of here on foot. We'll drive out in whatever we find," ordered C-One.

"Copy that shit," replied C-Five. He stood up to withdraw from the property. However, he only made it two steps before meeting the business end of Augustus' tactical knife.

Augustus plunged the knife deep into C-Five. From pure rage, more than from sheer strength, he lifted the two hundred plus pound mercenary off the ground. Augustus charged forward, to where C-Five had just arisen. He saw C-One preparing to leave. He threw C-Five onto C-One and fired into them the remaining rounds from his assault rifle.

The rounds mostly struck C-Five, killing him instantly. However, C-One managed to roll away from the barrage, suffering only two shots to his left leg. He stood up, showing no signs of weakness. In the blink of an eye, he retrieved his sidearm, pointed it at Augustus' head and pulled the trigger.

The shot from C-One's handgun went straight up into the air, his arm lifting in response to a blunt force thump from behind.

As C-One fell to the ground, Augustus caught sight of what brought this killer down. Pappy chambered the double-barreled weapon in his hands, looked at the smoking barrels and said – "Oh, yeah, I forgot to mention, that I always carry me a shotgun in my vehicles."

Augustus stepped to C-One and put a bullet into his head. He then said to Pappy – "No offense to your shotgun, I just want to make sure he stays down for good." He glanced towards Cal and saw that he had effectively neutralized those targets. Augustus ran back to the house.

Pappy yelled out to him – "Your family is safe, Auggie, Bo took care of it."

Augustus heard him, but needed to see for himself. He would not be able to breathe another second if anything happened to them…however slight.

He bolted inside. Bo was still standing watch over his family and had no idea that the attack was over. "It's me, Bo…it's me…Auggie."

Bo was wild-eyed, and did not recognize him for a second. "Auggie," he said slowly, motioning to the floor just off to their left. "I told him that he couldn't hurt no boy and his momma."

Augustus looked at the carnage and said – "You've done great, Bo. It's all over for right now…you've done real well." Augustus then went past him to be with his family.

ॐॐॐ

The scene at Arecibo was hectic. Every attempt at communicating with the pilots failed. Thermal images on the screen suggested to PSC that a threat approached the chopper. The atmosphere morphed into pandemonium as the imagery showed gunfire directed at the helo. That fact alone was disturbing. However, more disconcerting was that the attack came not from the images approaching the aircraft, but from those situated around it.

The circumstances worsened when the command center heard the pilot scream…followed by silence. The team watched in awe as three illusive heat signatures moved about the property with confidence.

"Satellite shutdown in 5, 4, 3, 2, 1…" called out the lieutenant. "You want it back up manually, sir?" he asked Boultry.

Boultry looked at Milken, who then replied – "No…there is nothing left to see." Milken went to an empty chair and took a seat, saying – "They were the most ruthless assets we ever had at our disposal. How in God's name could this have happened?"

Boultry responded – "The time is always right to ask yourself a deep and honest question. Are you operating so far from the acceptable limits of human dignity that the good Lord himself has decided to step in? Not to take sides, mind you, but to get things back in line with what He expects of us."

As Milken pondered these words, the overhead speakers crackled. A wrathful, haunting voice began to speak –

"You shoot my wife," the voice snarled. "And you try to shoot my son…a toddler…" The halls of the PSC echoed with a hissing sound from the speakers in between Augustus' words. "And…you continue to try…" The hissing filled the air for another twenty seconds. "You did these things to us because you believed I was a threat. However, I was not…my family was not. You instilled great fear in my family. That made you feel strong…and powerful. Those of you that can hear my voice have never experienced the fear that I will bring to your homes in the dead of night. You cannot fathom the degree of grotesque pain and suffering I have inflicted, in the name of country and honor…but you will. This time, it will be in the name of family. I am Augustus Peña. I am now exactly what you had so much wanted me to be…your greatest and most dreaded menace ever…"

Everyone remained frozen in place with fear. All that was audible within the PSC, for what seemed to be an eternity, was the sound of the overhead speakers – HSSSSSSSSSS…

Colonel Boultry ended the long silence, saying to Milken – "I can't say for sure whether the good Lord himself came here from the heavens to intervene in these matters. However, I do know this much to be true. The Devil does indeed walk amongst us. Satan, with all of his wickedness and hatred, will wreak havoc on us all…and we have just heard his voice."

⌘⌘⌘

THIRTEEN

Augustus powered down the helicopter and all of its systems. He exited the aircraft, and proceeded to drag the bodies of C-Two and C-Three to the chopper. After tossing their bodies inside, he returned to the field to retrieve the rest of them. Cal and Pappy where standing by the dead attackers. They did not say a word. Augustus grabbed one of the stiffs by both ankles and progressed to the chopper with it. Cal slung his weapon's harness over his shoulder, squatted, and grabbed the ankles of the corpse closest to him. He then dragged it to its final resting place.

Augustus made an inventory check after all the bodies had been stacked inside. Satisfied that he pilfered all he needed from the chopper, he jumped out. He grabbed two containers of diesel gasoline that he found in the shed. He saturated the bodies and the aircraft with the fuel.

He looked at Cal, who was holding four flares, and said – "Light it up."

The Seahawk was engulfed in flames. The temperature in and around the house increased substantially. The four men stared at the blaze transitorily. They then entered the house to start loading up their vehicles.

ॐॐॐ

Milken left the command center. He called Gates to update him on the mission and to offer some insight on how he would like to proceed. "We don't know where the Peña threat will take us. We can kick this can down the road and revive it, after we get what we need from the lobbyists. Kill the satellite," said Milken.

"I most certainly understand, Virgil," said Gates.

Milken's directive did not mean to suggest a curtailment in his desire to locate and eliminate Augustus. To the contrary, he developed a newfound sense of urgency. The multiple failures in this mission were catastrophic. A nudge from within begged him to step out of the shadows and to physically take charge of this pursuit. "Yes, I am quite convinced that this is what I need to do," whispered Milken. "Both NICO and XM assets have been useless…what an embarrassment." He then remembered - *XM still has an asset en route here. I will use him for damage control.*

"I trust XM is done screwing things up," Milken said in disgust. "I cannot recall a greater miscarriage of service or another occurrence of such an assassin's breach. The ramifications of this violation are going to be immeasurable."

࿊࿊࿊

Cal was on the phone, while everyone else loaded the vehicles for departure. "I'm telling you, this stinks something bad, and it goes straight to the top," he said to Cranston Hicks, the Marshal Service Special Operations Commander.

"I receive a call from a RAC I haven't dealt with for some time. He says he is looking into my status for a voluntary report but then calls it the biggest manhunt ever. That kind of shit is not voluntary…not ever. That call needed to be for a mandatory report, but it was not. That means it was for something else. And that something else, Hicks, was to provide my coordinates to the hit-team now smoldering in the helicopter they came here in less than an hour ago."

"I hear what you're saying, Caleb. I am inclined to buy into everything you have just told me. However, I need to know exactly what it is that you need. I must hear you say it. Do you understand?" said Hicks.

Cal replied – "This family needs protection and I don't mean basic witness protection. We need to place them in BOPS immediately. There is no time for delay. Moreover, since I am apparently on the target list as well, it is more than appropriate for me to run the op. My dad and bro need to come too. They would have been murdered, along with the rest of us, if we hadn't killed those bastards."

BOPS stood for Black Operations Protective Service. Overall, the agency regarded it as a myth. Only a handful of individuals knew of its existence. BOPS operated globally, at an unprecedented level, keeping endangered persons from the world's most influential and determined villains.

"I can do that," replied Hicks. "I can get everything that both of your families will need. Given the grave circumstances, I will open an op for five years. Hopefully, this will be enough to get this figured out."

Cal said – "Don't mind me saying, Hicks, but that was kind of on the spot authority. Is there something you are not telling me?"

"At the time that I received word, I thought nothing of it. However, after listening to you, I too am greatly concerned."

"Hear what?" pressed Cal.

"RAC Billings was found dead just a little while ago. He apparently crashed into a locomotive while crossing the tracks. His vehicle exploded into a fireball, almost making him unidentifiable." Cal placed his hand over his forehead in disbelief. Hicks then said – "I will contact you at the top of the hour. Stay safe."

☙☙☙

Cal ended the call, went to Augustus and said – "I just got off the phone with my agency's special operations commander. We got the green light to place both our families into BOPS…it is witness protection on steroids. The program is a total blackout, with zero data in the system. Even auditors do not know it exists. Your family is going to be safe, amigo. Oh, yeah…I'm running the op, since I need to be protected as well."

Cal placed his hand on Augustus' shoulder. He had a look of concern on his face. Cal did not know what to make of it, so he said – "Hey, amigo, I can vouch for Hicks…that is who I just spoke to. I mean, if there is anyone who would choose death before treachery, it is Cranston Hicks."

"Hermano," Augustus replied. "Your efforts are too incredible for words. I cannot thank you enough. What is causing me distress is the reality of what is to come."

"I don't understand."

Augustus explained – "I am not only a marked man, in need of protection, but am also a wanted fugitive. In the past seventy-two hours, I have killed to defend my family. This includes two federal agents in Iowa. You know, as well as I do, that the public does not know the truth surrounding this matter. I do not know if there exists a way to explain it to them. Undoubtedly, the very powers trying to kill me will distort my reputation. They will blame me for most, if not all, of the violence that has occurred. Moreover, a federal warrant for my arrest will most certainly be issued, if it has not already. You know what that means don't you?"

Cal answered – "It means that the US Marshal Service cannot protect you. Instead, we need to arrest you."

"That is correct," agreed Augustus. He then looked at Jennifer and Nathaniel as the men hoisted them into the vehicle. "It also means they have to go into protection without me."

Cal struggled for words, and then said – "Come with us, Augustus. Maybe I can work it out so that you can remain with your family while we get the truth out to the public."

"Cal, there is no point in making such an attempt," replied Augustus. "There is nothing you can say or do which will wash away all that I have done. This is my fate and I understand that. I brought these troubles on myself. My tribulations have now affected Jen, Nate, you and your family. This has been no one else's fault but my own."

"How can you say that?" cried Cal. "How can you be at fault for killer after killer coming to murder your wife and child? How can you say that, Auggie?"

"Because, it is true..."

"But it is NOT true! Don't you dare give those bastards an ounce of justification for what they have done...not one bit," shouted Cal.

"My service to this country has caused –"

"Your service was to protect our way of life, Auggie. None of this has to do with it. That was honorable service...this is nothing short of barbarism," said Cal loudly as Augustus made every attempt at getting a word in.

"Will you let me finish, Cal!" yelled Augustus. "My service was anything but honorable. None of the constraints set in place to govern civilized societies, and their militaries, applied to me. You, Cal, swore...you took an oath to defend the Constitution of the United States as well as to protect and honor her. I took no such oath."

"No...no...Auggie...I don't want to hear that...I don't."

"But you will hear it, Cal. You will hear it because it is the truth. If you, my brother, cannot stand to hear me out, then what goddamned chance would I have pleading my case to the American public?" shouted Augustus. Cal sat on the ground and crossed his legs Indian-style. He leaned forward, lowered his head and rested his arms on his legs. He then rocked ever so slightly as Augustus continued to speak.

"I took no oath because there was none to take. No vow on this planet could have addressed my depraved and wretched duties. My outfit did not swear to defend our Constitution because we wiped our asses with it on a daily basis. Our very existence, in and of itself, repulsed the rule of law wherever it could be found. Had our missions become known, every country we ever operated in would fight to put us before their firing-squads...including our own."

Augustus took a step backwards to get a better view of Cal. He then said – "Look at me, hermano...look up at me. If you are undertaking the responsibility of protecting the lives of my wife and son, then I need for you to look me in the eyes when I tell you this..."

Cal raised his head and looked at him with his tear-filled, bluish-green eyes.

Augustus then said – "Caleb, I was an assassin...a cold-blooded assassin for a paramilitary, ghost agency whose roots stem from the Vietnam War. While I cannot definitively say why this is happening, I suspect that I pose too great of a risk to remain alive. I am a threat to their anonymity. My remaining alive exponentially increases the probability of their exposure. Our elected officials would be burned at the stake if that ever happened." Augustus stepped to him, offering his hand.

Cal clasped it and stood up, saying – "I may not be an assassin, Auggie, but I will kill anyone whom I don't know that comes within 100 meters of your family, I promise." He then grinned and said – "By the way, I always suspected you were a stone-cold killer."

Cal hugged Augustus saying – "Come with us...at least to get them settled in. You should spend some time with them before heading off. If a warrant is issued for your arrest, I will make certain that you have more than enough time to disappear. I will not jeopardize your freedom, that's a fact."

Augustus agreed, and they went to assist the others for departure to their next destination.

కావావా

"**B**ird inbound sir," shouted the lieutenant to Boultry.

"I will check with Milken to see what he wants done. He might not need that guy anymore."

Boultry located him – "Sir, the bird with your asset is inbound. ETA five minutes...should we turn it back?"

"No, I have some use for him. Please bring him to me when he lands." Milken looked at his watch. He decided to call Iowa to see what other developments may have occurred.

"SAC Eggert, C. Virgil here. How goes the search?"

"Whew, it gets zanier by the minute," replied Eggert.

"Oh, how so?"

"Well shit sir, where the hell do I begin? When we last spoke, I told you about a tunnel-like entrance not far from the dead agents' vehicle. After my reinforcements arrived, we entered and walked the length of the road beyond it."

"Did you say a road?"

"That's right," replied Eggert. "The thing went for almost a mile...it's incredible. Anyway, we get to this domed structure. We immediately realized that this is some sort of militarized building, given all of the cameras embedded into it. We figured that it was either abandoned and booby-trapped or occupied and heavily defended. Consequently, we did not attempt a breach."

"Go on," said Milken, extremely curious as to what this structure could be.

Eggert continued – "We put some calls into the Governor's office, to see if we could get some answers. However, we needed to tread lightly regarding our activities. State law here is a bit ridiculous when it comes to what is public information. You can practically be required to release the time of the last shit you took, if you are a public official, and did it on official business. We were about to give up hope on finding out more info on this structure when we got a break. Our local ASAC received a voicemail from a state official claiming to be able to assist with the Peña search."

"Did you get back to him?"

"We are unable to," replied Eggert. "The official said he was in China, on formal state business, and could not be directly reached. He is apparently going to phone the ASAC again sometime in the next couple of hours."

"SAC Eggert, if you do not mind, I would like to go to Iowa and see these things that you speak of. I promise not to impede your investigation."

"The more the merrier. Come on out."

"Excellent," said Milken. "I will arrive in Des Moines with one of my foreign-service agents within the next six hours."

"Great. See you then."

ཚ་ཚ་ཚ

Mauricio exited the aircraft. A flight-deck officer greeted him – "Sir, welcome to Arecibo. Your presence is requested in the command center at once."

What in the hell is he saying? Mauricio thought, as he nodded and smiled at the officer. Mauricio's grasp of the English language was adequate. However, he often needed to prepare his mind before effectively discerning it. Meanwhile, his spoken English was always the same – broken and in need of an overhaul.

The flight-deck officer led Mauricio through a maze of military checkpoints. He continually referred to documents inside a folder when challenged by guards. *I am involved with something that not every soldier here knows about,* thought Mauricio, scrutinizing the interactions. They entered another area. This time, the officer did not reference the documents. Instead, he pointed at Mauricio. *Finalement, we are close to the decision maker, voilà.*

A multitude of men in black fatigues whisked Mauricio to the interior. He chuckled internally as he observed the drama unfold around him. *I could easily kill everyone here. Yet, they seem to think they are superior to anyone not associated with their ranks...fucking Americans.*

They arrived at an elevator door. One of the escorts punched a code into it. The door opened. Mauricio entered the small conveyor cautiously. The escort entered with him and closed the compartment. It moved sideways, contrary to what Mauricio had expected.

"This is like a little train, no?" he said to the escort.

The escort remained silent, made no eye contact, and did not react to the commentary.

A look of displeasure emanated across Mauricio's face as he thought – *Americans have the balls to suggest that French people are rude, pompous assholes. That is for shit.*

The conveyor stopped. The escort motioned for Mauricio to exit. He stepped out and the lieutenant greeted him.

࿔࿔࿔

"**M**ajor developments have occurred since our last communication," said the lieutenant.

Mauricio replied – "It is all done by now, yes?"

"To the contrary, I would say that it is just beginning. Come, our commander of operations will fill you in with the details." The lieutenant led Mauricio down the passageway and into a sizeable office.

As he entered, Mauricio observed an area just beyond where he stood. It appeared to be an auditorium with a large overhead screen.

"The commander will be here soon," said the lieutenant. "Please, make yourself comfortable. Food and drink will be here shortly. Also, there is a restroom at the rear of this office." The lieutenant departed and Mauricio sat down in one of the leather couches that lined the back wall.

Shortly thereafter, Milken entered saying – "No need to stand, you can call me commander."

"I did not contemplate the need to stand and I have no name that I wish to share," replied Mauricio.

"I can see we are going to get along real swell, aren't we?" said Milken, sarcastically.

Mauricio offered no response. He looked at Milken with a blank expression, mainly because he had no idea what swell meant.

Agitated by Mauricio's silence, Milken spoke – "Alright, hotshot. I am going to tell you the same thing I just told your bosses back in Belize. The mission that XM has been contracted to complete is all fucked up. There are people dead all over the place, but none of them is the target. Now, mind you, our folks were initially unable to get the job done. So I will make no bones about it, we screwed up too. However, that was before your involvement. We turn to XM when we require a higher level of efficiency than what we are able to provide. I don't know what happened on your Mediterranean slash Atlantic cruise, but it has caused us a world of shit. In light of the fact that your delay, in no small measure, caused today's catastrophic events, you will assist me with bringing this matter to fruition. You were part of the problem, monsieur, but you will now be responsible for fashioning a solution. Do you understand me?"

Mauricio replied – "No. I do not."

"What the fuck do you mean you do not?" shouted Milken. "Are you playing with me?"

Mauricio remained cool-tempered and did not match Milken's level of anger. He was not scared or intimidated. Rather, he did not know where he was, other than deep inside of a militarized location, from which he did not know how to leave.

"Monsieur commander," said Mauricio. "I most certainly am not playing with a man of your stature. I am simply curious. What happened to the others…the primary?"

"They are dead, all of them."

Mauricio responded – "I do not know why you take such a tone, Monsieur commander. It appears that you and my employer have made grave miscalculations, costing the lives of your respective personnel. It was those errors that caused the target to get away, not me."

Milken stared at Mauricio, astonished at the man's insolence. However, he decided against quarrelling with him. *This prick is a lot smarter than what he looks. Arguing with him will get me nowhere.* Milken stood up from his desk and said – "There is food on the way. I suggest you chow down then get yourself freshened up and groomed. I will have a suit brought to you. You are coming with me to Iowa, to see firsthand what all went wrong from the beginning. I am introducing you as one of my foreign-service agents, so your accent will not be a problem. I assume that in your duties for XM there would have been times requiring you to act in a civilized and official manner?"

Mauricio nodded in the affirmative.

"Good. We leave in one hour."

ॐॐॐ

The two vehicles arrived at the Baker ranch, after BOPS dispatched a team there to verify its safety and to protect the families. All through the trip, Jennifer held Nathaniel, quietly humming the songs he loved to hear. Although still in pain, she overcame her agonies for the sake of comforting her child. Nathaniel was awake and no longer groggy. However, he did not talk and cuddled silently in his mother's arms.

Doctor Broderson kept a close eye on both mother and child. He was prepared to sedate them again, to prevent them from falling into emotional shock.

"Mr. Peña," said Broderson. "I am keeping a very close eye on your family for any subtle signs of shock. We need to be extremely vigilant for this. In particular, I am worried about your son. He has not uttered a sound since waking up fully. I am hoping, praying really, that he does not suddenly experience an outburst of emotion, sending him into a psycho-traumatic spiral."

"I appreciate you very much doctor," replied Augustus. "I am confident you will do what is necessary for their recovery. I must tell you, though, that you will be responsible for their care with no more input from me."

"What do you mean?"

"I must leave, and I must do so at once. I will spend some time with them now, while everyone settles in. However, my presence will endanger them further, and that is something I cannot allow to happen."

"May I suggest that you break this news to your family as gently as possible? Doing otherwise has the potential for creating the requisite amount of stress needed for a total meltdown," said Broderson.

"Should I not tell them at all, doctor, and leave?"

"That is an option. However, if you perish, not having a final moment with you would be disastrous. I would tell them, gently, and then leave quietly."

Augustus reflected on the advice and then went inside to be with his family.

ବ୍ଧବ୍ଧବ୍ଧ

"How are you feeling?" He asked Jennifer.

Lying down in the master bedroom, with Nathaniel's head snuggled into her shoulder, she replied – "I am in pain, Augustus, but determined to get healed. Our boy needs us, both of us."

"Yes…yes he does. But, you know, I have to –"

"Stop," said Jennifer. "I know you need to leave. I would ask you to, if you did not. I love you, but we need this to stop. You are the only one who can figure out how to do that, but you cannot do it from here."

Augustus was never more proud to have Jennifer as his wife than at this moment. He looked at Nathaniel and touched his head. "Should I?"

"I will tell him that you are going to work…that would be best I think," she replied.

Augustus nodded in affirmation. He kissed Nathaniel softly on his head and then Jennifer on her lips – "I adore you, Jennifer. I will make this stop." Augustus rose and exited the bedroom.

ବ୍ଧବ୍ଧବ୍ଧ

Outside, Cal was on the phone with Marshal Hicks, discussing details of the BOPS operation. "Copy that, sir. I will be at those coordinates in thirty." Cal saw Augustus emerge from the house and said – "BOPS is air-dropping the first round of supplies we will need for our operation…cash, medicine, weapons, food…you name it. The coordinates for the drop point are thirty minutes away. The BOPS advance team will remain here to secure the perimeter. I can use a hand out there if you are up to it."

"I will go help you load the supplies onto the truck, but I will not return with you."

Cal's inclination was to protest his decision to leave so quickly. However, he could tell from the look on Augustus' face that it was a done deal. "I understand, amigo…I understand."

❮❮❮

The supply drop occurred on time, with no fanfare or drama. Most importantly, it was incident-free. The two friends loaded the truck with supplies. They then leaned against the vehicle to speak with each other before parting ways.

"Where to now?" asked Cal.

"I have some thoughts, but I can't say for sure."

"I don't suppose you will call or write?" Cal said, attempting to inject some levity.

"Maybe by carrier-pigeon, but you know, I cannot be depended on for a long-distance relationship," replied Augustus.

"You take care of yourself, amigo. I wish it didn't have to be this way, but –"

Augustus spoke over him. "But we both know this is what must happen right now." The comrades gave each other a firm handshake and Augustus said – "Hermano…how about a ride?"

Cal laughed and said – "Where to?"

"We passed a truck stop on the way here. I will start my journey from there."

"Hop on!" said Cal.

⌘⌘⌘

FOURTEEN

Cal dropped Augustus off just shy of the rest area. Holding onto the passenger door, as he prepared to close it, he said – "You do what needs to be done to protect my family. I will locate you when I am through." He then winked at Cal and shut the door.

Augustus walked away unhurriedly so as not to attract attention. He needed to identify a truck heading north; ideally, one going somewhere into Central Iowa. Unable to discern any of their destinations, he took a more direct approach.

He entered the diner, where many of the truckers were eating. Augustus went to the lunch counter and ordered a coffee. He then grabbed a food menu and said to the server – "I want a fritter."

"We have pork or chicken. Which one would you like?"

"I don't know," answered Augustus, injecting a slight Spanish accent into his voice.

"Well, what do you like to eat?"

Augustus answered – "I eat everything…but I do not know what is good here."

The server asked – "Where are you from?"

"Um, well, I am from a place that is far," he replied, attempting to come off as meek.

"Alright, look, I don't care where you are from. All I need to know is what you want to eat."

"I think that I will try the pig," said Augustus.

"The pig?" replied the server, flabbergasted. "You mean pork. I will get that right up to you in a few, just be mindful about how you refer to your food. Folks around here tend to take their meat very serious."

"Is there a difference?" pressed Augustus.

"Why hell yes there is!" shouted an elderly trucker from the rear of the diner. "I don't know where the hell you are from but out here it is either raised in Iowa or put together in Texas. It makes a world of difference let me tell you."

"Which one is this?" Augustus asked, pointing to the menu.

"I don't know where the devil that stuff comes from," replied the trucker. "But my truck is filled with Iowa pork!"

Augustus smiled. "I wanted to go to Iowa, but I no longer have a way to get there."

"How did you wind up in this joint?" asked the trucker.

"It was a terrible thing that happened to me, señor. I asked for a ride to Iowa from a man in a truck…and I paid him money. But, the man told me that he changed his mind and threw me out of his truck not far from here."

"That is just horrible," said the trucker. "I'll tell you what. I have a load of hogs on my rig that needs delivering to a slaughterhouse twelve miles from here. If you are fine with a little more delay in your travels, I can take you with me to the delivery and then get you up into Iowa. I am headed to a town named Cumming that's just south of Des Moines for another pickup."

"Bless you, señor. Yes, thank you very much," replied Augustus, sipping on his coffee.

ॐॐॐ

The trucker delivered the hogs and then hit the road, with Augustus on board, to Iowa. "You know, if you want to make some money, I can arrange it so that you are paid for helping me on these runs," said the trucker.

"Thank you," replied Augustus. "I am grateful for your kindness and generosity. However, I must decline. I have plenty of work waiting for me at the end of my travels."

"Well, suit yourself I suppose. Just let me know if you change your mind."

The trucker navigated his semi towards his destination. They agreed on a drop off point located fifteen miles south of the capitol complex area. When they arrived, Augustus thanked the driver, jumped off the rig and trotted into a busy travel plaza.

Just beyond the horizon, Augustus could see the towering presence of the city's tallest commercial building. The view caused him to pause and he whispered – "I am back home."

ॐॐॐ

A caravan of federal vehicles lined the tarmac. Milken scanned the vastness of the Des Moines airport as he disembarked the plane. He felt pleased by the lack of a media presence. *They are doing a fine job at keeping this suppressed,* thought Milken, as he and Mauricio entered the SUV waiting for them at the bottom of the stairs.

The agent driving the SUV did not introduce himself. "I take it you are not SAC Eggert," queried Milken.

"No, sir. I am taking you to meet him now. He is at the hospital."

They arrived at the emergency room entrance. The driver pointed out SAC Eggert to them. Milken went and introduced himself. Then, referring to Mauricio, he said – "This is one of our agency's foreign-service agents."

Mauricio jumped in – "Oui, monsieur…my name is Francois di Laureat…and…I am French." His attempt at humor boiled Milken's blood.

"Uh…yeah…that's great…great to meet you too," replied Eggert. "Say, let's get into an office so that I can brief you further on what we have."

☙☙☙

"What is the status of the trooper?" Milken asked.

"He is still pretty banged up, but he's a tough old dog, so he'll come through just fine."

"To be honest, SAC Eggert, I expected for us to meet at the special location we spoke of earlier," said Milken.

Eggert replied – "Me too. Yeah, I figured you would wonder why we are meeting here. Shortly before you landed, we breached the domed structure inside of the tunnel. The State official I told you about called again from China. He provided us with some interesting details about the place. Anyway, that is for a different conversation. Nevertheless, he gave us access codes and a description of the layout. We went in and it was as quiet as a church on Thursday morning. We searched the complex and boy did we get a surprise, we found yet another victim."

Milken was perplexed and asked – "Another dead person?"

Eggert replied – "Well, hell, that's what we all thought. But, as it turns out, the person was not dead…the guy was knocked out cold."

"It seems like Augustus has a thing for knocking people out if he decides not to kill them," opined Milken.

"Here's the thing, though," said Eggert. "He was not physically knocked out…like the trooper. No, this guy was medically sedated, and heavily."

"How do you know that?"

"It didn't take much investigative work," replied Eggert. "The syringe was right beside him. Whatever he took put him down hard, almost instantaneously. It looks like he barely had a chance to remove the needle after sticking himself. That is why we are here. The man is in ICU. The docs are trying to determine if he sustained any injuries. They are also trying to wake him."

"Have you identified this man?"

"His name is Chad Molander. He is the deputy director for Iowa's Safety and Intelligence Bureau …Augustus Peña's right hand man."

Milken meditated upon this information – *He sedated himself because he knew too much to remain conscious when the authorities arrived. This could very well be a problem for me. I am certain that he injected himself with the drugs at Augustus' request. That means they trust each other. I will have to kill him.*

Milken spoke quickly to further his assault on Augustus' character – "I am not convinced that the deputy director injected himself. Who is to say that Augustus did not try to kill the man by injecting him with a lethal dose of drugs just as he departed? I mean, given everything we have seen thus far…he is most certainly capable of doing so."

"That is definitely a possibility. We won't know for sure until he awakens," replied Eggert. "Earlier reports from the hospital indicate that a doctor was with them when Augustus and his family were evacuated. Maybe, that is how he was able to put together such a concoction."

"I would really like to be by his side when he wakes up," said Milken.

"Not a problem. Do you want to interview the trooper first? He's awake."

"I will spend some time with that trooper after I get what I need from the deputy director," replied Milken. "But, thank you. Oh, one more thing SAC Eggert, my deceased agents…have their bodies been…processed?"

"Yes sir. Both bodies are at the State Medical Examiner's Office. Oh, which reminds me…follow me." He led them out to his car, parked by the entrance doors. "They're with me," he said, to the three agents standing watch out front. SAC Eggert opened his car's trunk and pulled out a metallic briefcase. He opened it and gave the contents to Milken.

"These are your agents' credentials and personal effects. Their weapons are with their bodies at the SME's. I figured, given all we learned about how these agents came to be using our agency's credentials, that no other eyes needed to see these."

Milken took the bluish evidence bags, smiled at him and said – "That was an extremely thoughtful play on your part, SAC Eggert." He then handed the bags to Mauricio. "SAC Eggert, in the interest of full disclosure, I want to inform you that we will be retrieving the remains of our fallen comrades…regardless of whether the SME has completed their analysis."

Eggert replied – "That is not in my jurisdiction and I don't need to know. Nonetheless, thank you for giving me a heads up."

"Just one more thing, SAC Eggert," said Milken. "We require a vehicle, if you have one at your disposal. I did not requisition one for this trip."

"Absolutely, will an SUV work?"

Milken looked at Mauricio, then back at Eggert and said – "I think the bigger the better. Yes, that most certainly does."

"You gentlemen go grab a seat in the office. I'll make the arrangements for your vehicle."

Mauricio looked at the two bags in his hands and said to Eggert –"In France, if we give you a package, we give you the box as well so that you may carry it comfortably."

"Oh shit, what was I thinking," said Eggert, sheepishly. "Here, take the briefcase too…there's nothing else inside of it."

Milken feigned a chuckle and thanked him. Eggert departed to arrange for their vehicle while Mauricio and Milken walked to the office.

෩෩෩

Augustus entered the travel center to use the restroom. Adjacent to the stalls were pay-as-you-use showers, commonly utilized by interstate travelers. One of the showers was in use. Augustus observed that the person in the shower left their wallet in the back pocket of their blue jeans. The pants hung on a hook by a towel. Augustus needed cash. He was about to lift the wallet when he saw a partially opened envelope in the other pocket. It appeared to have money in it. He slowly removed the envelope and saw the handwritten marking – XYZ Co. spending cash. Augustus could not believe his luck. He tucked the envelope under his pants and exited the restroom.

On his way out, he heard a televised newscast from within the dining area. He went to check it out –

"Well, John, we don't always report on tragedies here at the news desk. This next story is a wonderful and exciting one. The State Lottery Commission has confirmed that the winning Hot Ticket from this weekends' drawing was sold right here in Iowa. The jackpot, if you recall, was a whopping $16.5 million dollars. Nobody has come forward to claim the prize just yet, so check your tickets to see if you are the winner!"

"Yes, Cheryl, this is much better news than the other major event we've been reporting on lately, and is the subject of our next story."

"Absolutely John, and what a tragedy this was indeed. State officials are keeping tight-lipped on the whereabouts of Director Augustus Peña and his family, after a series of attempts on their lives ended with heartbreak and bloodshed."

"It's like something straight out of a movie Cheryl. Our own Dawn Chamberlain is on the case with her live update. Dawn, what have we found out so far?"

"Well, John, as you just reported officials are not sharing details regarding the whereabouts of the Peña family. Nor are they commenting on these brutal attacks, other than to say that there is no threat to the public. State investigators are confident that these attacks specifically targeted the director and his family, albeit for unknown reasons. Back to you in the studio John…"

Augustus put on his sunglasses, exited the convenience store and walked towards downtown Des Moines. Getting there posed no problem for him. He knew this area well, from riding bicycle. Augustus strolled to a trailhead and stepped onto the tree-lined, paved path. The bike trail reduced the traveling distance to the downtown area significantly. He surmised he would arrive at his destination in about ninety minutes. Augustus was fine with this. It was the safest method for him to approach. Moreover, it allowed him to clear his head and gather his thoughts.

I have to assume that the Station has been discovered by now and that Chad has been found, he thought. *I will go to City Hospital to see if I can confirm this and, if possible, locate him.* City Hospital was not the only hospital in Des Moines. However, he deduced that Chad would wind up there since they had already been involved with this tragedy. *The newscast made no mention of the Station or Chad,* reflected Augustus. *Why is that? A reporter would salivate over that kind of story.* Augustus pondered on it some more and then said aloud – "Unless, of course, Milken has already asserted himself."

Augustus was convinced that Milken, or at least NICO management, had infiltrated the local level. He needed to strategize his method of insertion into the hospital. If his supposition held true, then he should expect a heavily guarded atmosphere. He looked at his watch and picked up his pace.

ஒஒஒ

Mauricio and Milken sat across from one another in the office.

Milken said - "Pass me those bags, will you?"

Mauricio removed the bags from the briefcase and put them on the table. Milken grabbed and tore them open, retrieving the dead agents' credentials.

"They won't need these anymore," said Milken, checking the credentials for completeness. After putting them into his suit jacket, he proceeded to slide the bags over to Mauricio.

"What am I to do with these?"

"You are a plunderer and pillager by nature. That is what you XM boys do, correct? Consider it booty…the spoils of your efforts."

Mauricio grinned, and looked inside of the bags, like a child inspecting their haul of trick-or-treat goodies. He did not remove any items. However, he was able to make out cash, jewelry, wallets and cell phones. Although seemingly a barbaric man, Mauricio was acutely aware of how the world of espionage worked. Consequently, upon seeing the devices he asked – "Are these special phones?"

"Hmm," said Milken. "I thought they would have remained with the weapons, being tools and all." He reached his hand out across the table and said – "I'll take those." Mauricio slid the phones over to him. Milken opened the back of one of them. He removed its SIM card, as well as another microchip-like item. He then replaced them with a fresh set that he took out of his front suit pocket.

"I never leave home without a few extra sets of these," he said lightheartedly, as he put the chips in and closed the back of the phone. He then slid it back to Mauricio saying – "Here you go, a brand new phone, for emergencies of course. Just dial seven, six and it will patch right into me."

"Maybe I get bored and do the phone sex with this, yeah?" clowned Mauricio, with a shit eating grin on his face.

Milken sat up straight saying – "You can have all the phone sex you want Frenchy, but make no mistake about it, I am not to be toyed with."

Mauricio conferred a dismissive look towards him in response.

Milken did not let the trivializing expression throw him off and said – "Now, when that fucking agent returns with that SUV, you are going to pay a visit to Augustus' old pals and put their lights out. Here is the address for one of them and here are their names. The second asshole apparently moved out just days ago. We do not have good address information for him. I'm sure you'll find a way to get it."

Mauricio took the paper and studied the names.

"This needs to be done ASAP and you need to get your ass out of here quicker than a French whore's period, do you understand me monsieur?"

"Oui," replied Mauricio. "What are the plans for my departure from here?"

"As I understand it, you possess a device that is exclusively used for communicating with your handlers in Belize, is that correct?"

"Oui, I do."

"They will be in contact with you shortly…to provide you those details." Milken glanced out the office window to the waiting area beyond. He saw an image on the television screen that grabbed his attention. He stepped out of the office to investigate –

"…that's right Chet. The reports we are receiving are that this was a NOAA satellite launched sometime in 2009. The satellite assisted in that agency's efforts at monitoring the movements of various aquatic species tagged with tracking devices. NOAA officials are telling the American News Bureau that they lost contact with the satellite last week. They discovered its downward trajectory towards earth late last night and contacted the military for emergency assistance. The Navy has scrambled its Seventh Fleet to this location to help with the satellite's recovery. Luckily, as with most of these types of incidents, the junk just plunged right into the ocean posing no threat to humans."

"Great reporting, Heidi, thank you."

Milken returned to the office mumbling quietly – "That took a little longer to accomplish than what I had expected but…all is well that ends well I suppose."

ॐॐॐ

SAC Eggert returned to the office with keys in his hands. He handed them to Milken saying – "She is all fueled up and ready for action…parked right out front."

"Excellent work SAC Eggert. Thank you for your hospitality. It has been exceptional, especially given agencies' reluctance to assist one another."

The two of them laughed while Mauricio looked at his watch, muttering something under his breath in French.

"My colleague will be taking the vehicle to conduct some intelligence gathering while I go await the deputy director's recovery." Milken then said – "Um, Francois, you do realize that we drive on the right-hand side of the road, do you not?"

Eggert laughed hard saying – "Awe shit, do I need to go get him a crash helmet?"

Mauricio produced the phoniest smile he could conjure. He took the keys from Milken, grabbed the briefcase and left.

ﺛﻌﺛﻌﺛﻌ

Augustus reached the downtown area. To get to the hospital, he had to walk several city streets. This exposure made him feel uncomfortable. He had an idea. He would use his physical appearance as a natural camouflage. He needed to gain entry to the hospital. To do so, he had to blend in and not appear as a threat.

During his time in Iowa, Augustus often found himself overcoming stereotypes about his cultural heritage. Iowa was primarily an agricultural state. Many of the workers in that industry hailed from Central America. Augustus continually corrected locals that he was of Puerto Rican descent, not Central American. Their response was usually the same – what is the difference? "American at birth, just like you," would be his answer.

This was not particularly troubling to him. He understood that this region of the country was not a popular destination for Puerto Ricans living on the mainland. However, recent political discourse on immigration caused many people to react dismissively towards those that either were, or appeared to be, of Hispanic heritage. The perception was they were in this country illegally and that they did not belong here, causing them to be scorned and ignored.

Augustus would play on these sentiments and use them to his advantage. He needed some clothing that would make him appear stereotypical…one of them. This would allow him to gain deeper access within the hospital. Ignorance is never a good thing. However, in this instance, it was going to assist in saving his family from slaughter.

ﺛﻌﺛﻌﺛﻌ

There was an interstate bus depot two blocks from the hospital. Augustus went in seeking a janitor closet. He needed to acquire work clothes. Anything would do, it did not matter. The clothing he wore looked too professional. He searched high and low, but was unsuccessful. Augustus needed a moment to think. He was certain there would be a closet with something in it he could throw on.

He sat on a bench beside him. He could see the hospital through the depot's large glass window. He became tempted to walk right up there to see what happened. Suddenly, he observed a man wearing a traditional mechanic uniform walk through the terminal. The man was almost twice his size. Nevertheless, it was something he was willing to work with.

Augustus pulled out the envelope with the travel money. *This guy must have been driving to Panama,* he thought. It was the first time he looked inside the envelope. "There is well over two thousand dollars in here," he whispered. August felt terrible for stealing the money. He knew that losing this amount of cash would cause the person their job. However, he could not focus on that right now. He needed to move forward. He pulled out a one hundred dollar bill and approached the man.

"Sir, I would very much appreciate it if you would sell me your clothing."

"Come again?"

"Your clothing, I need it. Would one hundred dollars be enough for you to part ways with it?" asked Augustus.

"You ain't trying to get frisky with me, are you son?"

Augustus said –"Please, sir. I cannot really explain it to you other than to say that, well, look at me. I need to go to a place where people don't dress the way I do."

"What you into I wonder?"

"Okay…two hundred dollars," said Augustus.

"Deal," replied the man. "Come on back to the garage with me. I will even give you a clean set of clothing. I work on the buses when they come in to make sure they are in good condition for their next trip."

Son of a bitch, thought Augustus, as the man led him to the depot's rear.

Minutes later, Augustus donned a good old-fashioned mechanic jumpsuit, with boots to match. He then walked up the steep hill to the hospital.

⁕⁕⁕

As he suspected, the hospital had heavy security. Augustus needed to think quickly. Every step placed him closer to the agents standing watch by the entrance.

A woman exited the hospital. She walked by Augustus. He started talking very rapidly to her in Spanish so as not to be understood – "Señora, adonde se puede encontrar la sala de maternidad?"

Unsurprisingly, the woman did not speak Spanish. He then motioned in front of his belly saying – "Bebe."

"Oh, baby! You are looking for the maternity ward. I'm sorry, I didn't make out what you were saying," said the woman. She then pointed to some doors. They were slightly away from the main entrance, where most of the agents gathered.

Augustus nodded and said – "Gracias…gracias." The agents barely paid attention to him. A non-English speaking immigrant, coming to check on a birthing mother, did not concern them.

He went through the set of doors the woman directed him to. Once inside, he snuck along the corridor, towards the posted agents. He came across a set of elevators. He prepared to jump inside one of them, to randomly exit and find a smock-room to change clothing again.

Augustus froze in his tracks. He saw a familiar physique down the hall. Three men had just exited a room. Augustus did not recognize two of them, but the third one set alarm bells off in his head. The man's build, his gait, and the way he carried himself, was distinctive of only one man Augustus had ever known…C. Virgil Milken.

⁕⁕⁕

Milken shook hands with Mauricio as they left the room saying – "All kidding aside, contact me immediately with any information." He winked at Mauricio, who then promptly left the hospital.

Milken turned to leave with Eggert when he caught some movement out the corner of his eye. He snapped his head toward the direction from which it emanated…but saw nothing. He did not come to his position in NICO by happenstance. He was an adept field operative, very much dialed in to the conditions around him. Most importantly, he learned to rely heavily on his highly evolved intuition.

"SAC Eggert, is this entire facility under guard?"

"We have agents stationed throughout the hospital. They are primarily local assets, drawn from federal agencies with a presence in this state. However, since we are contending with needing to keep this away from the media, it is not a show of force. Meaning, we are not staggered throughout the hospital at set intervals or checkpoints. Why do you ask?"

"Just a gut feeling," replied Milken. "Have your men check all ID's as well as stepping up their game a bit. I think we might have a fox in the hen house."

"Absolutely, sir," said Eggert. "I trust your judgment. Let me take you to the deputy director's recovery room while I make the call."

Eggert led him to Molander's recovery room as he issued orders over the radio consistent with Milken's suggestions.

࿐࿐࿐

Mauricio entered the SUV and leaned forward to access the dashboard mapping system. He input the street address Milken gave him and waited for directions. He then opened the briefcase, removed the bags and made a full accounting of his bounty.

"Ah…two nice watches," he said, holding up the dead agents' timepieces. He also pulled out one gold chain, two leather wallets, three gold rings, one of them diamond encrusted, and a large amount of cash. "This is not a bad taking," he whispered.

He returned the items to their respective bags and tossed them back into the briefcase. A piece of paper sailed out of one of them, onto the floor. It did not resemble money. Mauricio dismissed its importance but then decided against it. He figured it could contain a clue or some written instruction from Milken.

"Merde," he said as he uncomfortably reached under the passenger seat and retrieved it. He then sat back up to inspect it.

The mapping system spoke – "Directions…turn right onto…"

Mauricio said – "Oh, such a sexy voice. That is nice." He then put the piece of paper into his jacket without looking at it.

❧❧❧

Mauricio followed the directions as they were called out and said – "Okay, monsieur Billy Carter, let us see what you are doing for fun tonight." He arrived at the address within twenty-five minutes. A vehicle pulled out of the driveway. Mauricio drove past the house. He glanced at the driver to see if it matched the photo Milken gave him. It did. Mauricio kept watch in his rearview mirror, to see which direction the vehicle headed. He then maneuvered a U-turn and pursued.

He followed the car for almost five miles. It pulled into a strip mall. Mauricio suspected Billy would make one of these businesses his final destination, so he parked to observe from afar. The unsuspecting Carter got out of his car and entered an establishment. Mauricio sped to a parking spot much closer to it.

He got out, coolly walked to the entrance, and looked up reading its name aloud – "Bobby's Claddagh."

Mauricio entered the Irish pub and looked around. To the right were leather couches, inside of a spacious and slightly elevated room. To the left was the main dining area. Directly in front of him was a semi-circular bar. Only one bartender was working from what Mauricio could gather. The chairs that lined the bar were wood-framed and of good quality. Several patrons filled the pub, but no sign of Billy. Unable to locate him, Mauricio moved towards a sign for the patio. Suddenly, from somewhere behind him, a conversation ensued that caught his attention.

"Hey, Reggie…what's going on?"

"Hey Billy, long time no see," replied the bartender, apparently named Reggie.

"Yeah, it has been like, what, eighteen hours or something like that?" He and Reggie laughed loudly. Billy took a seat along the bar, his back facing Mauricio, and ordered a drink.

Mauricio shifted course and returned to the bar. He sat down two seats to the left of Billy. "Vinu," he said to Reggie.

"I'm sorry…what was that buddy?"

"Ah, excuse me, wine please," replied Mauricio. "Red wine…"

"Yeah, no problem, we've got it all here pal," said Reggie. "Any particular type? We've got California, some local stuff and a couple of Europeans…even have one from Argentina, if you can believe that."

Slightly annoyed by the bartender's joyful and talkative nature, Mauricio waved his hand dismissively saying – "It does not matter, really. An Argentinian will do."

"One Argentine red coming right up."

Mauricio glanced to his right. He looked at his prey, assessing his character, determining the best method for luring him in.

"Here's your wine, pal. Do you want to pay cash for the one or do you want to have a couple and start a tab?" queried Reggie, appearing with the libation.

"I will pay cash," said Mauricio. He handed Reggie a fifty-dollar bill, compliments of the recently deceased agents. Again, he glanced at Billy. The bartender returned.

"So…you from around here pal? I don't think I've seen you in here before."

"Mère de Dieu cet homme de ne pas arrêter de parler," he said, under his breath, frustrated about the bartender's constant chatter. "I am from Quebec."

"Oh, that's great. You must be here with one of the large insurance companies, right?"

"Yes, that is correct. I am here with the insurance companies."

"Oh, cool, which one are you with?"

Mauricio could not contain his anger and said – "I am with the one called 'I cannot sit down and enjoy my drink because the talkative servant will not shut his snout'…that one monsieur." He took a final glance at Billy, who was paying absolutely no attention to him, and slugged his wine.

As he left the pub, Reggie said – "Hey pal…I apologize…hopefully you'll come back. I promise I won't talk your ear off next time!"

&&&

Mauricio lit a cigarette to ponder his next steps. As he smoked, he observed the pub's patio. He wandered over to take a gander. It was nothing special…chairs, tables and a grill but it had a large television. It was on and a woman was talking. Mauricio thought she was very pretty, so he puffed on his cigarette and watched her speak.

She was a local newswoman and spoke of matters that he did not understand. She referred to a ticket, displayed on a picture in the backdrop of the screen. "This is odd," Mauricio said aloud. "What is the significance of that paper?" He moved in closer. He saw some words along the bottom of the screen. He could read English fairly well. The crawler said $16.5 million dollar winning ticket sold in Iowa. He then looked at the photo in the backdrop and read the name of the paper – Hot Ticket.

Mauricio finished his cigarette. He chuckled at the thought of someone winning such a large amount of money for doing no work. He thought nothing more of the newscast and returned to his car.

Mauricio started the engine, wondering whether he should return to Billy's home to wait for him, or try locating the other person. He had stuffed the paper Milken gave him in his jacket after mapping Billy's address. He reached for it to reference the other name. As he pulled it out, the other piece of paper glided onto his lap. It then slid off and fell onto the floor by his feet.

"What is with this blasted paper?" shouted Mauricio.

He exited the SUV, reached back inside and retrieved it from the floor mat. It was white with small red lettering. It looked official. Mauricio saw no messages on that side of the paper, so he turned it over. The other side had numbers displayed across it. Again, there were no notes. Mauricio tossed the paper. As it sailed away, he caught a glimpse of the typeface. Intrigued, he picked it back up. Towards the top of the side with the numbers on it, in bold black lettering, were the words – Hot Ticket.

He instantly associated these words with what he saw on television. He hurried back, hoping the newswoman was still talking about it…but she was gone. Something entirely different was playing.

"Merde," he said. "Could it be that this is a billet de loterie worth millions of American dollars? No, this is impossible. How could I have come across such a treasure?" He returned to the SUV. "This cannot be the billet she spoke of. I will go to the man's house and wait for him." Mauricio accessed the mapping system for the directions back to Billy's home.

࿇࿇࿇

Halfway through the drive he felt a pang of hunger. He did not know when Billy would return home or if he had items worth eating. Consequently, he pulled into a parking lot and entered a large grocery store to buy some food. He grabbed a handheld shopping basket and made his way to the produce area. After picking a few items, he went to the register and paid for them.

A sign on the customer service counter by the exit caught his attention. The sign read – check your lottery tickets here to see if you are a winner. Mauricio reached into his jacket and pulled out the ticket. He inspected both sides of it and walked over to the sign. Next to it was a red electronic device. It had an arrow with the words scan here below it.

Confused, he asked the manager behind the counter – "What do you do here?"

The manager pointed to the edge of the apparatus saying – "You scan the barcode there."

Mauricio showed the man the lottery ticket, shrugging his shoulders, indicating he did not understand. The manager reached out and Mauricio handed him the ticket. The manager pointed to two black squares located at the bottom of the ticket. He then pointed to the edge of the apparatus.

"I would scan it for you but I'm not allowed to."

Mauricio took the ticket from him. He glanced at it once more and placed the two black squares into a red beam of light. His first attempt was unsuccessful. A message appeared on the LED screen

– Unable to read. Please scan ticket again. Ah, this is such a waste of my time, thought Mauricio. Nevertheless, he scanned it again.

Instantaneously, an extremely loud and annoying voice shrieked from the devices' speakers saying – "YOU ARE A LOTTERY JACKPOT WINNER, CONGRATULATIONS!"

Mauricio bounded backwards with trepidation. The screaming box had lights on it that were now flashing. Mauricio looked up and saw a camera hanging from the ceiling, pointing right at him. The manager had a look of amazement. Mauricio noticed that people began heading towards him, with curiosity in their eyes.

"Oh…no!" shouted Mauricio, realizing what just happened. He then bolted out the grocery store with his purchases and a $16.5 million jackpot lottery ticket in hand.

ले ले ले

Augustus dove from Milken's line of sight not a moment too soon. He jumped into an open elevator and hit the button for it to close. *I wonder if he saw me,* thought Augustus. He assumed that Milken identified him. He randomly selected the fifth floor and exited the elevator.

He tiptoed slowly along the wall, listening for overhead announcements of a security breach. He heard nothing. Augustus came upon a small, empty visitor area and sat down. The personnel on the floor seemed to be moving about business as usual. *Maybe they decided to communicate amongst themselves and not make an announcement through the PA system.*

"Milken is going to kill Chad," whispered Augustus. "I have to find a way to thwart him." Anxiety swelled within him as he apprehended the risks of exposing himself in order to save Chad. *I could be killed,* he thought. If that happened, then nothing could stop the manic pursuit of his family. Yes, they were in the elusive BOPS program. Regardless, Milken and his minions would continue the chase until they eventually found them. Augustus had to choose between his family and a man, a boy in some respects really, that he handpicked for the position he held. Chad was the son of an extremely proud family. They had every right to be. Could he really allow the slaughter of Chad to occur for the sake of not taking the ultimate risk?

Augustus thought of young Nathaniel and of how beautiful and innocent he was. *What if, someday, he smilingly trusted, honored and showed loyalty to someone? Then, what if that person decided it was too hazardous for them to stop someone from murdering him?* The mere thought of this scenario crushed Augustus. It was so incredibly disturbing to him that he stood and went towards the nurse's station without an ounce of caution.

☙☙☙

Mauricio could not recall the last time he ran so fast. His breathing was heavy and rapid. He started the SUV's engine and peeled out the parking lot, screeching its tires. He drove randomly. He did not know the West Des Moines community where Augustus and his friends lived. He came across a district with several restaurants, and pulled in. Mauricio shut off the engine.

He sat motionless, weighing everything that just happened. He looked at the ticket again, shaking his head in disbelief. *Comment est-ce possible?* thought Mauricio, questioning how this could be possible. He finally accepted the reality that he had in his possession a ticket worth millions of US dollars.

However, he was now haunted with a complex issue. What was he to do with the ticket? Mauricio mulled it over – *Do I contact XM and tell them what I have in my possession? Do I disappear, say nothing to no one and return in the future to claim the money? Do I continue with this job for the client? This ticket is worth much more than the value of completing this operation.* In addition to these high-concept questions, Mauricio meditated upon more substantive issues – *How does one obtain the money for something like this? Where would I need to go? Do I have to reveal myself?* Mauricio then remembered the camera from when he checked the ticket and said – "They know my face."

This distressed Mauricio and he cursed – "Merde, I must notify XM at once."

He grabbed his communication device and punched in a code denoting an emergency. Afterwards, he sat back and took a deep breath. He looked out the window and observed the West Des Moines traffic along this major avenue. *It is pretty here,* thought Mauricio. *It is a much bigger place than what I expected.*

Mauricio heard an unfamiliar sound. He recalled Milken giving him a phone. He pulled it from its belt clip and watched it ring. "I am not going to talk to this man until I hear from XM." He then tossed the phone onto the passenger seat and resumed looking out the window…RING…RING…RING…RING…

જ્ર જ્ર જ્ર

Augustus hopped over the counter, stunning the nurse on duty. "I need to speak with hospital security. There is going to be a murder."

"What? What are you talking about? You can't be back here, get away!" shouted the nurse.

"The PA system, the one you use to page doctors. Access it now," demanded Augustus, shouting into her face. "I am Augustus Peña. My family and I lived through savage attacks some days ago. Now, the same people who attacked us are here, at this very moment, to kill my deputy director who is God knows where in this building!"

Augustus was lucid but he appeared manic, causing disbelief in his claims. A staff member several feet away from them called over his radiophone – "We have a 10-96 in progress. Fifth floor nurse's station…guy claims to be Augustus Peña but…yeah, no. Get a crew up here before someone gets hurt."

"Good," shouted Augustus, recognizing the official code the staffer used. It identified him as a mental subject. He continued ranting – "Was that security? Did you contact security? Good!" Augustus pushed the nurse aside. He cleared all of the items from her desk with his arm. They went crashing onto the floor. He examined the dials on her console and saw what he was looking for. The button marked P/A was tiny, and tucked away, where the corners of the console met. Augustus spun around and shouted – "How do you use this…How do you use this!" The nurse shook her head, quietly saying "No." However, her eyes looked at the phone, now on the floor.

Augustus snatched it and hung up the receiver, resetting the connection. He inspected it and saw a taped label that read P/A = *79. Augustus reached for the P/A button on the console and clicked it on. He then dialed *79…just as SAC Eggert's men arrived at the nurse's station.

The three agents tried to tackle Augustus. He anticipated their impact and prepared, by doing what his Japanese sensei described as "grounding" his center of gravity. The men bounced off Augustus. The P/A system came alive throughout the hospital, evidenced by a high-pitch screech. The agents got up off the floor, with stunned looks on their faces, and proceeded to wrap their arms around Augustus. They attempted to move him away from the console while simultaneously trying to strip the phone from his hand. Augustus utilized his martial training to the best of his ability. He needed to get his message out before these goons turned off the P/A button on the console to silence him.

৵৵৵

"Milken, you are an NSA assassin! I know this because I have killed on your command. Milken, you are here to kill Deputy Director Chad Molander because you think I told him about you! Do not kill him…Don't you dare kill him, Milken!" The words blared over the hospital P/A system.

The announcement triggered an immediate reaction of gasps, screams and shouts as people ran in every direction. Bedlam ensued. Panic swept over the staff members who were on duty the day of the attacks. "There are going to be more killings!" shouted some of the staff. "Lock all of the patient doors!" shouted another.

"Jesus Christ," yelled one of the agents holding onto Augustus. "What the fuck have you done?" Another agent said – "Take this piece of shit down already." The men grunted as they used all of their might to flatten Augustus onto the floor. Again, he anticipated this extra thrust of power. Still on his knees, he used their momentum against them. One by one, the agents hurled into the air as Augustus grappled, twisted and snapped their limbs.

The agents screamed from both terror and pain. They crashed violently onto the equipment and furniture around them, showing no signs of wanting to get up. Augustus rose to his feet. The few staffers that remained to watch this play out screamed wildly and ran for safety. A crackling sound emitted from one of the mangled agents. Augustus looked down and saw a two-way radio clipped onto the man's belt. He took the radio and ran swiftly down the hallway, disappearing into the hospital's cold darkness…

かかか

Milken sat alone in Chad's recovery room when the P/A system erupted with Augustus' voice. He jumped out of his chair. He could see the hallway through the room's window and saw people running wildly. Milken was in the midst of mulling over the best time to take Chad's life when the melee began. He looked back at Chad in frustration. This public outburst from Augustus meant he could not kill him.

Milken sighed and said to Chad's catatonic body – "Augustus has only bought you some time young man. He has not saved your life."

SAC Eggert and two other agents came rushing through the door with their guns drawn. "What the hell is going on Milken?"

Milken eyeballed the agents and replied – "This is most certainly an awkward moment for me gentlemen. I know that your heads must be spinning. However, I can assure you, that I am not here to kill this man."

"I don't know what the hell to think," said Eggert. "But I do know this – you need to get out of this hospital ASAP. This guy is running around looking for you. He has already critically injured some of my agents."

Milken nodded and said – "I agree. My suggestion to you, SAC Eggert, is that you leave these two agents here to guard this young man. The last thing I need is for him to get killed by that madman while I receive the blame for it."

He agreed and ordered the two agents to remain with Chad. He then left to escort Milken to safety.

かかか

Eggert took the lead, continuously establishing that every turn was clear of danger before moving forward. The pair came to a stairwell. Eggert opened the door leading into it. He checked high and low for any sign of peril. The stairwell was clear. Eggert motioned for Milken to enter.

Milken complied and quickly made his way down the stairs. He noticed the lack of cameras.

"I need to clear the next landing," whispered Eggert.

Milken gave the thumbs up.

Eggert positioned himself in front of Milken to look down the next flight of steps.

Milken struck Eggert's head with a small rubber baton that he carried for close-quarters fighting. The SAC fell forward, plummeting down the steep stairwell. Milken strolled to him and picked up his gun. He then fired two shots into SAC Eggert's chest and head, killing him instantly. He dropped the gun and then drew his own weapon. After going down another flight, Milken shot his weapon several times up and behind him, as if shooting at a pursuer. He then ran all the way down and barreled out of the stairwell onto the ground floor.

With his gun in his hand, he shouted to the agents and law enforcement personnel present – "I just got into a firefight with Augustus Peña in the stairwell…I think he killed SAC Eggert!"

The men ran into the stairway in pursuit of a ghost. Milken drifted out the hospital. He was not concerned about leaving SAC Eggert's gun behind after shooting him with it. Anything remotely resembling a fingerprint vanished from his hands many years before. Consequently, he would be leaving no trace evidence behind that could point to him as the shooter. Hell, he did not even exist.

Milken took his phone out and placed a call to Mauricio as he walked down the quiet Iowa streets.

⌘⌘⌘

FINAL CHAPTER

Augustus escaped the hospital by exiting through an empty patient room window. He slid down an exposed beam to the level immediately below. He then traversed the rooftop that extended out from that level, making his way to a fire escape and climbing down to the ground below.

Once on solid footing, he contemplated his next move. *Chad will be safe for the time being. It was the best I could do given the circumstances.* Augustus knew that Milken would stop at nothing to break his will…to make him a weaker target. *He will go after my mother.*

He hypothesized that his mother was under state and/or federal protection. However, Milken had already exhibited his willingness to pursue his agenda right under their noses, and with impunity. This concerned Augustus greatly. His mother was seventy-three years young, and fearless. She had recently moved to Iowa from his hometown in Brooklyn, New York, after learning he would be settling down here to raise Nathaniel. With his father having passed years prior, Mama Peña was willing to explore life elsewhere outside the Big Apple.

There was no doubt in Augustus' mind that his mother was giving a world of shit to her protective detail. Calling to inform her of the heightened threat would be futile. She would undoubtedly dismiss it as something she was not going to worry about or be afraid of. Consequently, Augustus knew what he had to do and where he needed to be.

๛๛๛

Mauricio kept looking at his watch. He became increasingly agitated at XM's lack of response. To the contrary, Milken's phone practically rang off the hook. Although his instinct was to avoid talking to Milken until he heard from XM, he decided to pick up, to preserve his sanity.

"Yes?"

"Where the fuck you been?" shouted Milken. "This place has gone to hell in a hand basket."

Mauricio feigned an apologetic tone – "Oui monsieur…merci."

"Whatever numb nuts, now listen up good," Milken shouted. "I need for you to cease your current assignment and shift your gears to a top priority strike. Do you even understand what the hell it is I'm saying to you?"

"I understand perfectly, monsieur."

"Uh huh…" said Milken, unconvinced. He provided the strike details and said – "I don't give a shit how clean it is…just get it done and get your French ass out of there. Call me when it's over so that I know you are on your way back to…wherever the hell you're going."

Mauricio looked at the phone after the conversation ended and said – "I would like to kill this talker of shit if I had the time." He then drove to his next target after entering the address into the SUV's mapping system.

ন্তনন্ত

Augustus went several blocks, deep into the lower middle class neighborhood that abutted the hospital. He knew that reports of theft from this area did not elicit swift responses from the local police department. He searched for a vehicle to steal. He identified a late model car and put his skills to work. In a matter of minutes, he gained entry to the vehicle and hotwired the engine. He then cautiously drove to his mother's house, less than eight miles away.

ন্তনন্ত

Mauricio arrived in the target's neighborhood. He looked for a place to park after identifying the home. Milken informed him the target was under federal protection. He would have to kill many. Mauricio exited the SUV and strolled towards his objective. As he got closer to the house, he scanned for any evidence of the protective detail. There were no indications that such a detail existed. However, he observed movement by the main level's window. He gave thought to the effectiveness of a full frontal assault on the house, when his XM device sounded.

"What is your emergency?" asked the voice.

Mauricio explained the situation in full as he continued on his trek. He walked past the house and used the opportunity to observe its entry points.

"Abort all activities immediately," ordered the voice. "Remove yourself from the area of hostilities at once. Another communication regarding your extraction will be forthcoming in ten minutes."

Mauricio turned the next corner and speedily walked back to the SUV. He fought all temptations to break out into a full-blown sprint. Doing so might attract the attention of any lookouts posted in the area. He had no reason to get into a battle with them now.

෯෯෯

Augustus arrived near his mother's house. He slammed on the brakes when he saw a man that was with Milken at the hospital. He was several blocks away. Augustus put the vehicle into reverse and sped backwards around the corner. He got out of the car. Augustus crept forward to get a line of sight on him, via gaps provided by backyards and driveways. The man closed in on his mother's house.

My God, thought Augustus. *This animal is suicidal. He is going to go right through the front door.* He almost charged the man, in a desperate attempt at saving his mother's life. However, he stopped himself. He observed the man listening to something as he walked past his mother's house.

"He is aborting," said Augustus aloud. "And he is coming this way."

Augustus ran back to the idling car. He looked over his shoulder to confirm the man was still walking in his direction…and he was. Augustus drove the car in reverse to the next intersection and took off, all without screeching his tires.

Mauricio's blood pumped with excitement. He loved engaging in immediate extractions from foreign soil. He entered the SUV and started its engine. The XM device hummed. Mauricio touched it to activate its speaker.

A masked voice said – "The extraction point is Omaha, Nebraska. Emergency Services Personnel will meet you there. You are to arrive at that location via railway. A freight rail system goes through the center of your current city. Be certain to board the next westbound train passing through two hours from now…and have the valuable item with you."

The XM device fell silent. Mauricio was about to shift the SUV's gear into drive when he heard a sound from behind.

His instinct proved correct. Mauricio put both hands in front of his neck, in a defensive position. By doing so, he successfully shielded his throat from the fishing wire Augustus had just swung over his head.

"Thanks for the line," snarled Augustus, pulling back extremely hard.

Mauricio's legs kicked up in front of him as blood spurted from his hands.

"What valuable item?" Augustus demanded. Mauricio kept kicking. Augustus realized he was trying to boot the horn to attract attention. He growled even louder – "What valuable item?"

Mauricio did not answer. Instead, he managed to kick the horn several times.

The sound of the klaxon echoed down the street. Augustus knew this would attract the attention of the agents in his mother's house, if he did not put an end to this. Augustus kept a grip on the wire with one hand. He then pulled out his serrated tactical knife with the other and plunged it into Mauricio's ribcage.

Augustus let go of the wire. As he expected, Mauricio lowered his hands toward his wound and slumped forward.

"Thank you," said Augustus, as he drove the knife through the back of Mauricio's neck, severing his spine.

Mauricio jerked slightly and then perished. Augustus leaned towards him to search for the valuable item the voice referenced. He had no idea what the item looked like or what it could possibly be. He kept searching, while maintaining watch, making sure he had not attracted unwanted attention.

Augustus pulled every item he could find out of Mauricio's pockets. He placed them in the back seat next to him, taking great care not to get blood on them. He was unable to identify anything that had the potential for great value. *I must search this entire vehicle.* He shifted his weight to start searching the cab from the front. As he did so, he put his hand down on the seat next to him for support. An item shifted and fell. Augustus looked to see what it was. The item that fell did not interest him. However, the lottery ticket on the cushion seat did.

He sat down and picked up the ticket. "Why would a NICO operative, contractor or otherwise, have a lottery ticket?" It seemed to be remarkably out of place with the nature of a mercenary's job. Its presence on Mauricio's person confused him.

"Unless…nah…" whispered Augustus. "There is no goddamned way…" Augustus recalled hearing about the recent winning lottery ticket sold in Iowa while at the travel center.

He recognized this SUV as belonging to the feds. He also knew they were typically equipped with onboard computers and internet access. He looked around the cabin and found what he was looking for. It was located in a dropdown tray, behind the front passenger seat. Augustus scooted over to the computer and typed in the web address for the Iowa Lottery.

Augustus looked at the ticket to see which game it was for. "Hot Ticket," he read aloud. "Well, let's just see how hot you really are." He located the Hot Ticket section of the website and read the banner prominently displayed along the top of the page – Check your Hot Ticket numbers now. Winning jackpot ticket of $16.5 million sold here in Iowa…Good Luck.

He compared the numbers on the screen to the numbers of the ticket in his hand. One by one, they matched. He felt a warm rush go through his body when the fifth number matched. He took a deep breath and compared the sixth and final number.

"This is most certainly a valuable item," he whispered as he sank back into the chair, gathering his thoughts.

Augustus exited the SUV quickly thereafter, but stopped when he heard a phone ring. He had already taken the device from which Mauricio had received his instructions. He was curious about who else might be trying to contact him. Augustus climbed back into the SUV and saw the ringing telephone. He pressed the button to activate the call and a very familiar voice began to speak.

"Tell me that the job is done and that you are just too much of a fuckup to remember to call," shouted Milken.

Augustus replied – "It is hard to be a fuckup when you are dead. How does it feel to be the hunted one, Milken?"

Hearing Augustus' voice come over the phone that he provided to Mauricio unraveled Milken to no end. "NO, NO, THIS CANNOT BE, NO!"

Augustus ditched the phone on the dead mercenary's lap. He returned to his still idling car and drove slowly past his mother's house. Augustus longed to see his mom one last time, but knew it could not be. He spoke softly towards her home as he passed by, apologizing and telling her he loved her, in Spanish. "Madre mía. Yo te amo mucho. Mi corazón está roto por no poder decirle adíos. Díos te bendiga Mamá, te amo."

�����

Milken was walking away from the downtown area when he learned of Mauricio's fate. Panic, and the feeling of defeat, set in as the possibility of NICO's exposure loomed over him. Milken scanned the area around him. He stood in the middle of this grand avenue, twisting in the wind. Dizziness set in. The lives taken, the destruction leveled and the exposure risked…it was all seemingly for nothing. Milken knew he would have hell to pay from Gates when he returned to The Chamber. He acknowledged to himself that he deserved it. Irrespective, a truth now remained. This thing he set into motion could not be undone. Augustus Peña was now on the run…and on the hunt.

Milken continued to walk somberly and placed a call – "This is Milken…I need an extraction."

�����

Augustus did not personally know Mauricio. However, he fathomed that the man was associated with the ghost mercenary conglomerate known as XM Investments. He did not need to know the particulars of the deal they had with NICO. He already knew something much more powerful than that. XM Investments called off their mercenary for something of great value to them…something that he now possessed.

XM chose fortune over service to their client. Their choice showed their weakness…greed. *I shall use their predilections to hunt them down.*

Close to two hours later, Augustus boarded the Omaha bound freight train on a journey into the unknown. Armed with a determination to strike with furious vengeance against those who attacked his exquisite family, he looked in his hand. He read the numbers aloud and realized that this was a winner, not for wealth, but for retribution. Augustus folded what had now become a Ticket of Death and placed it into his pocket. He then receded into the shadows of the train car until the time came for him to re-emerge…

About the Author

O. Nicholas Cicero is a native New Yorker, born and raised in the borough of Brooklyn. He currently resides in the Midwest, where he passed the bar examinations for Iowa and Minnesota. He received his Bachelor of Arts degree from The University of Iowa and Juris Doctorate from The University of Tulsa College of Law. Post law school, the author worked for federal and state regulatory agencies in various capacities.

To contact the author about this and other novels in this series, please contact him at AuthorONC@gmail.com

www.ingramcontent.com/pod-product-compliance
Lightning Source LLC
Chambersburg PA
CBHW071125170626
46809CB00002B/503